Hello, my name is:

_____,

(your signature)

BIG NATE'S #1 FAN

Also by Lincoln Peirce

Big Nate: In a Class by Himself
Big Nate Strikes Again
Big Nate on a Roll
Big Nate Goes for Broke
Big Nate Flips Out
Big Nate: In the Zone
Big Nate Lives It Up
Big Nate: What Could Possibly Go Wrong?
Big Nate: Here Goes Nothing
Big Nate: Genius Mode
Big Nate: Mr. Popularity

Lincoln Peirce

BiG NATE

FUN BLASTER

LAUGH DRAW RHYME DOODLE RHYME DRAW LAUGH DOODLE RHYME

HARPER
An Imprint of HarperCollins*Publishers*

Big Nate Fun Blaster
Copyright © 2012
by United Feature Syndicate, Inc.
www.harpercollinschildrens.com
www.bignatebooks.com

Go to www.bignate.com to read the *Big Nate* comic strip.

ISBN 978-0-06-234951-4

Typography by Andrea Vandergrift
15 16 17 18 19   PC/RRDH   10 9 8 7 6 5 4 3 2 1
❖
First paperback edition, 2015

For Big Nate Fans Everywhere—
Especially if you love
Nicknames,
Scribbling,
Secret codes,
Cartoons, and
Pop quizzes (Okay, forget that last one)

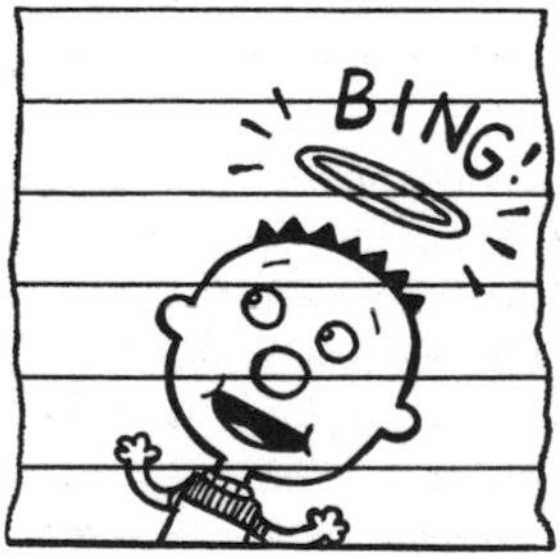
BING!

HOW WELL DO U KNOW NATE?

Do you surpass all others when it comes to Nate trivia? Test it out!

1. Nate's had it with Randy the bully. How does he get his revenge?

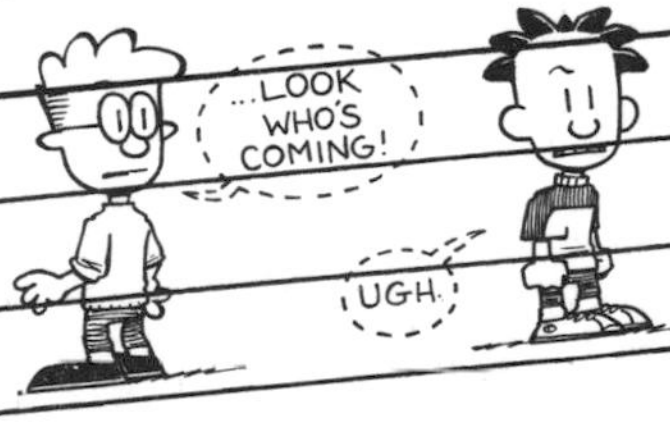
...LOOK WHO'S COMING!
UGH.

a. Beating him at dodgeball

b. Eating all his Cheez Doodles

c. Making him eat 10 lemon squares in a row

d. Throwing a pie in his face

e. Stealing his girlfriend

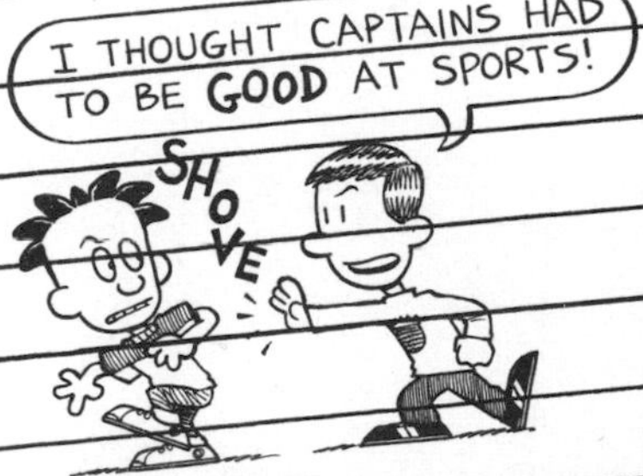
I THOUGHT CAPTAINS HAD TO BE GOOD AT SPORTS!
SHOVE

2. Nate became friends with Teddy when . . .

a. They joined the same fleeceball team.

b. Teddy gave Nate his egg rolls at lunch.

c. Teddy pretended his science lab squid was a booger.

d. Teddy moved next door.

e. Nate invited Teddy to join his band, Enslave the Mollusk.

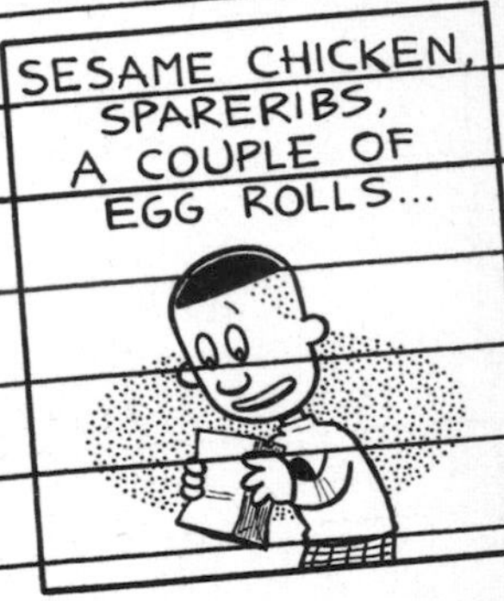
SESAME CHICKEN, SPARERIBS, A COUPLE OF EGG ROLLS...

3. Nate's sign

a. Virgo

b. Scorpio

c. Aquarius

d. Libra

e. Capricorn

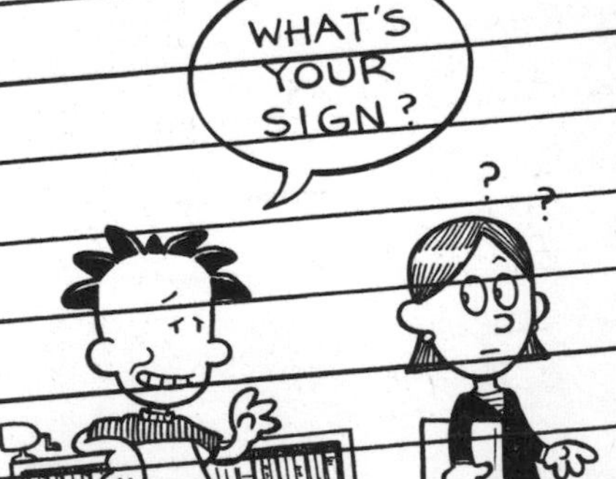
WHAT'S YOUR SIGN?
? ?

4. Nate's superhero self is called . . .

a. Super Nate

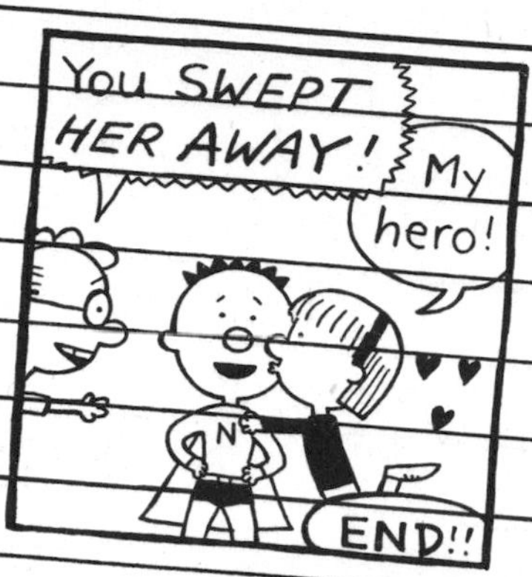
You SWEPT HER AWAY!
My hero!
N
END!!

b. Mr. Magnificent

c. Wonder Kid

d. Ultra-Nate

e. Nate the Notorious

5. Nate wanted his fleeceball team to have this name:

a. Killer Bees

b. Pumas

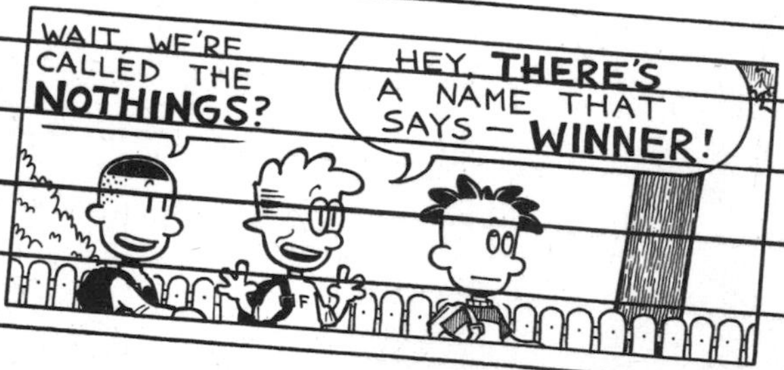
WAIT, WE'RE CALLED THE NOTHINGS?
HEY, THERE'S A NAME THAT SAYS — WINNER!

c. Chargers

d. Raptors

e. Psycho Dogs

CODE CRACKER

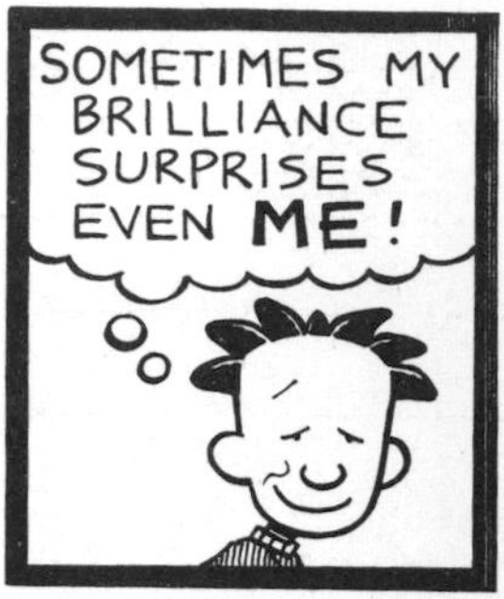
SOMETIMES MY BRILLIANCE SURPRISES EVEN ME!

Go undercover and help solve the secret messages using this code. Then circle whether they are true or false.

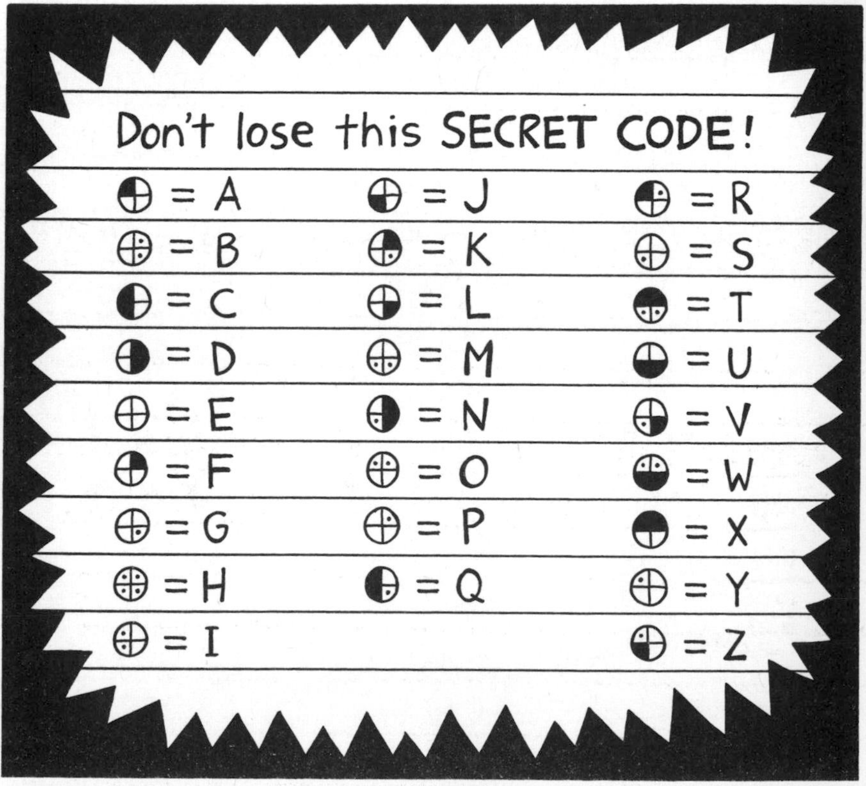
Don't lose this SECRET CODE!
= A = J = R
= B = K = S
= C = L = T
= D = M = U
= E = N = V
= F = O = W
= G = P = X
= H = Q = Y
= I = Z

VOILÀ!

T F

T F

T F

T F

T F

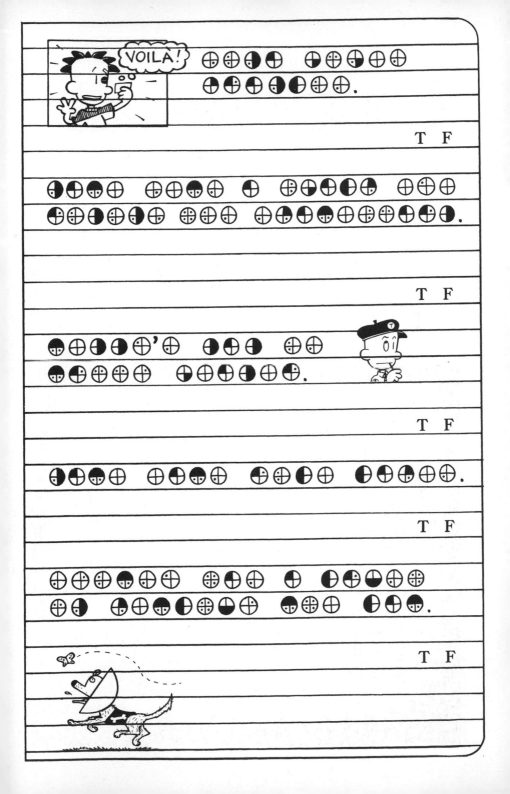

WHO AM I IN 20 YEARS?

Imagine what you will be like 20 years from now! Whoa . . . you'll be a grown-up! Write a letter from the future YOU. But first, a little review . . .

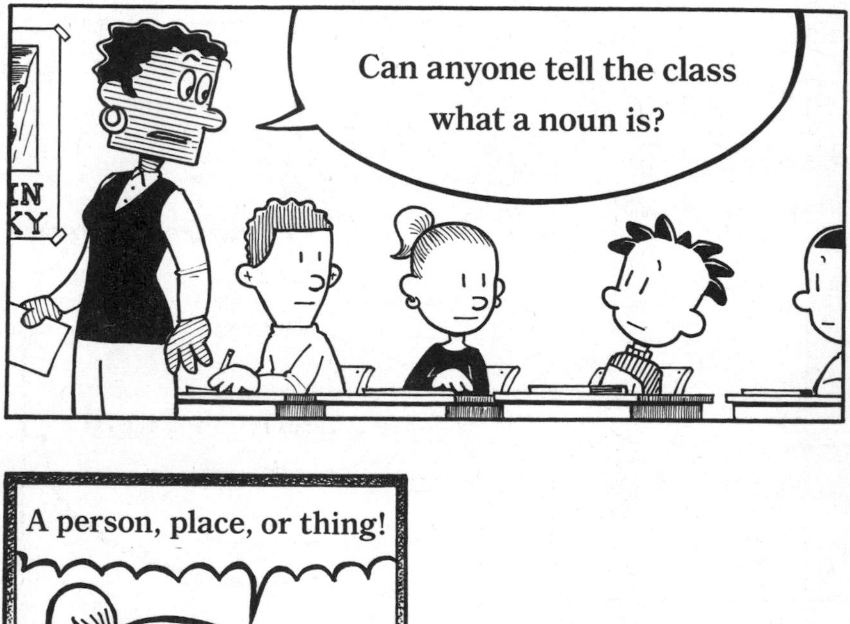

Can anyone tell the class what a noun is?

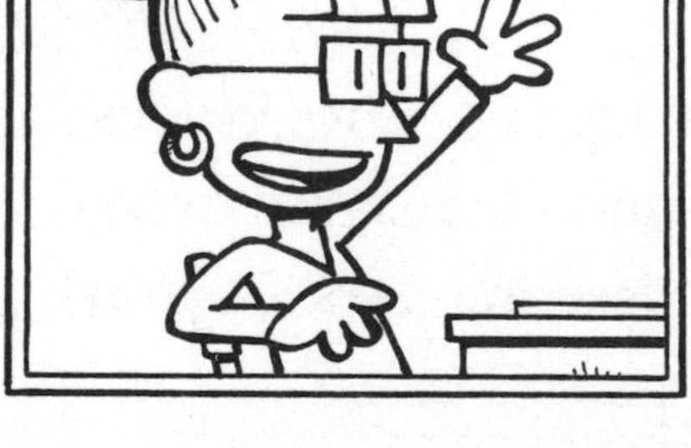

A person, place, or thing!

EXAMPLES: Bumble Boy (comic character), the cafetorium (place), green bean (thing)

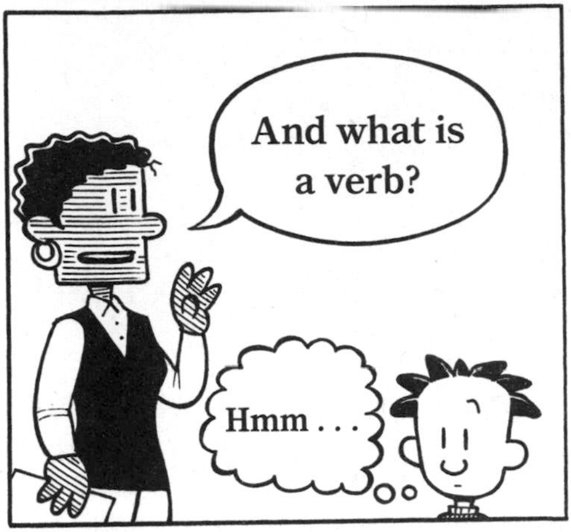
And what is a verb?
Hmm . . .

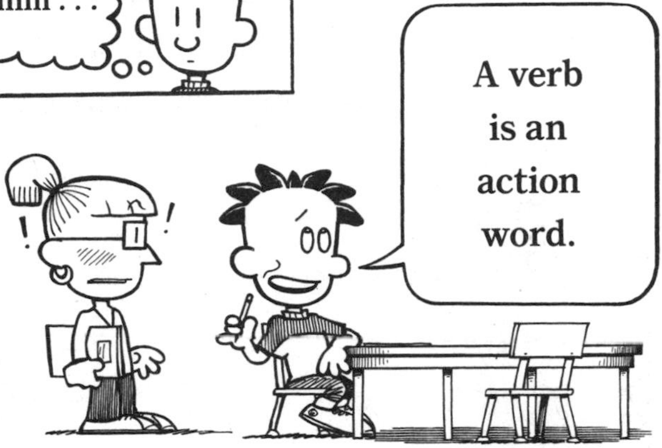
A verb is an action word.

EXAMPLES:
doodle, paint,
compete, yell

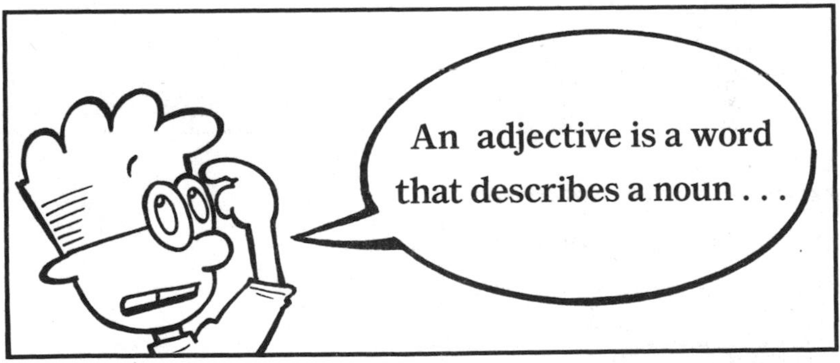
An adjective is a word that describes a noun . . .

EXAMPLES:
amazing (describes Pickles),
smart (describes Artur),
terrifying (describes Mrs. Godfrey)

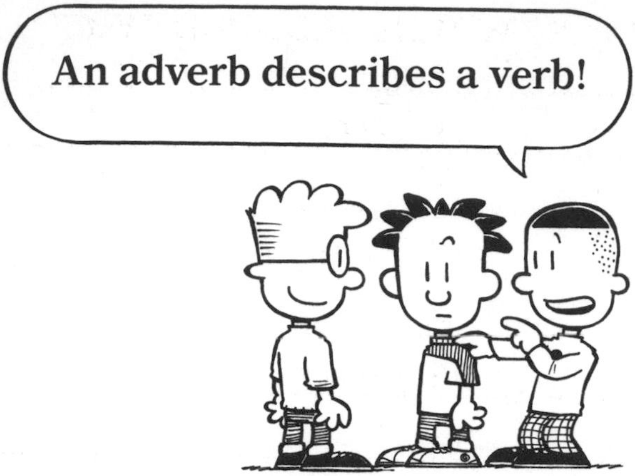
An adverb describes a verb!

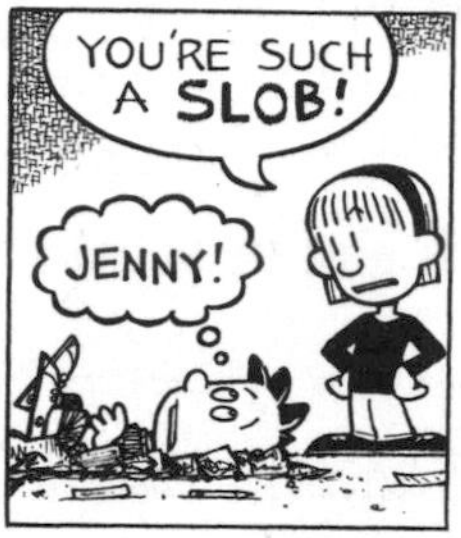
YOU'RE SUCH A SLOB!
JENNY!

AN EXAMPLE OF AN ADVERB IN A SENTENCE:
Francis and Teddy think Nate behaves *weirdly* around Jenny.

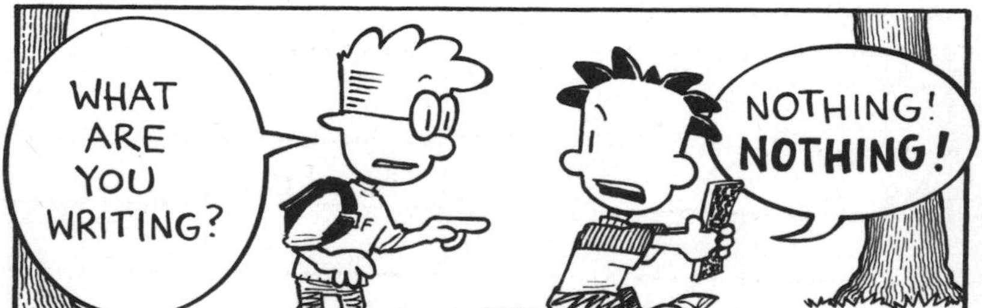
WHAT ARE YOU WRITING?
NOTHING! NOTHING!

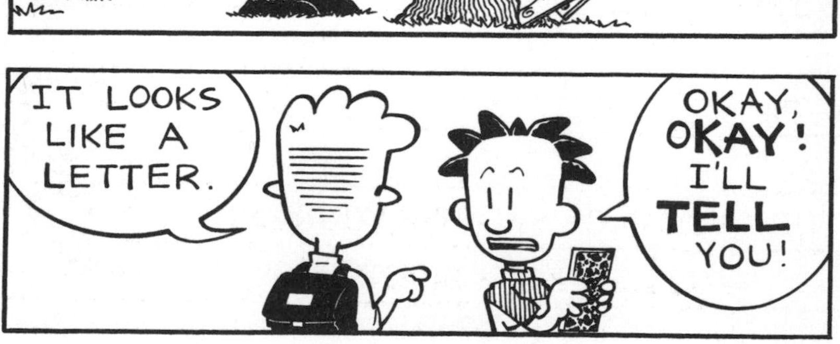
IT LOOKS LIKE A LETTER.
OKAY, OKAY! I'LL TELL YOU!

NOW MAKE A LIST OF WORDS ALL ABOUT YOU!

1. Your name:
2. Adjective:
3. Noun:
4. Adjective:
5. Adverb:
6. Verb:
7. Verb:
8. Noun:
9. Verb:
10. Plural noun:
11. Verb:
12. Plural noun:
13. Adjective:
14. Noun:
15. Noun:
16. Noun (place name):
17. Plural noun:
18. Plural noun:
19. Adverb:
20. Noun:

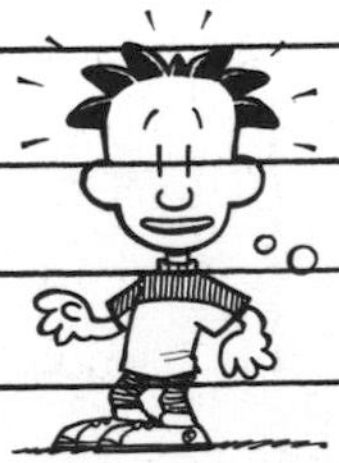

TURN THE PAGE AND USE YOUR LIST TO FILL IN THE BLANKS!

Dear ______________________ ,
1.

My life is pretty ________________ because I work as a
2.

______________ , which I find extremely ______________ .
3. 4.

After work I __________________ __________________ and
5. 6.

______________ . Every day is an ____________ because
7. 8.

I ______________ ______________ and ________________ .
9. 10. 11.

I think ________________ should make a reality show
12.

all about my ________________ ______________ . I live in
13. 14.

a ________________ in the country of ______________ ,
15. 16.

with ______________________ and ______________ . My
17. 18.

most exciting moment ever was when I ______________
19.

climbed __________________ !!
20.

THEN
I'm bored. Let's tax the colonists again.
NOW
I'm bored. Let's give the kids a standardized test.
DONUTS

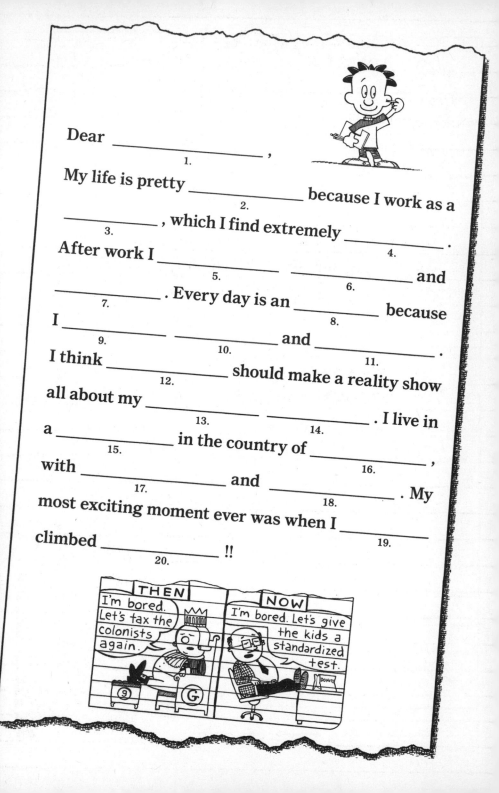

DOODLE CRAZE

Do you go crazy when you doodle? Well, what are you waiting for? Start by signing your name in crazy ways, just like Nate does here.

Nate Wright

Nate Wright

Nate Wright

WHAT A SAVE!

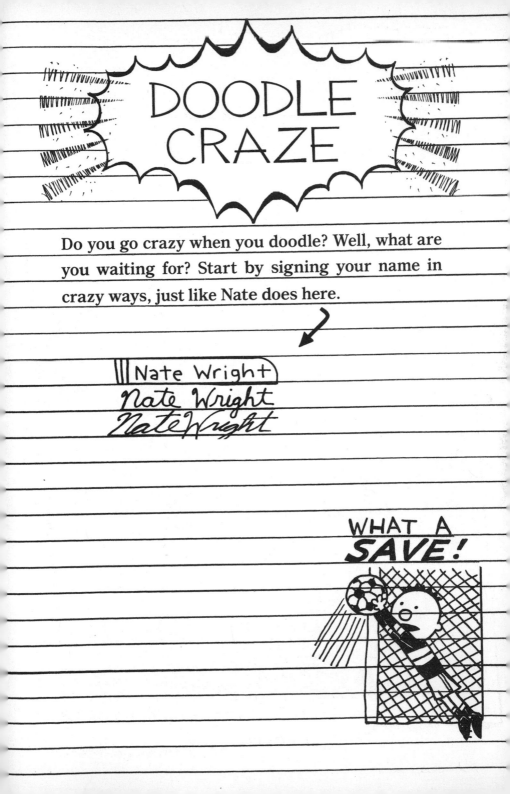

SCOUT'S HONOR

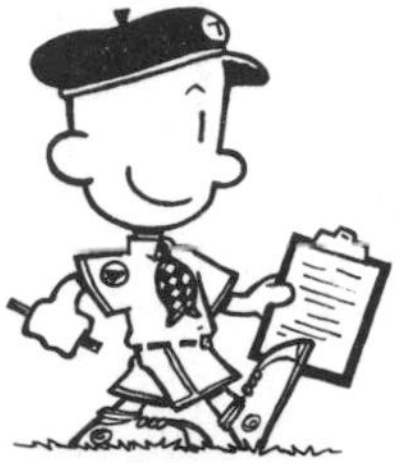

How many badges can Nate's troop earn? See if you can guess these merit badge activities!

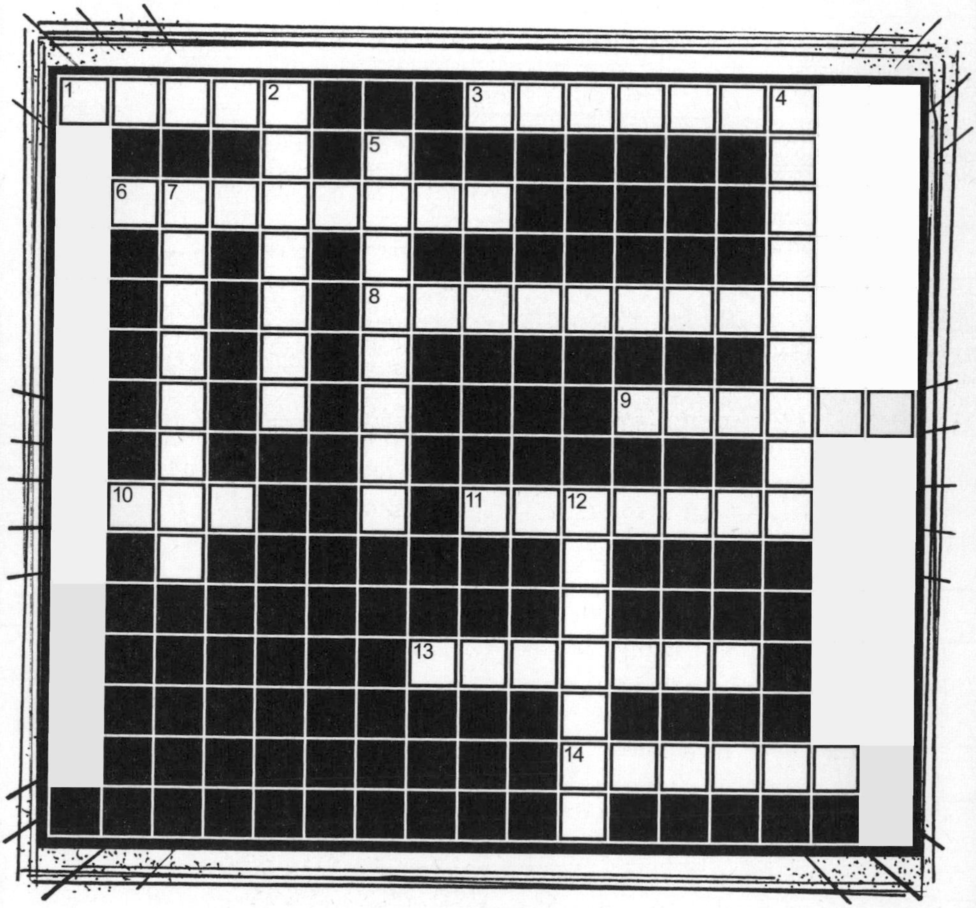
1
2
3
4
5
6
7
8
9
10
11
12
13
14

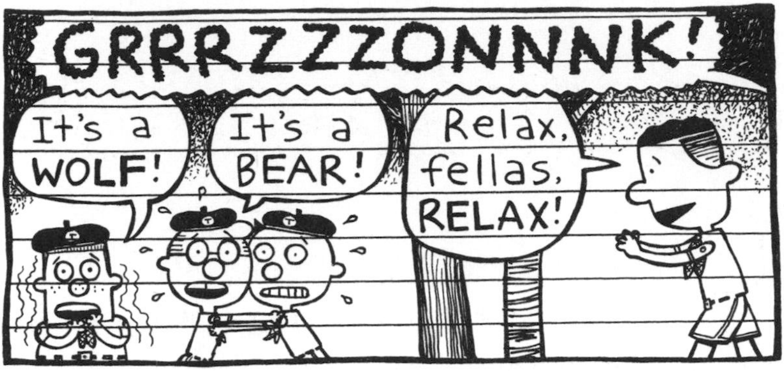
GRRRZZZONNNK!
It's a WOLF!
It's a BEAR!
Relax, fellas, RELAX!

ACROSS

1. Sing it, dance to it, or buy it for your iPod.

3. Mmmm, grilling hot dogs over the fire and making baked beans—better put on your apron for this.

6. Breaststroke, backstroke, butterfly—what is this?

8. Something you mold with clay. Rhymes with "vulture."

9. You'll need oars for this. Rhymes with "snowing." Don't get swept away in the current!

10. Draw! Paint! Create! You'll need your easel for this activity.

11. Take bait and a pole!

13. It rains, it snows, it's sunny or dry! What is this called?

14. The trees, the earth, Mother ________ .

DOWN

2. Don't forget your sleeping bag and tent.

4. If you have a green thumb, then you're very good at this!

5. What kit holds Band-Aids?

7. Build a birdhouse, get a badge in ________ing. First syllable rhymes with "could."

12. This can be done on ice or on concrete, and you'll need special shoes.

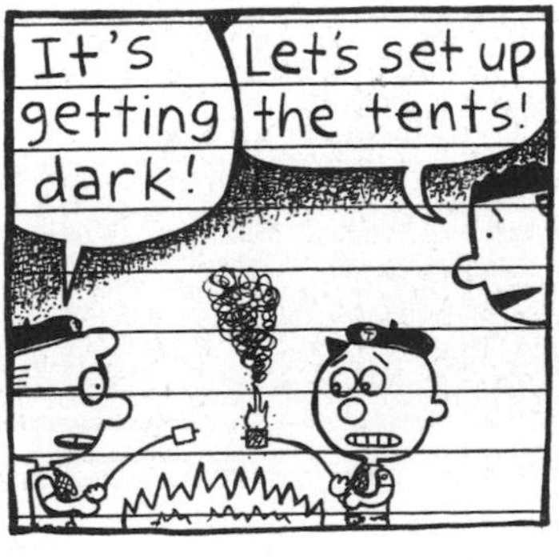
It's getting dark!
Let's set up the tents!

MOST VALUABLE PLAYER

Who made the game-winning save?
Solve the maze and find out.

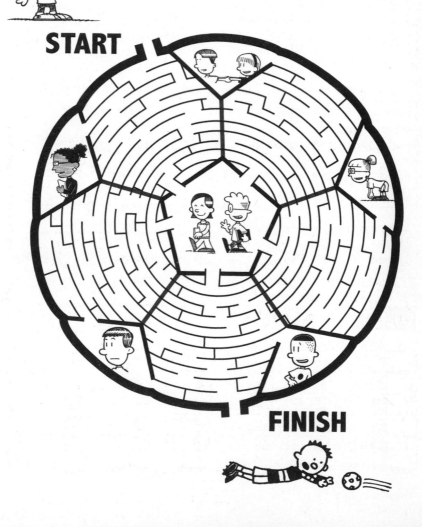

START

FINISH

SEMAPHORE SUPERSTAR

Nate invented a special semaphore code so that he and his friends Teddy and Francis can send secret messages that no one else can read—except you! Decode their first message below.

CODE CHART	Use this	
alphabet to decode the secret		☐ = U
messages in this book!		⊟ = V
•=A	❚=E	▽=I	◖=M	⊠=Q	◎=W
⊟=B	⊠=F	◪=J	◣=N	÷=R	▧=X
◸=C	✕=G	▣=K	⊞=O	▪=S	■=Y
◉=D	⊟=H	⊟=L	❚=P	◆=T	⊠=Z

UN-YUMMY TREATS

Nate loves Cheez Doodles, but his house is a no-snack zone! Help him avoid these gross foods by filling in the blanks so only one of each food appears in every row, column, and box.

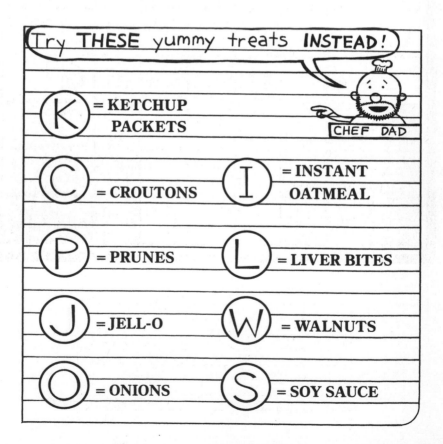

Try **THESE** yummy treats **INSTEAD!**

(K) = KETCHUP PACKETS

CHEF DAD

(C) = CROUTONS   (I) = INSTANT OATMEAL

(P) = PRUNES   (L) = LIVER BITES

(J) = JELL-O   (W) = WALNUTS

(O) = ONIONS   (S) = SOY SAUCE

UNHAPPY EATING!

K	O	S		J	W	C		L
J	I		K		L	O		P
	P	W	C	I				S
I					S	K	L	O
C		K	I	O	P		J	W
	W		L			P	C	
W			O	P			S	
O	C	L		W		I	P	J
	S				C			K

• One box of lime Jell-O
The freshness date expired BEFORE I WAS BORN!

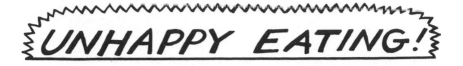

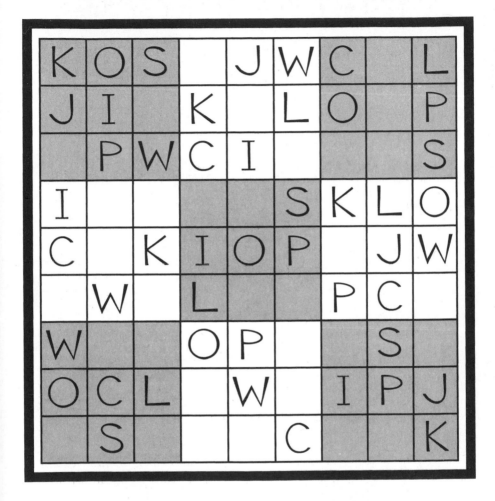

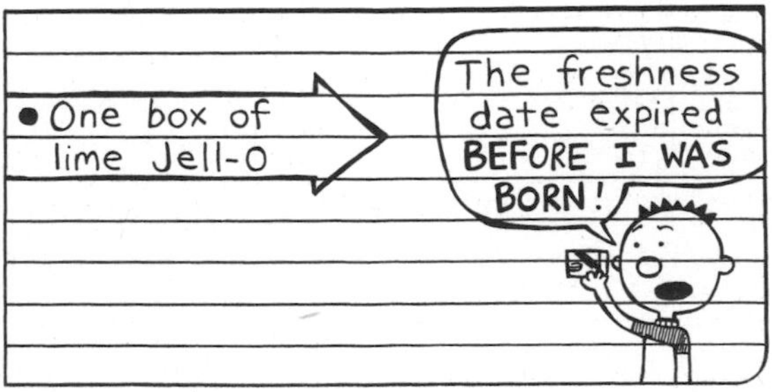

NATE WRIGHT, FOOD CRITIC

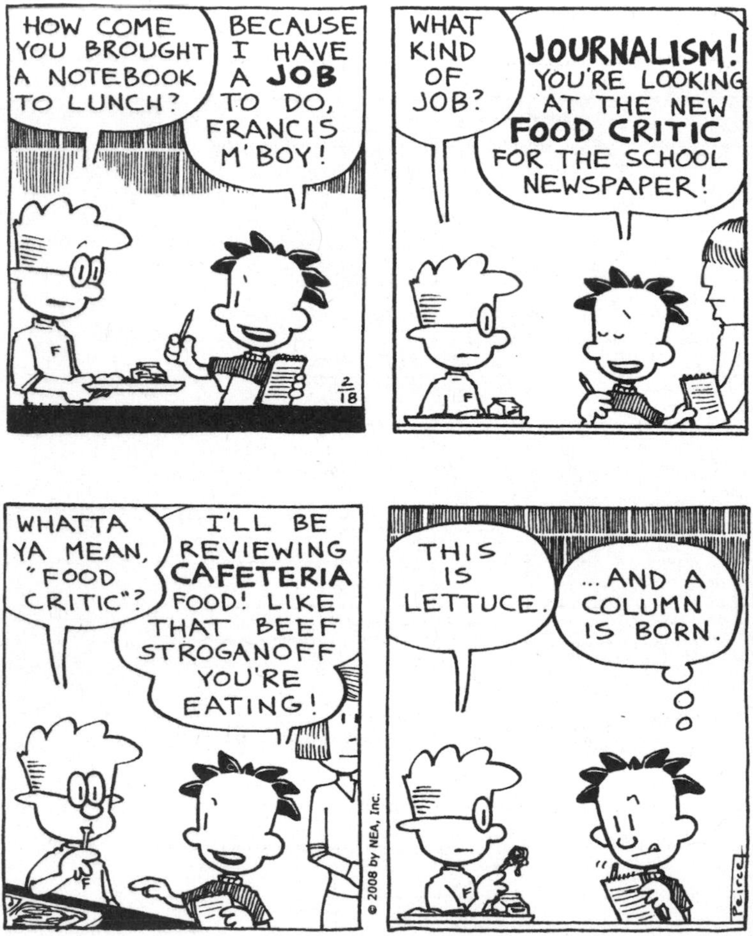

HOW COME YOU BROUGHT A NOTEBOOK TO LUNCH?
BECAUSE I HAVE A **JOB** TO DO, FRANCIS M'BOY!
2/18
WHAT KIND OF JOB?
JOURNALISM! YOU'RE LOOKING AT THE NEW **FOOD CRITIC** FOR THE SCHOOL NEWSPAPER!
WHATTA YA MEAN, "FOOD CRITIC"?
I'LL BE REVIEWING **CAFETERIA** FOOD! LIKE THAT BEEF STROGANOFF YOU'RE EATING!
© 2008 by NEA, Inc.
THIS IS LETTUCE.
...AND A COLUMN IS BORN.
Peirce

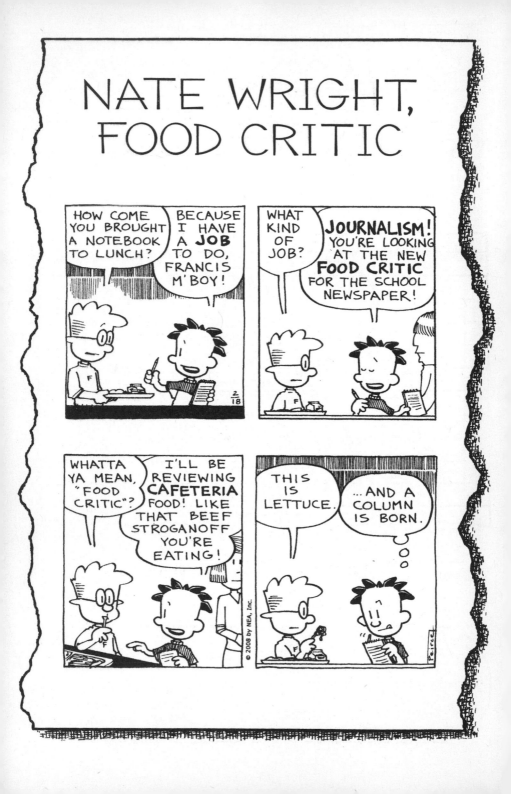

SUPER SCRIBBLE GAME

Turn your super scribble into . . .

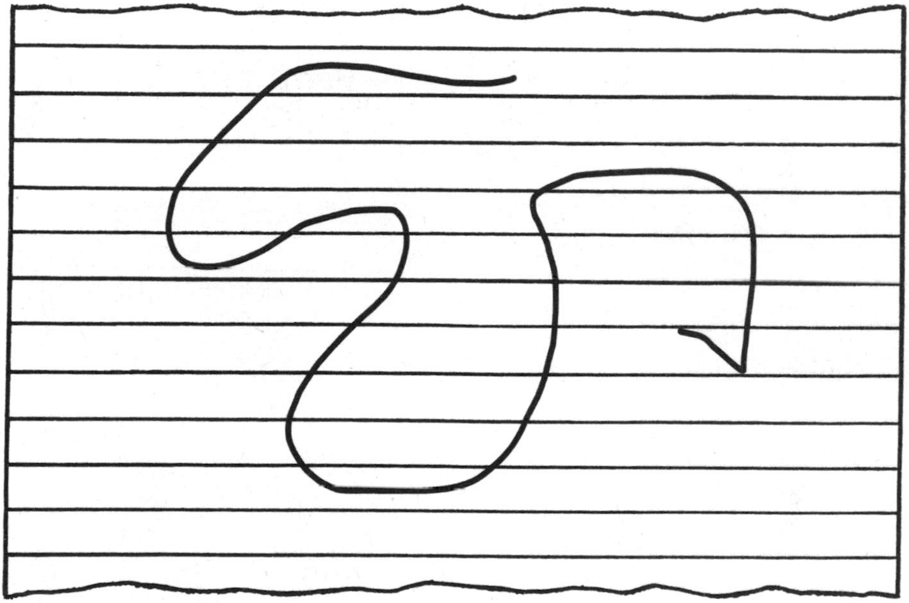

Don't forget to write a caption for it:

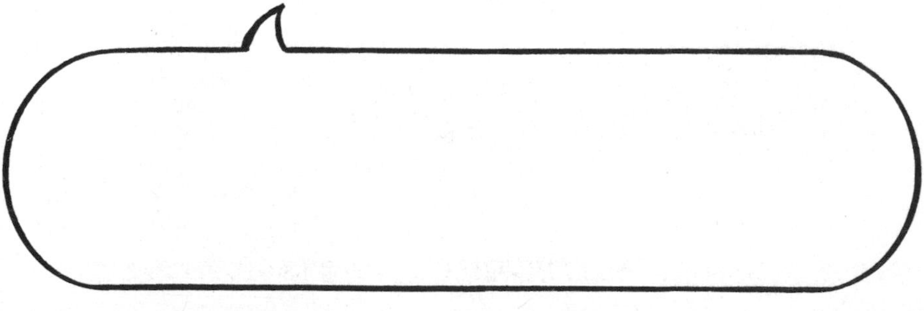

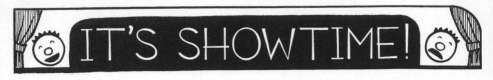

IT'S SHOWTIME!

You're in the spotlight! Guess the clues and take the lead. If you haven't memorized the semaphore code, use the chart on page 15.

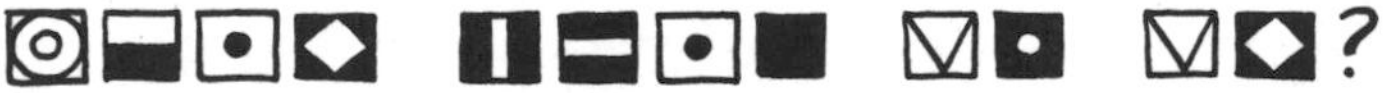

SOLVE THE PUZZLE AND FIND OUT!

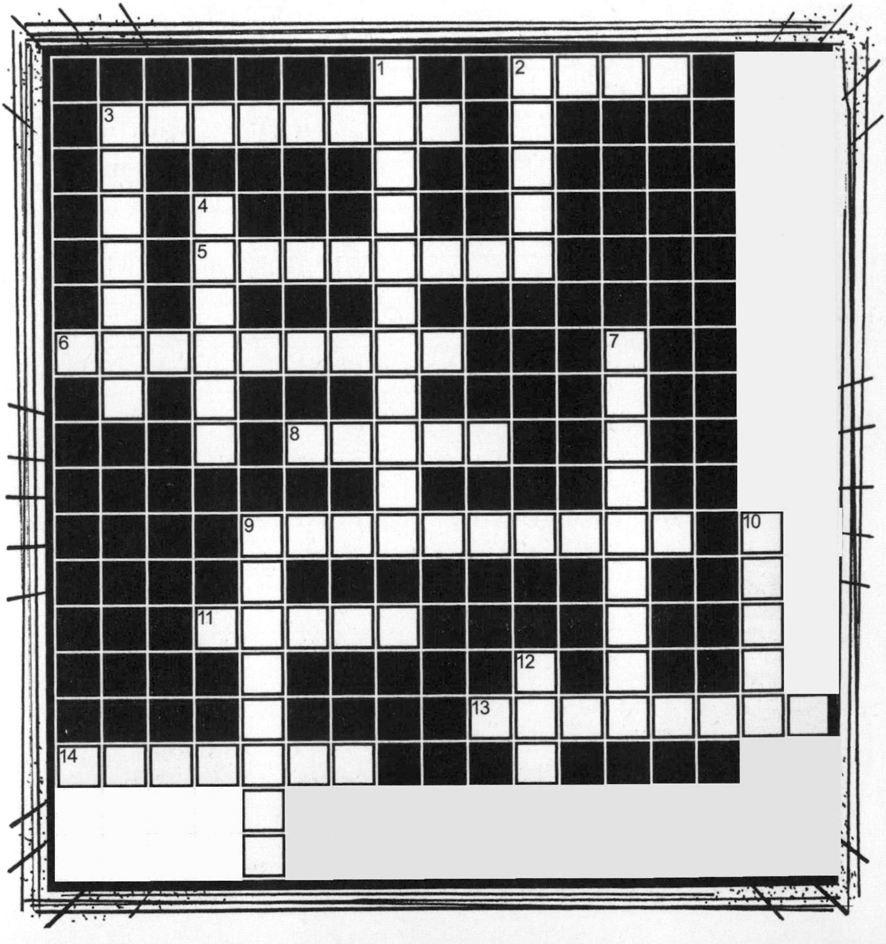

ACROSS

2. Seen in the the night sky, or as the lead in a play.

3. The boy who flies!

5. Many hands clapping for the performers at the end of the play.

6. A faraway magical place where people don't grow old.

8. Weapon that is long and sharp.

9. Rhymes with "wink her tell."

11. She follows her brothers out the window and into the night sky.

13. These are the young men who will never grow up.

14. Usually red cloth, this lifts and drops to mark the beginning and end of the show.

DOWN

1. His hand was eaten by a crocodile.

2. Where all the action in a play happens.

3. They wear eye patches and plunder ships.

4. Actors wear this on their faces so their features can be seen from far away.

7. Shines brightly in a circle on the stage. Nate loves this!

9. On a ship, you must walk _____ _____ if you're found to be an enemy.

10. A tiny creature with wings.

12. Take a _____ . Rhymes with "cow."

GINA SAYS, NATE SAYS

It's no secret that Nate and Gina are all-time enemies! Whatever Gina says, Nate thinks the opposite, like this:

GINA SAYS...
I SAY...
I'm SO much smarter than you are!
No, you get better GRADES, because all you ever do is STUDY!
I've never been sent to detention! EVER!
Translation: You have no life.
I'm Mrs. Godfrey's all-time favorite student!
...because you're a complete SUCK-UP!

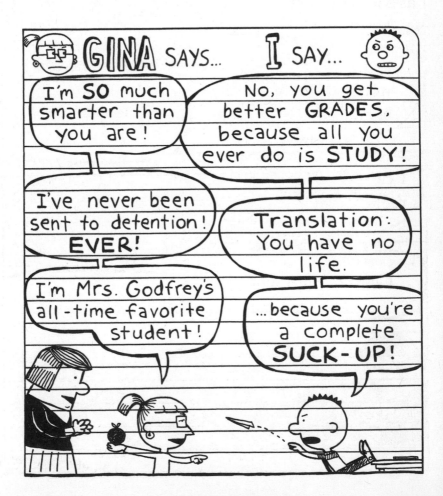

NOW YOU TRY GUESSING WHAT NATE WOULD SAY!

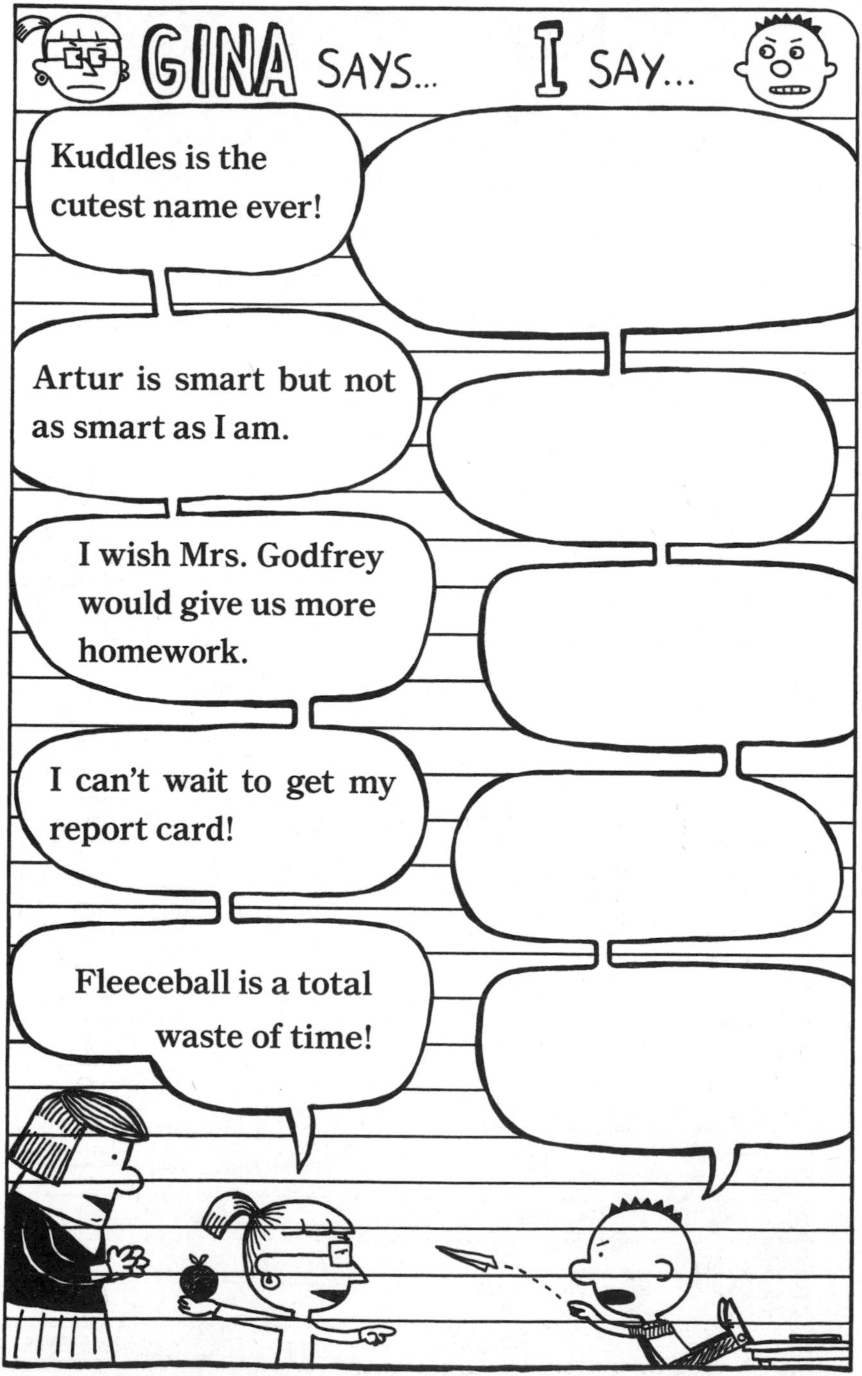
GINA SAYS...
I SAY...
Kuddles is the cutest name ever!
Artur is smart but not as smart as I am.
I wish Mrs. Godfrey would give us more homework.
I can't wait to get my report card!
Fleeceball is a total waste of time!

FAST AND FURIOUS FLEECEBALL

Get ready to play ball! Using the letters that spell Nate's favorite SPOFF, let's see if you can create more than 20 other words!

FLEECEBALL

1. Lab	12.
2.	13.
3.	14.
4.	15.
5.	16.
6.	17.
7.	18.
8.	19.
9.	20.
10.	21.
11.	22.

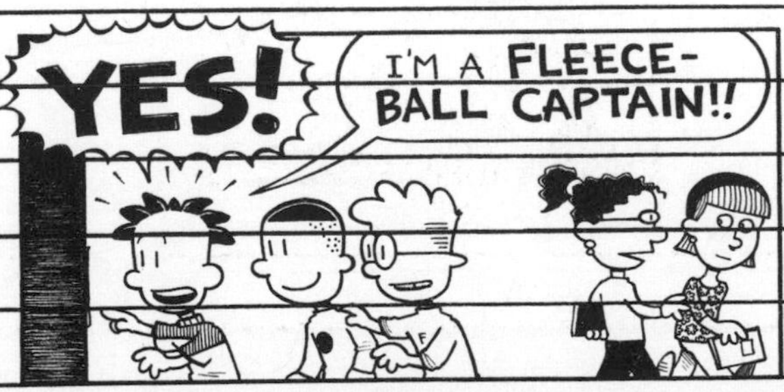
YES!
I'M A FLEECE-BALL CAPTAIN!!

HEADLINERS

Extra, extra, read all about it! Pretend you're a reporter and write a headline for each scene.

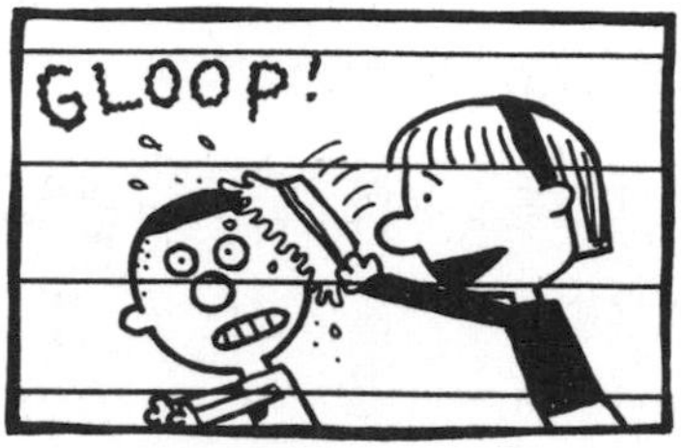
GLOOP!

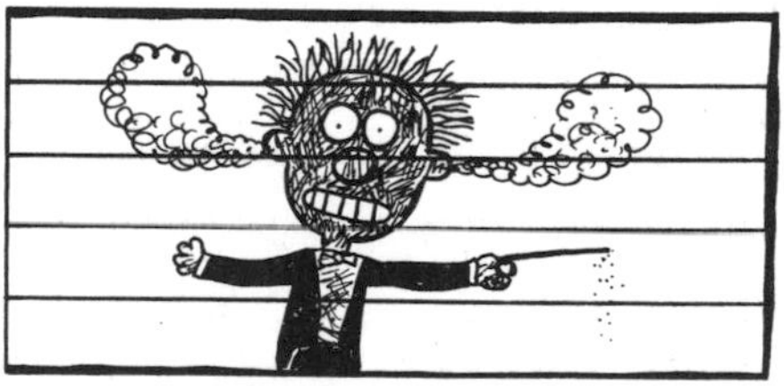

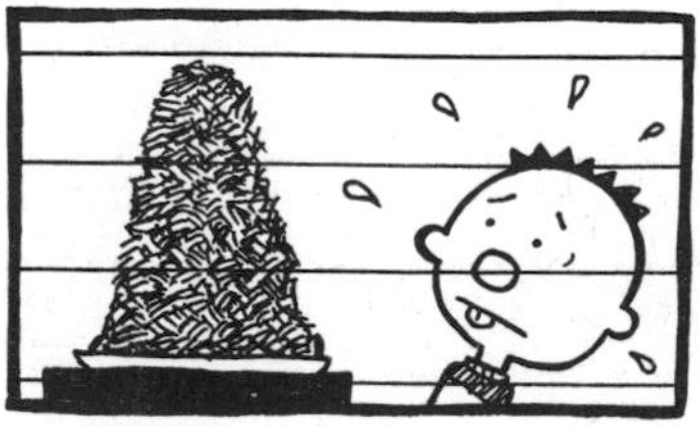

CLASSROOM CHATTER

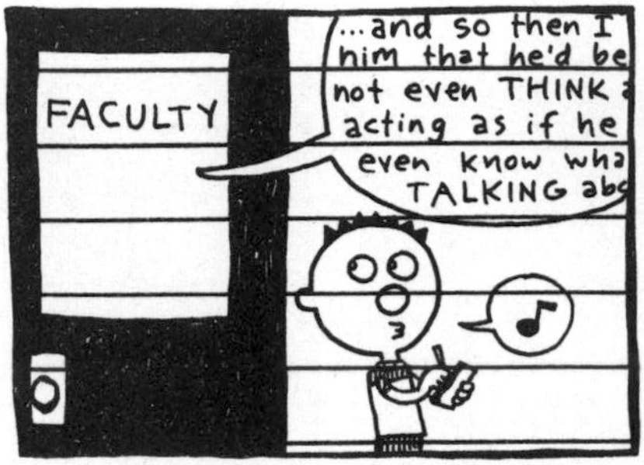
FACULTY
...and so then I
him that he'd be
not even THINK
acting as if he
even know wha
TALKING ab

Nate's got lots of talents, but he's especially skilled at eavesdropping! He writes the gossip column for the school paper. It's called Classroom Chatter! How does he get the best scoop? From hanging out in front of the teachers' lounge!

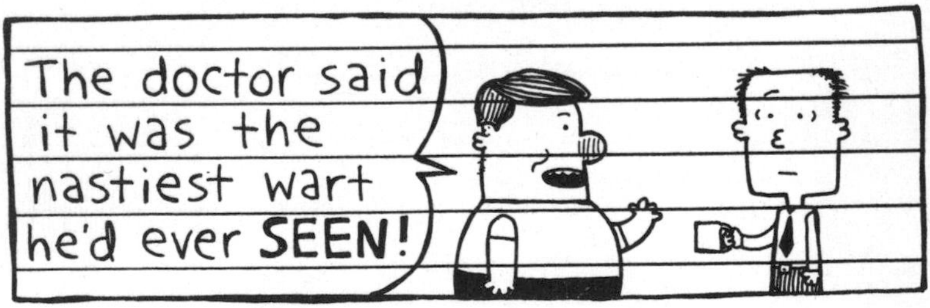
The doctor said it was the nastiest wart he'd ever **SEEN!**

On pages 6–8, Ms. Clarke refreshed your memory about the parts of speech.

WRITE THE MOST GOSSIPY WORDS YOU CAN THINK OF!

1. Noun (person):
2. Adjective:
3. Noun (plural):
4. Noun (person):
5. Noun (person):
6. Noun (person):
7. Adjective:
8. Noun:
9. Verb (ending in -ing):
10. Verb (ending in -ing):
11. Noun (person):
12. Noun:
13. Noun:
14. Noun (person):
15. Adjective:
16. Noun:

TURN THE PAGE TO GET THE SCOOP!

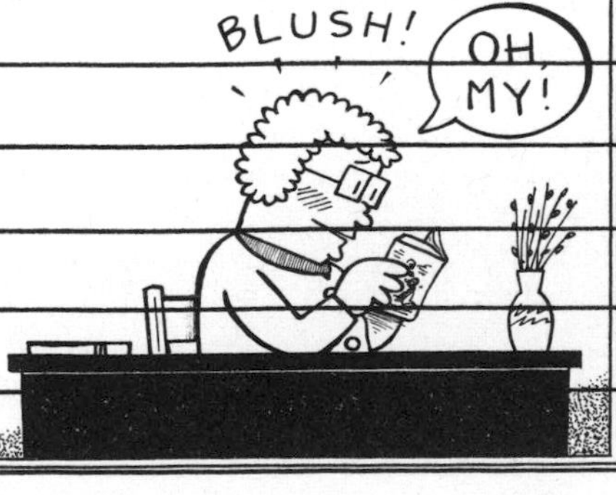
BLUSH!
OH, MY!

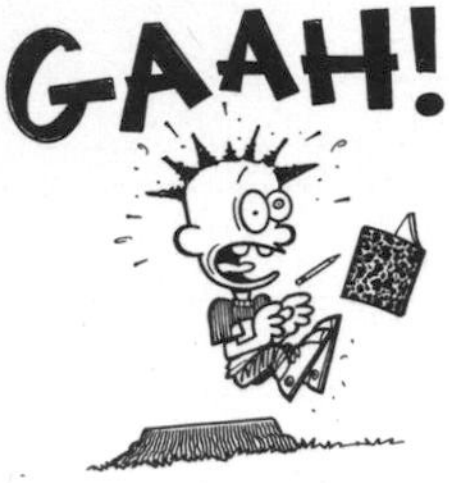
GAAH!

EXCLUSIVE NEWS!

YOU HEARD IT HERE FIRST!

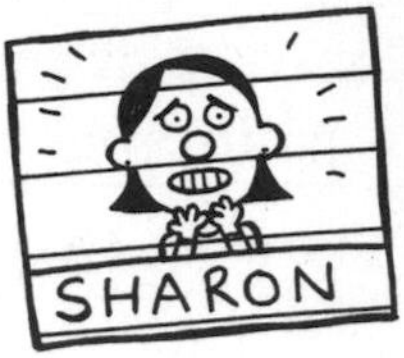
SHARON

____________ (1.) was seen throwing ____________ (2.)

____________ (3.) with ____________ (4.) near

____________ (5.) 's locker after school.

____________ (6.) was seen throwing ____________ (7.)

____________ (8.) and secretly ____________ (9.) after

publicly ____________ (10.) at recess.

Will ____________ (11.) have a change of ____________ (12.)?

Or is the ____________ (13.) over for good?

Only ____________ (14.) knows the ____________ (15.)

____________ (16.).

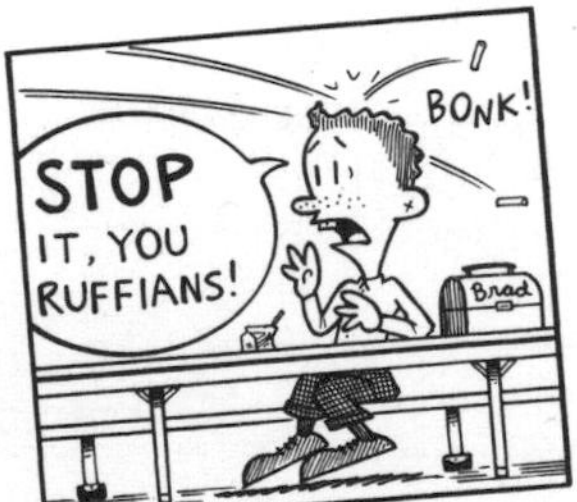
BONK!
STOP IT, YOU RUFFIANS!
Brad

HIKE TO NOWHERE

What awaits Nate at the end of his hike? Solve the maze and find out!

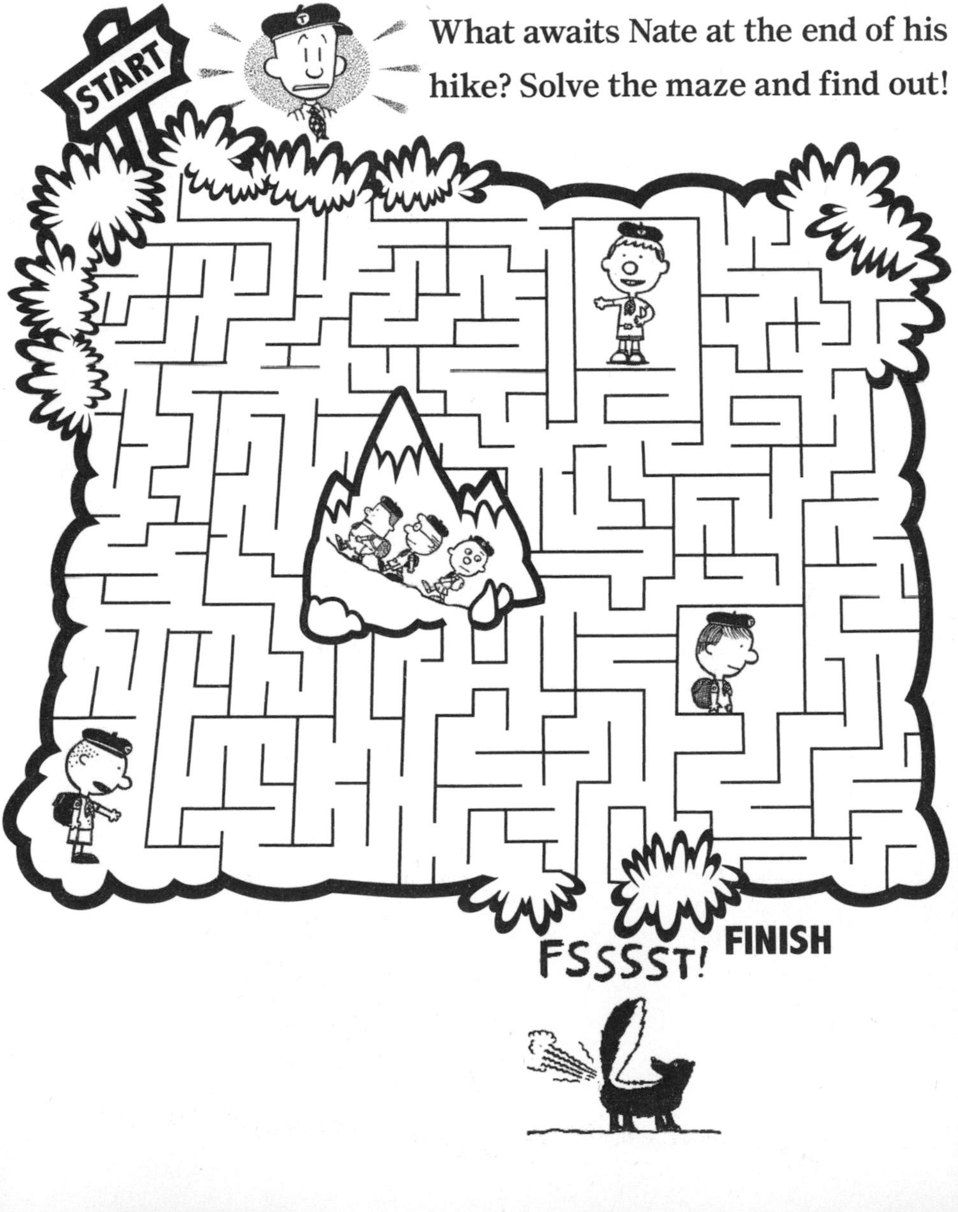
START
FSSSST!
FINISH

TIMBER SCOUTS

Nate, Teddy, and Francis are Timber Scouts. Now they need to make room for . . . Artur! Make sure each boy's initial appears only once in every row, column, and box.

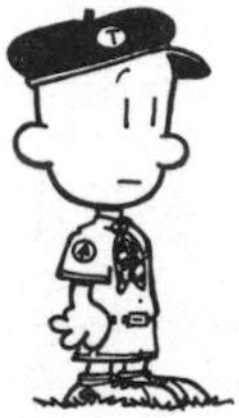

N **= NATE**

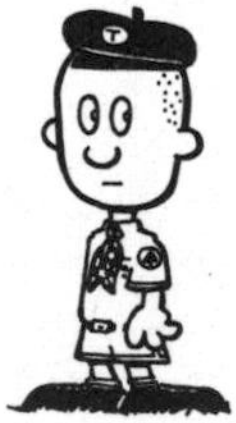

T **= TEDDY**

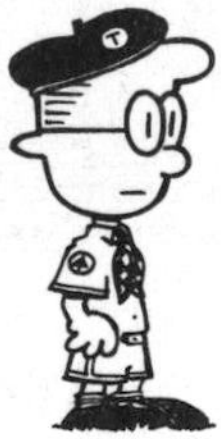

F **= FRANCIS**

A **= ARTUR**

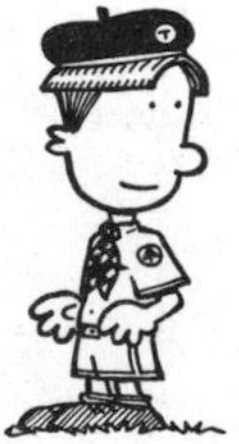

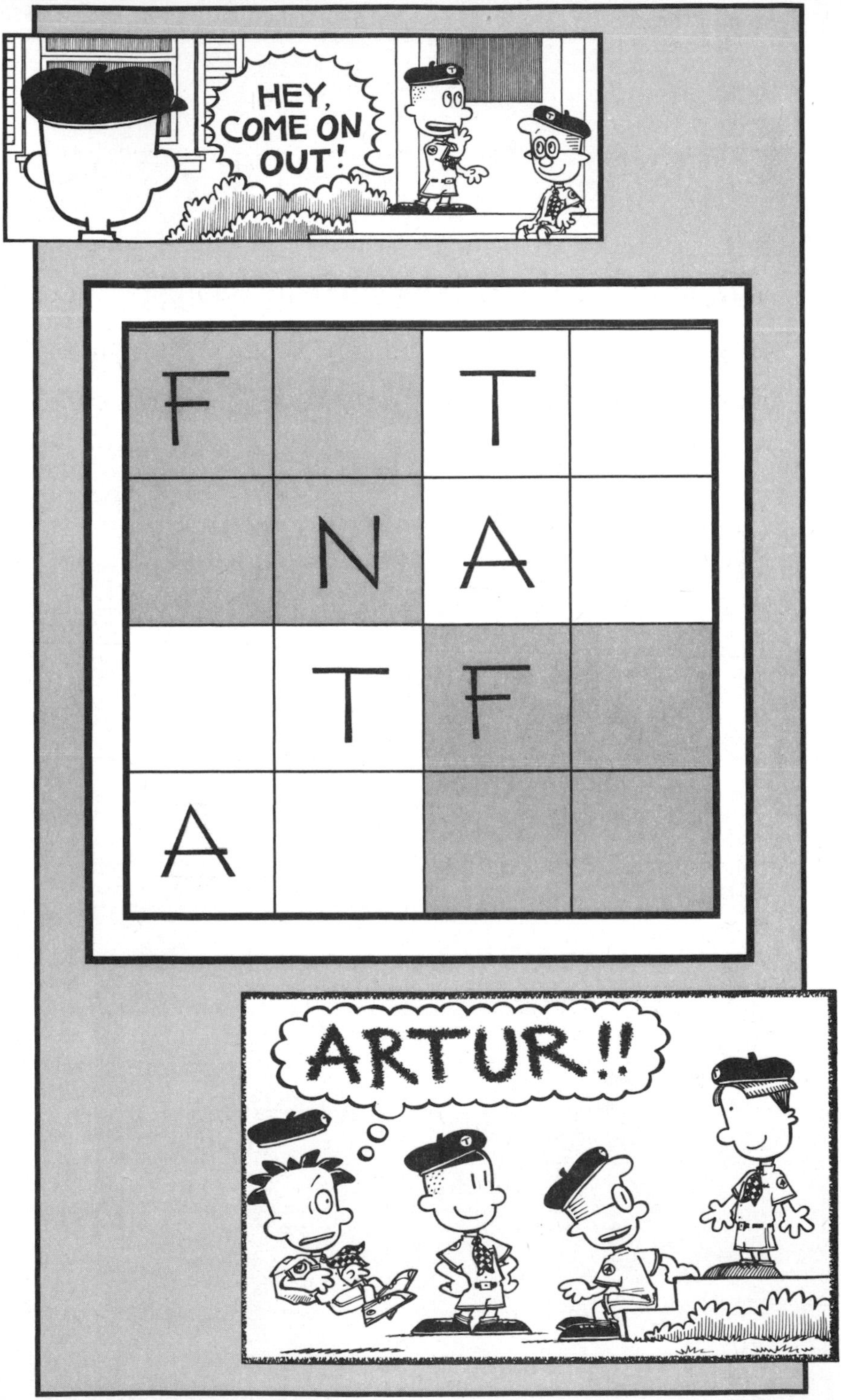
HEY, COME ON OUT!
F T
N A
T F
A
ARTUR!!

TIME TO RHYME

**Nate likes to rhyme,
more than mime,
all of the time!**

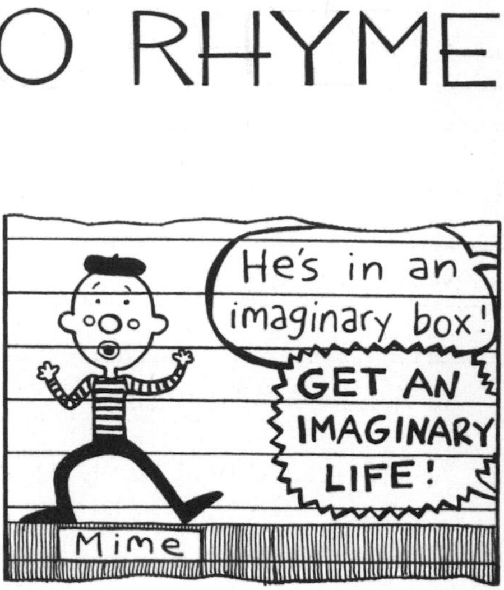
He's in an imaginary box!
GET AN IMAGINARY LIFE!
Mime

Create pairs of rhyming words that match these funny definitions.

EXAMPLES:

1. Extra large feline __fat__ __cat__

2. Rodent dwelling __mouse__ __house__

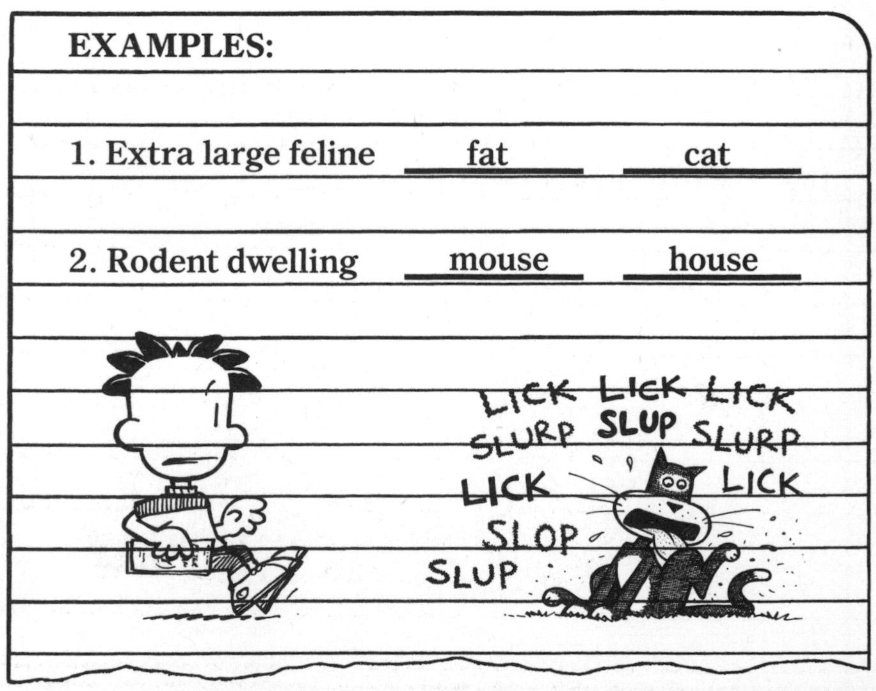
LICK LICK LICK
SLURP SLUP SLURP
LICK LICK
SLOP
SLUP

NOW YOU TRY!

3. Silly rabbit ______ ______

4. Peaceful mother calm ___

5. Angry father ___ ___

6. Wacky white-petaled flower ______ ______

7. Weird ape funky _______

8. Reading corner _____ nook

9. Not the right tune ______ _____

10. Pleasure-filled race fun ___

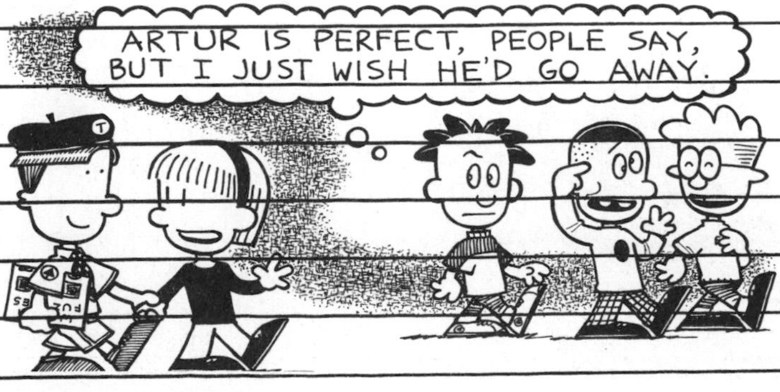
ARTUR IS PERFECT, PEOPLE SAY, BUT I JUST WISH HE'D GO AWAY.

TEDDY'S ULTIMATE SPORTS TRIVIA

Teddy is wild about sports. Can you decode his secret messages?

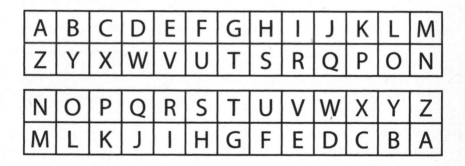

A	B	C	D	E	F	G	H	I	J	K	L	M
Z	Y	X	W	V	U	T	S	R	Q	P	O	N

N	O	P	Q	R	S	T	U	V	W	X	Y	Z
M	L	K	J	I	H	G	F	E	D	C	B	A

,

$\overline{H}\ \overline{S}\ \overline{Z}\ \overline{J}\ \overline{F}\ \overline{R}\ \overline{O}\ \overline{O}\ \overline{V}$ $\overline{L}\ \overline{M}\ \overline{V}\ \overline{Z}\ \overline{O}$

$\overline{D}\ \overline{V}\ \overline{Z}\ \overline{R}\ \overline{H}$ $\overline{G}\ \overline{S}\ \overline{V}$ $\overline{L}\ \overline{Z}\ \overline{R}\ \overline{T}\ \overline{V}\ \overline{H}\ \overline{G}$

$\overline{H}\ \overline{S}\ \overline{L}\ \overline{V}\ \overline{H}$ $\overline{R}\ \overline{M}$ $\overline{G}\ \overline{S}\ \overline{V}$ $\overline{M}\ \overline{Y}\ \overline{Z}$.

$\overline{H}\ \overline{R}\ \overline{A}\ \overline{V}$ **22!**

$\overline{G}\ \overline{S}\ \overline{V}$ $\overline{G}\ \overline{L}\ \overline{F}\ \overline{I}$ $\overline{W}\ \overline{V}$ $\overline{U}\ \overline{I}\ \overline{Z}\ \overline{M}\ \overline{X}\ \overline{V}$

$\overline{Y}\ \overline{R}\ \overline{X}\ \overline{B}\ \overline{X}\ \overline{O}\ \overline{V}$ $\overline{I}\ \overline{Z}\ \overline{X}\ \overline{V}$

$\overline{O}\ \overline{Z}\ \overline{H}\ \overline{G}\ \overline{H}$ **21** $\overline{W}\ \overline{Z}\ \overline{B}\ \overline{H}$' $\overline{Z}\ \overline{M}\ \overline{W}$

$\overline{O}\ \overline{Z}\ \overline{M}\ \overline{X}\ \overline{V}$ $\overline{Z}\ \overline{R}\ \overline{N}\ \overline{H}\ \overline{G}\ \overline{R}\ \overline{L}\ \overline{M}\ \overline{T}$

$\overline{S}\ \overline{Z}\ \overline{H}$ $\overline{D}\ \overline{L}\ \overline{M}$ $\overline{Z}$ $\overline{I}\ \overline{V}\ \overline{X}\ \overline{L}\ \overline{I}\ \overline{W}$

7 $\overline{G}\ \overline{R}\ \overline{N}\ \overline{V}\ \overline{H}$!

SUPER SCRIBBLE GAME

Ready. Set. Scribble!

Don't forget to write a caption for it:

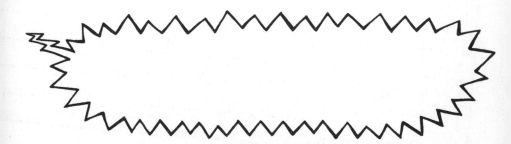

FRIENDS FOREVER

Nate's super tight with his buddies Francis and Teddy! Who are your favorite amigos?

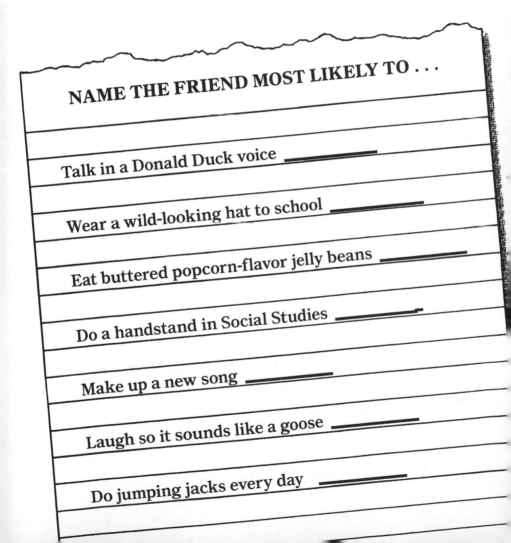

NAME THE FRIEND MOST LIKELY TO . . .

Talk in a Donald Duck voice _____

Wear a wild-looking hat to school _____

Eat buttered popcorn-flavor jelly beans _____

Do a handstand in Social Studies _____

Make up a new song _____

Laugh so it sounds like a goose _____

Do jumping jacks every day _____

Try out for the soccer team _____

Recite lines from a favorite book _____

Get an A in science class _____

Draw comix featuring
out-of-this-world characters _____

Take the team to victory in kickball _____

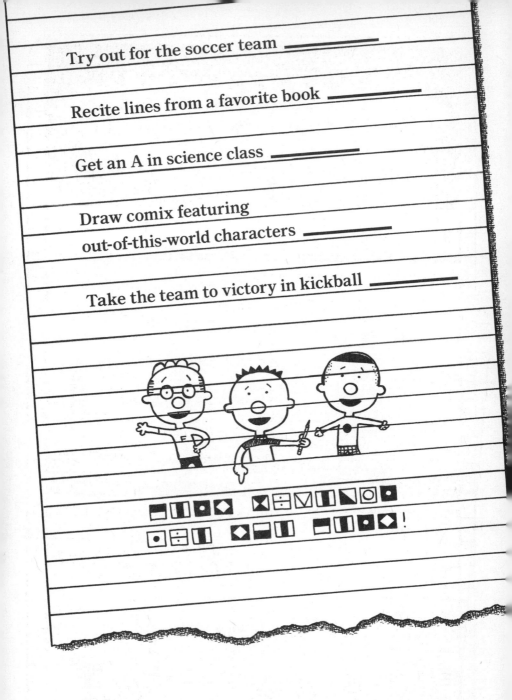

CAMPER DAD COMIX

Why is Nate's dad so clueless? Fill in the speech bubbles and create your own comix.

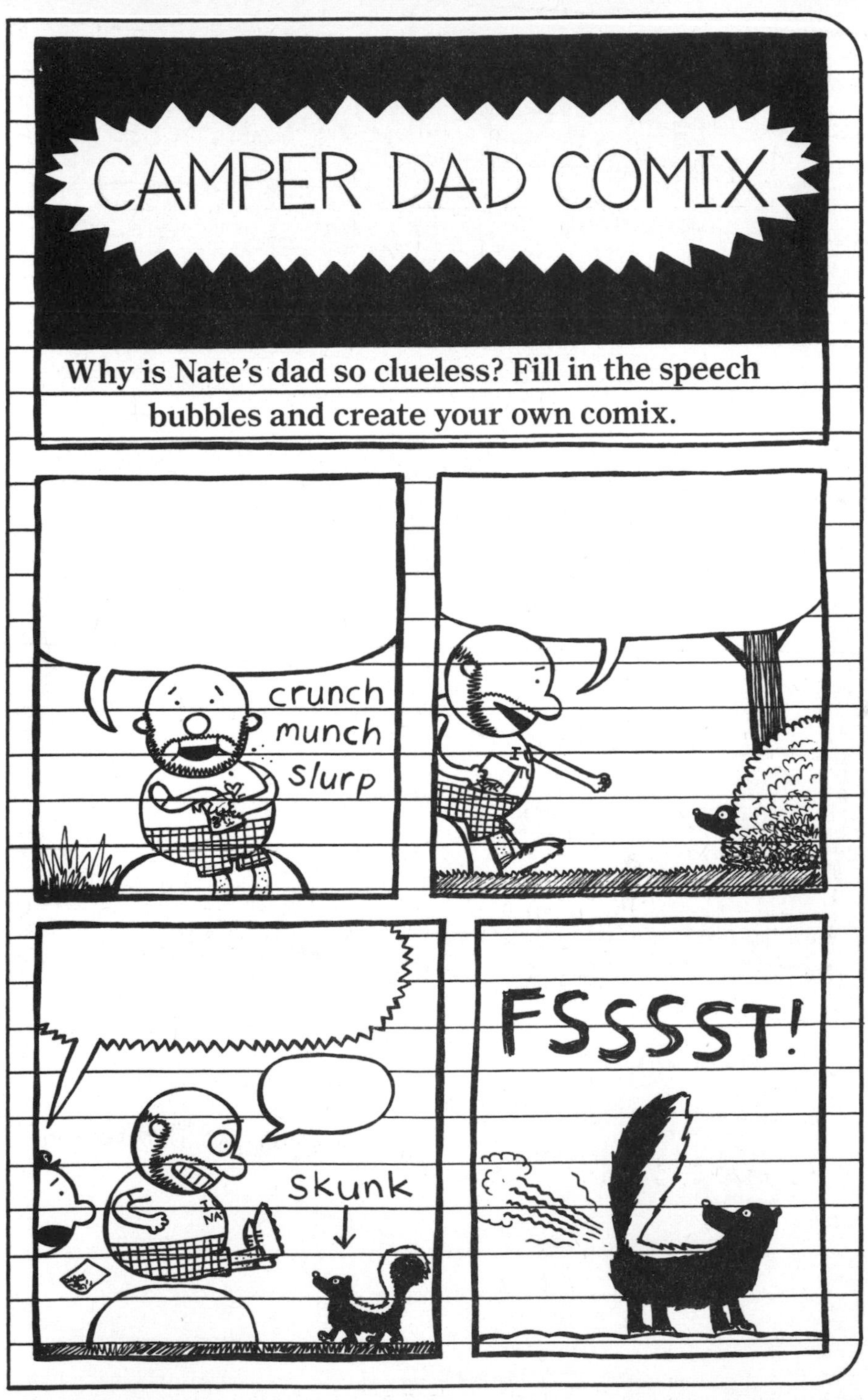
crunch
munch
slurp
skunk
FSSSST!

DOG DAZE

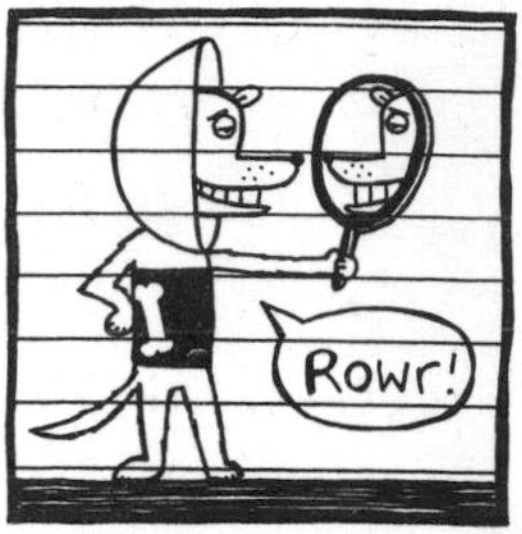
Rowr!

Nate thinks his neighbor's dog, Spitsy, is pretty cool . . . if you ignore the fact that Spitsy wears a goofy-looking dog sweater!

What kind of dogs do you love?
See if you can find all the different dogs in this hidden word puzzle!

BASSET HOUND
BEAGLE
BULLDOG
CHIHUAHUA
COCKER SPANIEL
DALMATIAN
GOLDEN RETRIEVER
GREYHOUND
IRISH SETTER
LABRADOR
MALTESE
NEWFOUNDLAND
POMERANIAN
POODLE
PUG
SAINT BERNARD
SCOTTISH TERRIER

R	G	B	D	N	N	B	R	O	R	U	E	E	P	L	A	R
E	L	E	I	N	A	P	S	R	E	K	C	O	C	I	A	I
V	U	A	D	R	Y	O	U	T	I	S	M	A	T	N	N	R
E	R	G	S	P	D	G	S	G	R	E	Y	H	O	U	N	D
I	S	L	P	O	L	N	E	C	R	S	E	R	E	D	D	D
R	N	E	N	O	G	D	U	A	E	G	A	A	A	E	R	D
T	I	N	T	D	T	T	N	O	T	U	O	B	H	A	N	B
E	U	A	N	L	E	I	H	A	H	R	L	D	N	A	A	B
R	L	I	O	E	A	E	H	A	S	T	E	R	L	I	R	W
N	A	T	E	N	C	M	U	L	I	R	E	D	A	L	I	E
E	B	A	P	H	R	H	N	N	T	B	N	S	I	I	U	N
D	R	M	R	O	I	Y	E	H	T	U	L	S	S	L	N	B
L	A	L	I	H	E	T	N	N	O	E	D	E	N	A	O	L
O	D	A	C	G	O	D	I	F	C	A	D	I	T	A	B	R
G	O	D	B	R	T	A	W	E	S	E	I	U	D	E	O	P
I	R	I	S	H	S	E	T	T	E	R	P	N	U	L	D	P
U	A	I	M	S	N	E	O	N	T	D	H	A	R	I	E	D

HOW DOES THAT SOUND, SPITSY?
WURF!

YOU'LL HELP ME THINK OF SOME-THING, RIGHT?
WUFF!

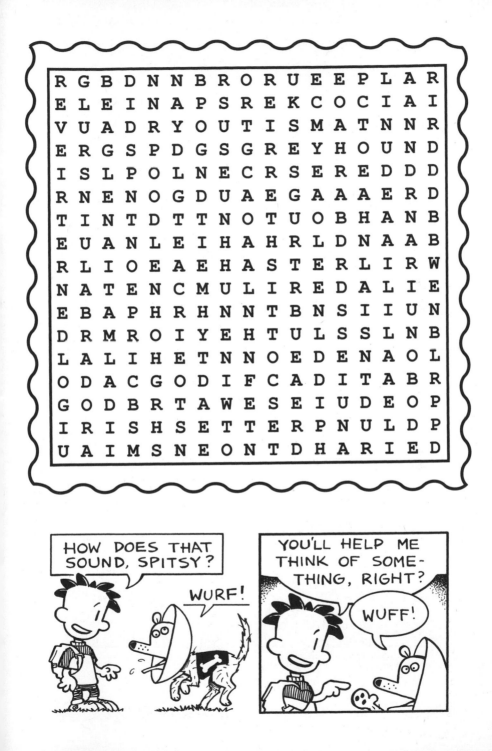

SPITSY, CHAMPION DOG

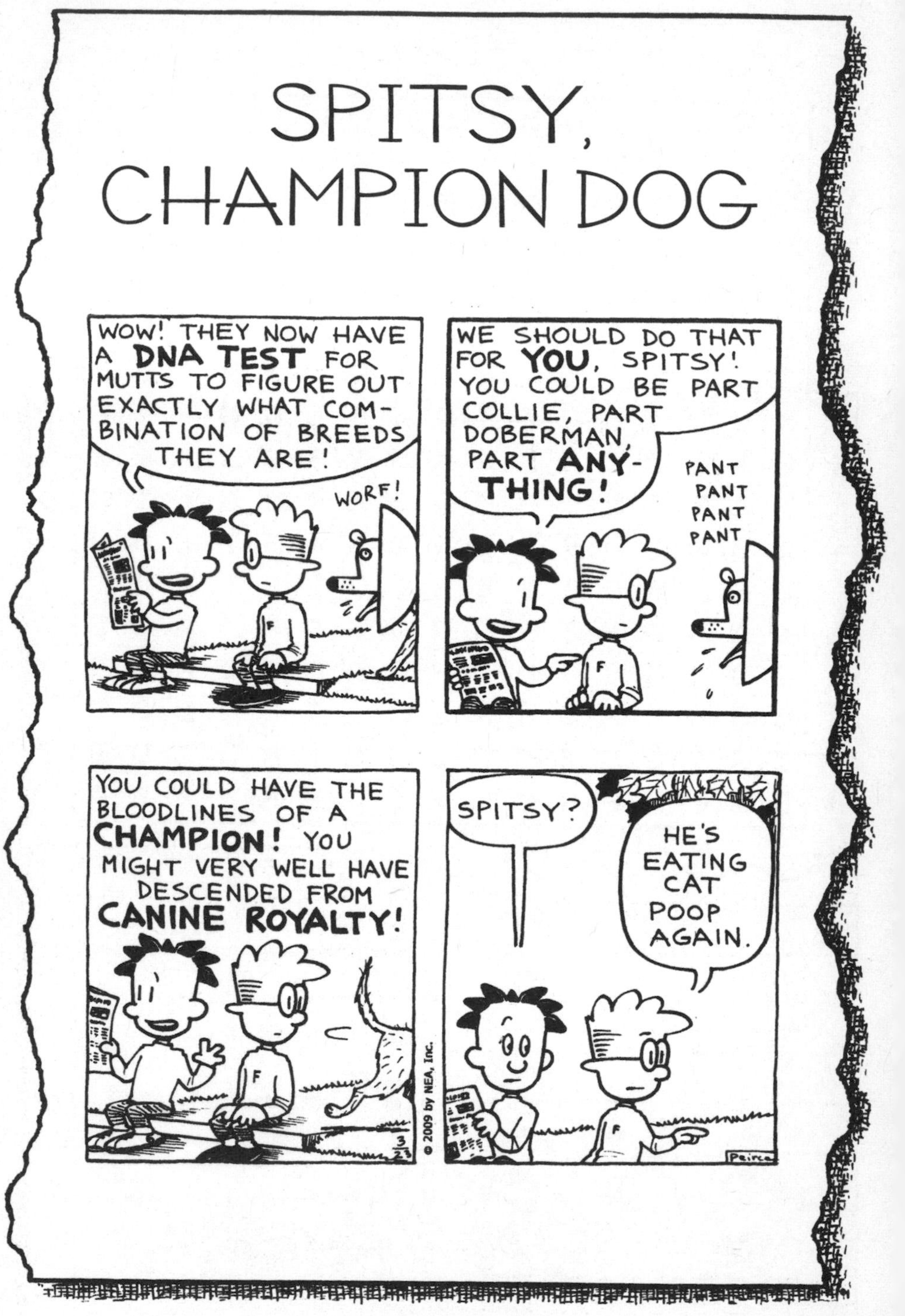
WOW! THEY NOW HAVE A **DNA TEST** FOR MUTTS TO FIGURE OUT EXACTLY WHAT COMBINATION OF BREEDS THEY ARE!
WORF!
WE SHOULD DO THAT FOR **YOU**, SPITSY! YOU COULD BE PART COLLIE, PART DOBERMAN, PART **ANYTHING**!
PANT PANT PANT PANT
YOU COULD HAVE THE BLOODLINES OF A **CHAMPION**! YOU MIGHT VERY WELL HAVE DESCENDED FROM **CANINE ROYALTY**!
© 2009 by NEA, Inc.
SPITSY?
HE'S EATING CAT POOP AGAIN.
Peirce

COMIX GENIUS

What is the name for a comix genius? A cartoonist, of course! Turn on your genius and see if you can make more than 20 other words with these letters!

CARTOONIST

1.	12.
2.	13.
3.	14.
4.	15.
5.	16.
6.	17.
7.	18.
8.	19.
9.	20.
10.	21.
11.	22.

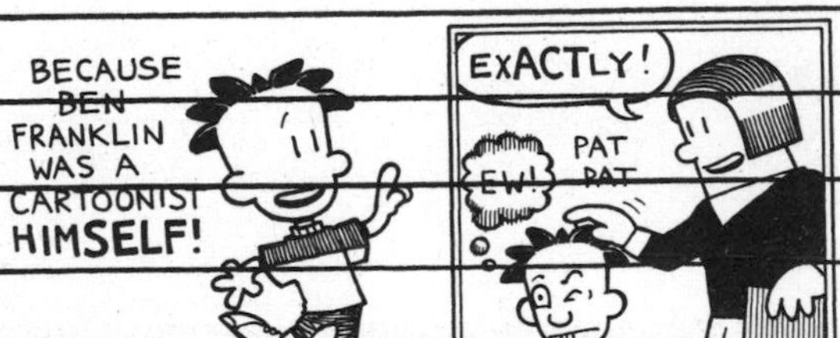
BECAUSE BEN FRANKLIN WAS A CARTOONIST HIMSELF!
EXACTLY!
PAT PAT
EW!

BREAKFAST BOOK CLUB

At BBC, Breakfast Book Club, the kids at P.S. 38 talk about books!

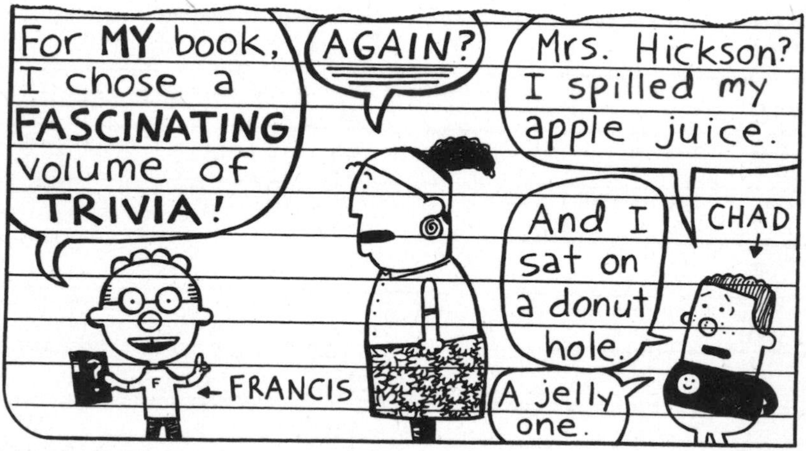
For MY book, I chose a FASCINATING volume of TRIVIA!
AGAIN?
Mrs. Hickson? I spilled my apple juice.
And I sat on a donut hole.
A jelly one.
CHAD
FRANCIS

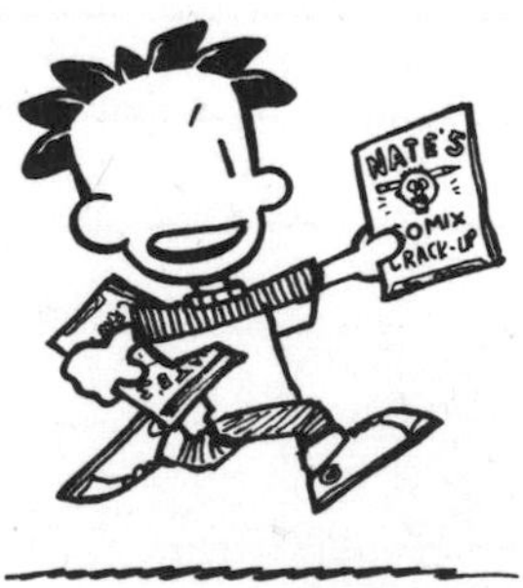
NATE'S COMIX CRACK-UP

List the most memorable books you've read. Then grade them from A to F!

BOOK TITLE	GRADE
1.	
2.	
3. *Big Nate: In a Class by Himself*	A
4.	
5.	
6. *Big Nate Strikes Again*	A
7.	
8.	
9. *Big Nate on a Roll*	A
10.	
11.	
12. *Big Nate Goes for Broke*	A

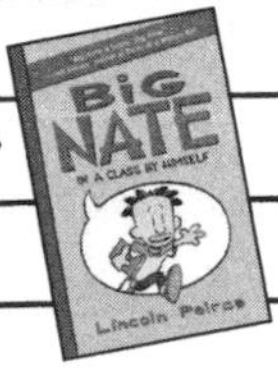
BIG NATE
IN A CLASS BY HIMSELF
Lincoln Peirce

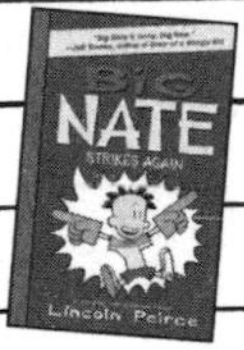
BIG NATE
STRIKES AGAIN
Lincoln Peirce

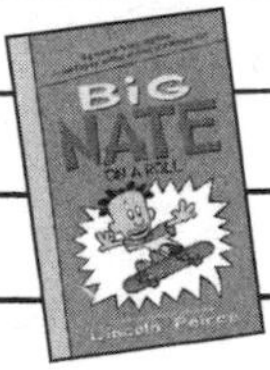
BIG NATE
ON A ROLL
Lincoln Peirce

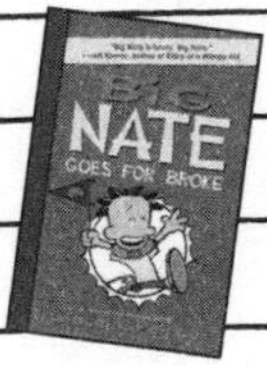
BIG NATE
GOES FOR BROKE

DOOR-TO-DOOR DISASTERS!

Nate has had some unfortunate door-to-door selling encounters. Fill in the blanks so that each letter shows up once in every box, row, and column.

W = WARM FUZZIES

P = WRAPPING PAPER

C = CANDY BARS

S = SCENTED CANDLES

M = MAGAZINE SUBSCRIPTIONS

R = RAFFLE TICKETS

This was the worst! Decode the message on page 47 to find out why.

AACK! I'M ALLERGIC TO WAX!
CALL 911!
"ocean mist"

M			W		
P			M	R	S
			R	P	M
R	P	M			
S	R	P			W
		W			R

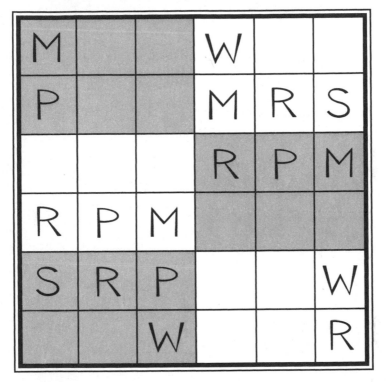

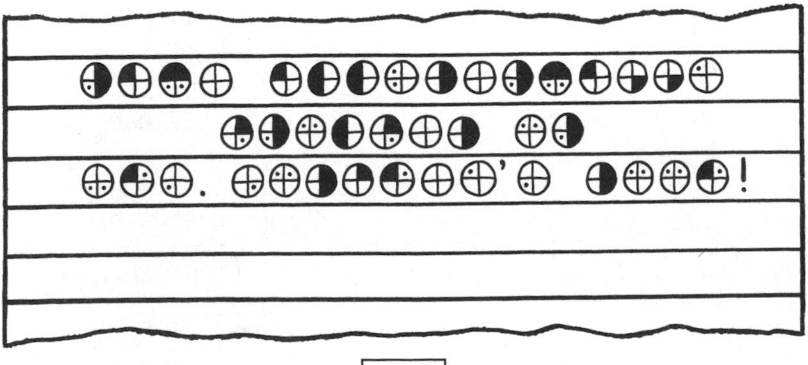

INVENTION CONVENTION

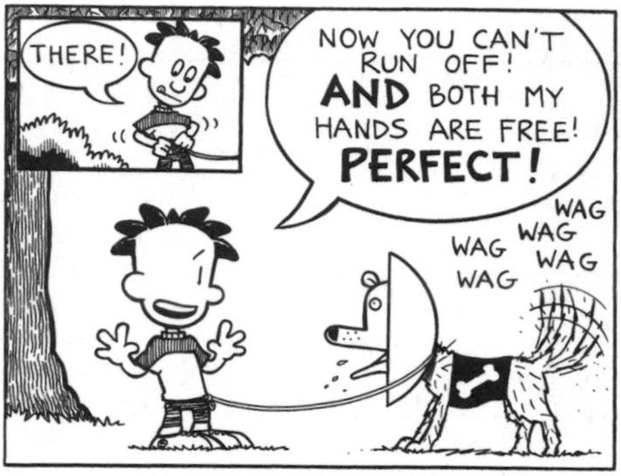
THERE!
NOW YOU CAN'T RUN OFF! AND BOTH MY HANDS ARE FREE! PERFECT!
WAG WAG WAG WAG WAG

Nate is super creative when he's making things up, like excuses when he hasn't finished his homework, teacher nicknames, or funny new inventions, like the Belsh! Now it's your turn to invent!

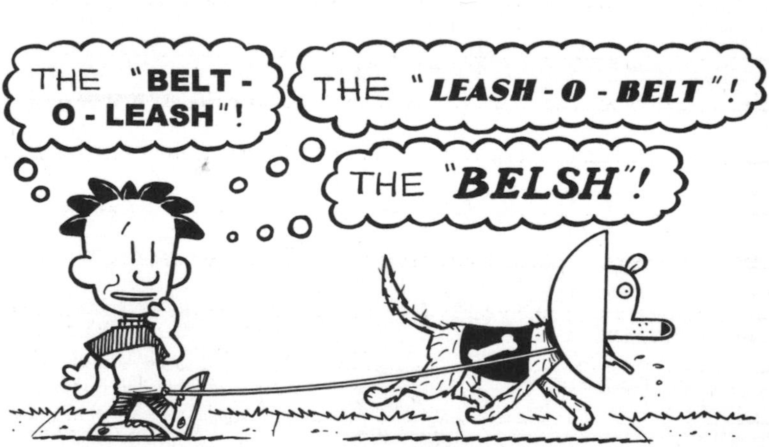
THE "BELT-O-LEASH"!
THE "LEASH-O-BELT"!
THE "BELSH"!

WATCH + PEN = __________

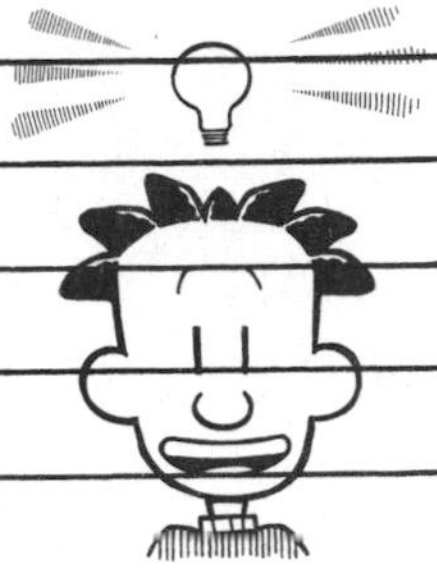

SCARF + HAT = __________

CAMERA + GLASSES = __________

FLIP-FLOPS + FAN = __________

UMBRELLA + __________ = __________

BALL + __________ = __________

__________ + __________ = __________

__________ + __________ = __________

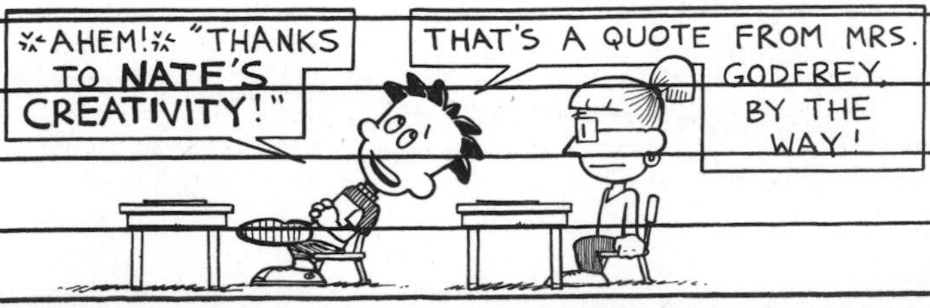
AHEM! "THANKS TO NATE'S CREATIVITY!"
THAT'S A QUOTE FROM MRS. GODFREY, BY THE WAY!

LAUGH RIOT

Teddy's a jokester. Decode (see page 34) his favorite jokes!

Q: $\overline{\underset{D}{}}\ \overline{\underset{S}{}}\ \overline{\underset{Z}{}}\ \overline{\underset{G}{}}\ \overline{\underset{W}{}}\ \overline{\underset{L}{}}\ \overline{\underset{B}{}}\ \overline{\underset{L}{}}\ \overline{\underset{F}{}}$

$\overline{\underset{X}{}}\ \overline{\underset{Z}{}}\ \overline{\underset{O}{}}\ \overline{\underset{O}{}}\ \overline{\underset{Z}{}}\ \overline{\underset{H}{}}\ \overline{\underset{O}{}}\ \overline{\underset{V}{}}\ \overline{\underset{V}{}}\ \overline{\underset{K}{}}\ \overline{\underset{R}{}}\ \overline{\underset{M}{}}\ \overline{\underset{T}{}}$

$\overline{\underset{X}{}}\ \overline{\underset{L}{}}\ \overline{\underset{D}{}}$?

A: $\overline{\underset{Z}{}}\ \overline{\underset{Y}{}}\ \overline{\underset{F}{}}\ \overline{\underset{O}{}}\ \overline{\underset{O}{}}\ \overline{\underset{W}{}}\ \overline{\underset{L}{}}\ \overline{\underset{A}{}}\ \overline{\underset{V}{}}\ \overline{\underset{I}{}}$!

HA! HA! HA!

Q: DSB WRW GSV YLLTVI XILHH GSV ILZW?

A: YVXZFHV SV DZH YVRMT KRXPVW LM!

WA HA HA HA
OH HO HO HO
HA
HA
HA
HO

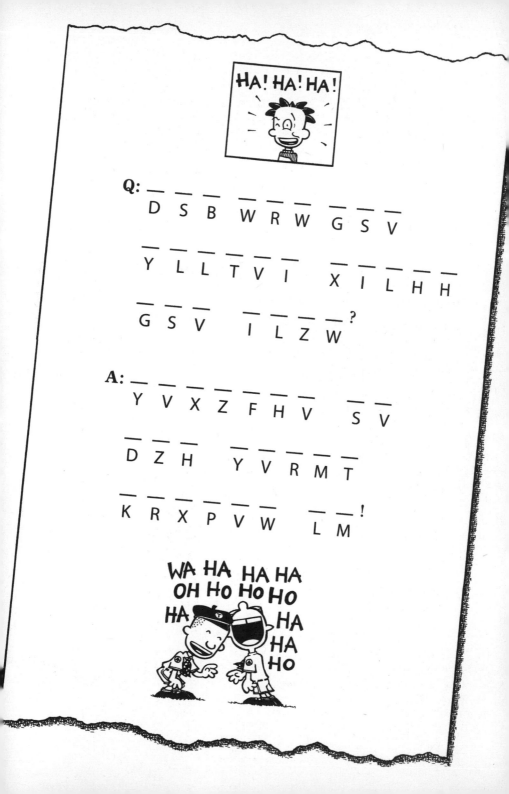

LIFE WITH ELLEN

Look at Nate as a little kid! This is how Nate remembers his big sister, Ellen. Now pretend you're Ellen and tell the same story from HER point of view.

Me and Ellen

Need help with definitions of the parts of speech? Visit Ms. Clarke's class on pages 6–8.

MAKE A LIST OF WORDS
THAT ELLEN WOULD USE!

1. Noun:	7. Verb:
2. Verb (ending in -ing):	8. Adverb:
3. Noun:	9. Verb:
4. Noun:	10. Noun:
5. Adverb:	11. Noun:
6. Adjective:	12. Noun:

WE'RE GETTING BACK OUR
BOOK REPORTS, WHICH I
KNOW I DID WELL ON!
AND I'M TRYING OUT FOR
THE SCHOOL MUSICAL!
AND I'M RUNNING FOR
CLASS PRESIDENT! AND
THEN [...]NG TO WORK
ON A[...]TINE[...]AT
CHE[...]NG PRA[...] SO
TO[...] R[...] THE GIR[...] BUT
W[...] HAV[...]T DECIDED [...] I'M
[...] ABOUT [...]EN
[...] [...] WHEN

TURN THE PAGE TO READ

ELLEN'S SIDE OF THE STORY!

When Nate was a _____ , he was always
$\quad$ 1.

_____ around the _____
$\quad$ 2. $\qquad\qquad\qquad\qquad\qquad$ 3.

and spitting up _____ . I was a
$\qquad\qquad\qquad\qquad$ 4.

_____ _____ big sister and
$\quad$ 5. $\qquad\qquad\qquad$ 6.

taught him how to _____
$\qquad\qquad\qquad\qquad\qquad$ 7. $\qquad\qquad$ 8.

and _____ . Deep down, he knows
$\qquad$ 9.

I am a _____ , because it's obvious I'm
$\qquad\qquad$ 10.

a super _____ . Too bad he's a little
$\qquad\qquad\qquad$ 11.

_____ !
$\quad$ 12.

ALL-STAR CARDS

TEDDY ORTIZ
KUDDLE KITTENS
KUDDLE KITTENS
NATE WRIGHT
Francis Pope
Kuddle Kittens

Become an all-star athlete—draw your very own trading card featuring YOU!

KUDDLE KITTENS

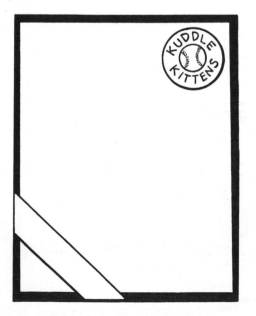

LATER, SKATER

Nate is one super skateboarder. But there's one thing he wants most of all—his own customized skateboard!

CUSTOMIZED
SKATEBOARD!
55mm wheels
cast aluminum truck assembly
YOU DESIGN THE BOARD YOU WANT!

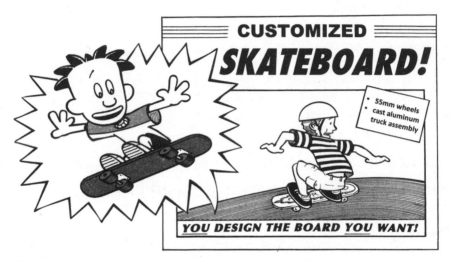

DESIGN YOUR DREAM SKATEBOARD!

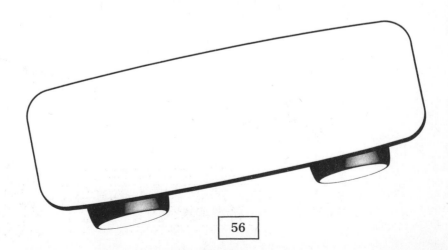

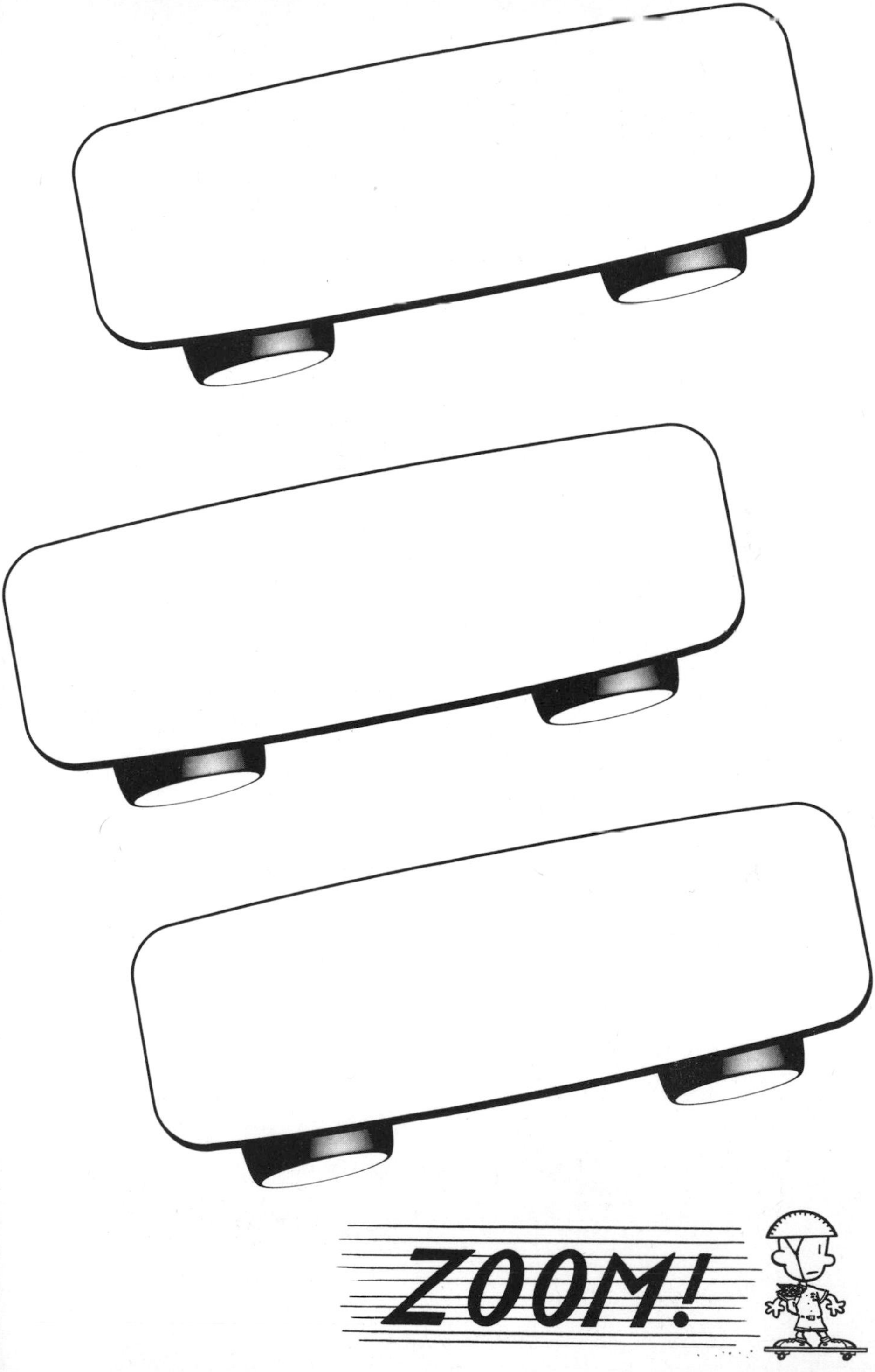
ZOOM!

FRANCIS'S CLASSIFIED CODE

No one will ever guess my code!

What number should F be?

Francis made his own secret alphabet. But Nate can decode Francis's messages . . . and so can you!

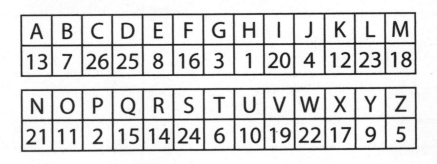

A	B	C	D	E	F	G	H	I	J	K	L	M
13	7	26	25	8	16	3	1	20	4	12	23	18

N	O	P	Q	R	S	T	U	V	W	X	Y	Z
21	11	2	15	14	24	6	10	19	22	17	9	5

I know I can figure it out!

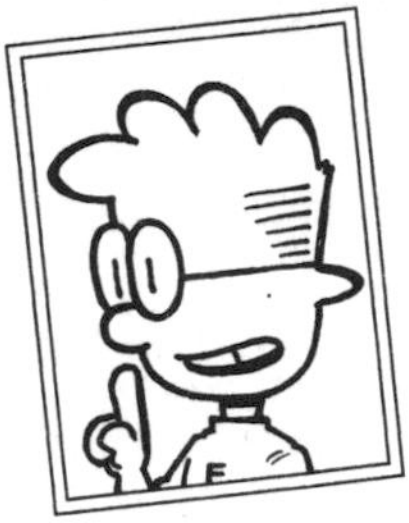

24 26 20 8 21 6 20 24 6 24

20 21 2 8 14 10

16 11 10 21 25 13 3 20 13 21 6

2 8 21 3 10 20 21 6 1 13 6

23 20 19 8 25 6 1 20 14 6 9 -

24 20 17 18 20 23 23 20 11 21

9 8 13 14 24 13 3 11 .

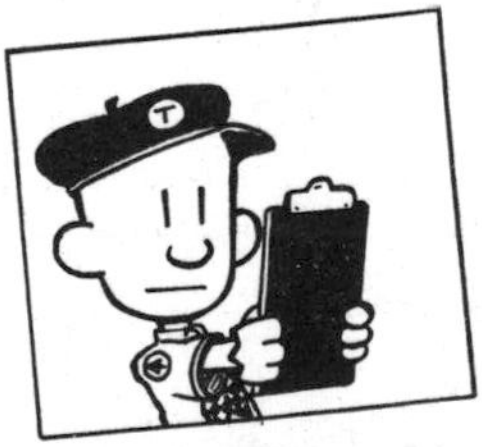

BADGE BONANZA

How many Timber Scout merit badges does Nate have? Fill in the blank squares so each badge letter appears once in every column, row, and box.

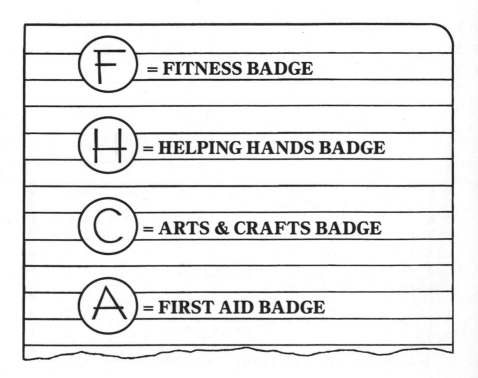

$\left(\text{F}\right)$ = FITNESS BADGE

$\left(\text{H}\right)$ = HELPING HANDS BADGE

$\left(\text{C}\right)$ = ARTS & CRAFTS BADGE

$\left(\text{A}\right)$ = FIRST AID BADGE

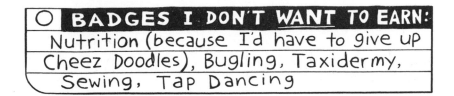

BADGES I DON'T WANT TO EARN:

Nutrition (because I'd have to give up Cheez Doodles), Bugling, Taxidermy, Sewing, Tap Dancing

F
H
F
C
A

Put your arms around him, Nate! Then SQUEEZE!
Teddy's dad
I'm TRYING!

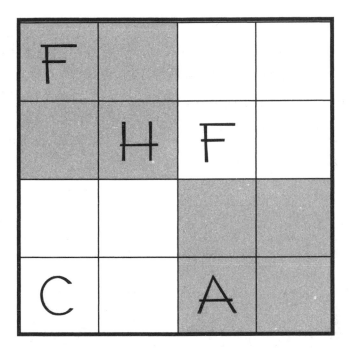

NAME THAT GNOME

Nate has one VERY odd job—moving garden gnomes! See if you can come up with more than 10 funny gnome names!

1.	11. Jolly Wally
2.	12.
3.	13.
4.	14.
5. Funny Face	15.
6.	16.
7.	17.
8.	18.
9.	19.
10.	20.

ON THE BOTTOM OF EACH ONE, YOU'LL FIND A NAME!

Wobbly

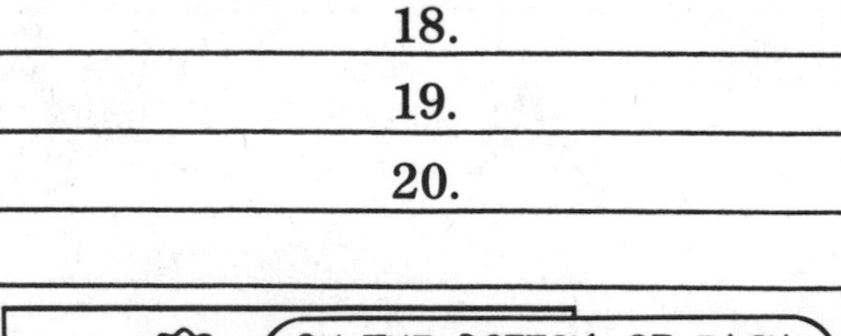

BONUS ROUND: Speaking of little guys, can you name all the dwarfs from Snow White?

1. H_ _ _ _
2. B_ _ _ _ _ _
3. G_ _ _ _ _
4. Doc
5. Sleepy
6. D_ _ _ _
7. S_ _ _ _ _

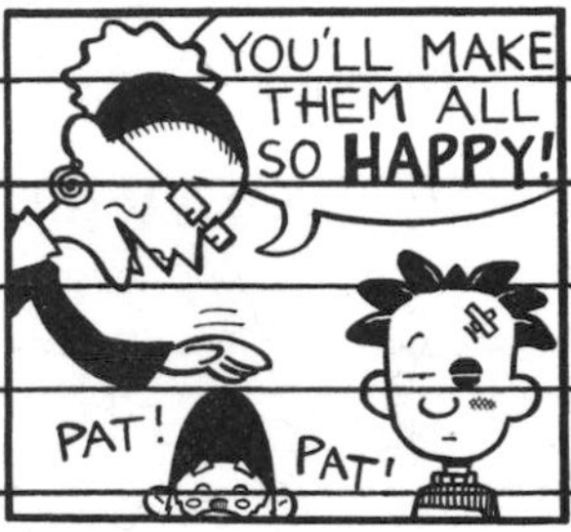
YOU'LL MAKE THEM ALL SO HAPPY!
PAT!
PAT!

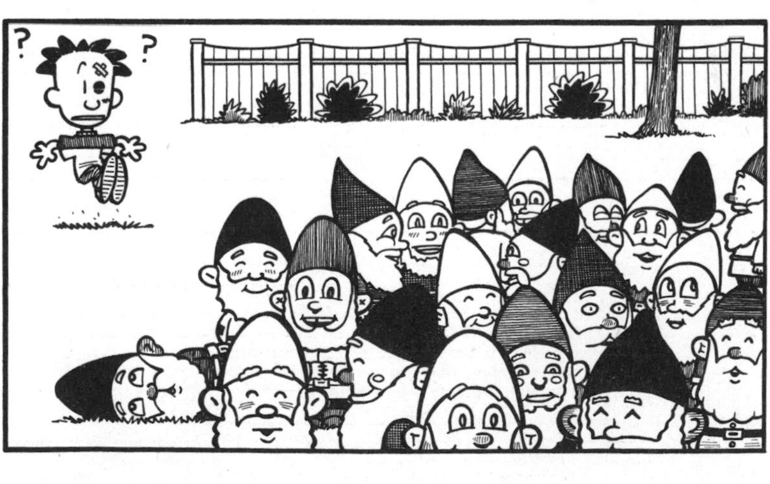
?
?

HAPPY HAIKU

Nate's quite a poet. How about you? Nate even writes haiku!

Haiku is a kind of poem with only 17 syllables.

The first line has 5 syllables.

The second line has 7 syllables.

The third line has 5 syllables.

JUST LIKE THIS:

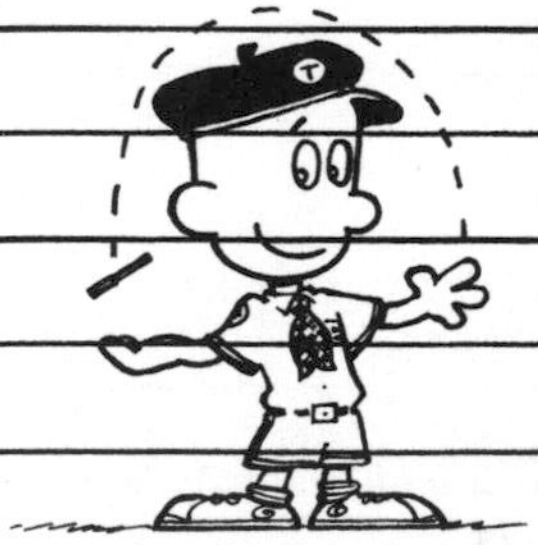

HAIKU by Nate Wright

```
You have Cheez Doodles.
Fresh. Crunchy. Puffalicious.
Give me one right now.
```

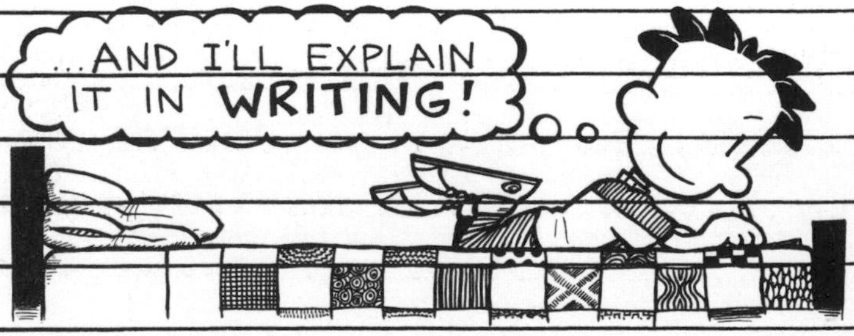
...AND I'LL EXPLAIN IT IN WRITING!

HERE'S ANOTHER HAIKU:

Nate's locker smells gross,
Like Cheez Doodles and gym socks.
Papers falling out.

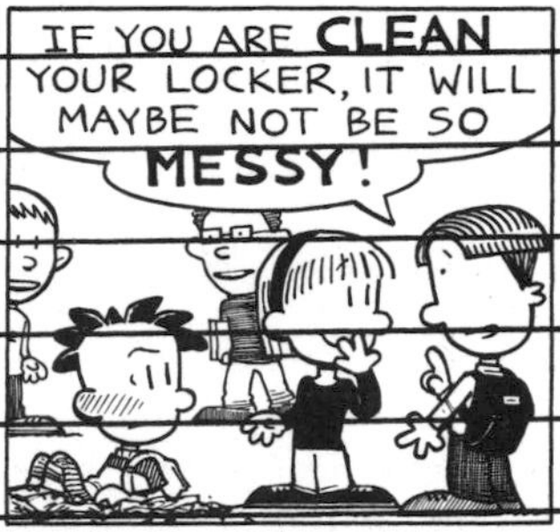
IF YOU ARE CLEAN YOUR LOCKER, IT WILL MAYBE NOT BE SO MESSY!

NOW YOU TRY!

1. **Detention again.**
2. ______________________
3. ______________________

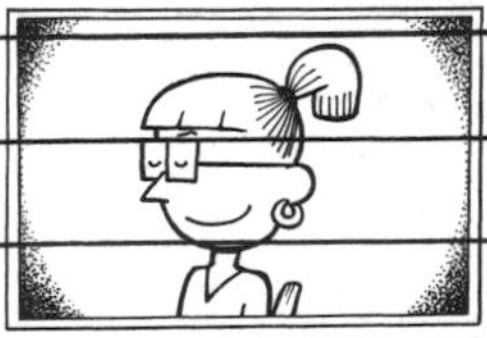

1. **Gina gets an A.**
2. ______________________
3. ______________________

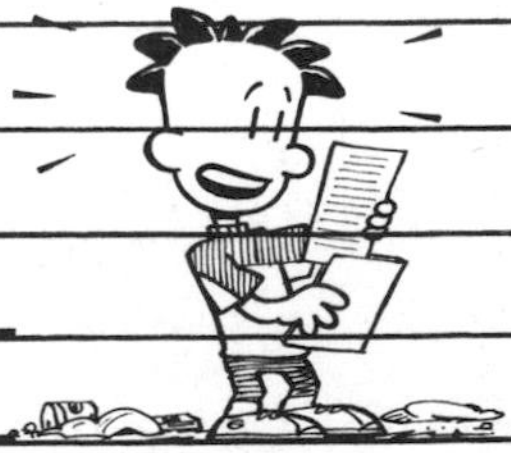

1. **The nickname czar rules.**
2. ______________________
3. ______________________

ALIAS

Nate has many different nicknames for Mrs. Godfrey, his horrifying social studies teacher. Fill in the blanks so only one of each Godfrey alias appears in every row, column, and box.

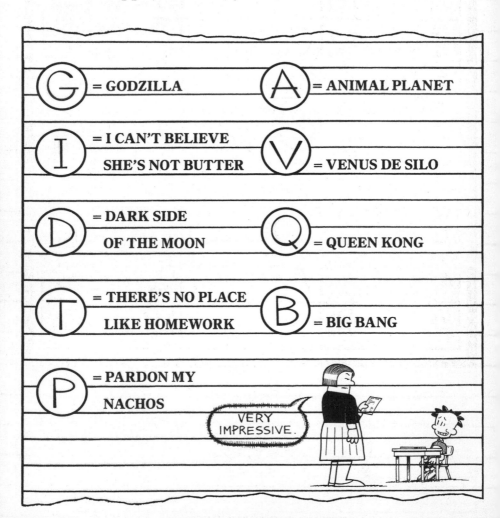

(G) = GODZILLA   (A) = ANIMAL PLANET

(I) = I CAN'T BELIEVE SHE'S NOT BUTTER   (V) = VENUS DE SILO

(D) = DARK SIDE OF THE MOON   (Q) = QUEEN KONG

(T) = THERE'S NO PLACE LIKE HOMEWORK   (B) = BIG BANG

(P) = PARDON MY NACHOS

VERY IMPRESSIVE.

CRACK!!
Peel me a GRAPE!
Q

G	B	T		Q	I	D	A	
		A			B	I		
I		V	G	D			Q	
B	V		I					Q
		G	Q		V	B	D	T
T		Q	D		P	G		I
D		I	V		Q	P	B	
V			A		G	Q	I	D
A		P				V		G

HISSS!..
HISSS!..
HISSS...
BWA HA HAA!
GRRRRRRRRR...

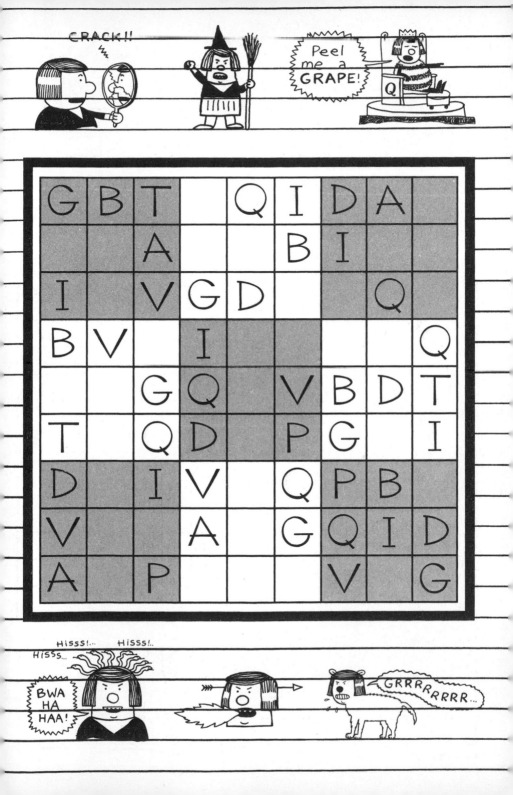

SUPER SCOUT CHALLENGE

Being a scout means rising to the challenge! Just ask Nate. See if you can find all the key scouting words in the puzzle.

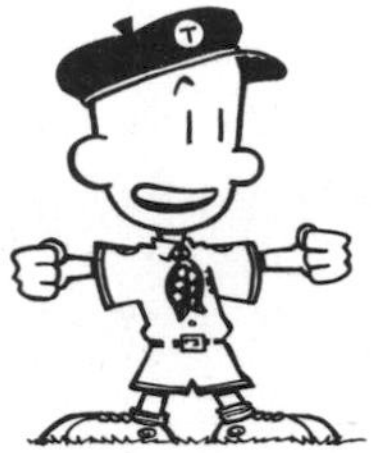

MARSHMALLOW
HONOR
TROOP
FORT
CLIMBING
HIKING
SURVIVAL
OATH
CAMPFIRE

BADGES
UNIFORM
WALKING STICK
ARCHERY
SLEEPING BAG
CABINS
HANDSHAKE
FRIENDSHIP
OUTDOORS

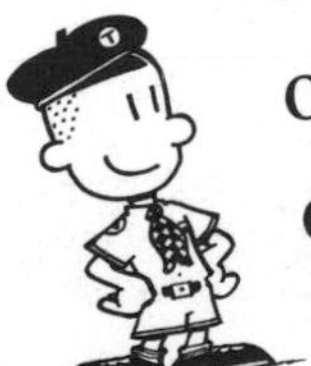

G	H	C	G	I	O	I	B	R	O	C	G	H
N	A	A	S	I	I	A	L	C	H	M	D	P
I	N	B	B	R	D	I	A	T	P	R	W	K
K	D	I	G	G	O	M	A	I	E	O	P	C
I	S	N	E	N	P	O	H	H	L	F	L	L
H	H	S	S	F	I	S	D	L	O	I	C	P
A	A	U	I	M	D	P	A	T	M	N	C	O
R	K	R	L	N	N	M	E	B	U	U	O	O
R	E	V	E	A	H	W	I	E	O	O	P	R
K	C	I	T	S	G	N	I	K	L	A	W	T
R	R	V	R	S	G	T	N	Y	I	S	R	R
F	K	A	R	C	H	E	R	Y	A	O	O	G
S	M	L	G	T	L	A	A	E	F	B	N	N

JUST TELL ME WHAT HAPPENED DURING THE TROOP MEETING.

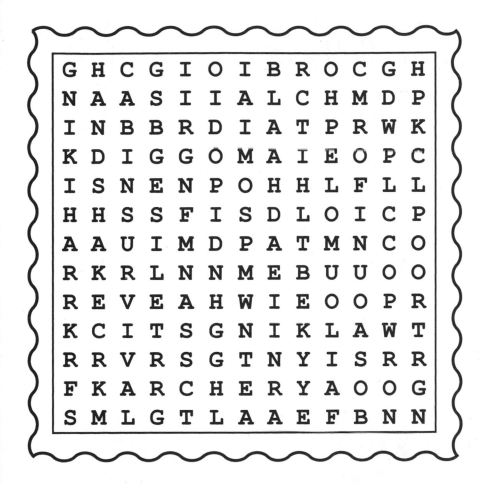

YOU ARE THE INVENTOR

What new thing would you invent?

Draw it!

COOL! IS IT **REAL?**

BACKPACK / SNACK DISPENSER

HEADBAND / FAN

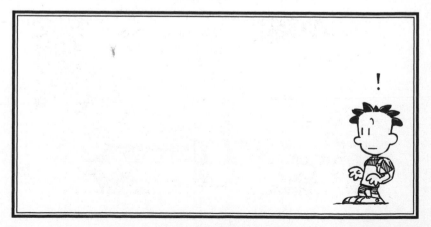

MAKE UP YOUR OWN WACKY INVENTION!

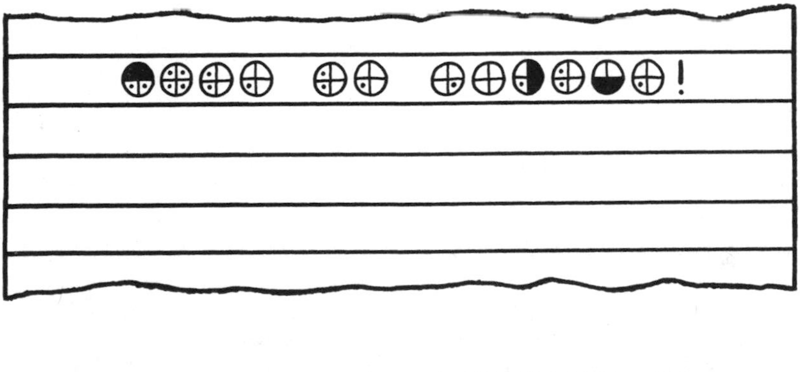

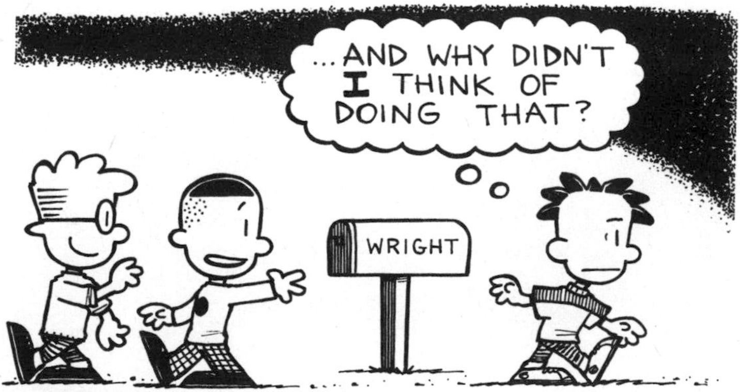
...AND WHY DIDN'T I THINK OF DOING THAT?
WRIGHT

OPEN FOR BUSINESS

Nate is the master of all jobs, big and small! Name 20 jobs where you shine!

1. ______________________________
2. ______________________________
3. ______________________________
4. ______________________________
5. Selling cookies
6. ______________________________
7. ______________________________
8. ______________________________
9. ______________________________

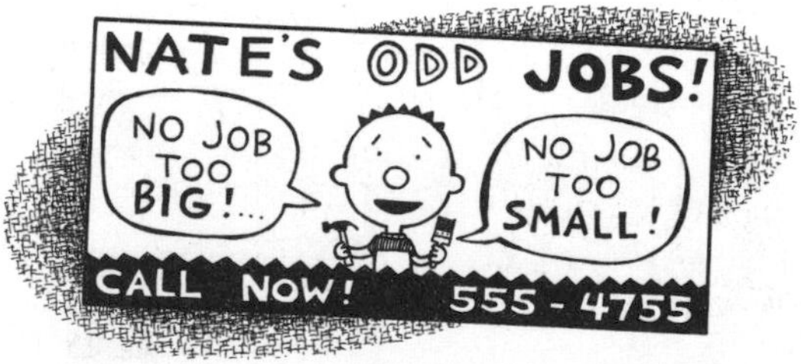
NATE'S ODD JOBS!
NO JOB TOO BIG!...
NO JOB TOO SMALL!
CALL NOW! 555-4755

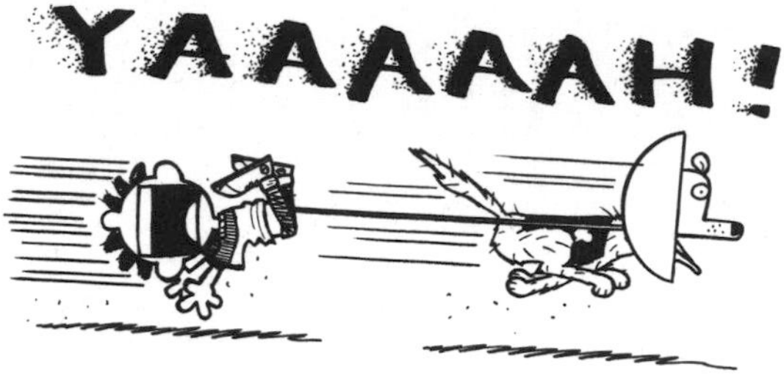
YAAAAAH!

10. Walking the dog
11.
12.
13.
14. Making comic books
15.
16.
17.
18.
19.
20.

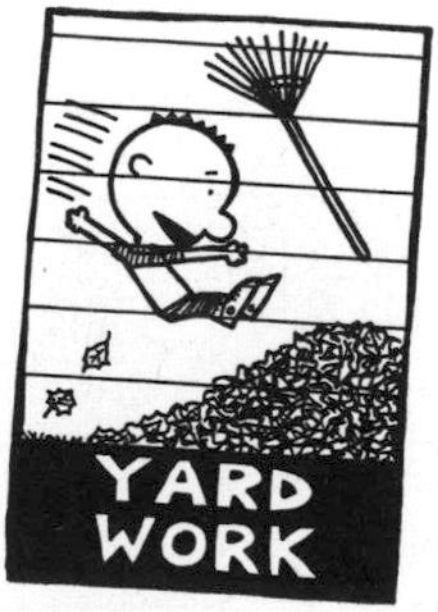
YARD WORK

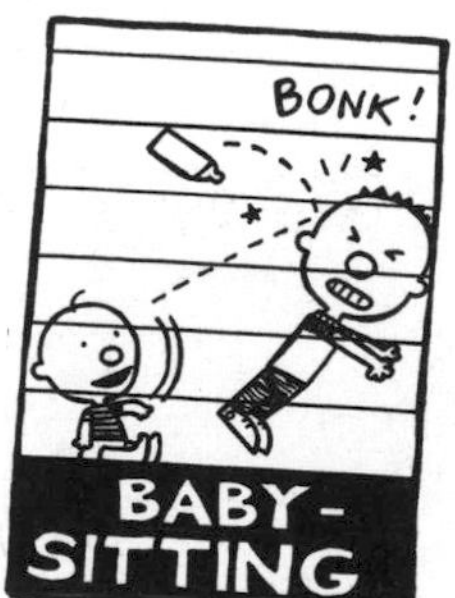
BONK!
BABY-SITTING

COVER CRAZE

Are you an artist extraordinaire or a daring designer? Check out these cool covers!

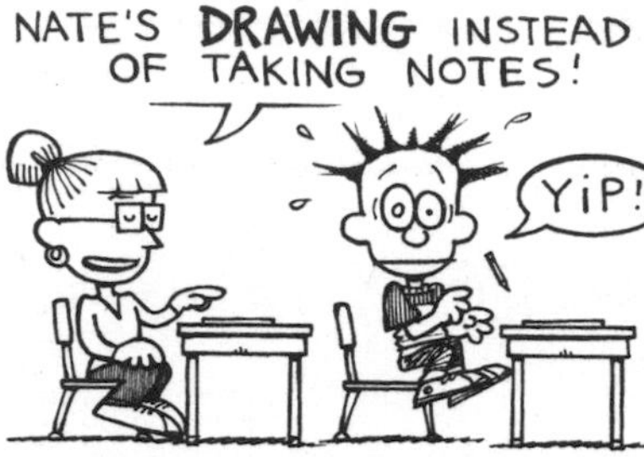

NATE'S **DRAWING** INSTEAD OF TAKING NOTES!
YiP!

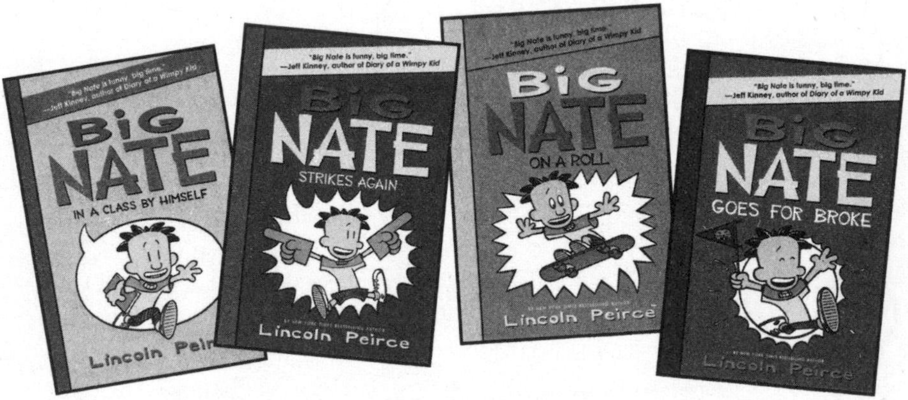

BiG NATE
IN A CLASS BY HIMSELF
Lincoln Peir
"Big Nate is funny, big time."
—Jeff Kinney, author of Diary of a Wimpy Kid
BiG NATE
STRIKES AGAIN
Lincoln Peirce
BiG NATE
ON A ROLL
Lincoln Peirce
"Big Nate is funny, big time."
—Jeff Kinney, author of Diary of a Wimpy Kid
BiG NATE
GOES FOR BROKE
Lincoln Peirce

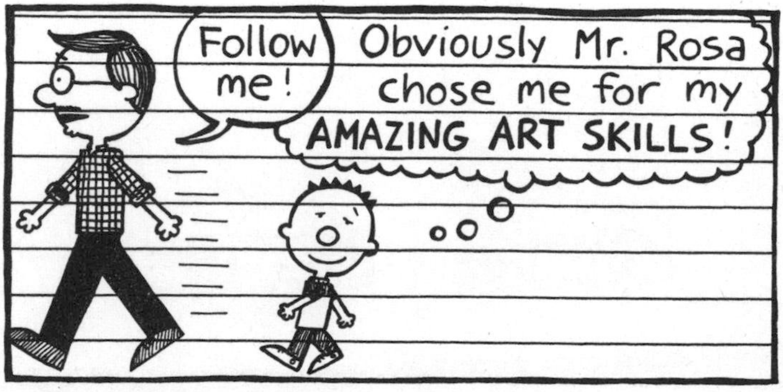

Follow me!
Obviously Mr. Rosa chose me for my AMAZING ART SKILLS!

NOW DRAW YOUR OWN COVER
FOR THE NEXT BIG NATE BOOK!

SUPER SCRIBBLE GAME

Got nothing to do? It must be scribble game time!

Don't forget to write a caption for it:

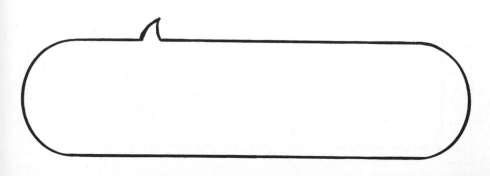

WHAT'S ANNOYING?

What's super annoying? List 10 things that make you crazy.

1. Stepping on gum

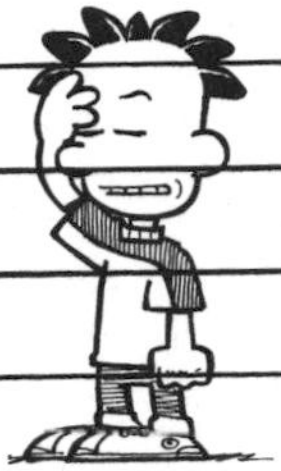

2. Bad haircut

3. Eating peas

4.

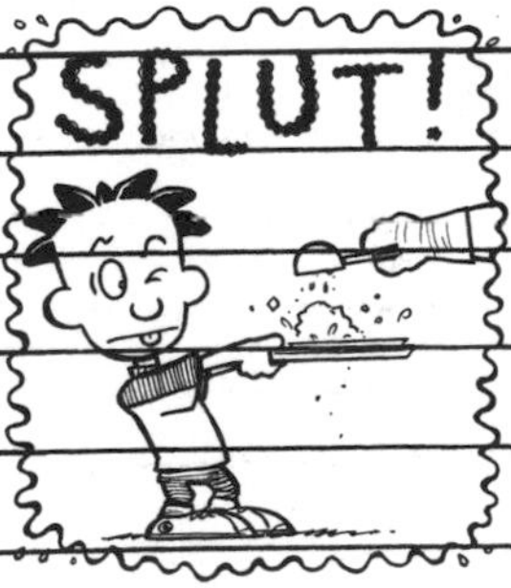
SPLUT!

5.

6.

7.

8.

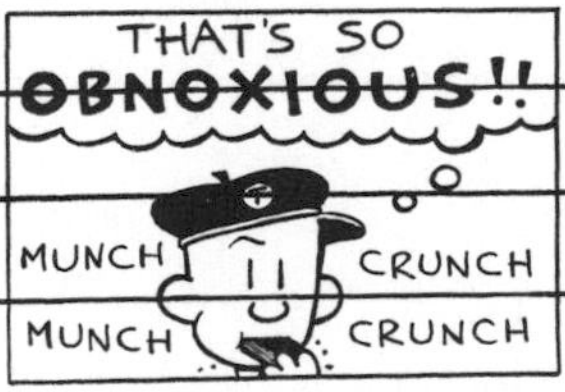
THAT'S SO OBNOXIOUS!!
MUNCH
MUNCH
CRUNCH
CRUNCH

9.

10.

FAR-OUT FACTOIDS

Francis is a serious fan of factoids. Can you decode these wacky facts using Francis's secret code on page 58?

$\overline{1}\ \overline{10}\ \overline{18}\ \overline{13}\ \overline{21}\ \overline{24}$

$\overline{1}\ \overline{13}\ \overline{19}\ \overline{8}$

$\overline{11}\ \overline{19}\ \overline{8}\ \overline{14}$

$\overline{24}\ \overline{8}\ \overline{19}\ \overline{8}\ \overline{21}\ \ \ \ \overline{6}\ \overline{1}\ \overline{11}\ \overline{10}\ \overline{24}\ \overline{13}\ \overline{21}\ \overline{25}$

$\overline{25}\ \overline{20}\ \overline{16}\ \overline{16}\ \overline{8}\ \overline{14}\ \overline{8}\ \overline{21}\ \overline{6}$

$\overline{16}\ \overline{13}\ \overline{26}\ \overline{20}\ \overline{13}\ \overline{23}$

$\overline{8}\ \overline{17}\ \overline{2}\ \overline{14}\ \overline{8}\ \overline{24}\ \overline{24}\ \overline{20}\ \overline{11}\ \overline{21}\ \overline{24}$.

20 21 13 21 13 19 8 14 13 3 8

23 20 16 8 6 20 18 8, 9 11 10

22 20 23 23 7 14 8 13 6 1 8

13 14 11 10 21 25 24 20 17

1 10 21 25 14 8 25

18 20 23 23 20 11 21

7 14 8 13 6 1 24.

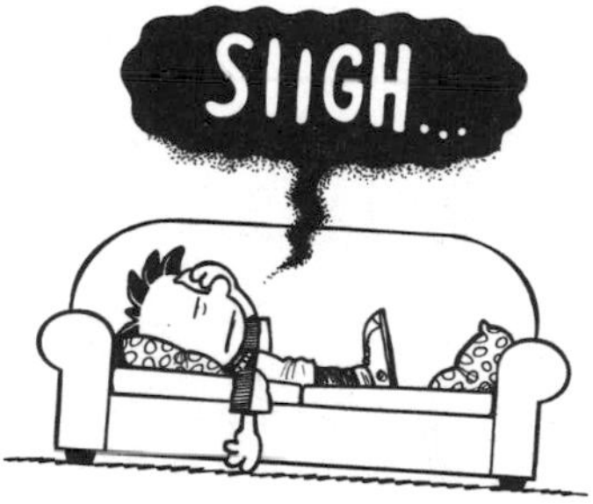
SIIGH...

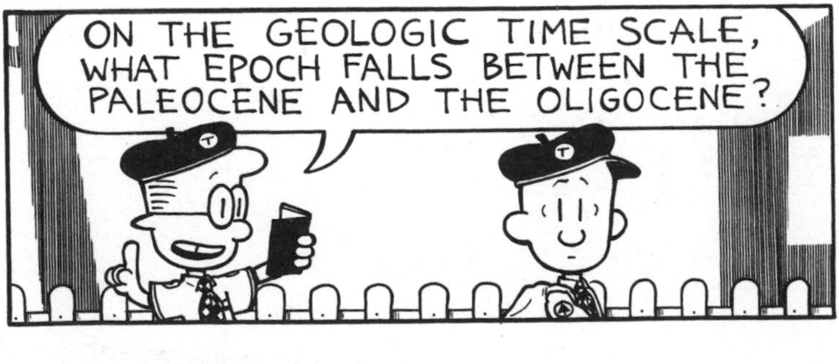
ON THE GEOLOGIC TIME SCALE, WHAT EPOCH FALLS BETWEEN THE PALEOCENE AND THE OLIGOCENE?

GYM IS A DISASTER

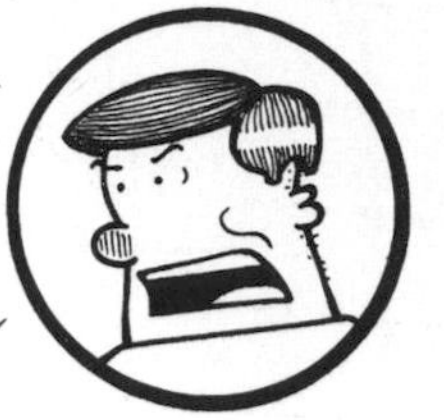

Nate once had to run wind sprints with his stomach full of green beans, in shorts that were way too big. Talk about uncomfortable! Name your biggest gym disasters.

1.

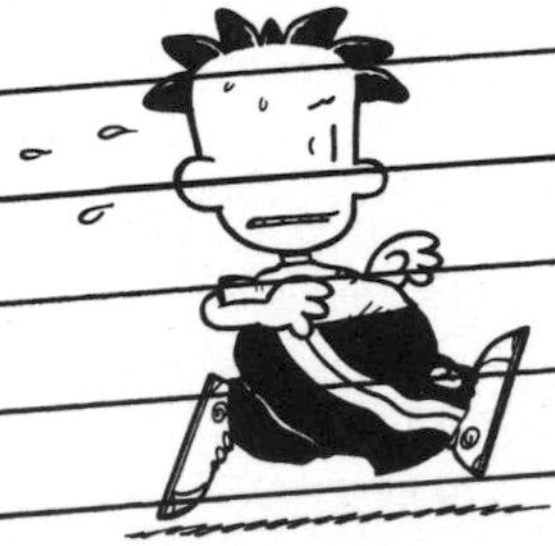

2.

3.

4.

5. Watching your crush be assigned to the other team

6.

7.

8.

9. Climbing the rope to the ceiling and having to pee SO bad!

10.

11.

12.

13.

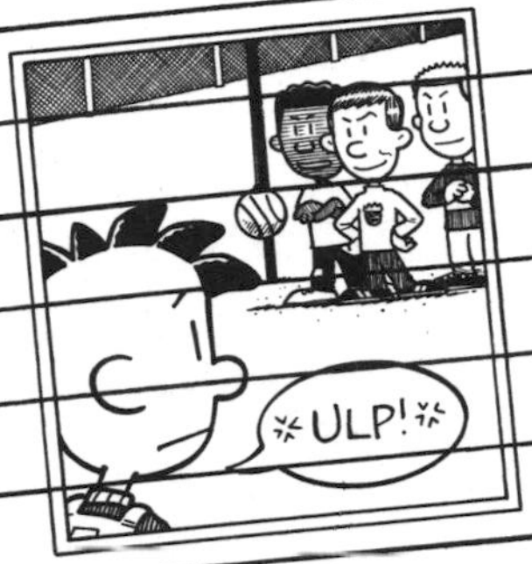
ULP!

14.

15. Facing down the school bully in dodgeball

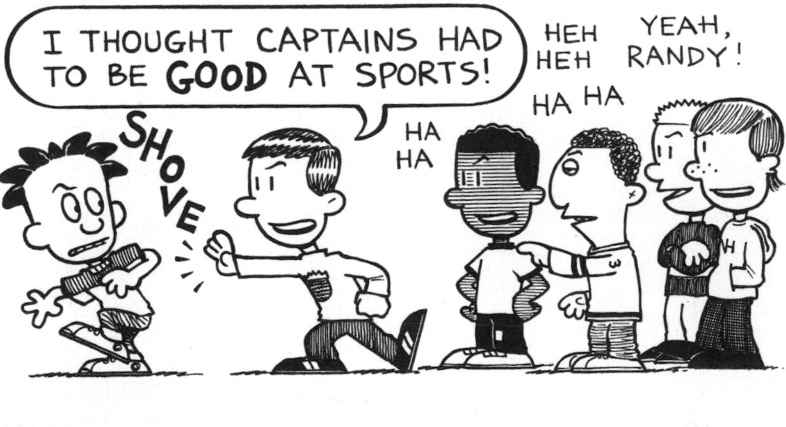
I THOUGHT CAPTAINS HAD TO BE **GOOD** AT SPORTS!
HEH HEH
YEAH, RANDY!
HA HA
HA HA
SHOVE

ADVENTURES OF ULTRA-NATE

Help Nate save the day!

Fill in the speech bubbles . . . fast!

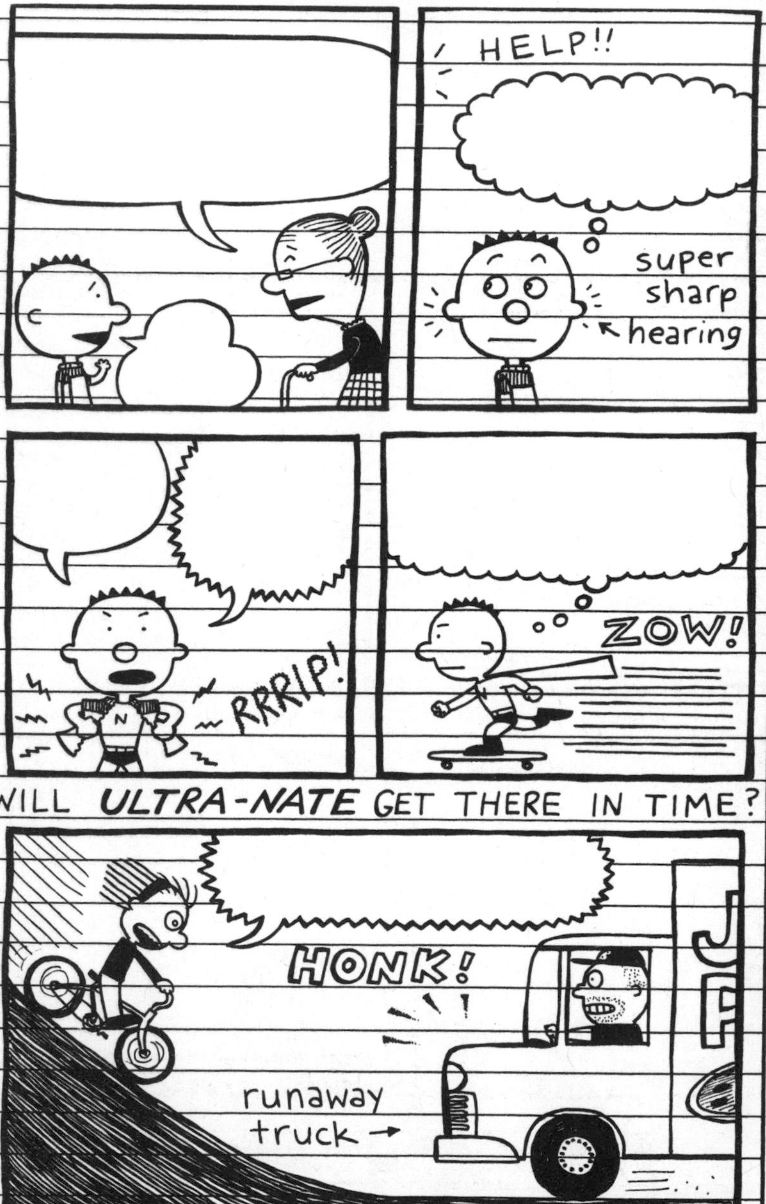

HELP!!
super
sharp
hearing
RRRIP!
N
ZOW!
WILL ULTRA-NATE GET THERE IN TIME?
HONK!
runaway
truck

NOW WHAT HAPPENS? YOU DECIDE!

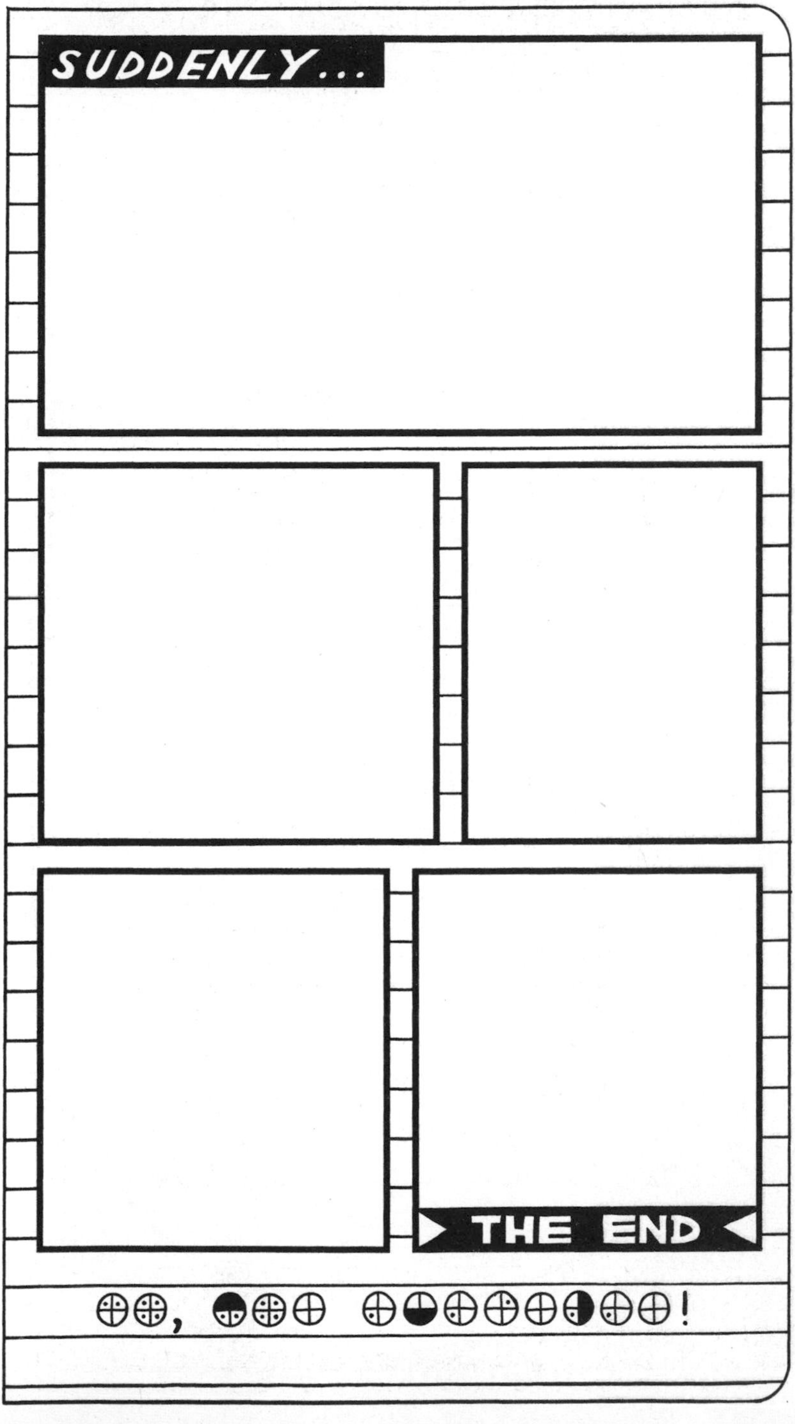
SUDDENLY...
THE END

MAD FOR BADGES

Nate does cool things to earn his merit badges. Check out his sharp Timber Scouts uniform!

ARTS & CRAFTS
HELPING HANDS
FITNESS
FIRST AID

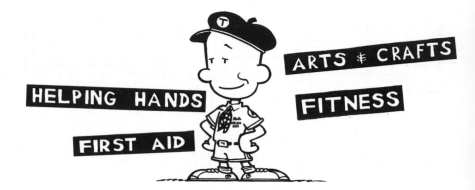

DESIGN YOUR OWN MERIT BADGES FOR EACH ACTIVITY!

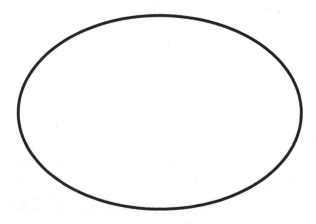

WILDERNESS SURVIVAL

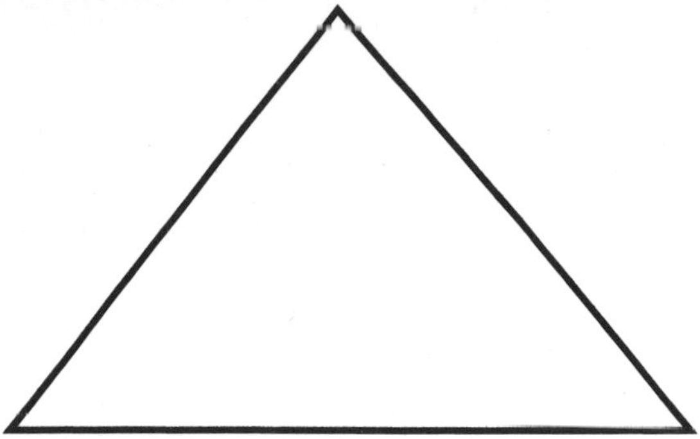

MUSIC

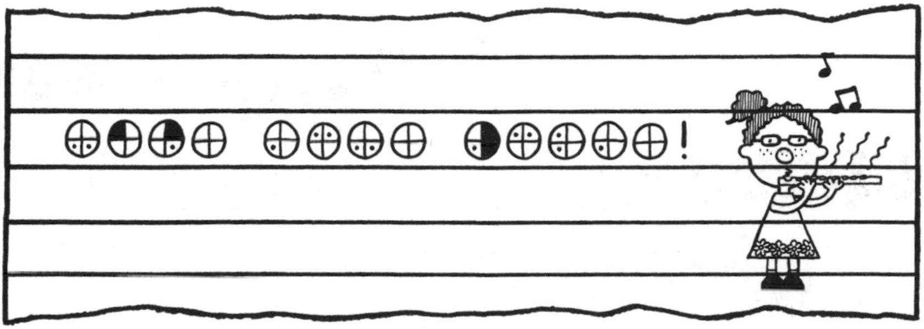

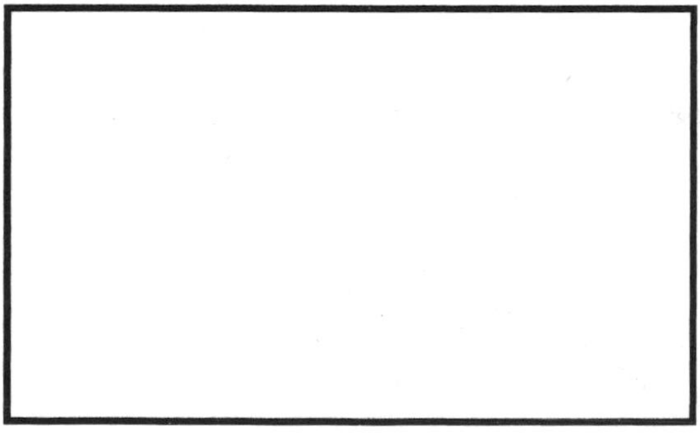

ASTRONOMY

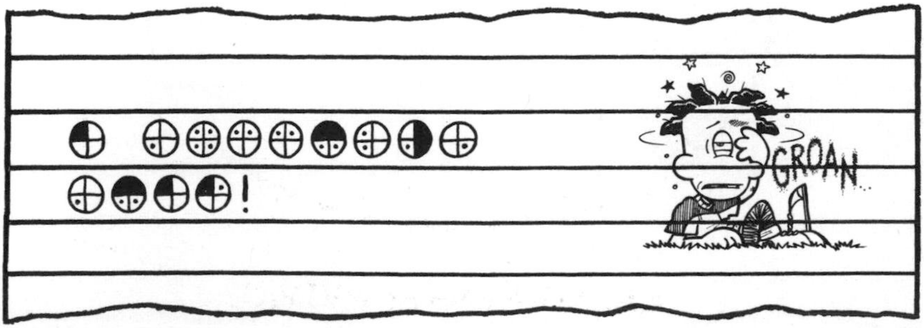
GROAN

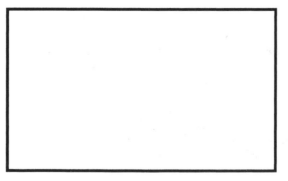

COOKING

...OR FRANCIS'S FRENCH FRIES?
OOH! HOW ABOUT TEDDYS TACOS?
WRIGHT

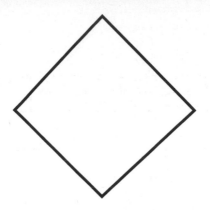

X-TREME SPORTS

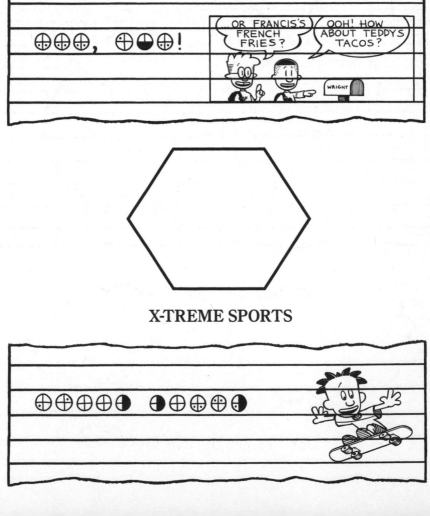

SCRIBBLE BREAK

Take a breather and turn this scribble into a masterpiece!

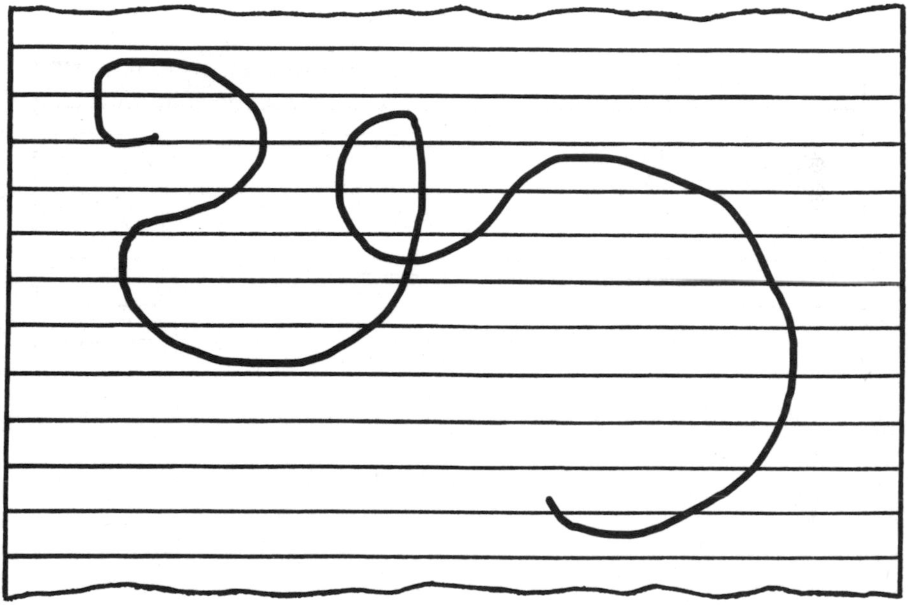

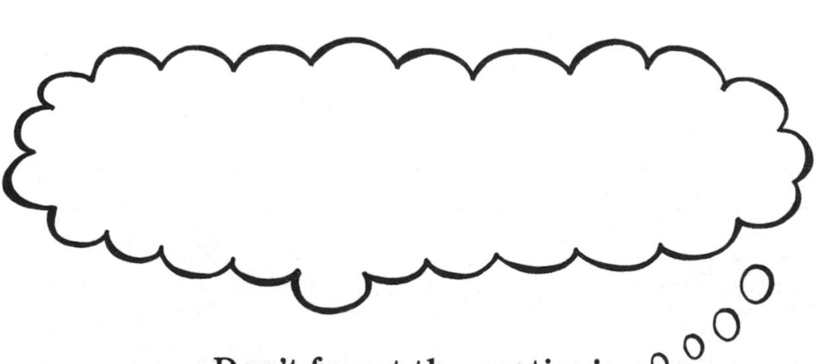

Don't forget the caption!

RHYME-A-THON

Are you a rhyming champ like Nate? Decide which pairs of rhyming words will match the funny clues.

HEY, THAT RHYMES!

1. Group of friends you just met

___ ___   ___ crew ___

2. Royal leader's finger jewelry

_____'s   _____

3. Quiet and bashful man

___ shy ___   ___

4. Super 6th grader who likes Cheez Doodles

___ great ___   _____

5. Beautiful cat   _____   _____

6. Circus performer's city

clown's ____

7. Gloomy opposite of night

gray ___

8. Not heavy, a toy you can fly in the sky

_____ kite

9. This black bird doesn't move fast

____ ____

10. A very large hog

___ pig

There once was a fellow named Nate,
Who was king of P.S. 38.
Then Artur moved to town.
Now he's stealing Nate's crown.
How come everyone thinks **HE'S** so great?

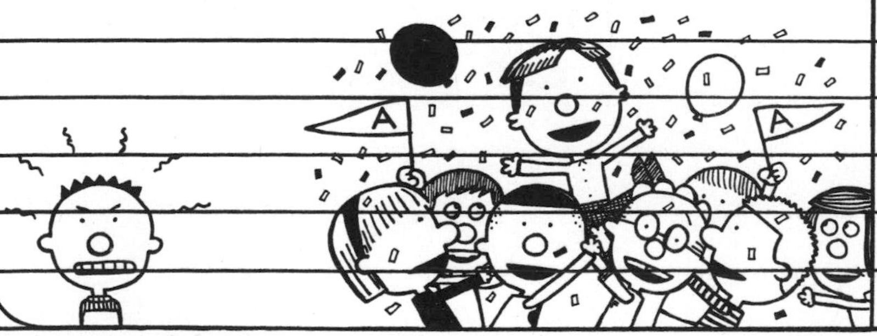

A
A

CREATE-A-COMIX!

Pick up your pencil and let your imagination run wild! Create a comic using Nate, green beans, and Teddy.

+

+

YOU GONNA EAT THOSE GREEN BEANS?

=

?

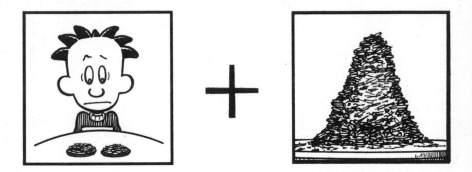

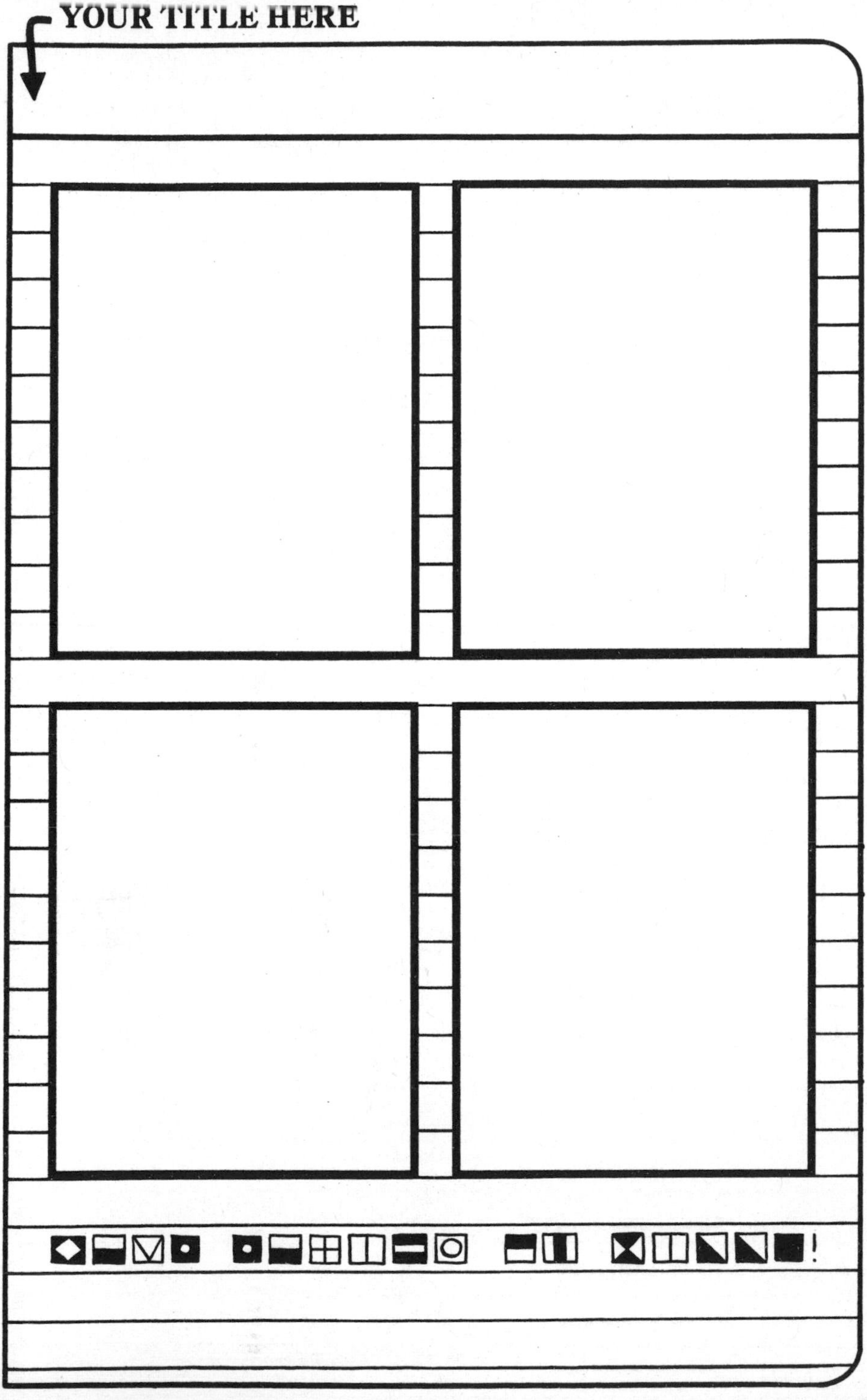
YOUR TITLE HERE

SKATER SCRAMBLE

Dude! Nate can skate. He's got wicked cool moves! Now let's see what you can do. Using the letters in "skateboard," see how many words you can create!

SKATEBOARD

1.	11.
2.	12.
3.	13.
4.	14.
5.	15.
6.	16.
7.	17.
8.	18.
9.	19.
10.	20.

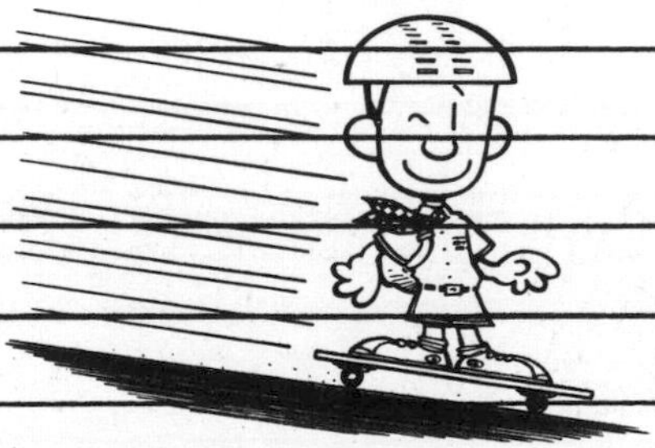

BONUS:

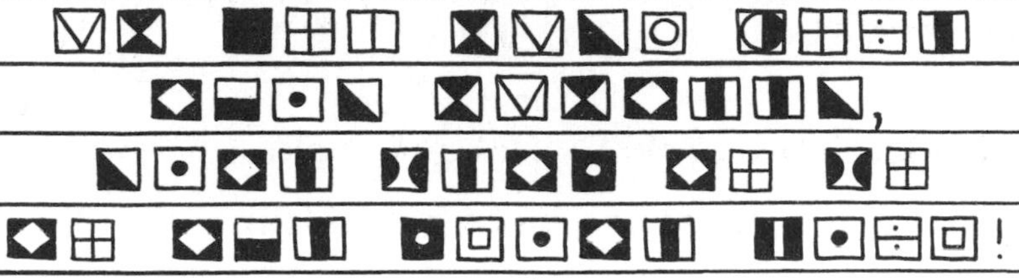

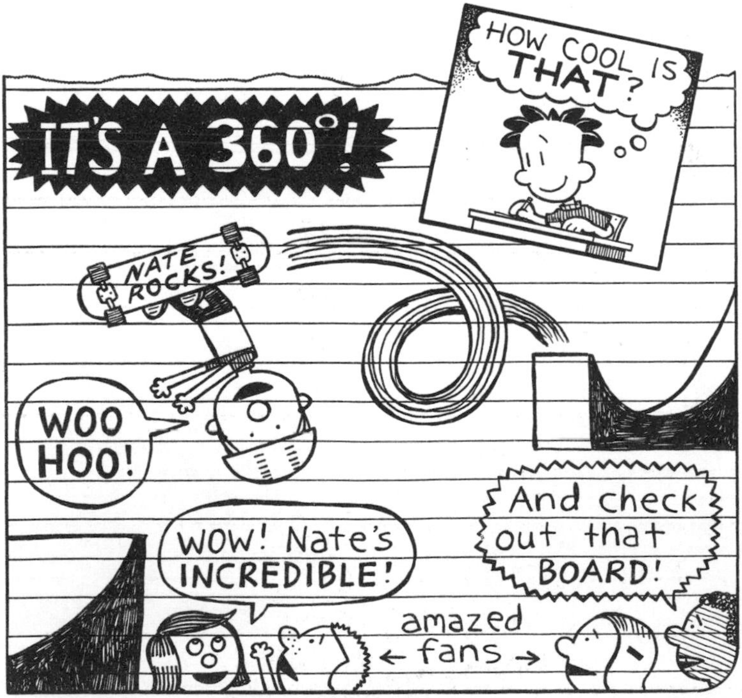
HOW COOL IS THAT?
IT'S A 360°!
NATE ROCKS!
WOO HOO!
WOW! Nate's INCREDIBLE!
And check out that BOARD!
amazed
← fans →

TOP 5 DOGGONE FACTS

Nate's neighbor's dog, Spitsy, is a little bit strange!
Fill in the rest of these funny facts.

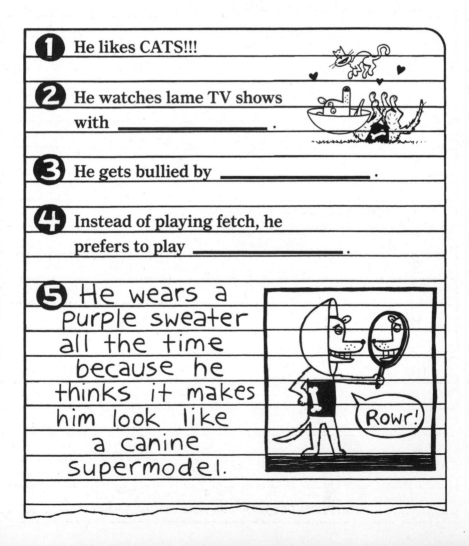

1 He likes CATS!!!

2 He watches lame TV shows with _____ .

3 He gets bullied by _____ .

4 Instead of playing fetch, he prefers to play _____ .

5 He wears a purple sweater all the time because he thinks it makes him look like a canine supermodel.

Rowr!

HOW ABOUT YOUR PET? LIST HIS OR HER WILD AND WACKY FACTS HERE!

1.

2.

3. Drinks out of the toilet

4.

5.

6.

7.

8.

9.

10.

11.

12.

13.

14.

15. Rubs his face on everything

16.

17.

18.

19. Eats daisies

20.

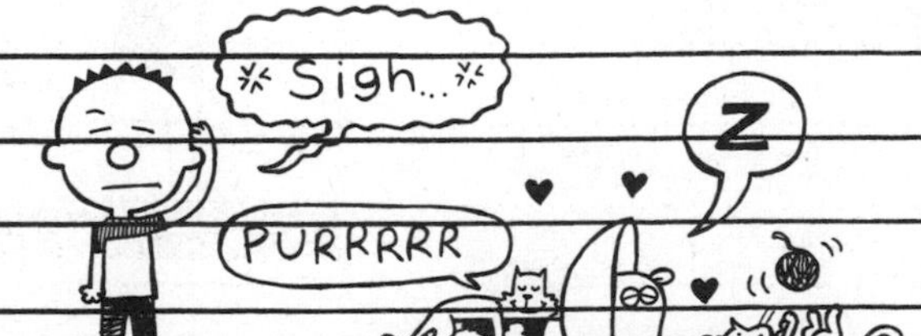

Sigh...
PURRRRR
Z

MY BEST FRIEND IS A SPORTS CHAMP

Create a player card that stars your best friend! Name the sport! Name the team!

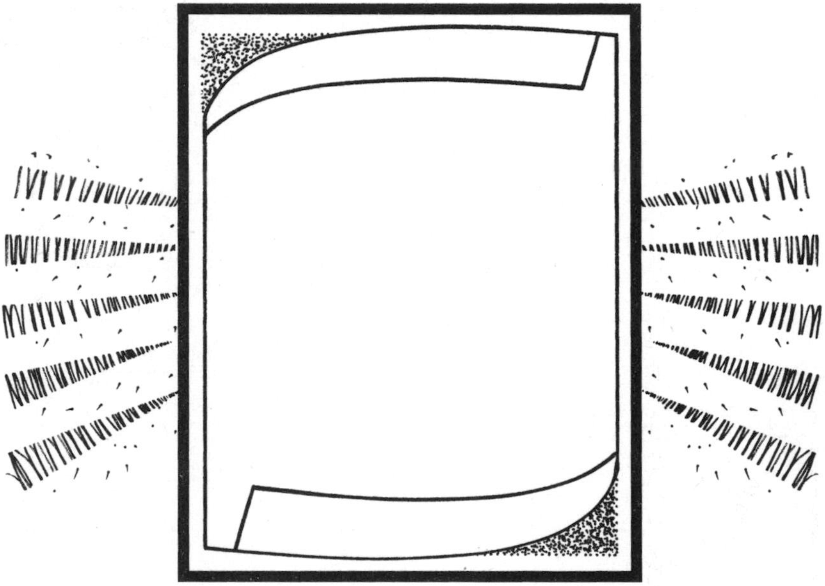

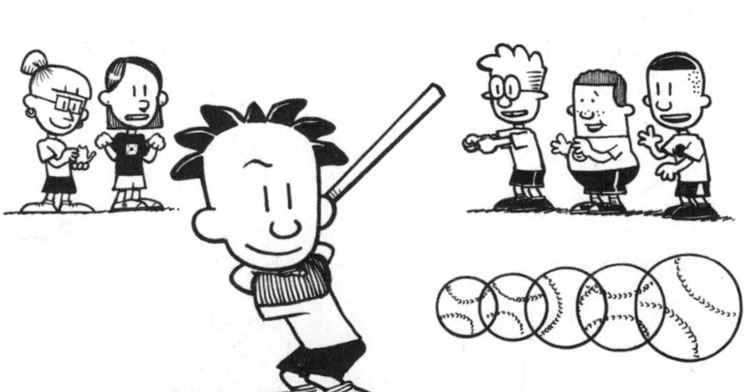

DOODLE 'ROUND THE CLOCK

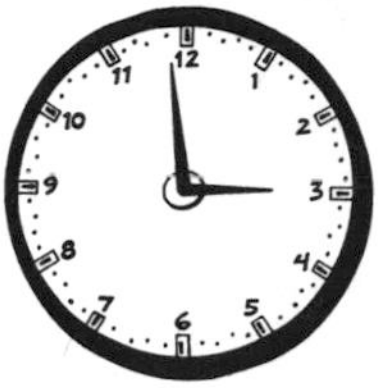

Fill this page with doodles!

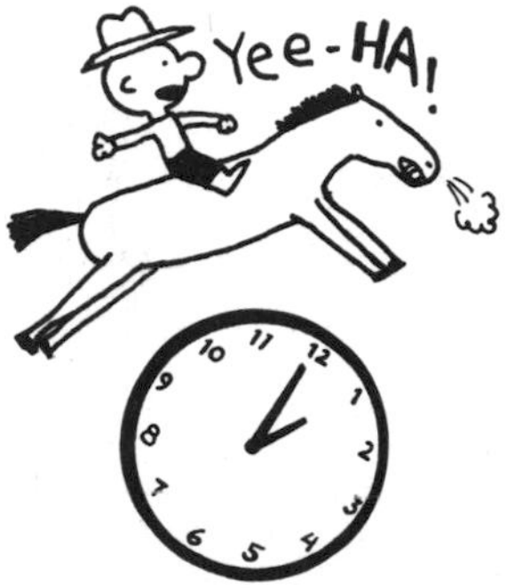
Yee-HA!

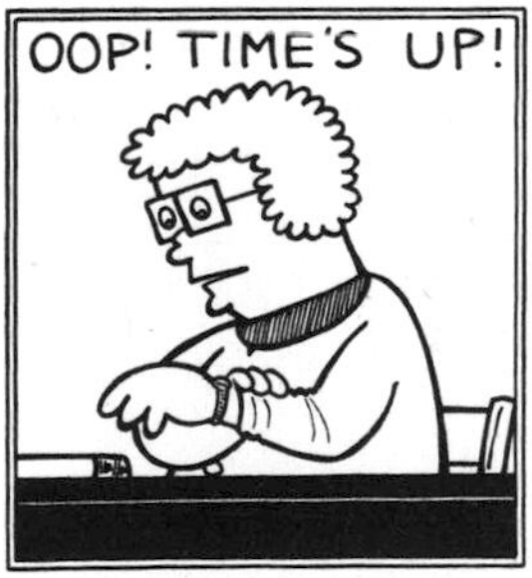
OOP! TIME'S UP!

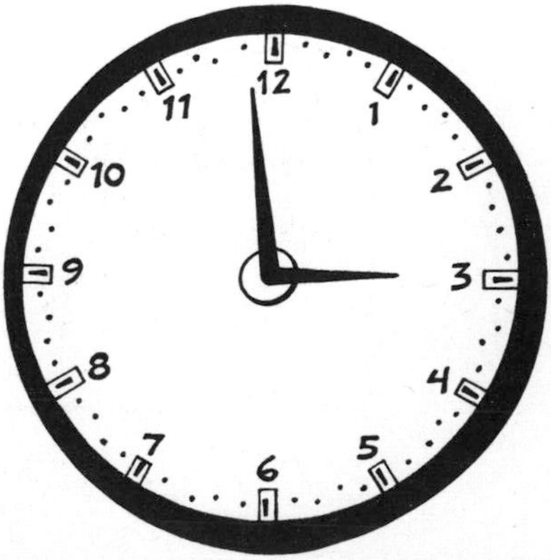

DRAMATIC FLASHBACK!

What happened before? You decide and draw it!

HOW DID NATE GET A BLACK EYE?

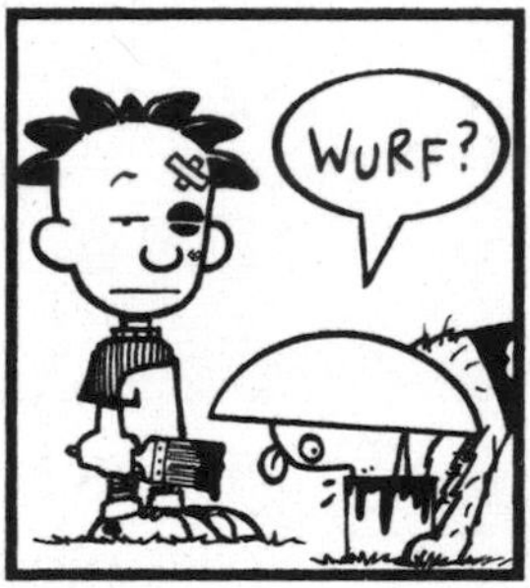
WURF?

WHY DID SPITSY GO CRAZY?

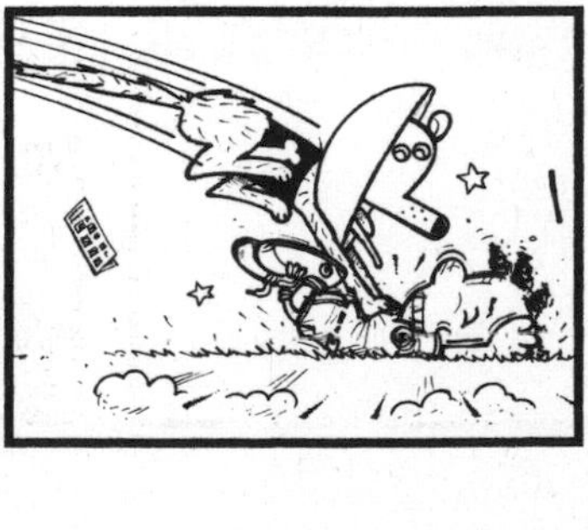

WHY IS NATE IN TROUBLE AGAIN?

YOU'RE SUCH A SLOB!
JENNY!

IS NATE GOING TO THE PRINCIPAL'S OFFICE? WHY?

I'D LIKE TO SEE YOU IN THE HALLWAY, NATE.
OOOOOOOOOOOOOH!

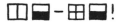

THE FORTUNE-TELLER

Nate's loves knowing his fortune, even if it means eating too many fortune cookies! Nate just went to Pu Pu Panda—help him decode all of his fortunes.

HERE! HAVE A FORTUNE COOKIE!

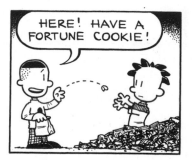

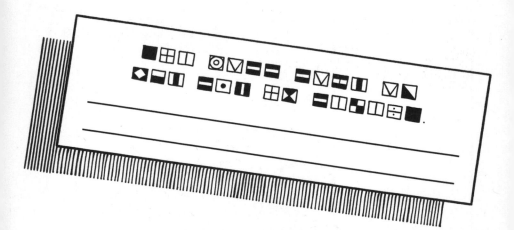

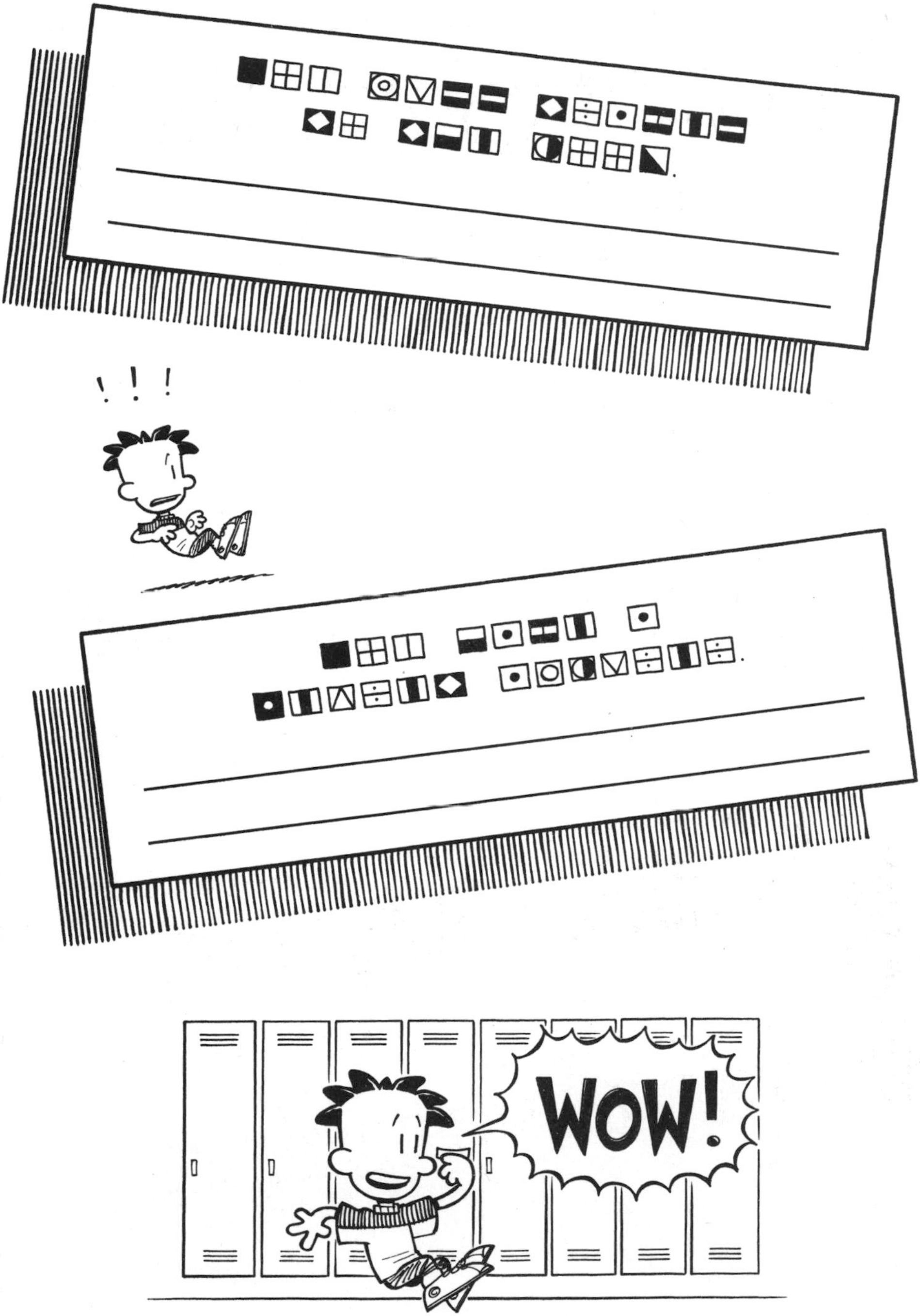
! ! !
WOW!

RAGE-O-METER

What drives you crazy? How do these rank on your RAGE-O-METER?

1. You have to leave your friend's birthday party early.

☐ MIFFED **☐ HACKED OFF**

☐ MAD **☐ BALLISTIC**

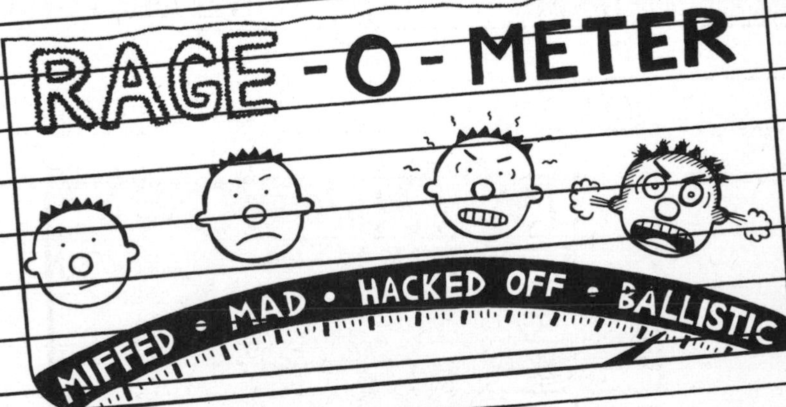
RAGE-O-METER
MIFFED • MAD • HACKED OFF • BALLISTIC

2. Your dad is snoring super loud during your favorite movie.

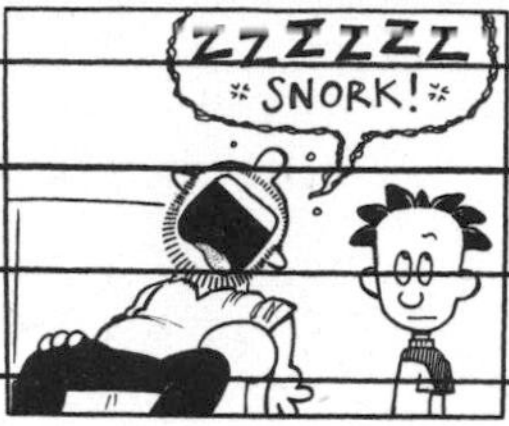
ZZZZZZ
SNORK!

☐ MIFFED ☐ HACKED OFF

☐ MAD ☐ BALLISTIC

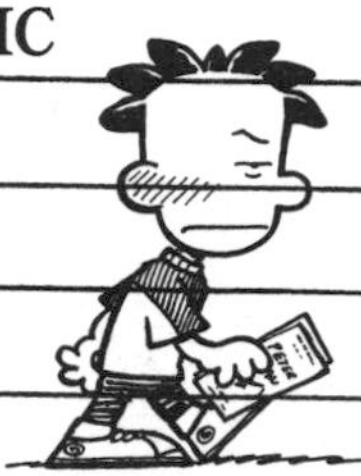

3. You lose your lucky hat.

☐ MIFFED ☐ HACKED OFF

☐ MAD ☐ BALLISTIC

4. Your dog throws up in your room.

☐ MIFFED ☐ HACKED OFF

☐ MAD ☐ BALLISTIC

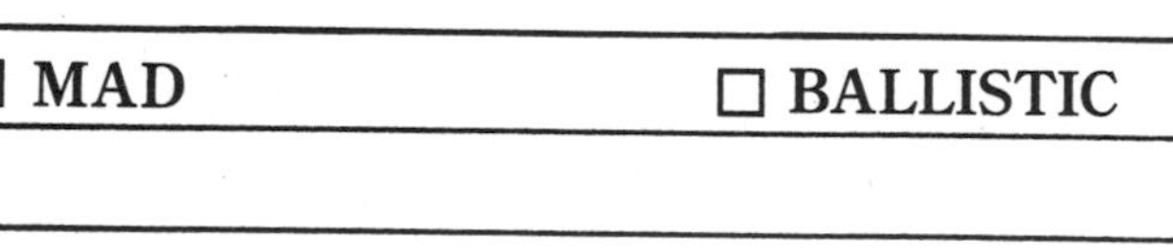
SPITSY! NO!!
NOT ON THE RUG!
GRUNT.

5. You spill grape juice on your white T-shirt.

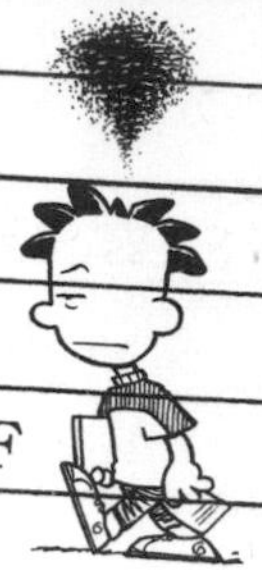

☐ MIFFED ☐ HACKED OFF

☐ MAD ☐ BALLISTIC

6. You slip and fall in a mud puddle on school picture day.

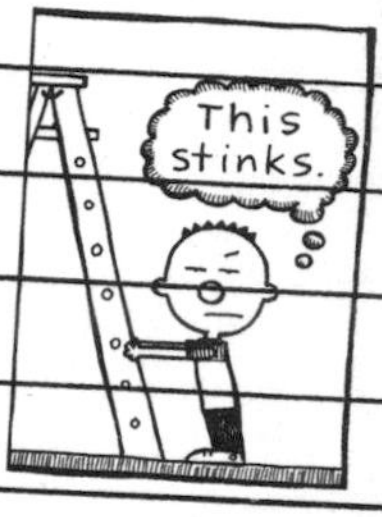
This stinks.

☐ MIFFED ☐ HACKED OFF

☐ MAD ☐ BALLISTIC

7. Your social studies teacher surprises you with a pop quiz.

☐ MIFFED ☐ HACKED OFF

☐ MAD ☐ BALLISTIC

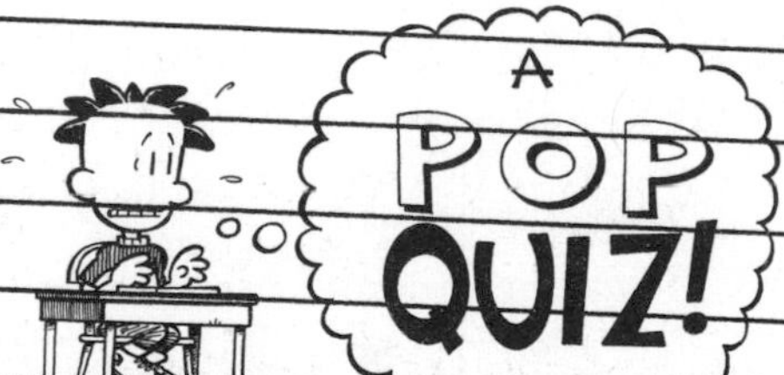
A POP QUIZ!

8. You get floor burn while playing fleeceball in gym class.

FLOOR BURN!
SQUEEEEEK!
What's the score?
Wood one, skin zero!

☐ MIFFED ☐ HACKED OFF

☐ MAD ☐ BALLISTIC

9. Your archenemy beats you in chess.

☐ MIFFED ☐ HACKED OFF

☐ MAD ☐ BALLISTIC

Before Artur...	After Artur...
I was the #1 player on the chess team.	He knocked me down to #2.
Check-mate! stunned expression	Nice tries, Nate! Sigh...

ZAPPED!

Everyone knows that Ben Franklin flew kites. Did you know that Ben taught himself how to swim?

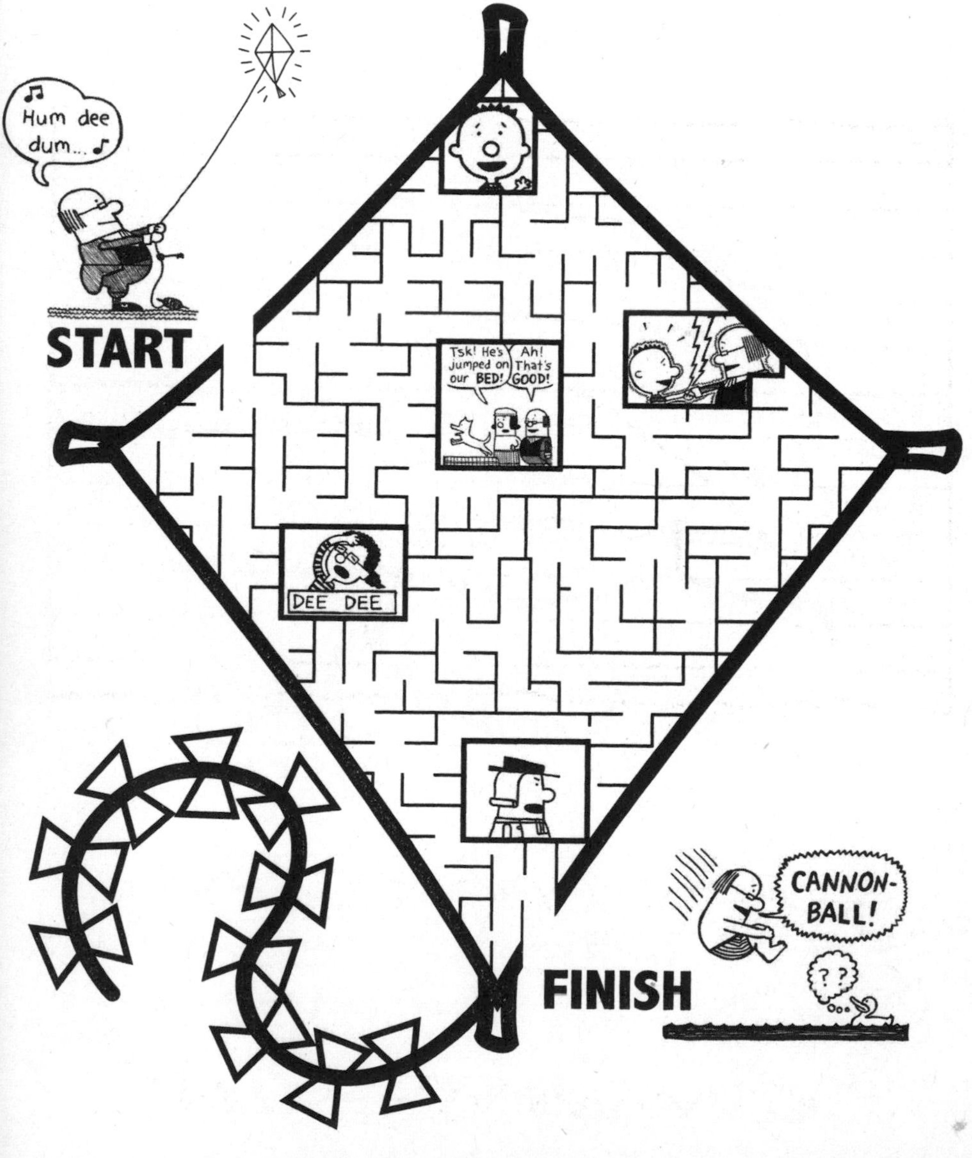

Hum dee dum...
START
Tsk! He's Jumped on our BED!
Ah! That's GOOD!
DEE DEE
CANNON-BALL!
??
FINISH

SUPER SCRIBBLE GAME

My scribble is a . . .

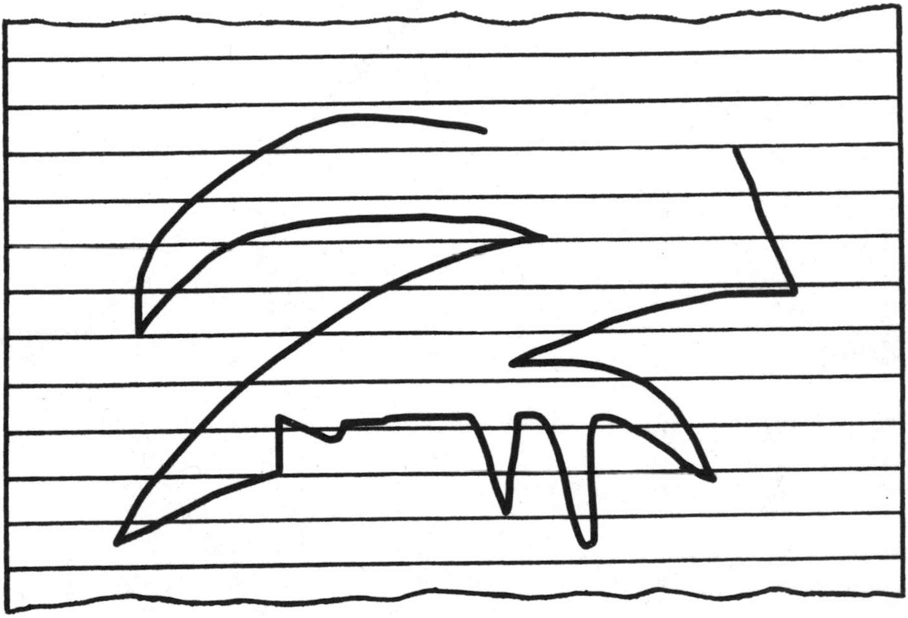

My caption:

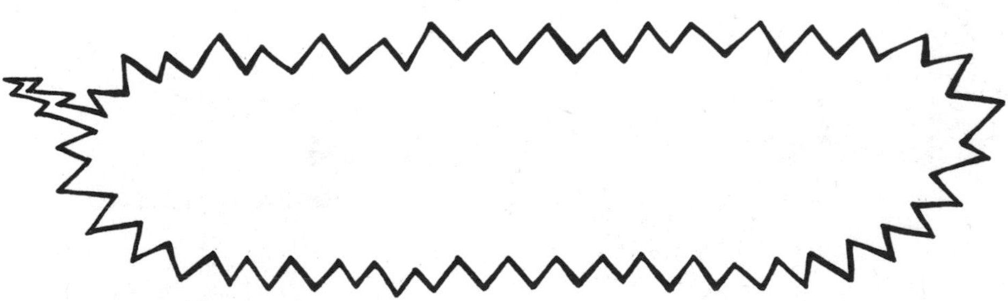

FACT-TASTIC TRIVIA

Can you decode the answers to questions in Francis's *Fact-tastic Trivia* book? Use his code on page 58.

Q: What do you call the offspring of a male tiger and a female lion?

A: $\overline{}_{13}$ $\overline{}_{6}$ $\overline{}_{20}$ $\overline{}_{3}$ $\overline{}_{23}$ $\overline{}_{11}$ $\overline{}_{21}$.

Q: What bird, extinct by 1681, was named for the Portuguese word for "stupid"?

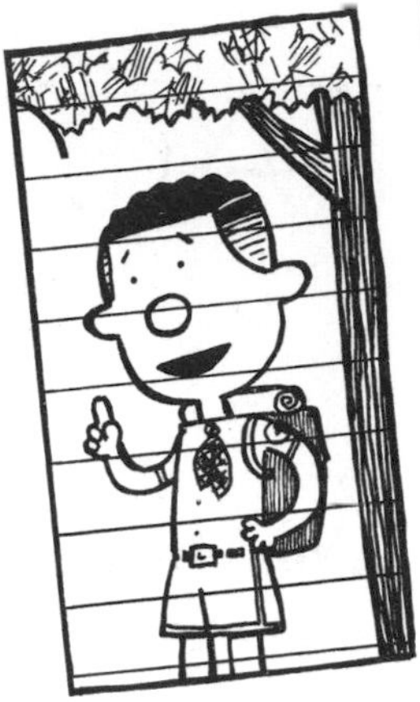

A: ___ ___ ___
6 1 8

___ ___ ___ ___ ___ ___ ___ ___.
25 11 25 11 7 20 14 25

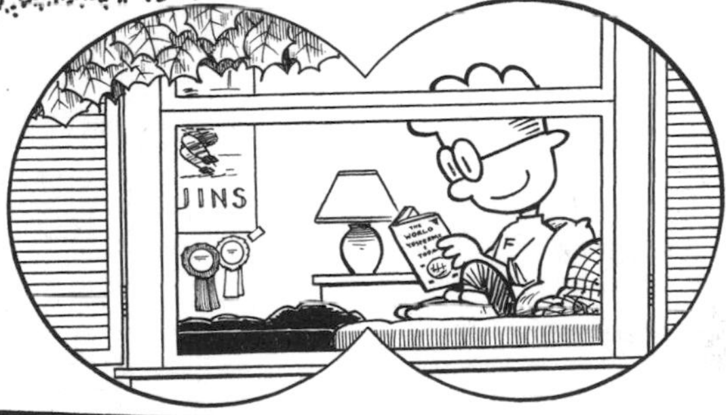
JINS

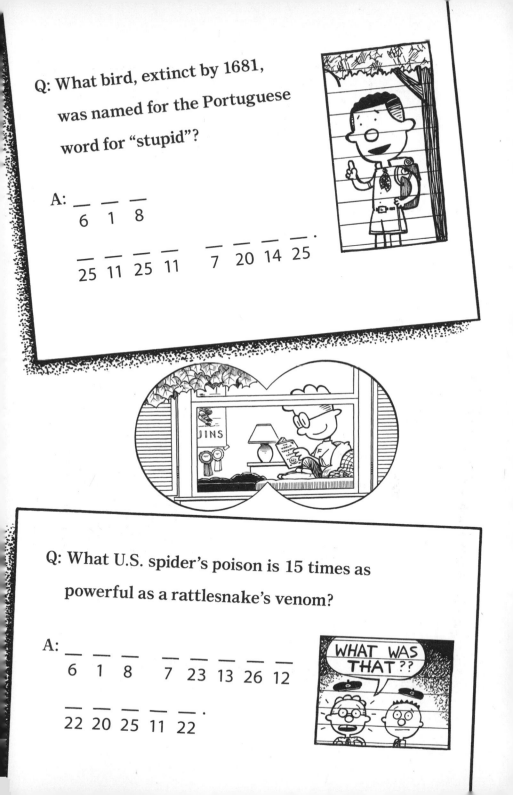

Q: What U.S. spider's poison is 15 times as powerful as a rattlesnake's venom?

A: ___ ___ ___ ___ ___ ___ ___ ___
6 1 8 7 23 13 26 12

___ ___ ___ ___ ___.
22 20 25 11 22

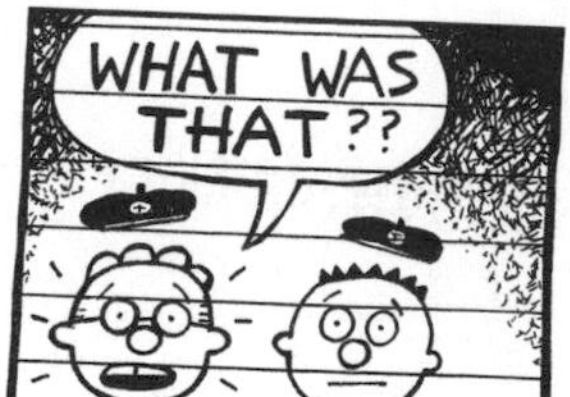
WHAT WAS THAT??

FAMILY REUNION

Here's a snapshot from Nate's family reunion.

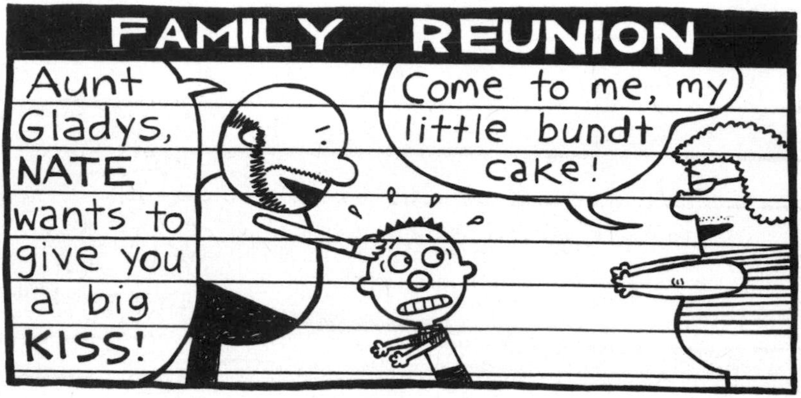
FAMILY REUNION
Aunt Gladys, NATE wants to give you a big KISS!
Come to me, my little bundt cake!

WHAT DOES YOURS LOOK LIKE?
DRAW IT!

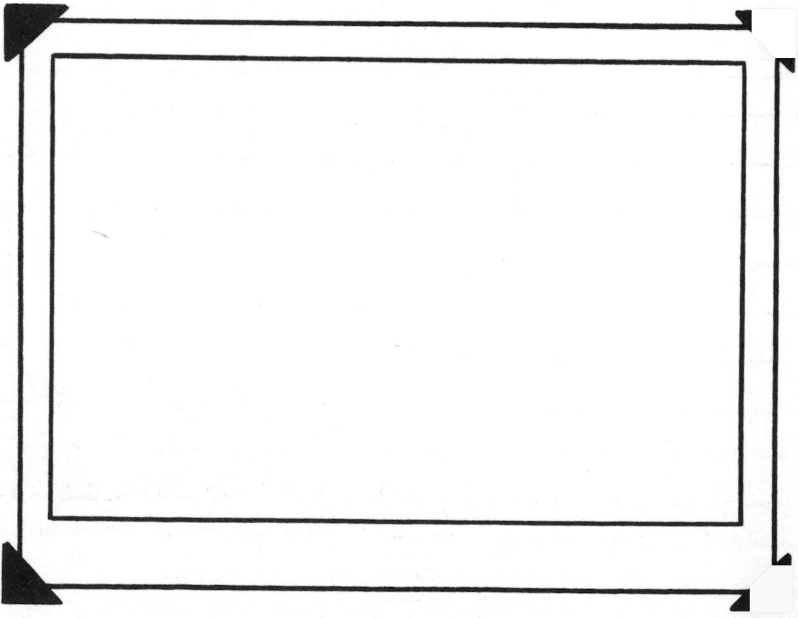

WRITE DOWN THE FAVORITE PART OF YOUR FAMILY REUNION.

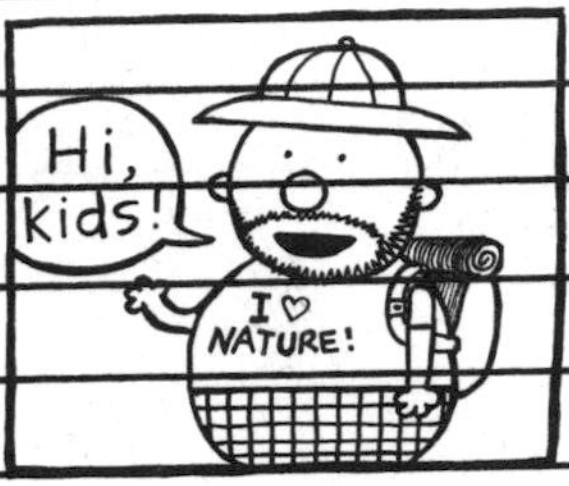
Hi, kids!
I ♡ NATURE!

WRITE DOWN THE MOST ANNOYING PART OF YOUR FAMILY REUNION.

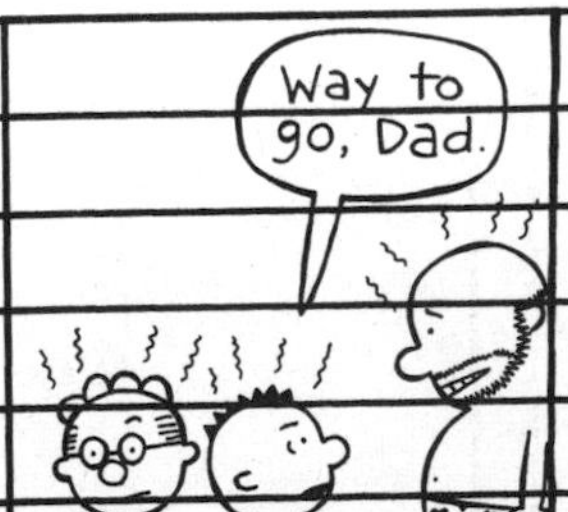
Way to go, Dad.

ADVENTURES WITH ARTUR

Poor Nate! He's up against his archrival, Artur, again, and this doesn't look good! Fill in the speech bubbles and finish this comic.

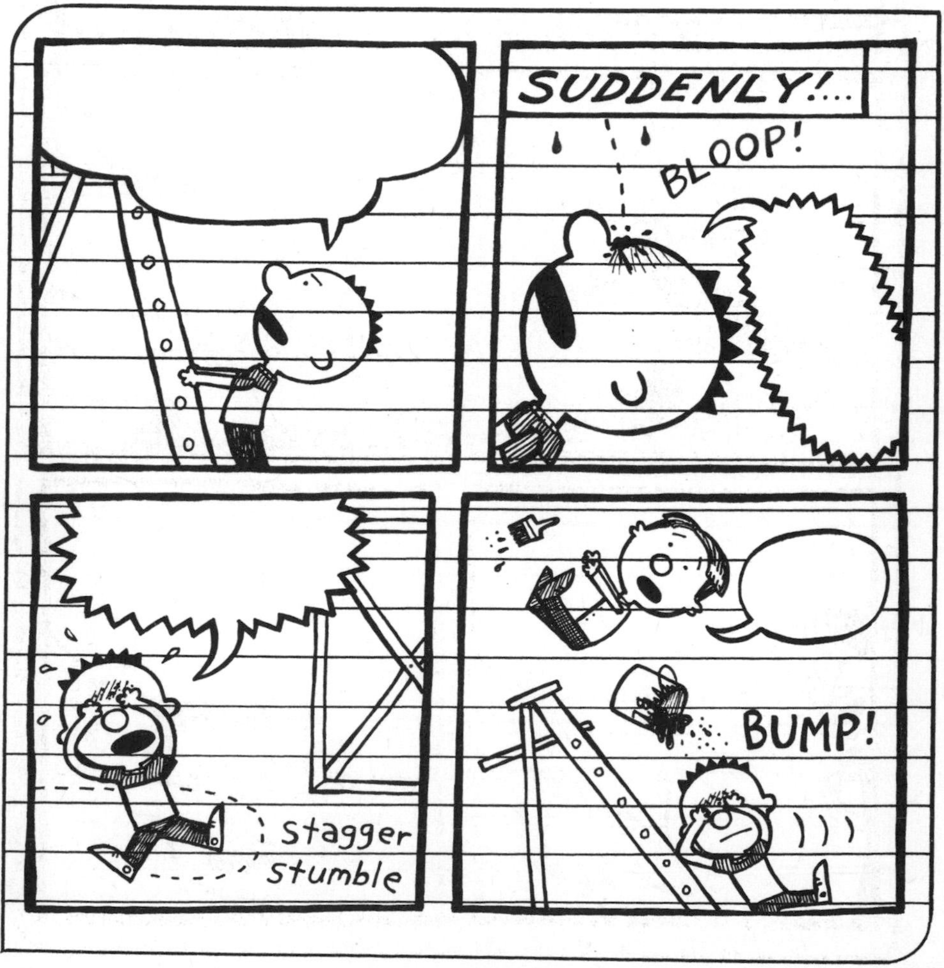
SUDDENLY!...
BLOOP!
stagger
stumble
BUMP!

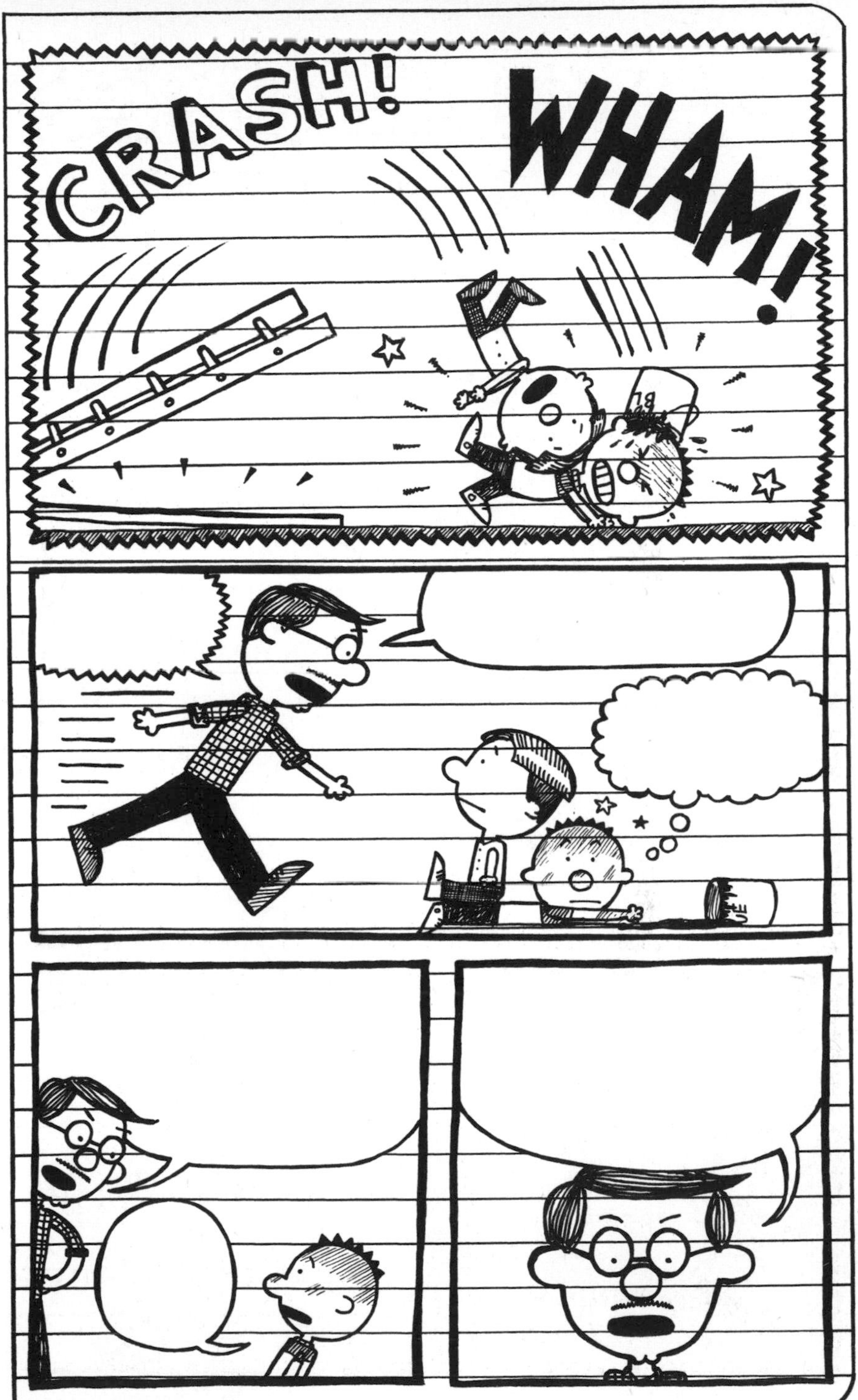
CRASH!
WHAM!

PSYCHO DOGS RULE

Nate's superstar fleece-ball team (the Kuddle Kittens, according to Gina) has a lineup of nine kids. Can you hit a home run and arrange each initial so that it only shows up once in each row, column, and box?

(N) = NATE

(P) = PAIGE

(T) = TEDDY

(S) = SARAH

(F) = FRANCIS

(M) = MARCIE

(G) = GINA

(C) = CHAD

(W) = WILL

dribble dribble dribble

N		T		F	G	W		
	W		P					G
G		S				F		M
	M		N				W	
P				W	F	S		
T				G				N
C		M			P	T	F	
	S		G			M	P	
					S			C

COME ON, NATE!
IT'S UP TO YOU!
CLAP CLAP
CLAP CLAP
CLAP
RELAX, GUYS! I'M ALL OVER IT!

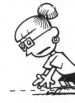

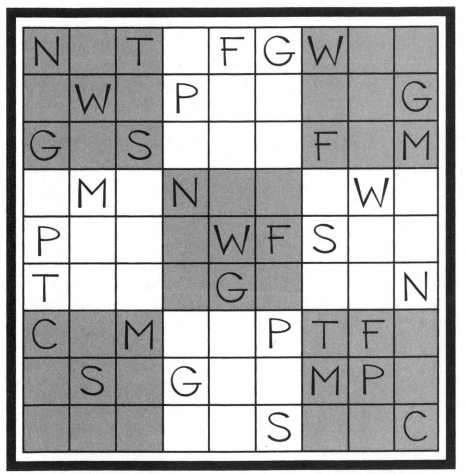

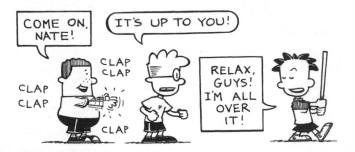

THE HERO

Who will come to Jenny's rescue?

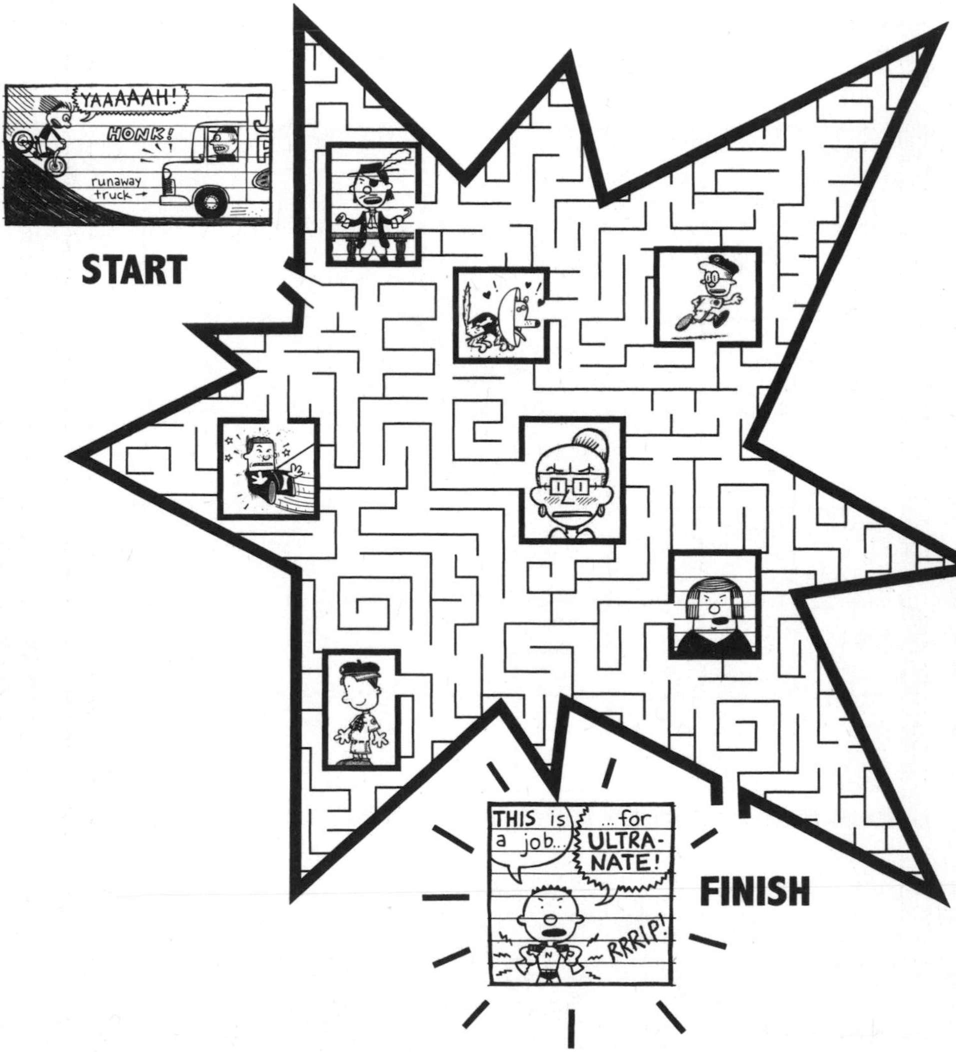

YAAAAAH!
HONK!
runaway truck →
START
THIS is a job...
...for ULTRA-NATE!
RRRIP!
FINISH

PAGE O' DOODLES

**Bust that boredom! It's doodle time—
see how fast you can fill the page.**

"LUNCH"   by NATE

KING OF JOBS

THERE MUST BE **SOMETHING** I CAN DO, OR SELL, OR...

Someday Nate would love to be a professional cartoonist. What if you could have a job that nobody else had? Combine the words below and create the most exciting jobs you can think of.

SENIOR
DESIGNER
LUXURY
EXPERT
DREAM
TRUCK
PONY
TEACHER
RACER
CROSS COUNTRY
HOT-AIR BALLOON

SAILBOAT
HAT
CIRCUS
DRIVER
MARSHMALLOW
ENGINEER
SALESPERSON
SINGING
SPORTSCAR
OCEAN
RACING HORSE

TASTER
PAINTER
CREATOR
TAP DANCER
TESTER
BUILDER
DIVER
HAMMOCK
RESORT
ICE CREAM
SCULPTOR

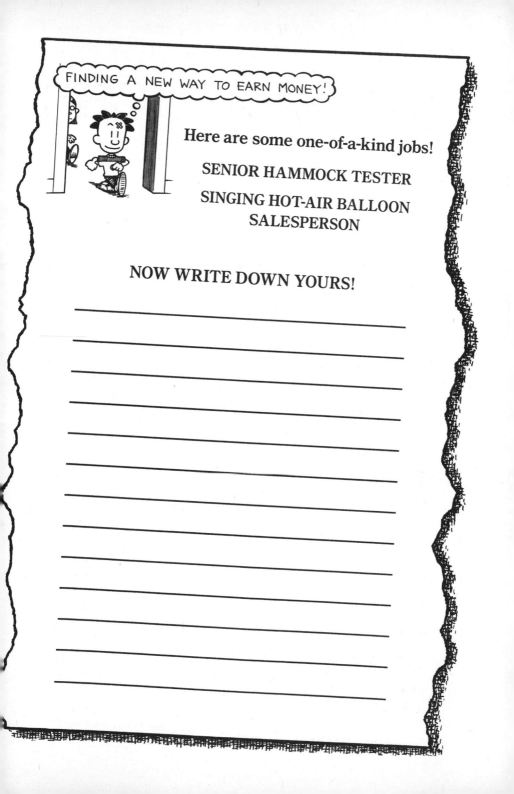

FINDING A NEW WAY TO EARN MONEY!

Here are some one-of-a-kind jobs!

SENIOR HAMMOCK TESTER

SINGING HOT-AIR BALLOON SALESPERSON

NOW WRITE DOWN YOURS!

IT'S YOUR CALL!

What will happen when brainiac Francis goes up against Randy the bully? Will Mrs. Hickson save the day? You decide! Create a comic that tells the story.

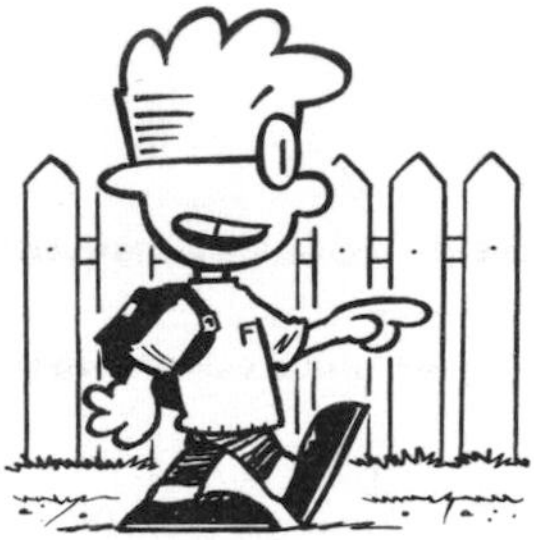

+

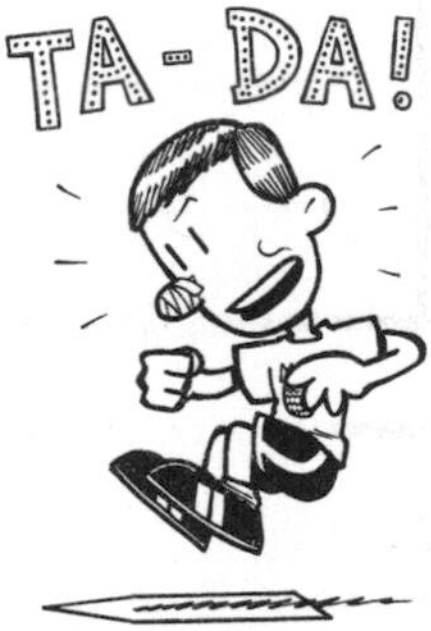
TA-DA!

+

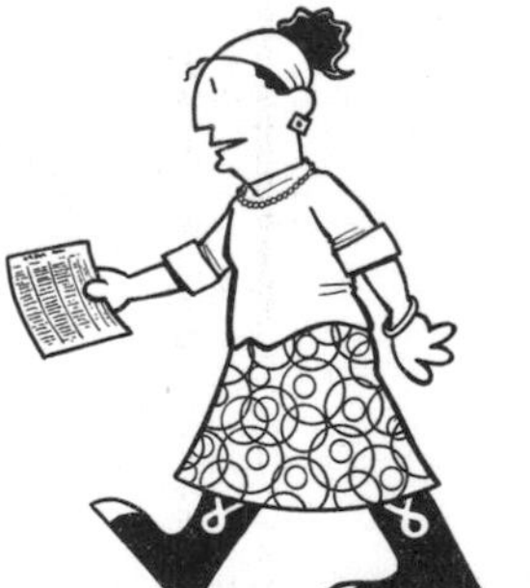

=

?

YOUR TITLE HERE

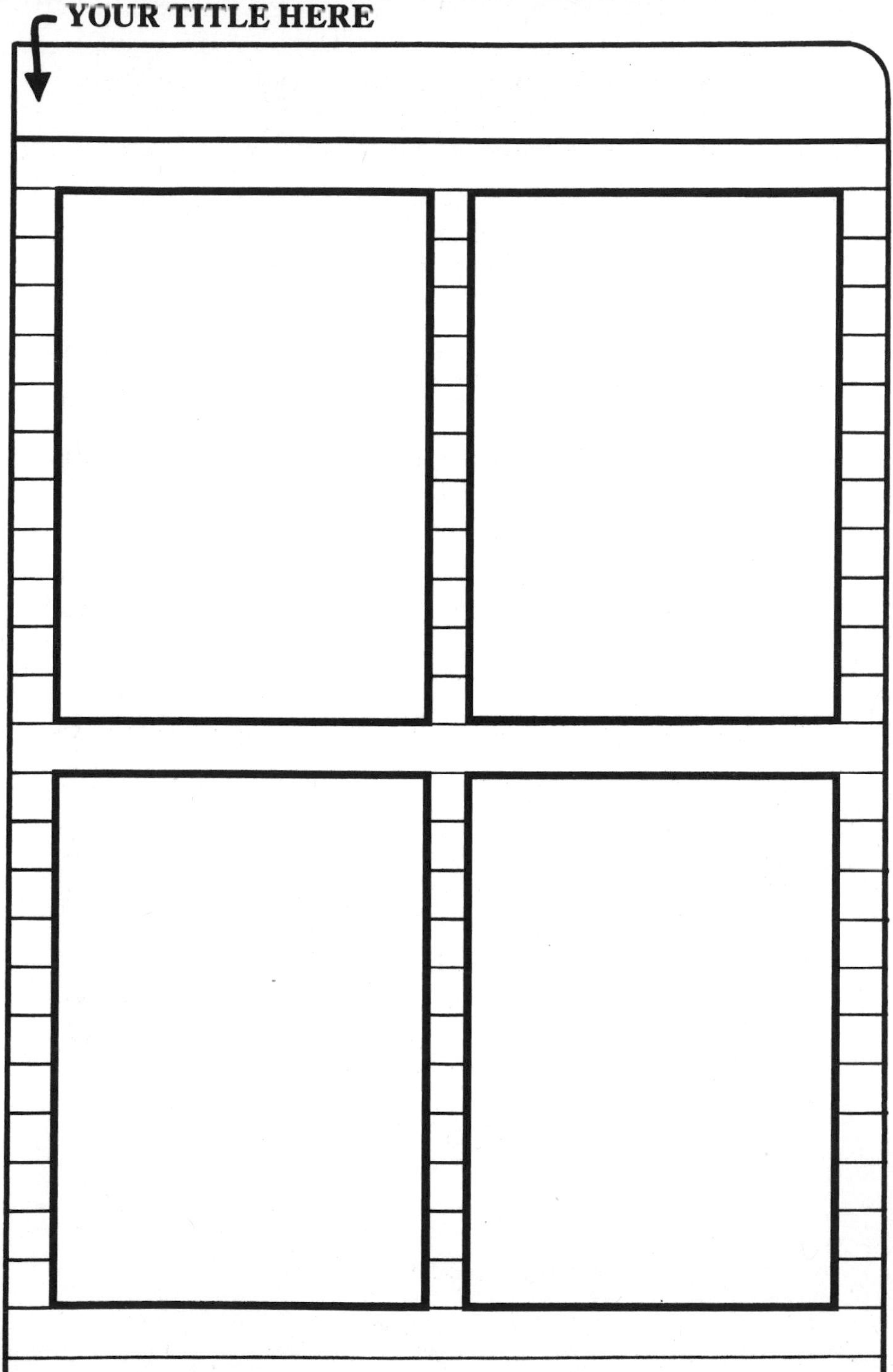

JOKIN' AROUND

Teddy likes to clown around with Nate, and joke telling is his specialty! Use his special code on page 34 to decode the punch lines to these silly jokes.

Q: What do you call a fairy that hasn't taken a bath?

A: $\frac{}{H} \frac{}{G} \frac{}{R} \frac{}{M} \frac{}{P} \frac{}{V} \frac{}{I} \frac{}{Y} \frac{}{V} \frac{}{O} \frac{}{O}$

Q: What did the chewing gum say to the shoe?

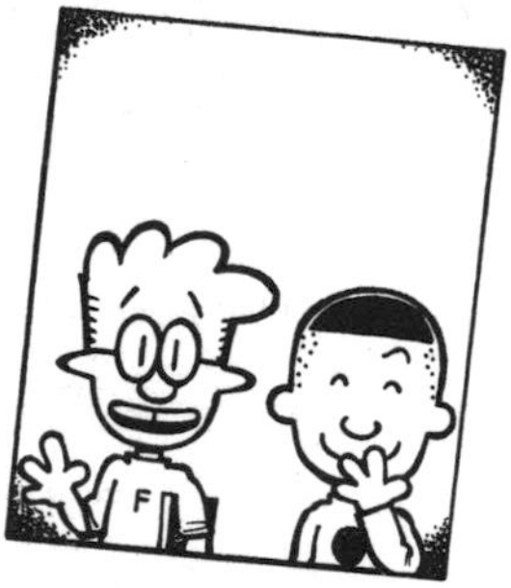

A: _'_ _ _ _ _ _ _ _ _ _ _.

R N H G F X P L M B L F

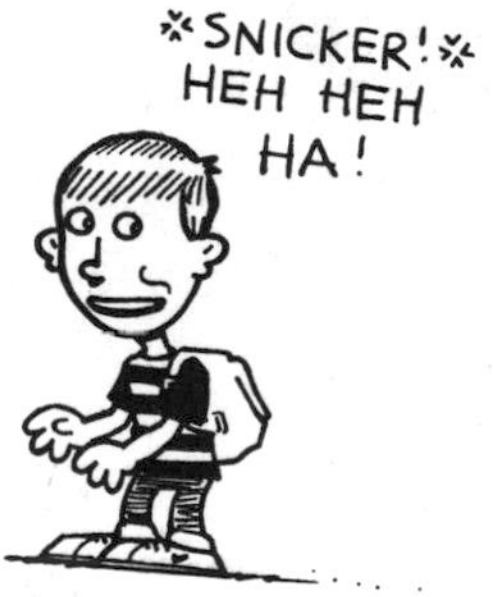
SNICKER!
HEH HEH
HA!

Q: What is the difference between here and there?

A: _ _ _ _ _ _ _ _ _ "_".

G S V O V G G V I G

U R CAR2NING!

Create your own comic using Gina's toy, Kuddles, plus Nate and Coach!

WILL YOU RUB MY TUMMY?

+

+

COACH

=

?

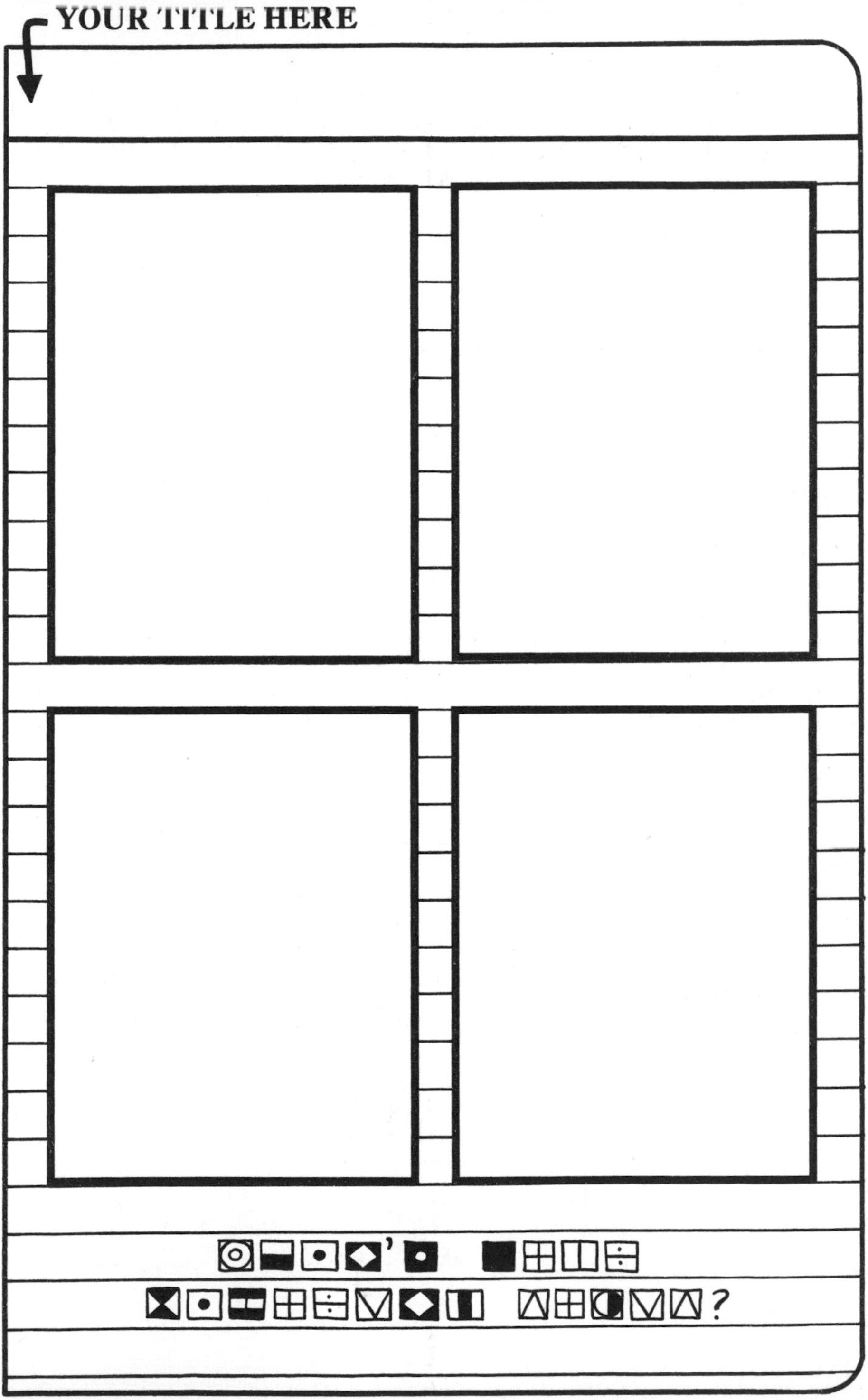
YOUR TITLE HERE

DESTINED FOR GREATNESS

How will Nate surpass all others? He has so many talents. Fill out the grid so that the first letter of each skill shows up only once in every row, column, and box.

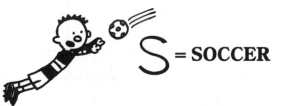 **= SOCCER**

 **M** = MUSIC

 **C** = CARTOONING

 **T** = TABLE FOOTBALL

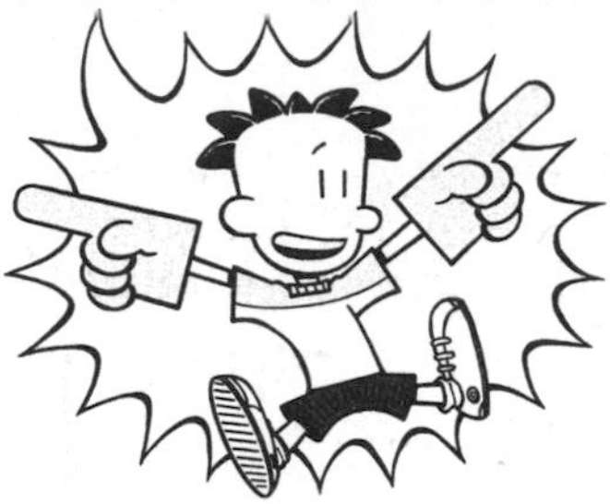

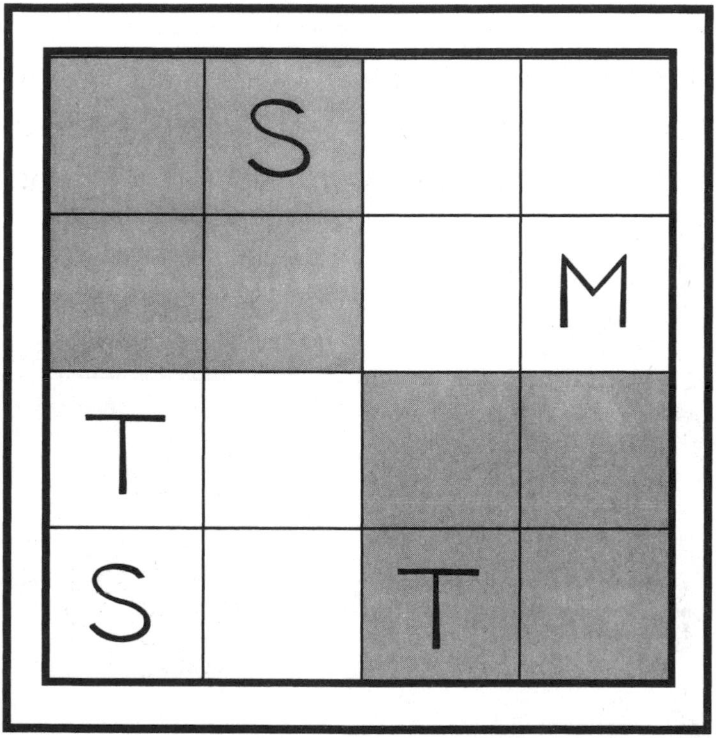
S
M
T
S
T

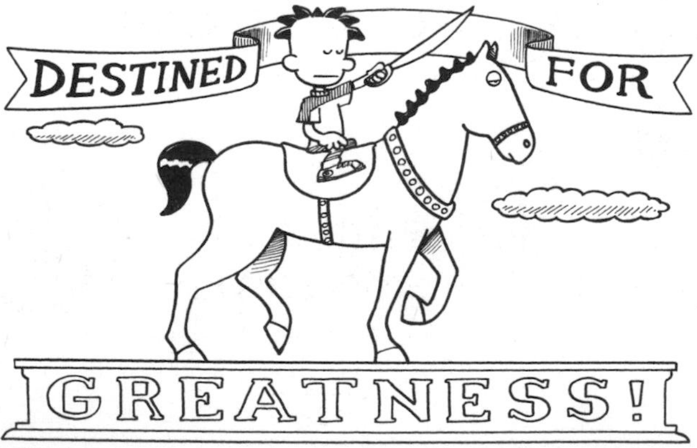
DESTINED
FOR
GREATNESS!

THE DOCTOR IS IN!

Uh-oh! What is Doctor Cesspool up to?

Fill in the speech bubbles and decide what's happening!

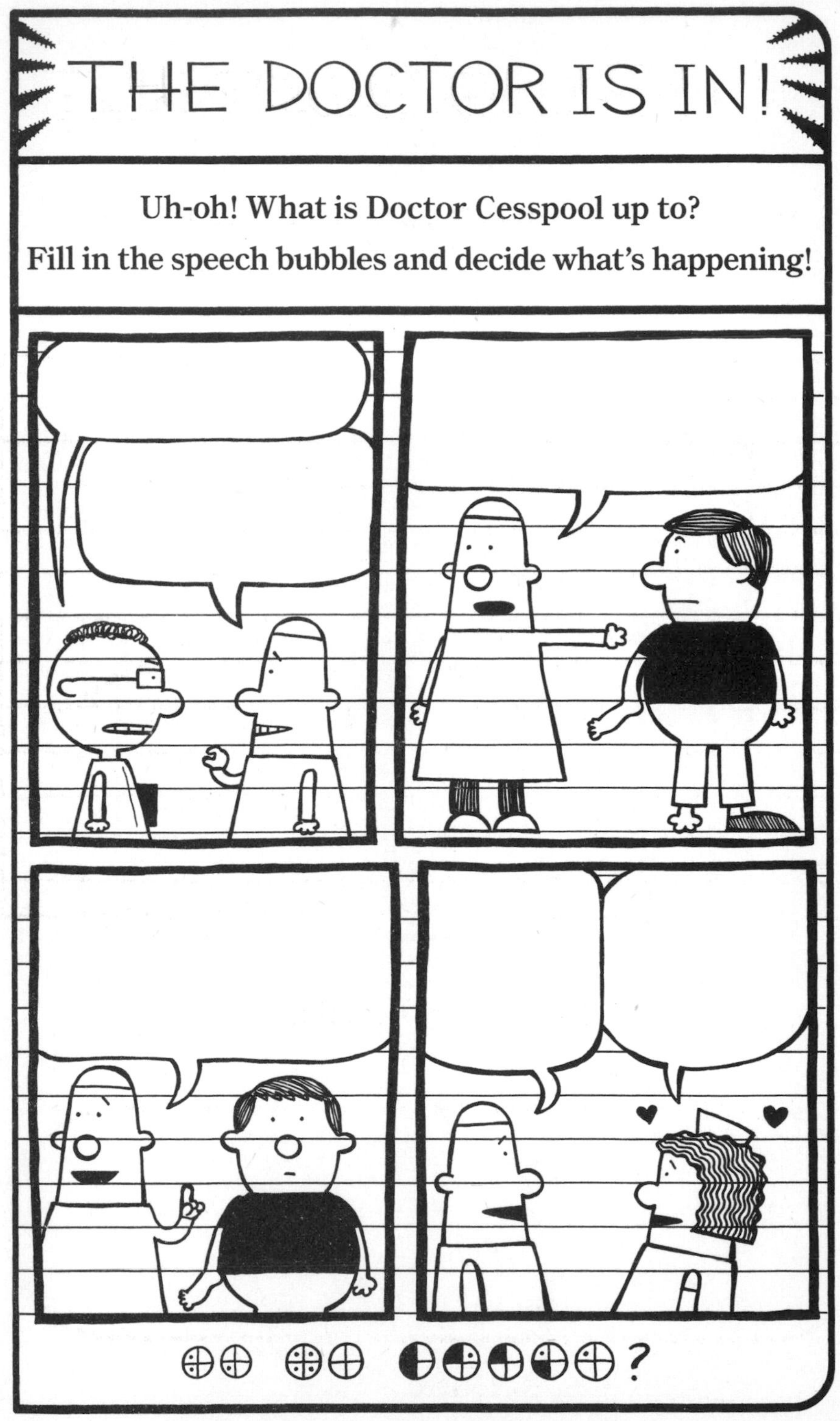

SCRIBBLE, SCRIBBLE

Turn this scribble into a _____________ picture.

(beautiful, scary, weird, funny . . .)

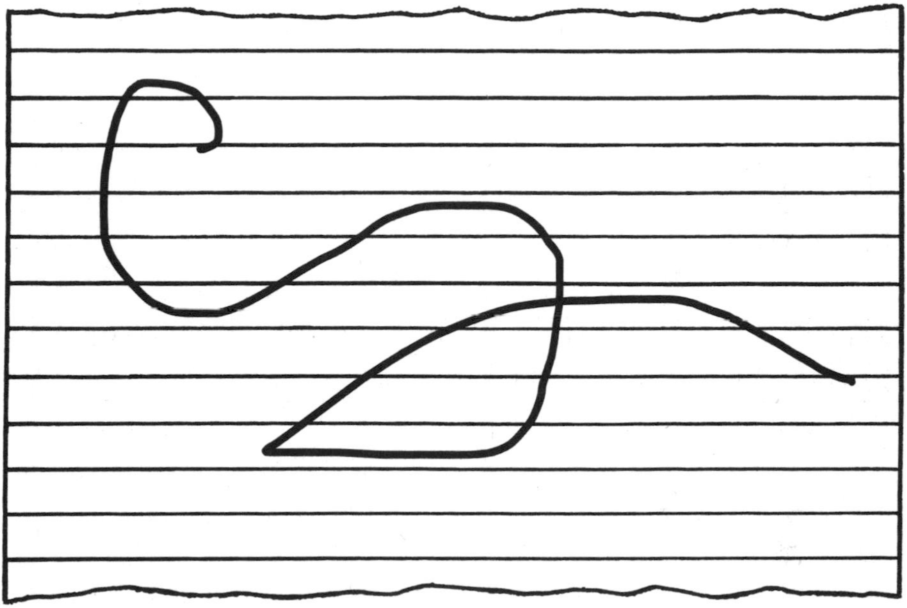

Give your art a caption!

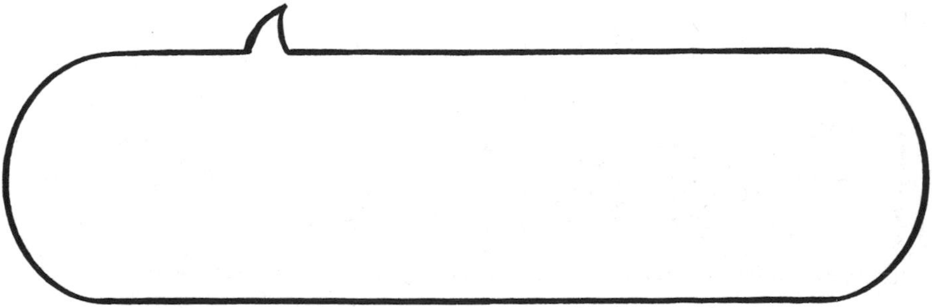

SUPER TROOPER

Nate is really proud to be a member of the Timber Scouts. If you could create your own troop name, what would it be? Mix and match the names below!

BRAVE

RIVER

RACING

DARING

DAUNTLESS

CAMELS

SUN

COURAGEOUS

RUNNING

PLATYPUSES

BADGERS

MOUNTAIN

BEARS

HAWKS

FLYING

FEARLESS

WARRIOR

HAPPY

MOON

PURPLE

RAVENS

EXPLORERS

HOUNDS

KITTENS

EAGLES

GUIDES

PEACOCKS

CATS

BULLS

LUCKY

LIST YOUR TOP TROOP NAMES HERE!

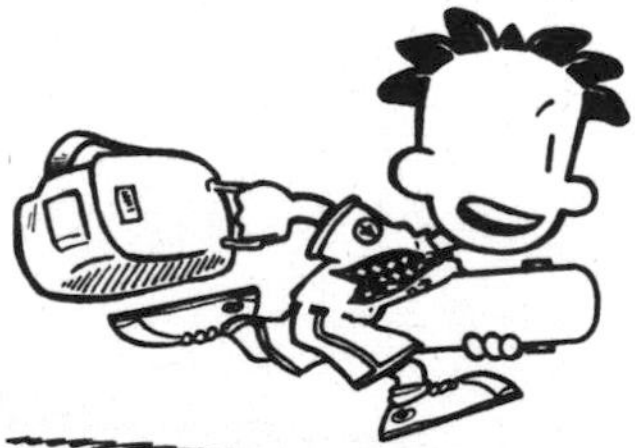

THE GRAND PRIZE

Help Nate land the first prize!

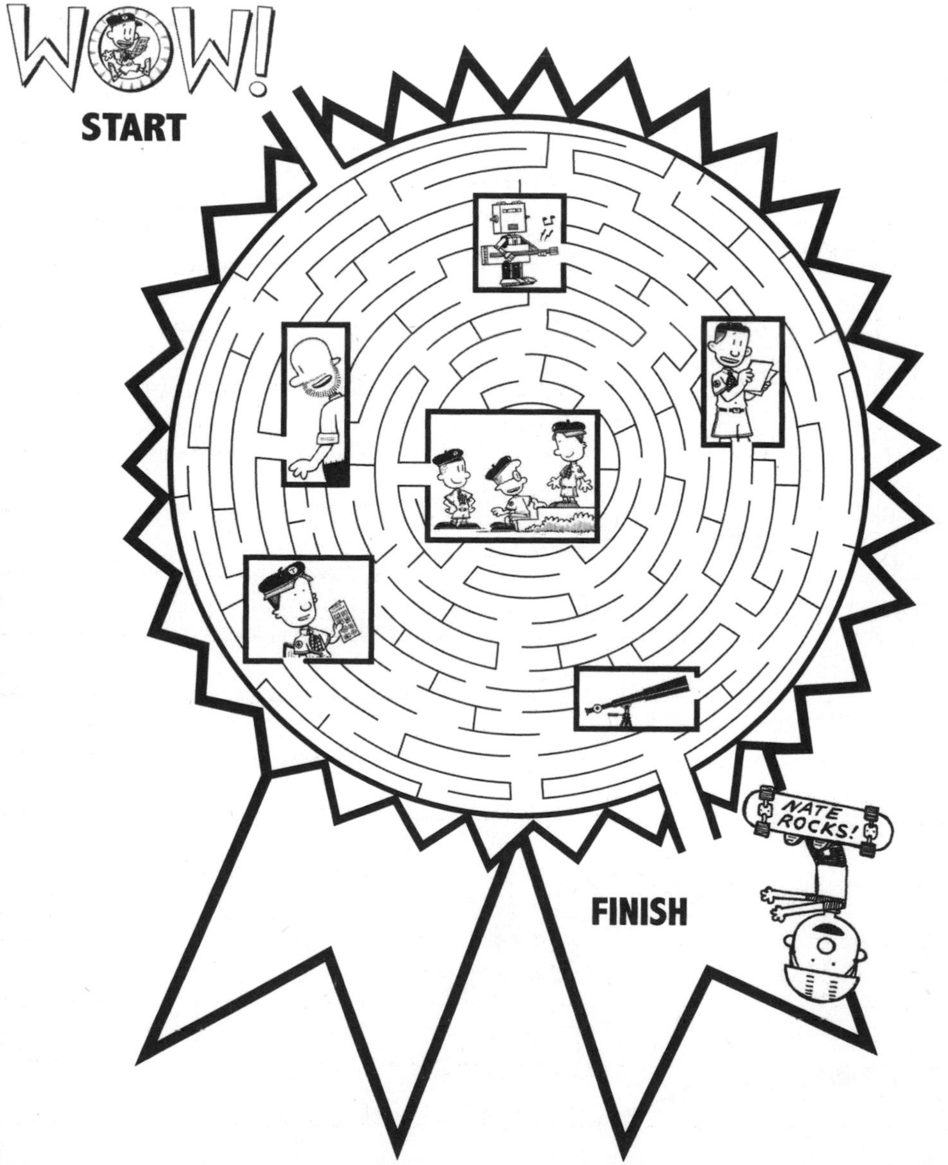
WOW!
START
FINISH
NATE ROCKS!

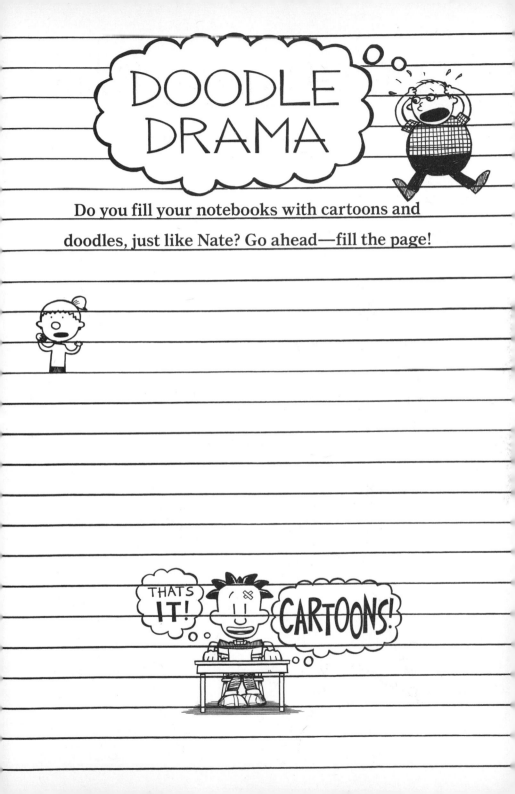

DOODLE DRAMA

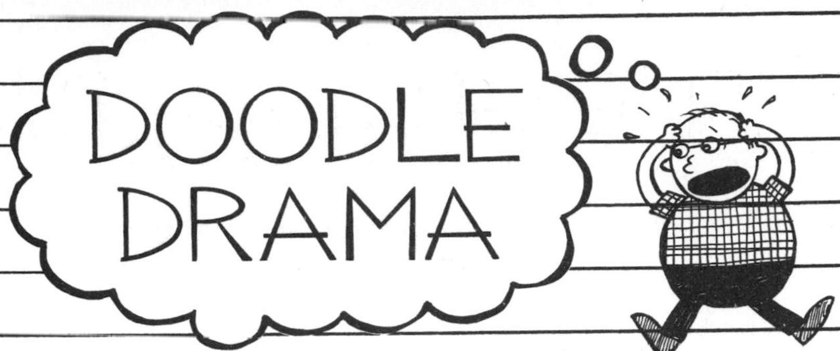

Do you fill your notebooks with cartoons and doodles, just like Nate? Go ahead—fill the page!

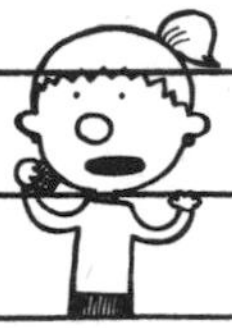

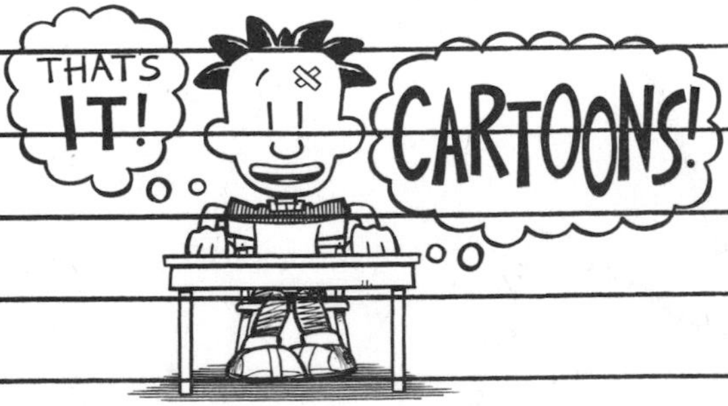
THATS IT!
CARTOONS!

U DRAW IT!

Anything could happen! Create a comic using all three characters below.

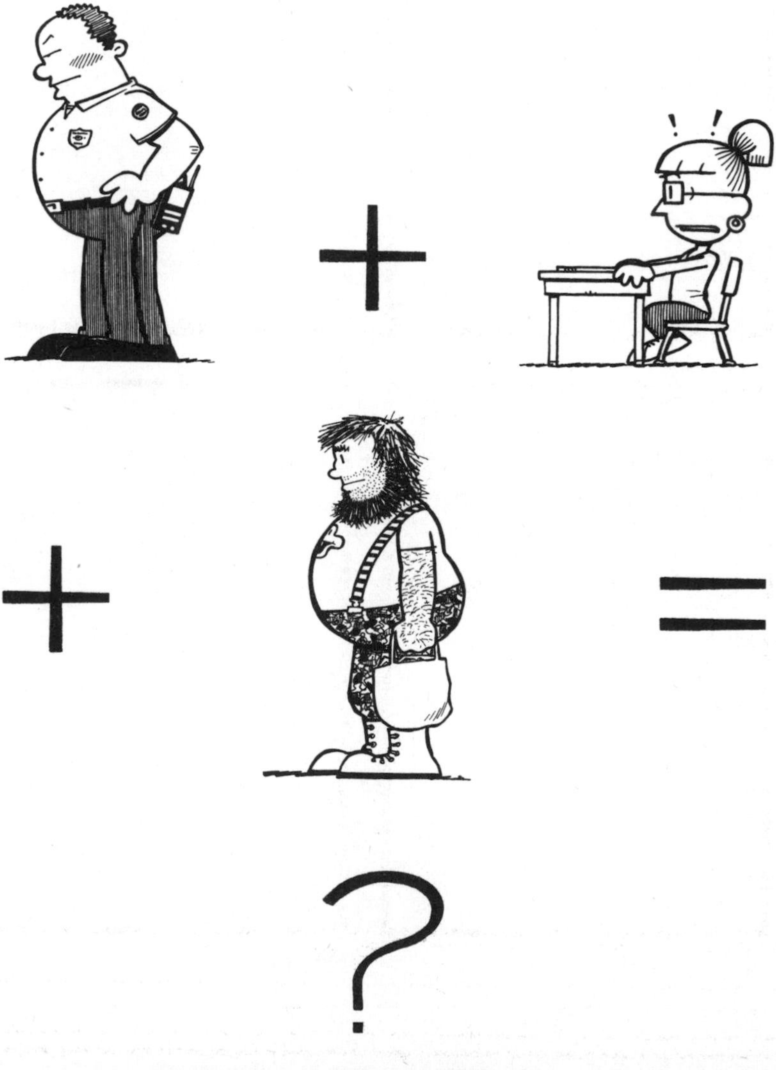

YOUR TITLE HERE

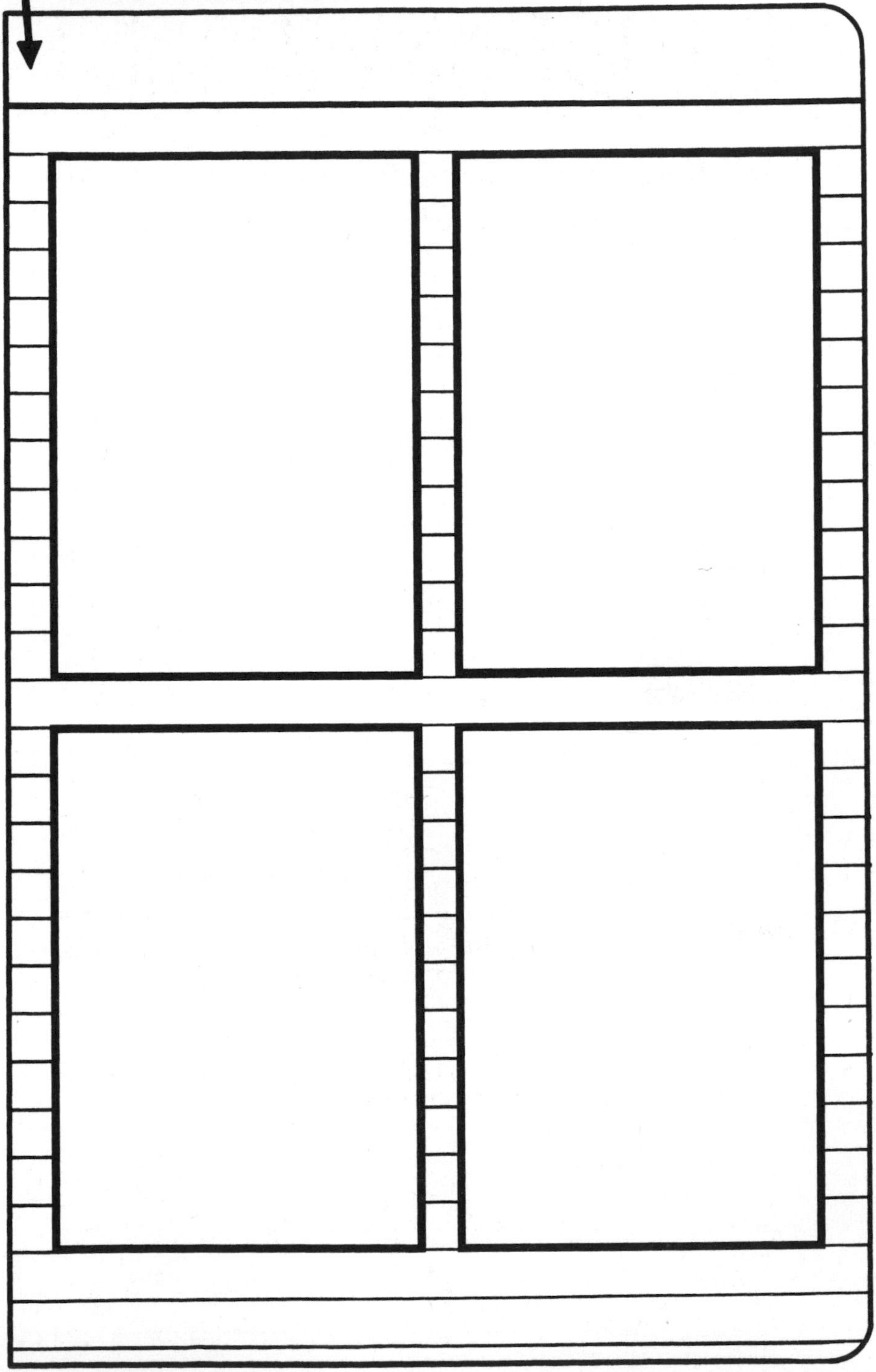

HIDDEN WORDS

Are you a wordsmith? Let's see your skills! Using the letters in "Timber Scout" below, see if you can create at least 20 other words!

TIMBER SCOUT

1. met	11.
2.	12.
3.	13.
4.	14.
5.	15.
6.	16.
7.	17.
8.	18.
9.	19. tore
10.	20.

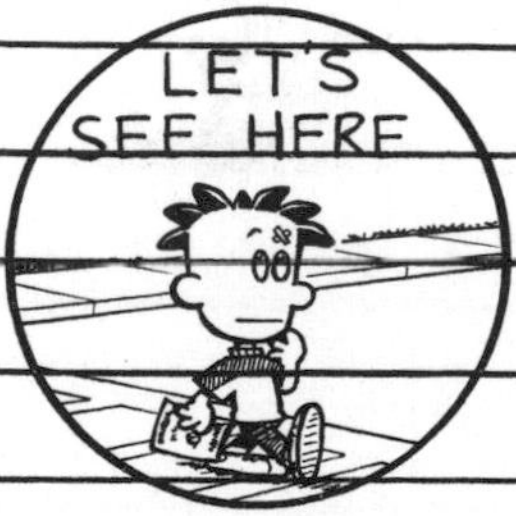
LET'S SEE HERE

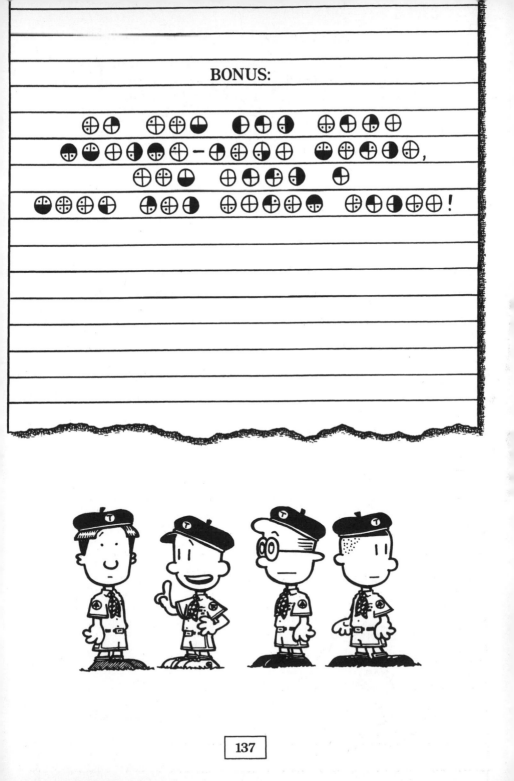

BONUS:

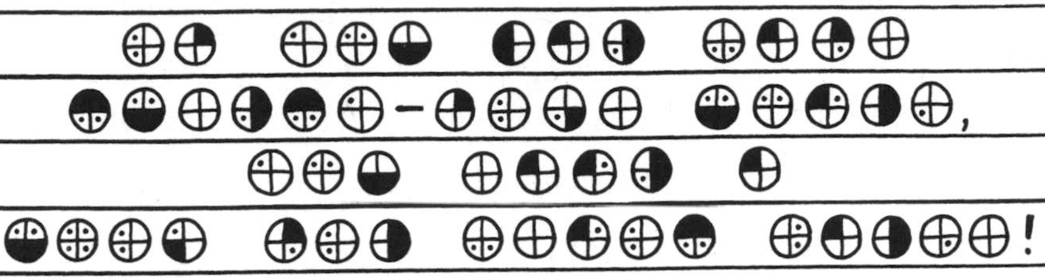

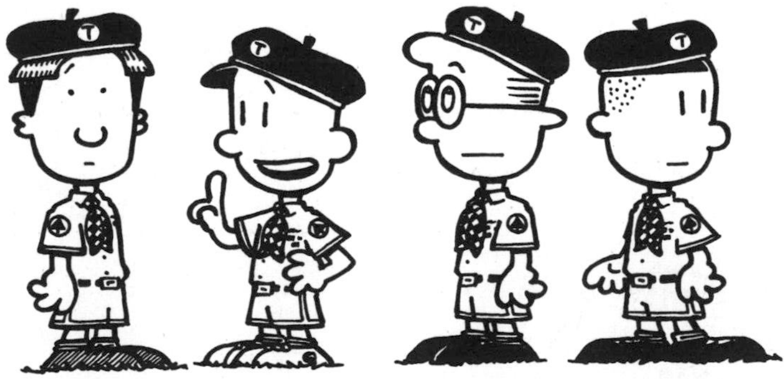

BELIEVE IT OR NOT?

Francis is like a walking encyclopedia. Use his code on page 58 to find out what he knows.

$$\overline{19}\ \overline{8}\ \overline{21}\ \overline{10}\ \overline{24}\quad \overline{20}\ \overline{24}\quad \overline{6}\ \overline{1}\ \overline{8}$$

$$\overline{11}\ \overline{21}\ \overline{23}\ \overline{9}\quad \overline{2}\ \overline{23}\ \overline{13}\ \overline{21}\ \overline{8}\ \overline{6}$$

$$\overline{6}\ \overline{1}\ \overline{13}\ \overline{6}\quad \overline{14}\ \overline{11}\ \overline{6}\ \overline{13}\ \overline{6}\ \overline{8}\ \overline{24}$$

$$\overline{26}\ \overline{23}\ \overline{11}\ \overline{26}\ \overline{12}\ \overline{22}\ \overline{20}\ \overline{24}\ \overline{8}.$$

$$\overline{13}\quad \overline{25}\ \overline{10}\ \overline{26}\ \overline{12}\ \overline{24},$$

$$\overline{15}\ \overline{10}\ \overline{13}\ \overline{26}\ \overline{12}\quad \overline{25}\ \overline{11}\ \overline{8}\ \overline{24}$$

$$\overline{21}\ \overline{11}\ \overline{6}\quad \overline{8}\ \overline{26}\ \overline{1}\ \overline{11}.$$

$\overline{18}\ \overline{11}\ \overline{24}\ \overline{6}\quad \overline{25}\ \overline{10}\ \overline{24}\ \overline{6}$

$\overline{2}\ \overline{13}\ \overline{14}\ \overline{6}\ \overline{20}\ \overline{26}\ \overline{23}\ \overline{8}\ \overline{24}\quad \overline{20}\ \overline{21}$

$\overline{9}\ \overline{11}\ \overline{10}\ \overline{14}\quad \overline{1}\ \overline{11}\ \overline{10}\ \overline{24}\ \overline{8}\quad \overline{13}\ \overline{14}\ \overline{8}$

$\overline{18}\ \overline{13}\ \overline{25}\ \overline{8}\quad \overline{16}\ \overline{14}\ \overline{11}\ \overline{18}$

$\overline{25}\ \overline{8}\ \overline{13}\ \overline{25}\quad \overline{24}\ \overline{12}\ \overline{20}\ \overline{21}\ .$

$\overline{6}\ \overline{1}\ \overline{8}\quad \overline{8}\ \overline{23}\ \overline{8}\quad \overline{2}\ \overline{1}\ \overline{13}\ \overline{21}\ \overline{6}\quad \overline{20}\ \overline{24}$

$\overline{6}\ \overline{1}\ \overline{8}\quad \overline{11}\ \overline{21}\ \overline{23}\ \overline{9}$

$\overline{18}\ \overline{13}\ \overline{18}\ \overline{18}\ \overline{13}\ \overline{23}$

,

$\overline{6}\ \overline{1}\ \overline{13}\ \overline{6}\quad \overline{26}\ \overline{13}\ \overline{21}\ \overline{6}\quad \overline{4}\ \overline{10}\ \overline{18}\ \overline{2}\ .$

GREAT NATE FACTS

How well do YOU know Nate Wright? Take this quiz and find out!

1. Nate once spilled egg salad on this person's head.
   a. Randy
   b. Jenny
   c. Gina
   d. Dad

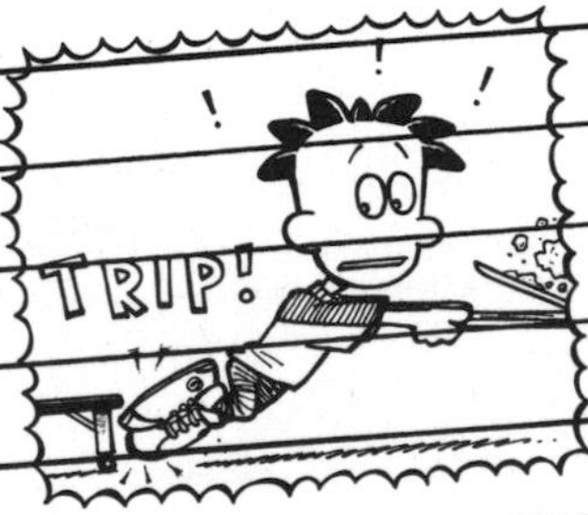

! ! !
TRIP!

2. Nate lost this, his most prized possession, in a creek!
   a. Comic book
   b. Soccer ball
   c. Skateboard
   d. Timber Scout beret

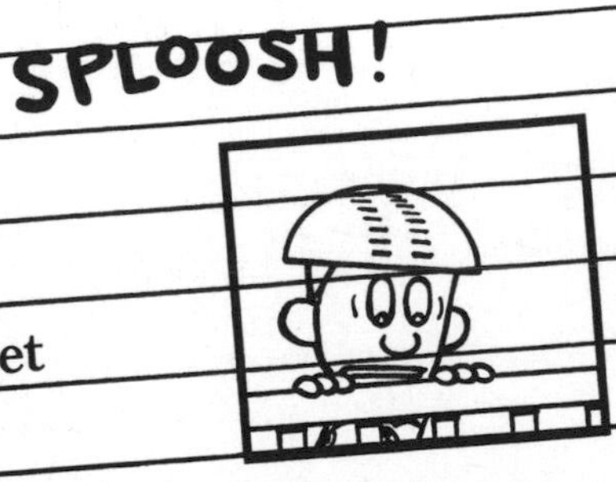

SPLOOSH!

3. This is not one of Nate's after-school jobs.

a. Arranging garden gnomes

b. Pulling weeds for Mr. Galvin

c. Walking Spitsy

d. Selling comic books to Gordie

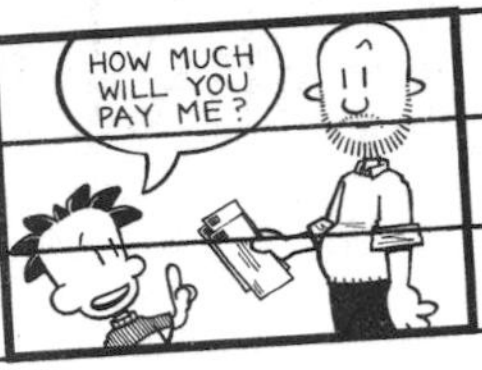
HOW MUCH WILL YOU PAY ME?

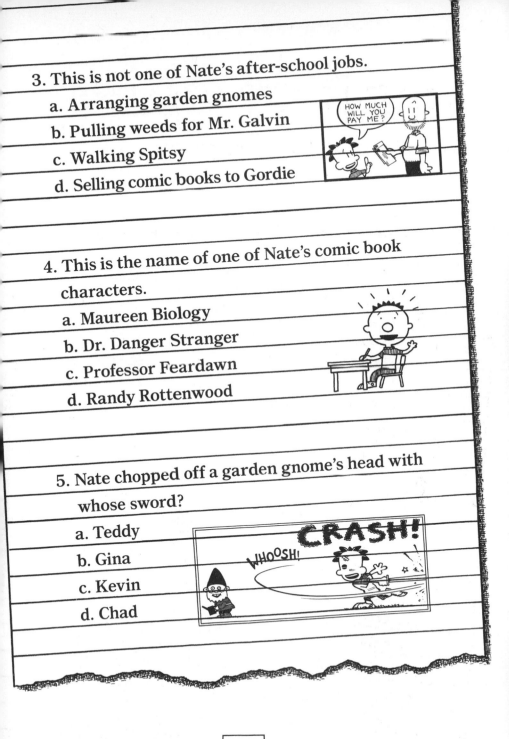

4. This is the name of one of Nate's comic book characters.

a. Maureen Biology

b. Dr. Danger Stranger

c. Professor Feardawn

d. Randy Rottenwood

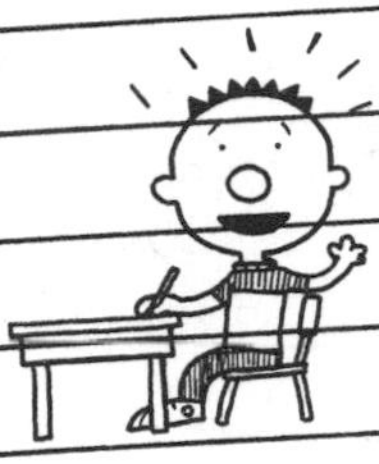

5. Nate chopped off a garden gnome's head with whose sword?

a. Teddy

b. Gina

c. Kevin

d. Chad

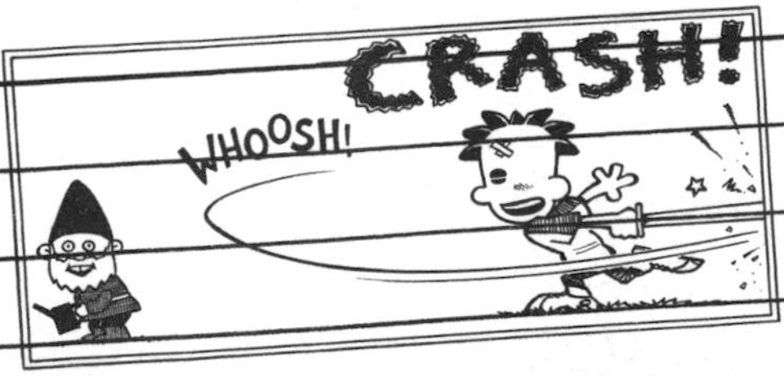
CRASH!
WHOOSH!

DESIGN TIME

Using your super scout names from page 131,
design a troop symbol for each one!

HERE'S NATE'S TIMBER SCOUT SYMBOL:

NOW DRAW YOURS!

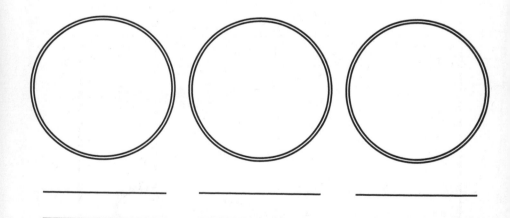

**WRITE THE MATCHING
SCOUT NAME BELOW EACH INSIGNIA.**

Check out Nate's cool scout uniform—
the beret, the necktie, and the arm patch
with his scout symbol!

BERET

TIMBER
SCOUT
INSIGNIA

CLIP-ON
NECKERCHIEF

MERIT
BADGES

NAME
STITCHED
ON SHIRT

SPORTY
STRIPE

DESIGN YOUR OWN AWESOME UNIFORM:

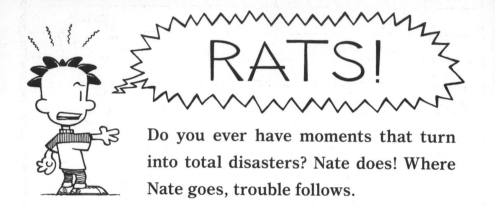

RATS!

Do you ever have moments that turn into total disasters? Nate does! Where Nate goes, trouble follows.

LIST YOUR WORST DISASTER MOMENTS HERE!

1.

2.

3.

4.

5.

6.

7. You get picked dead last for kickball in gym class.

8.

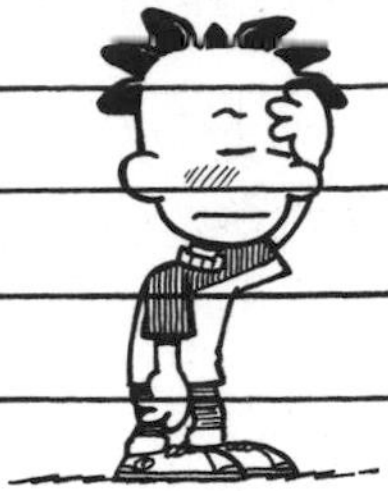

9.

10.

11. First you slip and fall in throw up in the school hallway, then you have to wear ugly pants from the Lost & Found for the rest of the day!

12.

13.

14.

15.

16. Your brother eats all the double chocolate cupcakes and doesn't even save one for you.

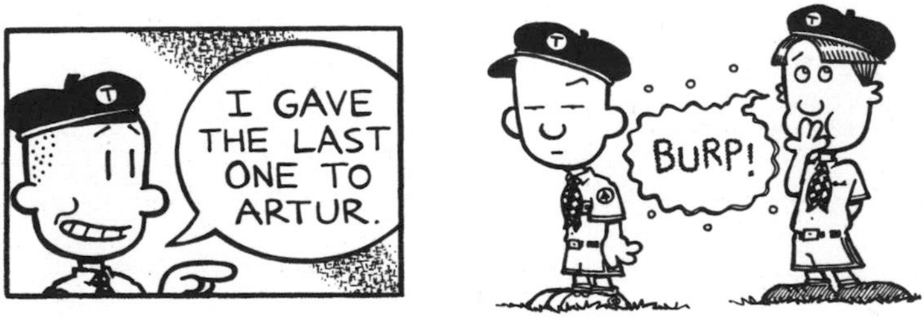
I GAVE THE LAST ONE TO ARTUR.
BURP!

TEACHER'S PET

What happens when you put 3 Goody Two-Shoes in a room with Mrs. Godfrey? You decide! Create a comic with these characters:

Goody Two-Shoe #1   Goody Two-Shoe #2

Goody Two-Shoe #3

YOUR TITLE HERE

LOTSA LIMERICKS

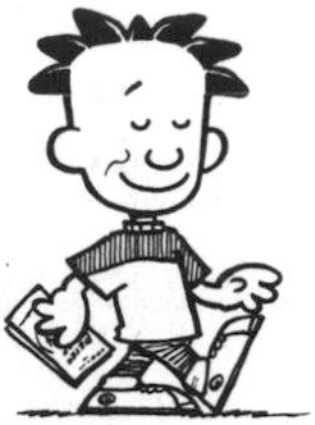

Nate's a master of rhyme.
With verse he is fine.
But he's given the sign—
It's your turn this time!

Try writing a limerick. That's a poem with 5 lines, where the 1st, 2nd, and 5th lines rhyme, and the 3rd and 4th lines rhyme.

HERE'S NATE'S EXAMPLE:

LIMERICK by Nate Wright

I have feasted on all sorts of noodles,
I have tried an assortment of strudels.
Of the foods that I've eaten,
Only one can't be beaten:
An extra-large bag of Cheez Doodles.

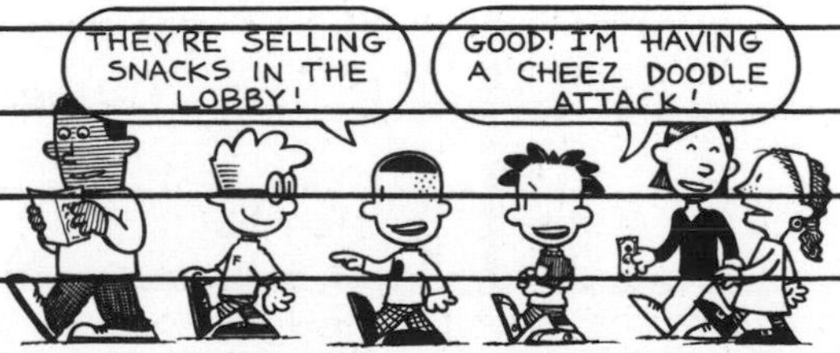
THEY'RE SELLING SNACKS IN THE LOBBY!
GOOD! I'M HAVING A CHEEZ DOODLE ATTACK!

NOW, YOU TRY!

There once was a kid from Peru,
Who came down with a terrible __________.
He gave out a cry,
And yelled out "Oh, __________,"
Then left on a train right at two.

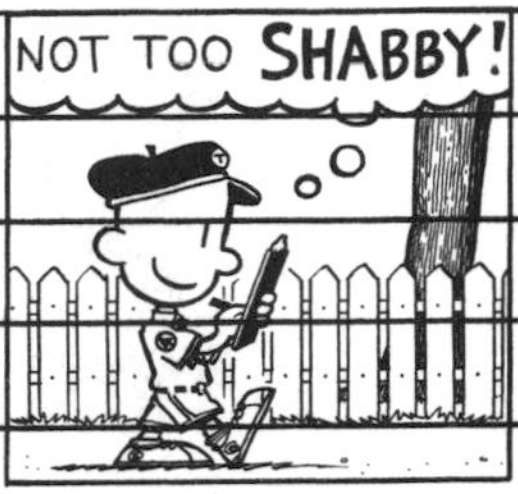
NOT TOO SHABBY!

A little girl wanted a llama,
She decided to go ask her __________,
It ran and it ate,
And never was __________,
But still it caused all kinds of drama.

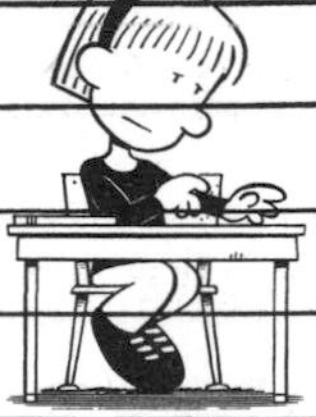

The class clown of P.S. 38,
He goes by the name of Big __________.
He loves to eat oodles
Of orange Cheez __________
And thinks that he's awesome and __________!

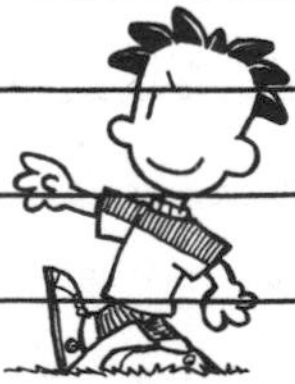

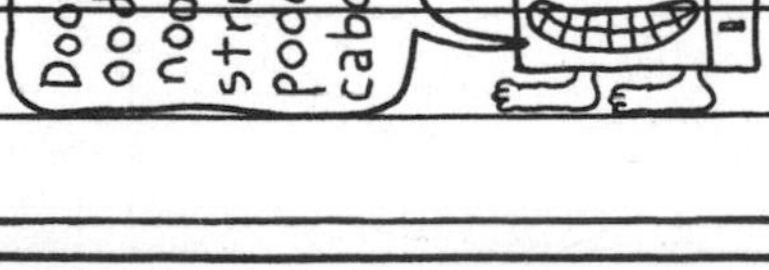
Doodle
oodle
noodle
strudel
poodle
caboodle
ON
OFF

WRITE YOUR OWN LIMERICKS!

There once was a fellow named Chad,

______________________________,

______________________________,

______________________________,

______________________________.

WHAM!

Oh, how I love pizza with cheese,

______________________________,

______________________________,

______________________________,

______________________________.

...BUT LET'S AVOID ANY MORE POEMS ABOUT JUNK FOOD, SHALL WE?

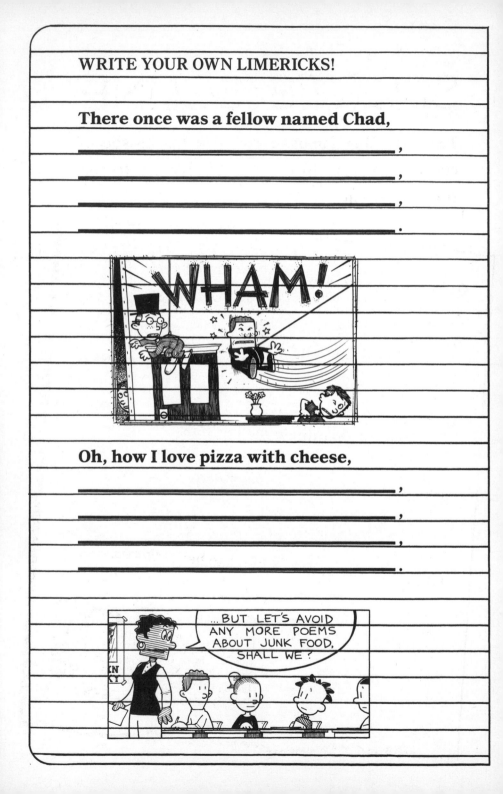

SPORTS SCENE

Teddy is a huge fan of sports trivia. Use his special code on page 34 to decode the answers to this super sports quiz!

Q: What gem do baseball players play on?

A: $\overline{}\ \overline{\underset{Z}{}}\ \overline{\underset{W}{}}\ \overline{\underset{R}{}}\ \overline{\underset{Z}{}}\ \overline{\underset{N}{}}\ \overline{\underset{L}{}}\ \overline{\underset{M}{}}\ \overline{\underset{W}{}}$.

SNAG!

Q: What are the most home runs hit by one player in a single major league game?

A: $\overline{\underset{U}{}}\ \overline{\underset{L}{}}\ \overline{\underset{F}{}}\ \overline{\underset{I}{}}$.

POW!

Q: How many events are in the heptathlon?

A: $\overline{\underset{H}{}}\ \overline{\underset{V}{}}\ \overline{\underset{E}{}}\ \overline{\underset{V}{}}\ \overline{\underset{M}{}}$.

SAY IT LOUD!

What's going on in each picture? It's up to you! Fill in the speech bubbles and finish each story.

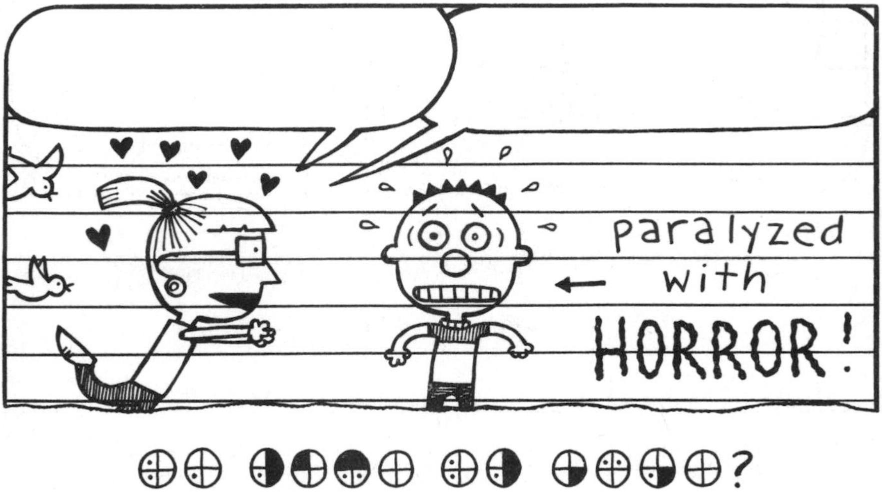
paralyzed with HORROR!

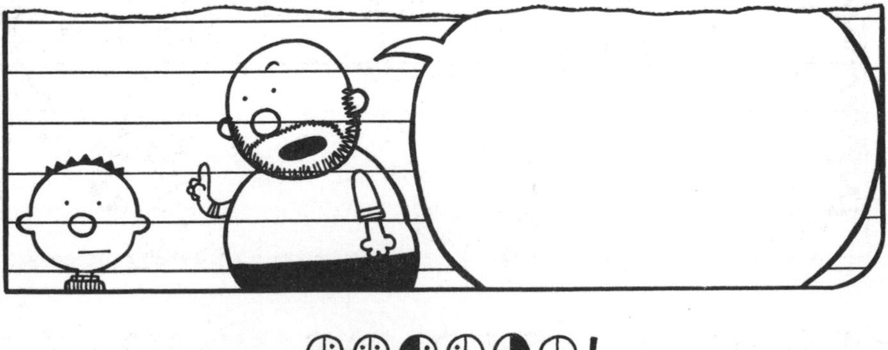

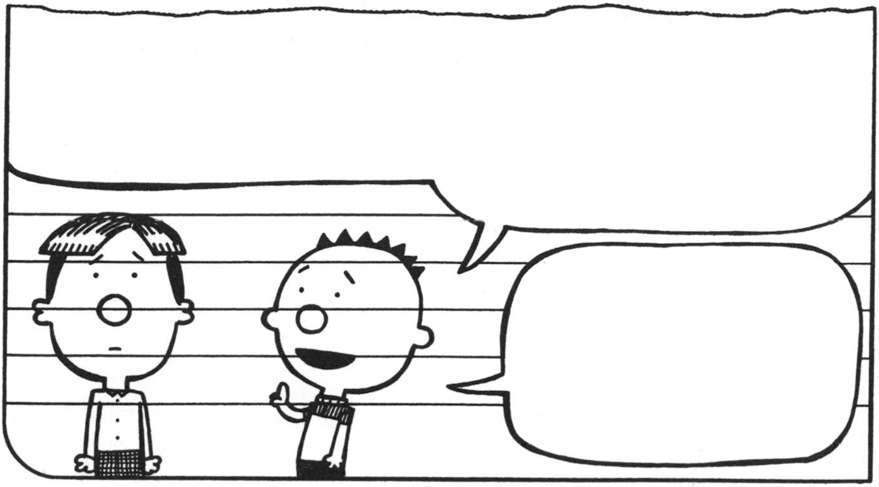

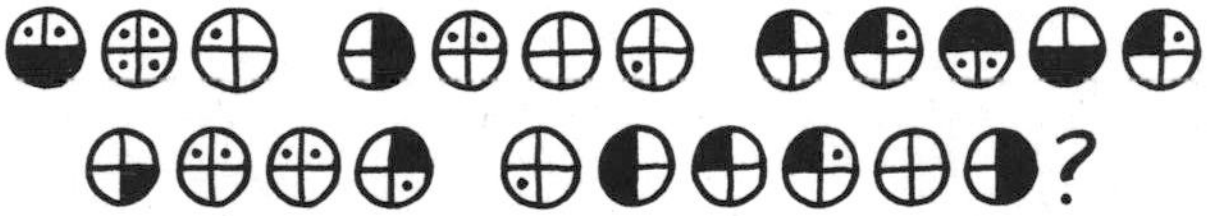

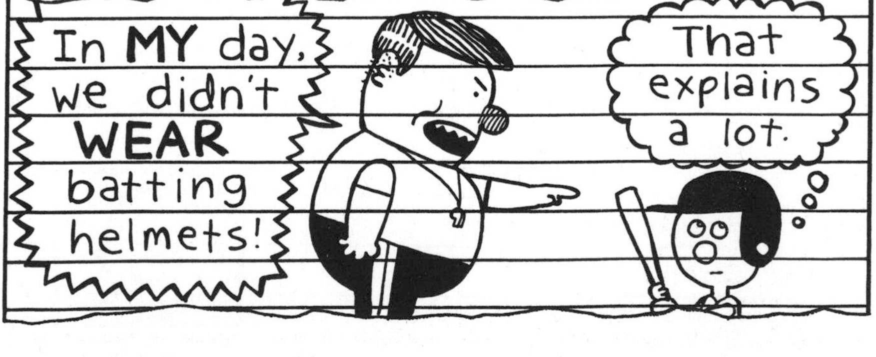
In MY day, we didn't WEAR batting helmets!
That explains a lot.

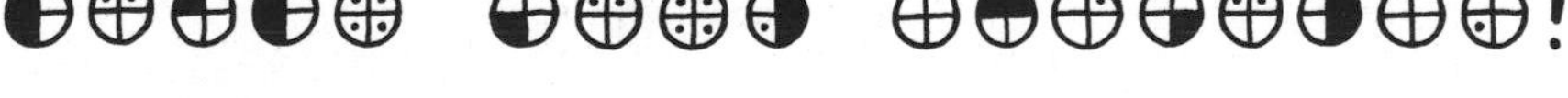

SCHOOL PICTURE DAY

Nate draws comix based on his own true-life moments! The best AND the worst!

SCHOOL PICTURE DAY
How do I look?
GREAT!
Except for that little zit there!

NOW YOU TRY!

WRITE DOWN YOUR FAVORITE PART OF SCHOOL PICTURE DAY.

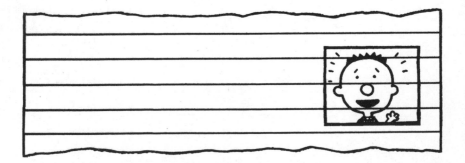

WRITE DOWN THE MOST ANNOYING PART OF SCHOOL PICTURE DAY.

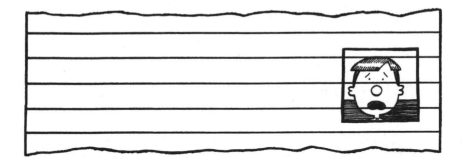

DRAW YOURSELF ON SCHOOL PICTURE DAY!

CAPTION CAPTAIN

I FOUND YOUR "WARM FUZZIES" BROCHURE ON THE KITCHEN FLOOR.

For his scout troop, Nate has to sell cheesy wall hangings called Warm Fuzzies. Check out these off-the-wall captions!

YOU'RE MY SWEETIE PIE!

I'M A NUT!

HANG IN THERE!

NOW CREATE YOUR OWN CAPTIONS FOR THE FOLLOWING FUNNY POSTERS!

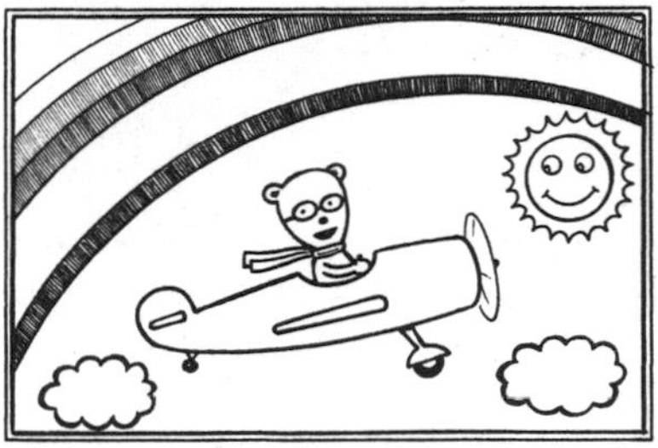

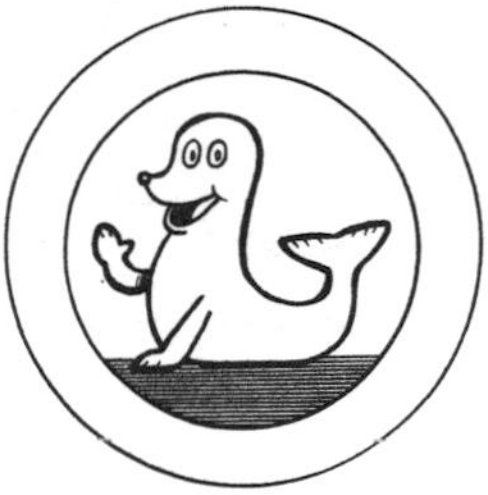

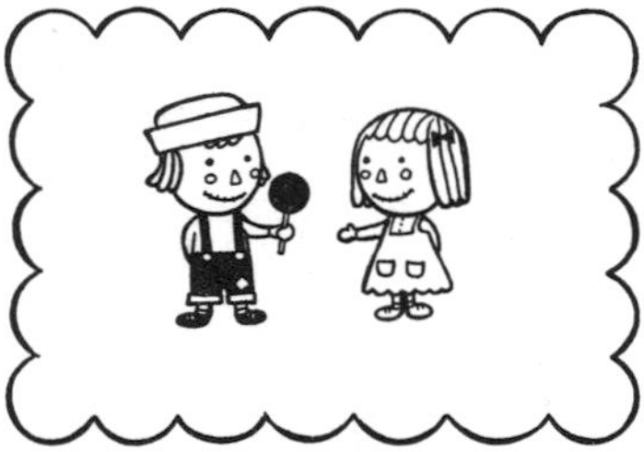

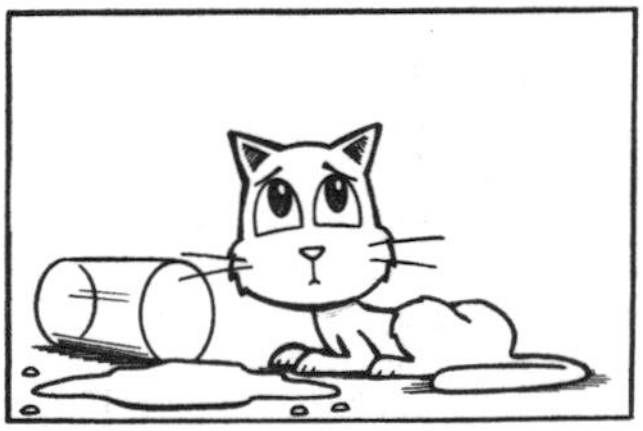

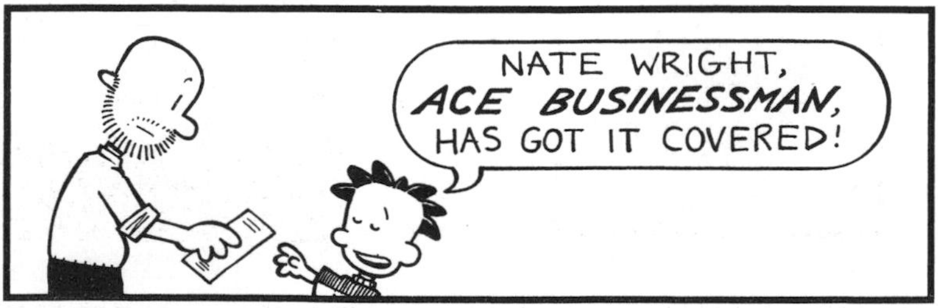
NATE WRIGHT, *ACE BUSINESSMAN*, HAS GOT IT COVERED!

WHO'S A
BRAINIAC?

Francis is one smart scout! And he loves learning strange factoids. Use his code on page 58 to uncover this weird and funny trivia.

$$\overline{24}\ \overline{11}\ \overline{18}\ \overline{8}$$

$$\overline{6}\ \overline{10}\ \overline{14}\ \overline{6}\ \overline{23}\ \overline{8}\ \overline{24}$$

$$\overline{26}\ \overline{13}\ \overline{21}$$

$$\overline{7}\ \overline{14}\ \overline{8}\ \overline{13}\ \overline{6}\ \overline{1}\ \overline{8}$$

$$\overline{6}\ \overline{1}\ \overline{14}\ \overline{11}\ \overline{10}\ \overline{3}\ \overline{1}$$

$$\overline{6}\ \overline{1}\ \overline{8}\ \overline{20}\ \overline{14}\ \quad \overline{7}\ \overline{10}\ \overline{6}\ \overline{6}\ \overline{24}.$$

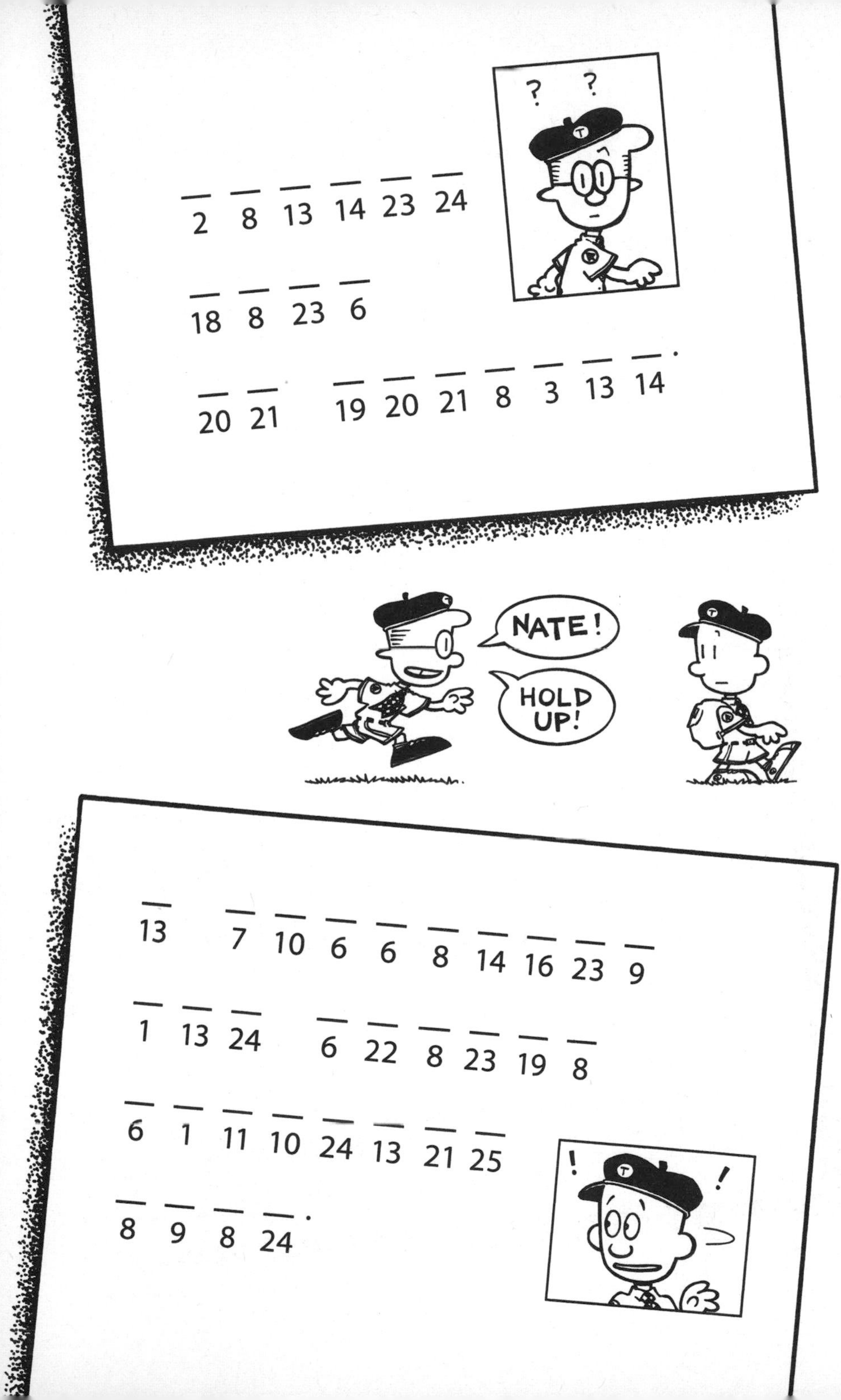

2 8 13 14 23 24
18 8 23 6
20 21 19 20 21 8 3 13 14.
NATE!
HOLD UP!
13 7 10 6 6 8 14 16 23 9
1 13 24 6 22 8 23 19 8
6 1 11 10 24 13 21 25
8 9 8 24.

LAUGH-A-THON

...AND THE DUCK SAYS, "PUT IT ON MY BILL!"
HA! HA! HA! VERY FUNNY, SIR! HA! HA!

Nate's math teacher, Mr. Staples, always tells lame jokes. What makes you laugh out loud? It's time to joke around! Fill in the punch lines!

Q: What kind of dog tells time?
A: A ______________ dog!

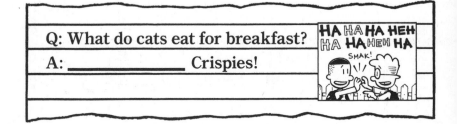

Q: What do cats eat for breakfast?
A: ______________ Crispies!

HA HA HA HEH
HA HA HEH HA
SMAK!

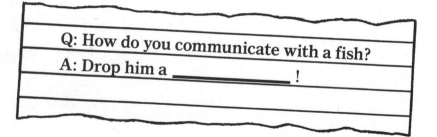

Q: How do you communicate with a fish?
A: Drop him a ______________ !

WHAT COULD GO WRONG?

How will Nate's walk to the park with Spitsy turn out?

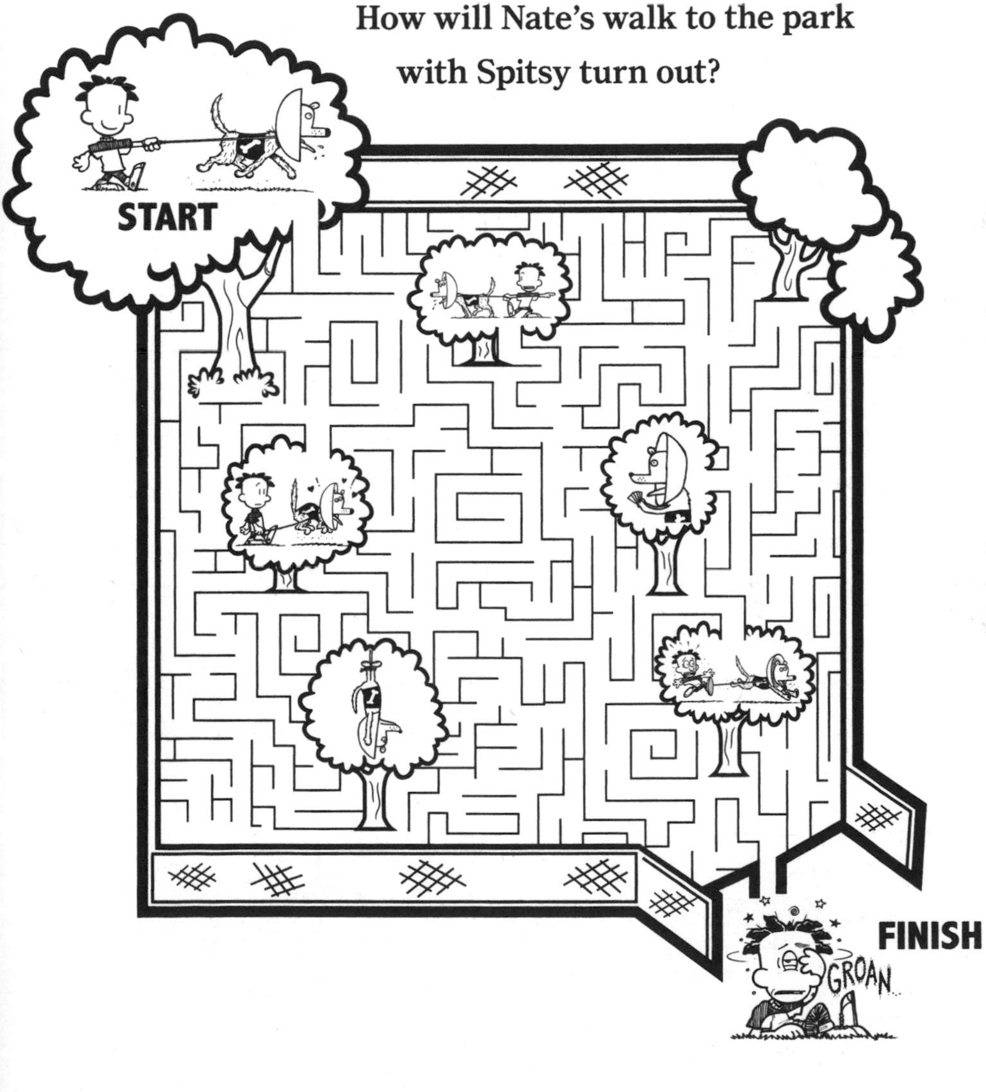
START
FINISH
GROAN...

EXCLAMATION STATION

What's going on in each picture? You decide!

Fill in the speech bubbles below.

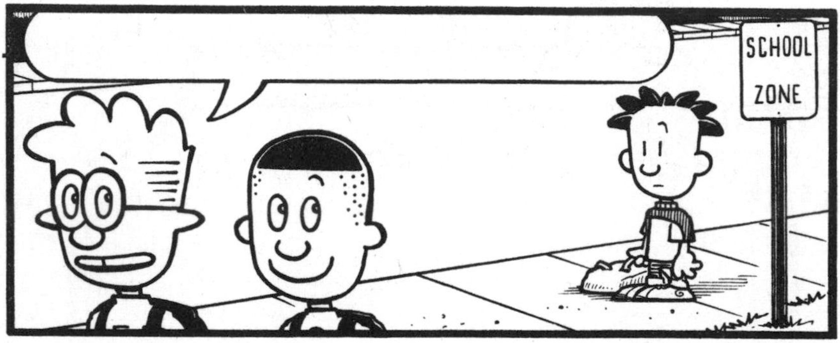
SCHOOL ZONE

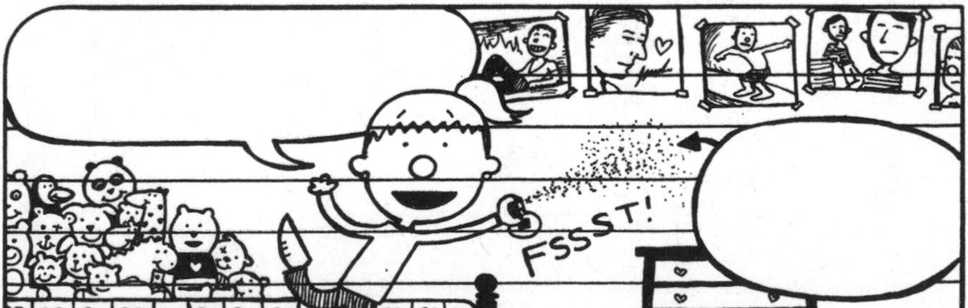
FSSST!

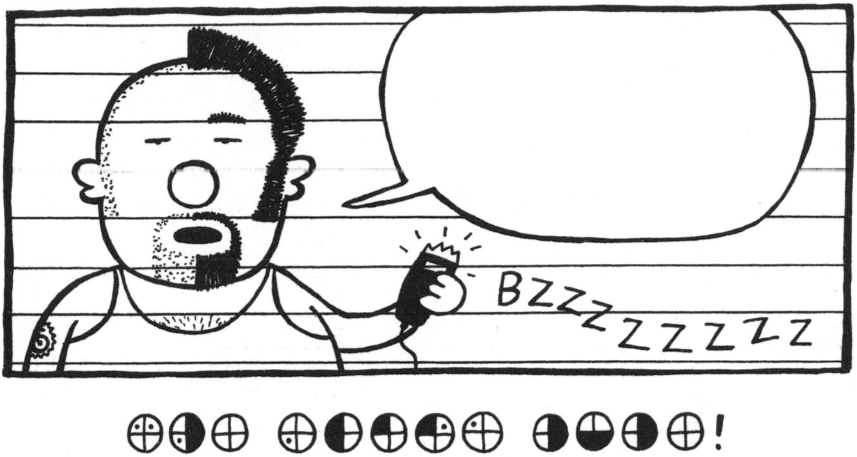
BZZZZZZZZZ

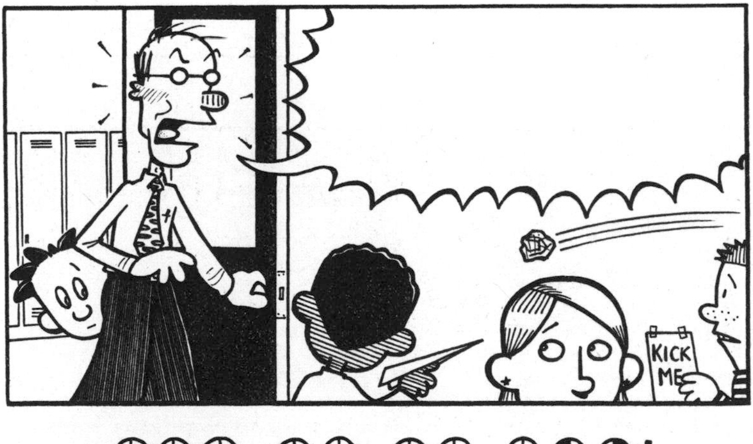
KICK ME

FUNNY BUSINESS

Teddy's one funny guy! Use his secret code on page 34 to uncover the punch lines to his favorite jokes below.

Q: Why was the belt arrested?

A: $\underline{U}$ $\underline{L}$ $\underline{I}$ $\underline{S}$ $\underline{L}$ $\underline{O}$ $\underline{W}$ $\underline{R}$ $\underline{M}$ $\underline{T}$
$\underline{F}$ $\underline{K}$ $\underline{G}$ $\underline{S}$ $\underline{V}$ $\underline{K}$ $\underline{Z}$ $\underline{M}$ $\underline{G}$ $\underline{H}$.

Q: Why are teddy bears never hungry?

A:

Y V X Z F H V

G S V B Z I V

Z O D Z B H

H G F U U V W.

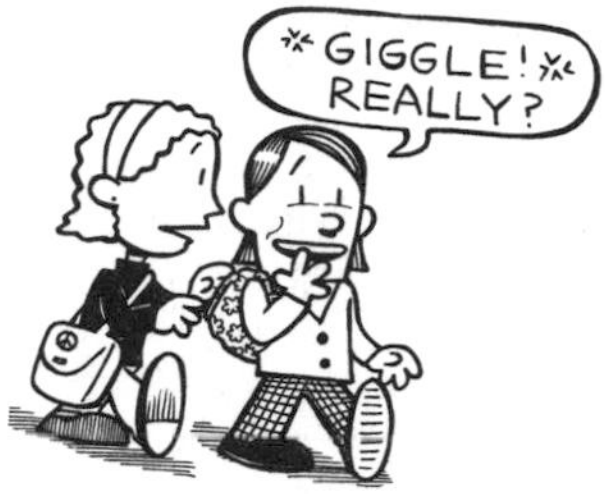

GIGGLE! REALLY?

Q: Why didn't the hot dog star in the movie?

A:

G S V I L O V H

D V I V M'G

T L L W

V M L F T S.

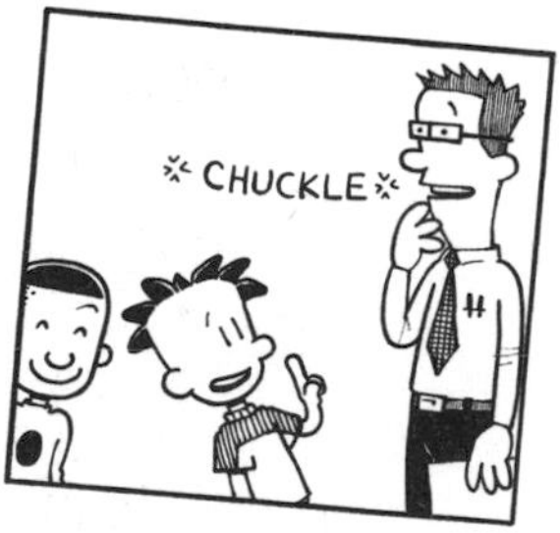

CHUCKLE

SCRIBBLE MASTER

Who's the scribble master? You are!
Make a work of art out of this scribble!

Remember the caption!

NATE'S NAME GAME

Nate invented a name game. For each letter in a person's first name, write down an adjective (see page 7 for the definition) or phrase that describes him or her, beginning with that letter!

HERE'S WHAT
NATE WROTE
FOR ARTUR,
HIS RIVAL.

ANNOYING

REASONABLY NICE

TALENTED

UNFORTUNATELY,

REALLY IRRITATING

NOW YOU TRY!

N _____

A WESOME

T _____

E _____

E ______________________

L OVES UNICORNS

L ______________________

E ______________________

N ______________________

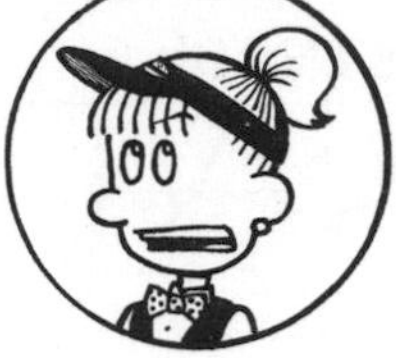

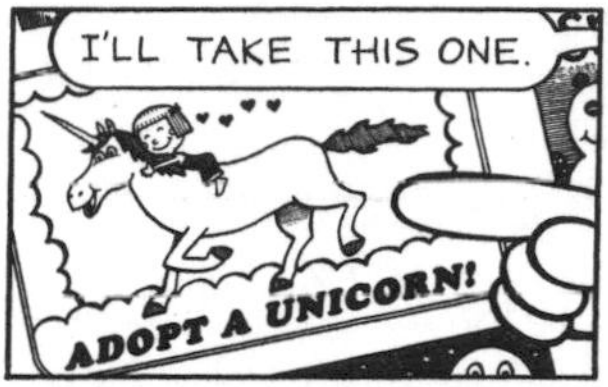
I'LL TAKE THIS ONE.
ADOPT A UNICORN!

G RADE OBSESSED

I ______________________

N ______________________

A ______________________

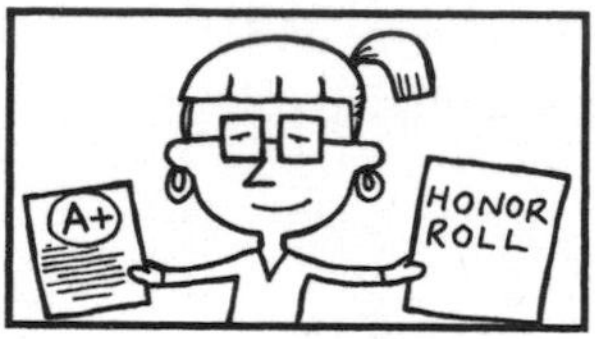
A+
HONOR ROLL

F ACT FINDER

R ______________________

A ______________________

N ______________________

C ______________________

I ______________________

S ______________________

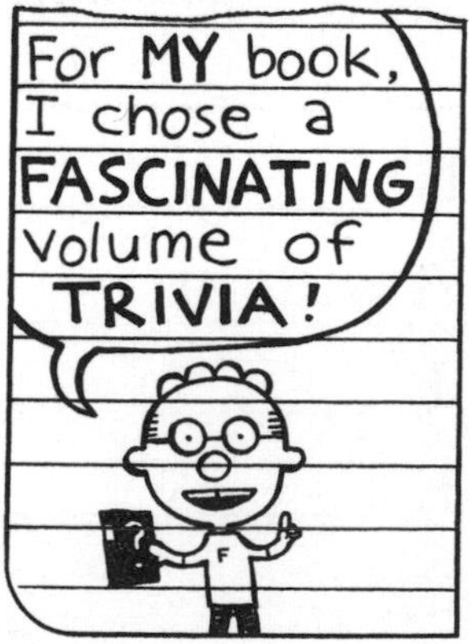
For MY book, I chose a FASCINATING volume of TRIVIA!

TELLS JOKES

E _____

D _____

D _____

Y _____

J _____

E _____

N ATE'S DREAM GIRL

N _____

Y _____

NOW TRY YOUR NAME!

_____

_____

_____

_____

_____

_____

_____

YOUR PORTRAIT

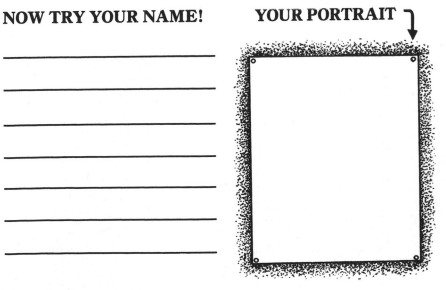

LOCKER DISASTER

Watch out! Nate's locker is overflowing . . . AGAIN. Solve the clues to the puzzle and find every item inside!

ACROSS

3. Nate wears this to scout meetings—the beret is the best part!

5. It's filled with numbers, and Nate needs to read it for Mr. Staples's class. Rhymes with "bath hook."

7. After school, Nate sometimes kicks this around with his friends.

9. Mmm, orange and puffalicious, these are Nate's favorite snack.

10. Nate loves to draw these, especially where he's Ultra-Nate, the superhero.

11. This little piece of pink paper means that Nate has to stay after class!

12. Nate cruises the neighborhood on these cool wheels. Riding this is like surfing, only better!

DOWN

1. Nate gets them at Pu Pu Panda, and thinks they taste like Styrofoam.

2. Nate's feet are smelly, so these can get gross after gym class.

4. Nate didn't get a very good grade in Mrs. Godfrey's class on his _______ .

6. Nate wrote this rhyming masterpiece to Jenny, his crush, in Ms. Clarke's class.

8. Nate would rather be cartooning than doing this. Not schoolwork, but _______ .

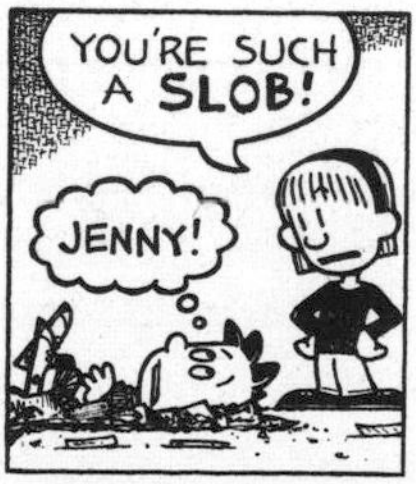
YOU'RE SUCH A SLOB!
JENNY!

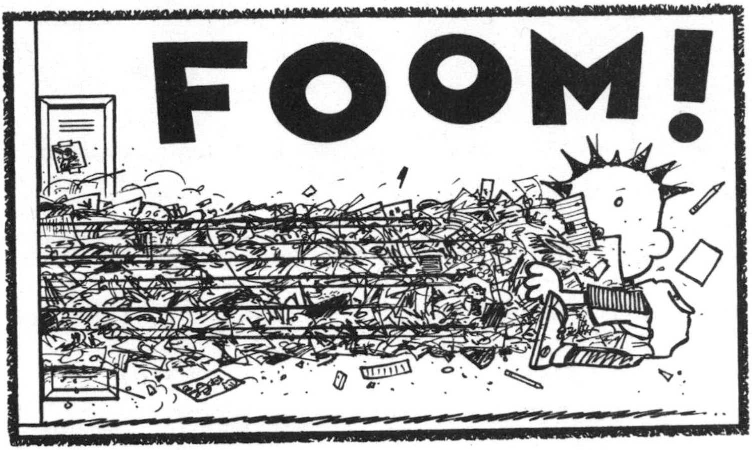
FOOM!

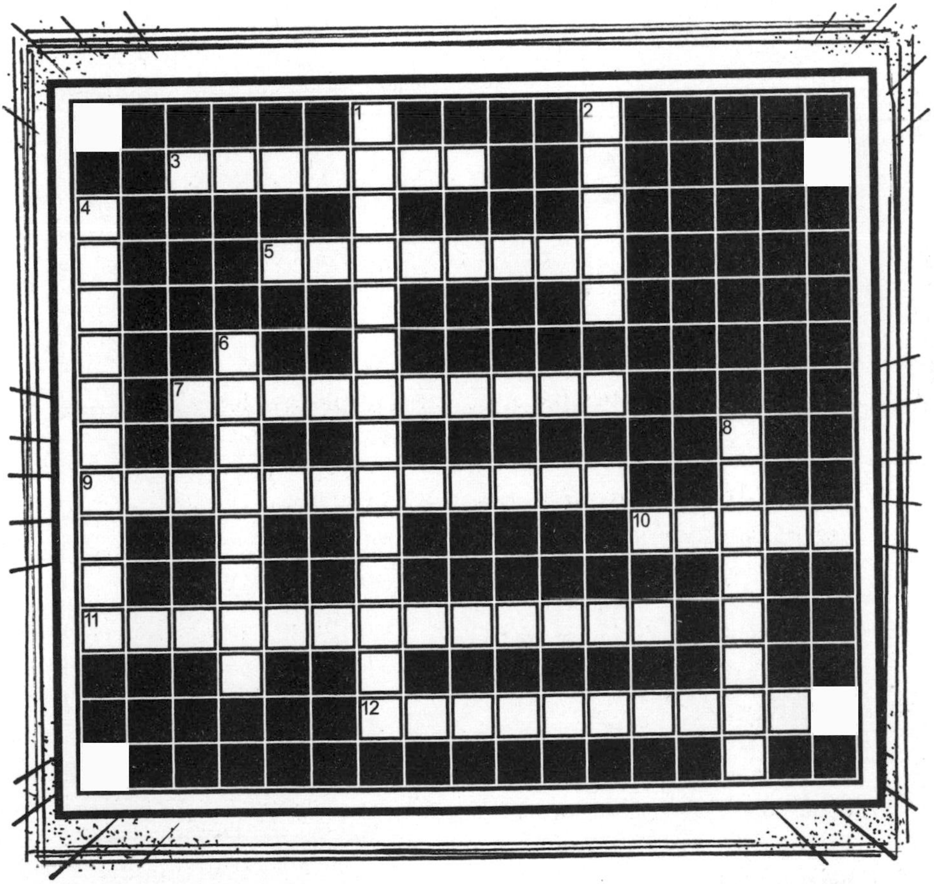
1
2
3
4
5
6
7
8
9
10
11
12

COPY CAT

Are you an awesome
artist? Test your skills.
Try drawing each of
these characters in the
blank boxes below.

WHAT WAS THE QUESTION AGAIN?

Francis is one smart student. He even listens to Mr. Galvin! Use his code on page 58 to find the answers to these cool questions about the Earth.

What is the name of the largest ocean on Earth?

$\overline{2}$ $\overline{13}$ $\overline{26}$ $\overline{20}$ $\overline{16}$ $\overline{20}$ $\overline{26}$

$\overline{11}$ $\overline{26}$ $\overline{8}$ $\overline{13}$ $\overline{21}$.

The mass of the Earth is made up mostly of which two elements?

$\overline{20}$ $\overline{14}$ $\overline{11}$ $\overline{21}$

$\overline{13}$ $\overline{21}$ $\overline{25}$

$\overline{11}$ $\overline{17}$ $\overline{9}$ $\overline{3}$ $\overline{8}$ $\overline{21}$.

Outside of Antarctica, what is the largest desert in the world?

$\overline{6}$ $\overline{1}$ $\overline{8}$

$\overline{24}$ $\overline{13}$ $\overline{1}$ $\overline{13}$ $\overline{14}$ $\overline{13}$.

HAPPINESS IS... WARM FUZZIES

Sell the most wall hangings for the Timber Scouts and win a GREAT prize. Fill in the blanks so that each wall hanging is represented only once in every row, column, and box!

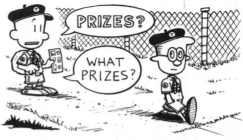

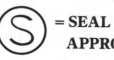

PRIZES?
WHAT PRIZES?

(N) = I'M A NUT

(W) = WHO ME?

(S) = SEAL OF APPROVAL

(F) = FOLLOW YOUR RAINBOW

(U) = ADOPT A UNICORN

(H) = I NEED A HUG!

(G) = DON'T YOU LOVE . . . GRANDMAS?

(L) = LOVE IS . . . SHARING

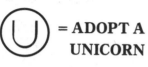

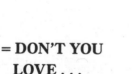

I'M A NUT!

I NEED A HUG!

DON'T YOU LOVE...
GRANDMAS?

WHO, ME?

S	U	W		L		F	
		F					N
				H		G	
H	G	L			N		W
W	S	H			L		F
			L	W		U	
							S
G	L	N		F			

FOLLOW YOUR RAINBOW!

"SEAL" OF APPROVAL

I'LL TAKE THIS ONE.
ADOPT A UNICORN!

HANG IN THERE!

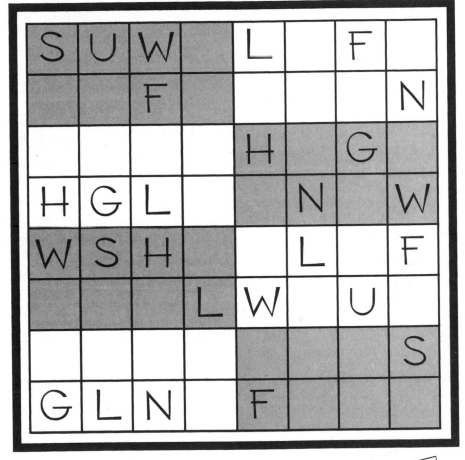

BUBBLE TROUBLE

Nate's in trouble, again. Fill in the speech bubbles and find out what's happening!

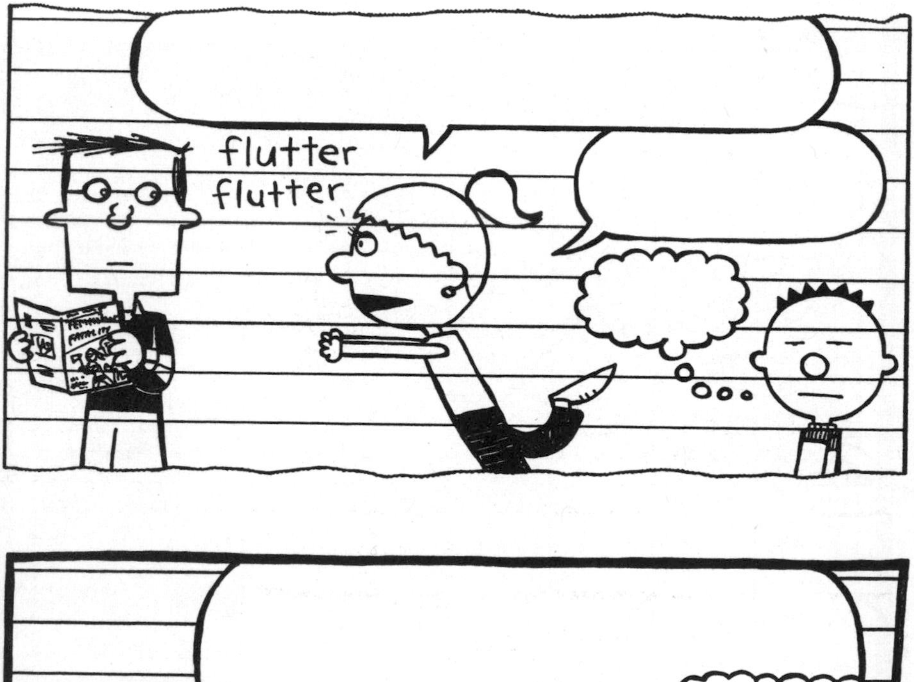
flutter
flutter

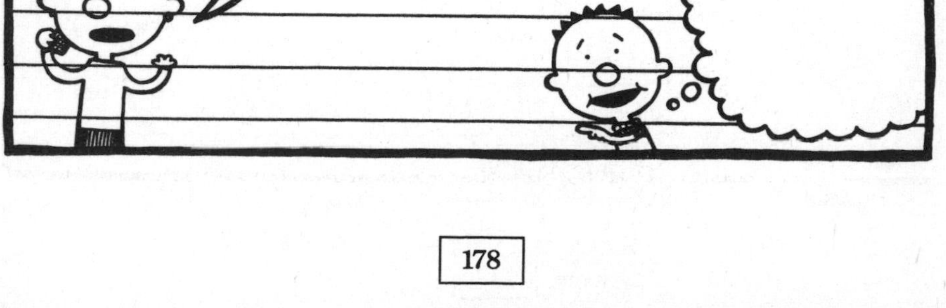

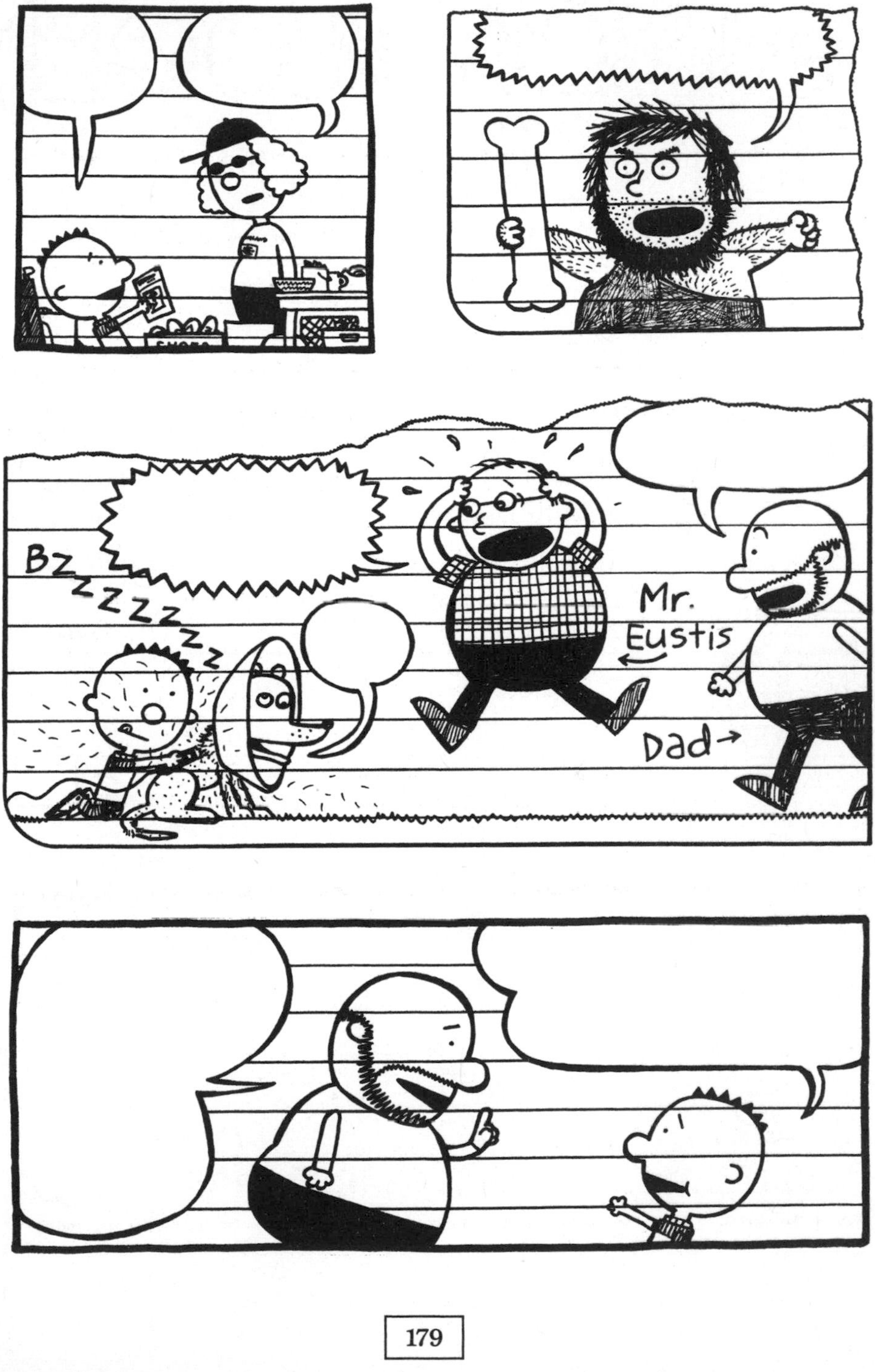
Bzzzzzzzz
Mr. Eustis
Dad

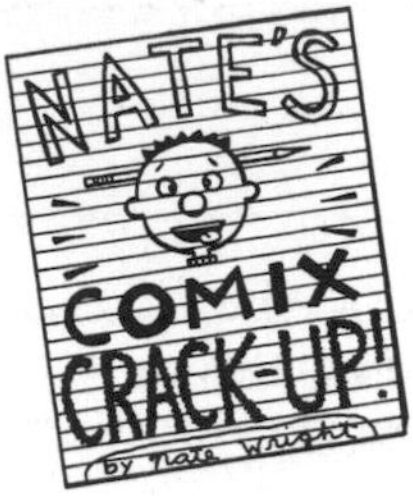
NATE'S
COMIX
CRACK-UP!
by Nate Wright

CARTOON CRAZE

Nate's a master at cartooning. He even has his own comix collection with characters he's created, like Doctor Cesspool. Create your own comix villains and heroes by mixing and matching the following names!

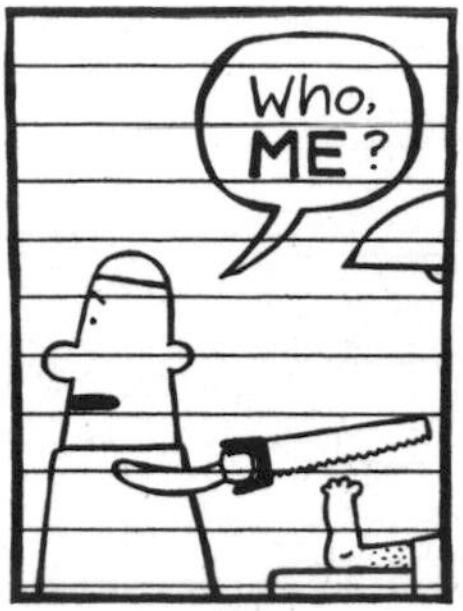
Who, ME?

DARING	SILVER	PROFESSOR
MAGNIFICENT	DETECTIVE	______
INVISIBLE	BLOB	CLIMBER
______	MASTERMIND	______
OUTRAGEOUS	PRINCE	DISASTER
MYSTERIOUS	HEIRESS	LICORICE
MAD	______	MIDNIGHT
SLIMY	MAGICIAN	PILOT
MAGNETIC	CLOWN	GOLD TOOTH
ULTIMATE	DISAPPEARING	PINK

HERE ARE SOME

WILD CHARACTER NAMES:

Slimy Prince Disaster

Professor Licorice Midnight

NOW MAKE UP YOUR OWN!

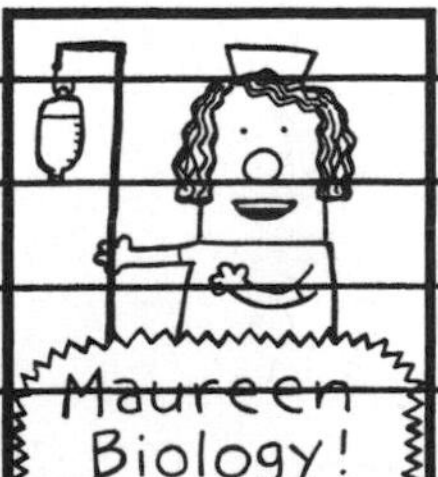
Maureen
Biology!

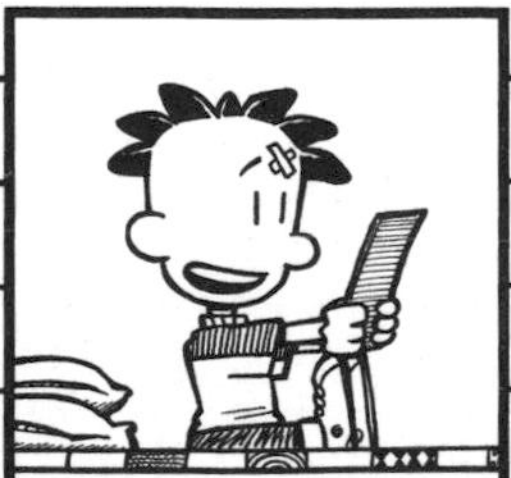

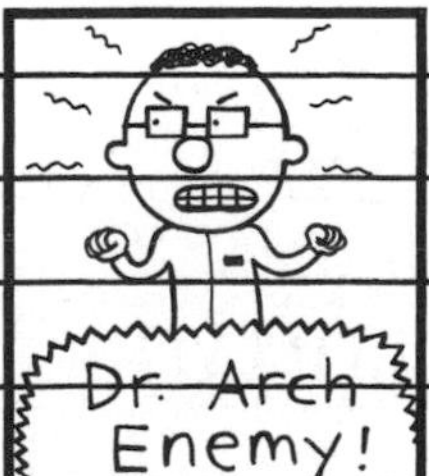
Dr. Arch
Enemy!

ALL MIXED UP!

What do all of these words have in common? Each one adds to the action in *Big Nate on a Roll*, book 3, where Nate runs into all kinds of trouble!

ARTUR
MALL COP
MATH OLYMPIAD
JAMBOREE
GORDIE
BUMBLE BOY
TOY POODLE
SCENERY
BROWNIES
MR. EUSTIS
SKATEBOARD
WARM FUZZIES
GNOMES
SPITSY
COMIC BOOK
PRIZES
FUNDRAISER
ROCKIN' ROBOT
TELESCOPE
TIMBER SCOUTS

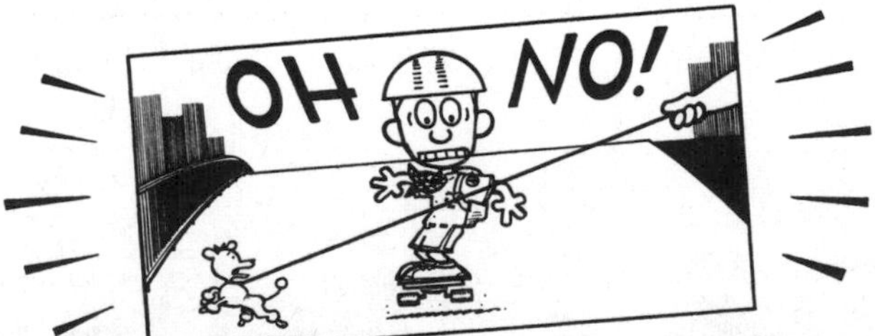
OH NO!

Find more than 15 of the words in the puzzle below and help Nate in his mission to beat Artur, aka Mr. Perfect!

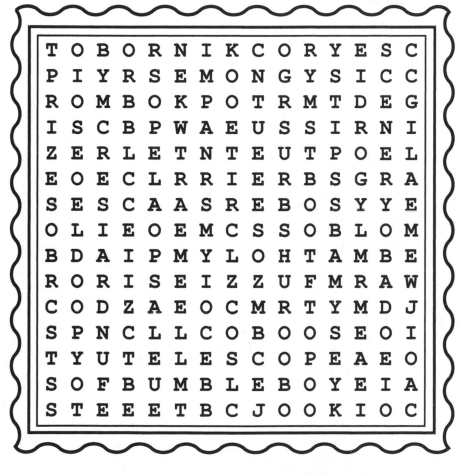

```
T O B O R N I K C O R Y E S C
P I Y R S E M O N G Y S I C C
R O M B O K P O T R M T D E G
I S C B P W A E U S S I R N I
Z E R L E T N T E U T P O E L
E O E C L R R I E R B S G R A
S E S C A A S R E B O S Y Y E
O L I E O E M C S S O B L O M
B D A I P M Y L O H T A M B E
R O R I S E I Z Z U F M R A W
C O D Z A E O C M R T Y M D J
S P N C L L C O B O O S E O I
T Y U T E L E S C O P E A E O
S O F B U M B L E B O Y E I A
S T E E E T B C J O O K I O C
```

HE'S *PERFECT!*

LOOOVE IT!

What do you love most?
Rate these from 1 to 10.
10 = BIG LOVE
1 = JUST O.K.

	RATING
Hot fudge sundae	_____
A water slide	_____
When your teacher gives you an A	_____
Going camping with your family	_____
Breakfast for dinner	_____
Playing at the beach	_____
Slumber party with your best friends	_____
Making a super-cool video or drawing	_____

Getting a puppy	——
Watching fireworks	——
Finding out your crush likes you back	——
Dancing like crazy	——
Summer vacation	——
Opening birthday presents	——
Climbing a tree	——
Performing in a killer band	——
Becoming captain of the team	——
Eating the last cookie	——

NATE'S COMIX CRACK-UP

Nate's comic book is a masterpiece. Solve the maze and figure out who's dying to buy a copy!

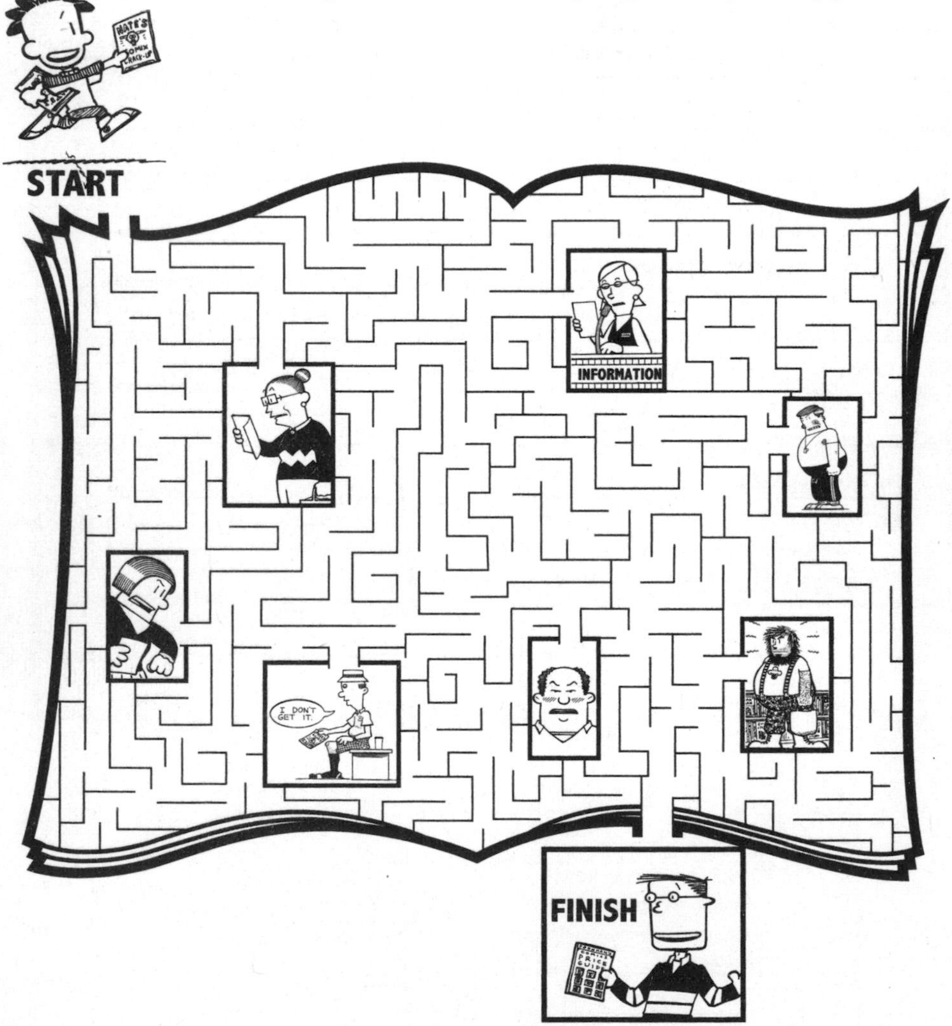
START
INFORMATION
I DON'T GET IT.
FINISH

TAKE A HIKE

Nate and his scout troop are on the move.
Fill in the speech bubbles and finish the story!

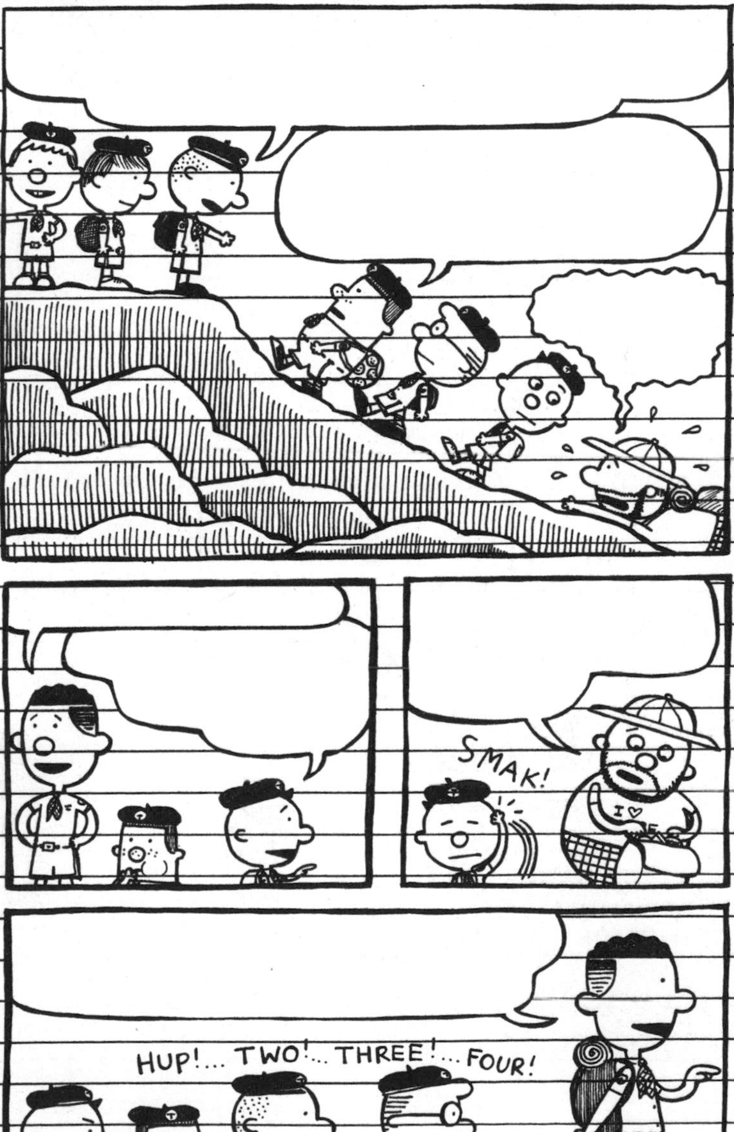
SMAK!
HUP!... TWO!... THREE!... FOUR!

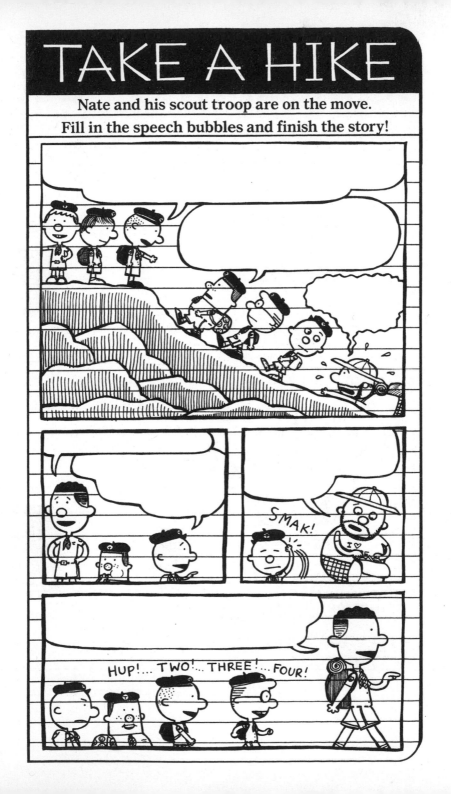

SUPER WRITER

Nate's a superstar at making
up silly rhymes. Now you try!
Answer each of these clues with
a two-word phrase that rhymes!

EXAMPLE:

Overweight feline   <u>F</u> <u>A</u> <u>T</u>   <u>C</u> <u>A</u> <u>T</u>

1. Friendly rodents   <u>N</u> _ _ _   _ _ <u>C</u> _

2. Feathered animal,
   a group of them   <u>B</u> _ _ _   _ _ _ <u>D</u>

3. Beach-covered
   sweets   _ _ _ <u>D</u> _   <u>C</u> _ _ _ _ _

4. A long distance away,
   it twinkles in the night sky   _ _ <u>R</u> _ <u>T</u> _ _

5. You just bought it,
   and you wear it on your foot   <u>N</u> _ _   _ <u>H</u> _ _

6. What your dog drinks from ___ ___ P ___ C ___ ___

7. Color that rhymes with “head”
The place where you sleep ___ E ___ ___ ___ D

8. A partner who isn’t on time
___ ___ T ___ M ___ ___ ___

IT’S YOUR TURN!
MAKE UP TWO-WORD PHRASES THAT RHYME
AND WRITE CLUES THAT DESCRIBE THEM.

9.

10.

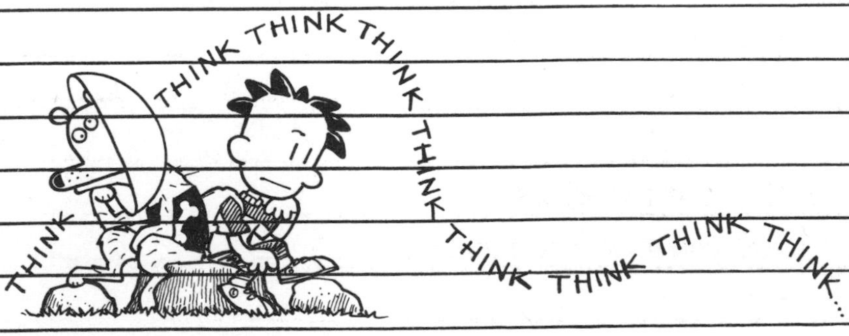
THINK THINK THINK THINK THINK THINK THINK THINK THINK THINK...

WHO'S A
SPORTS GENIUS?

Are you a sports whiz like Teddy?

Use his code on page 34 to decipher the answers.

Q: Which three events make up the triathlon?

A: $\overline{}\,\overline{}\,\overline{}\,\overline{}\,\overline{}\,\overline{}\,\overline{}\,\overline{}$,
   H D R N N R M T

$\overline{}\,\overline{}\,\overline{}\,\overline{}\,\overline{}\,\overline{}\,\overline{}$, $\overline{}\,\overline{}\,\overline{}$
X B X O R M T   Z M W

$\overline{}\,\overline{}\,\overline{}\,\overline{}\,\overline{}\,\overline{}$.
 I F M M R M T

RACE YOU GUYS TO THE FLAGPOLE!

Q: What sport features strikers and sweepers?

A: $\underline{\ }\ \underline{\ }\ \underline{\ }\ \underline{\ }\ \underline{\ }\ \underline{\ }$.
H L X X V I

Q: What racket sport involves hitting a bird?

A: $\underline{\ }\ \underline{\ }\ \underline{\ }\ \underline{\ }\ \underline{\ }\ \underline{\ }\ \underline{\ }\ \underline{\ }\ \underline{\ }$.
Y Z W N R M G L M

Q: What are the steps in the triple jump?

A: $\underline{\ }\ \underline{\ }\ \underline{\ }$, $\underline{\ }\ \underline{\ }\ \underline{\ }\ \underline{\ }$,
S L K   H P R K

$\underline{\ }\ \underline{\ }\ \underline{\ }\ \underline{\ }\ \underline{\ }\ \underline{\ }$.
Z M W Q F N K

COMIX-O-RAMA!

It looks like detention is calling. . . . What happens when Nate runs up against his dad AND a substitute teacher in one day? It's up to you!

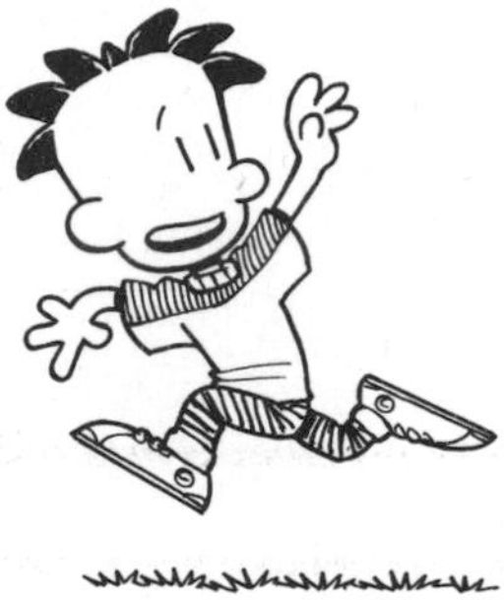

+

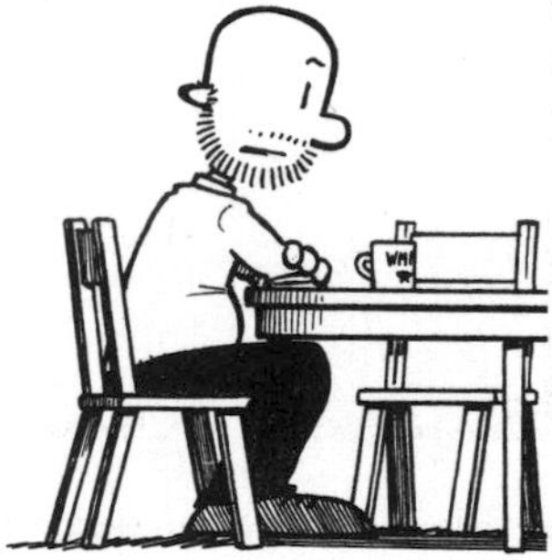

+

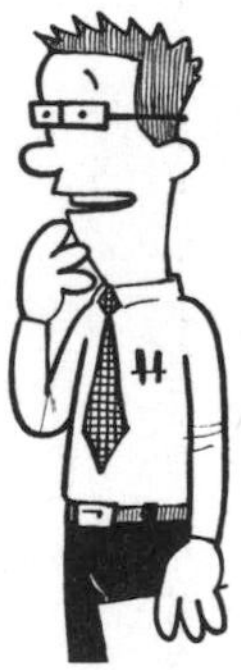

=

?

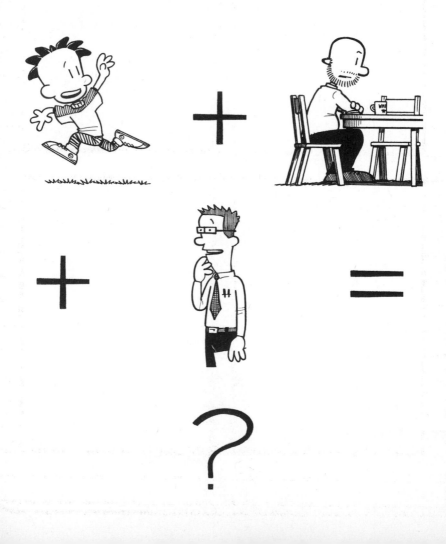

YOUR TITLE HERE

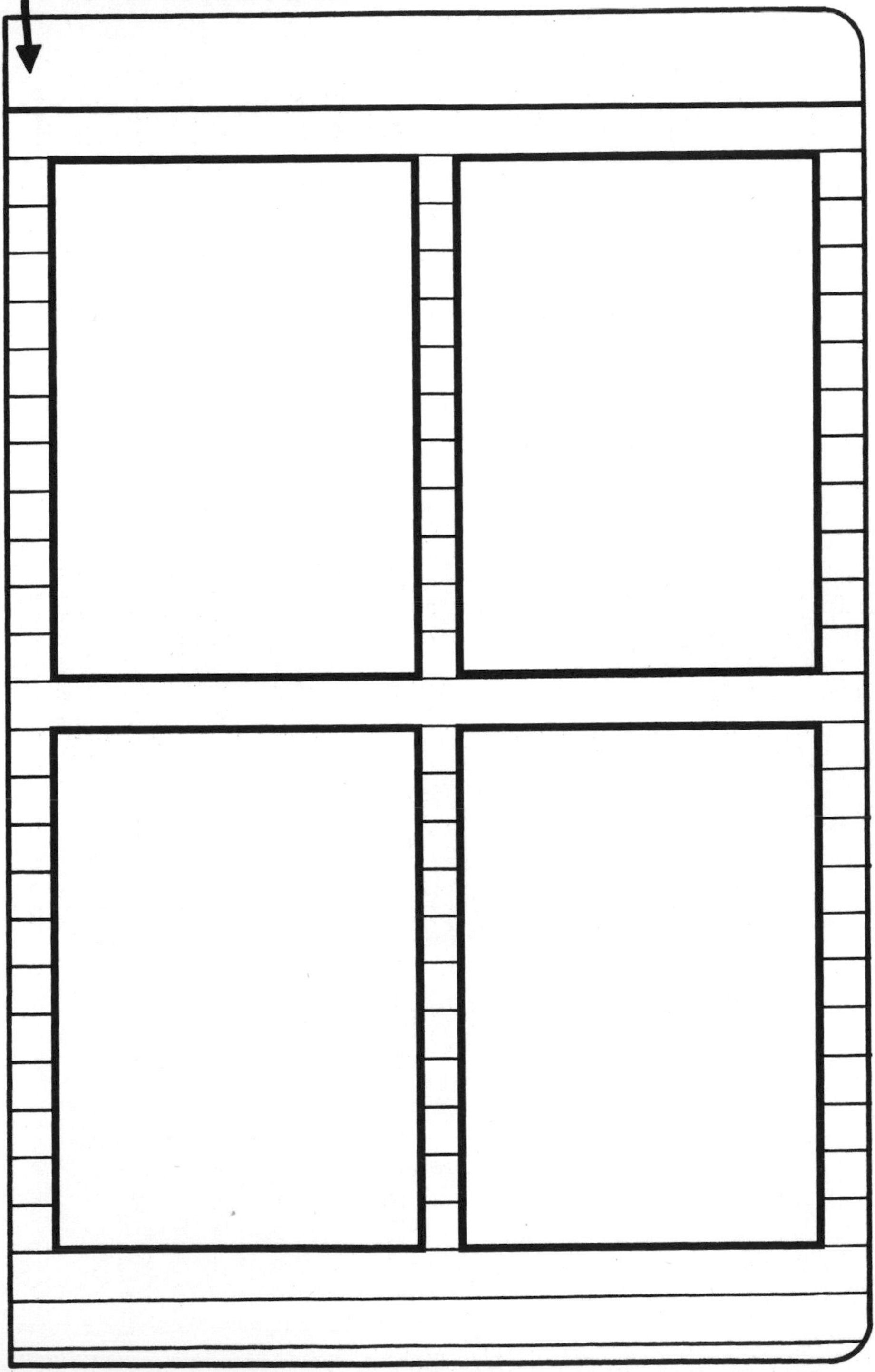

CATS AND DOGS

Spitsy has a serious crush on Francis's cat, Pickles. But how much do cats and dogs really have in common? Solve the clues to the puzzle and find out!

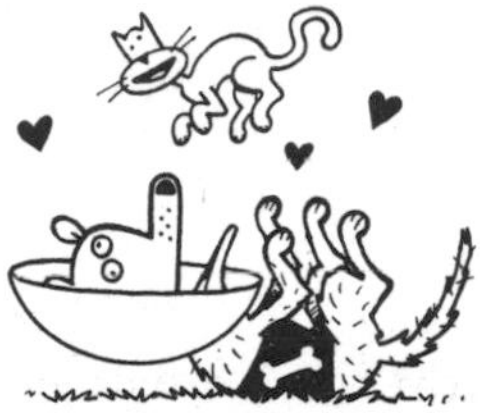

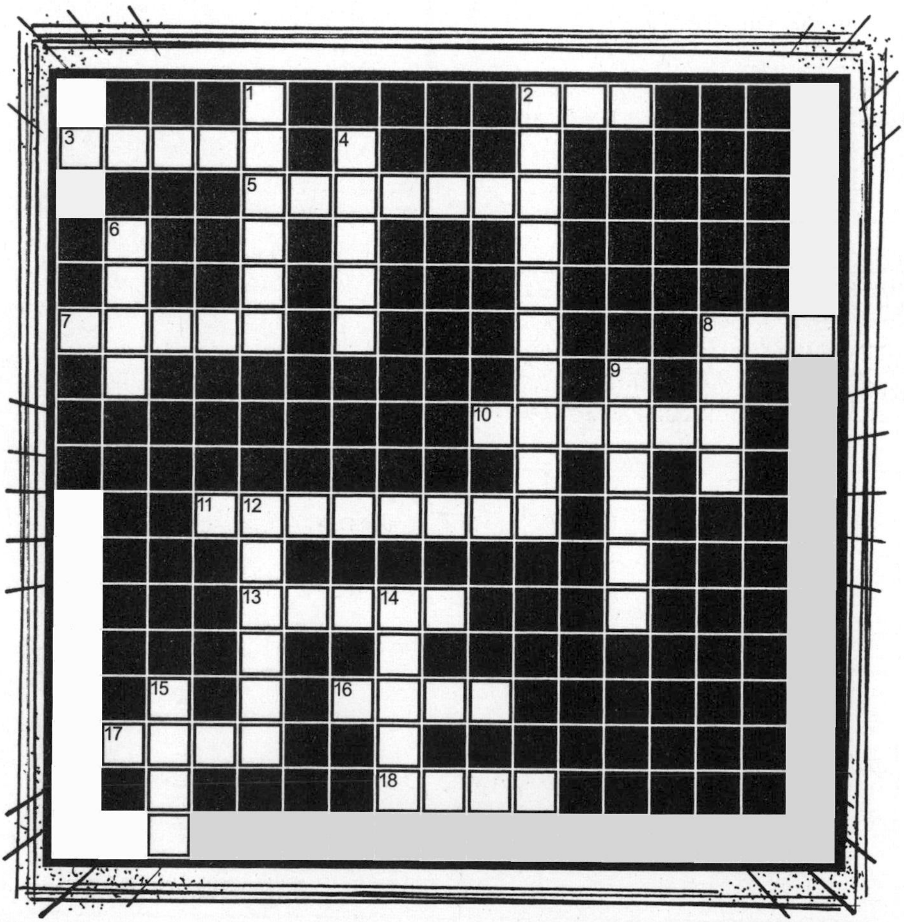
1
2
3
4
5
6
7
8
9
10
11
12
13
14
15
16
17
18

ACROSS

2. A cat will almost never meow at another ________. This sound is reserved for humans.

3. Dalmatian puppies are pure ________ at birth.

5. A dog's nose works about one ________ times more efficiently than the human nose.

7. Most pet owners say their pet makes them really happy. They ________ more than once a day.

8. Superman's ________ was named Krypto.

10. Charlie Brown's dog is named ________.

11. Cats usually have 12 ______ on each side of their noses.

13. An adult cat has 30 teeth in its ________.

16. Cats are carnivores, which means they eat ________.

17. Dogs sweat from the pads on their ________ (rhymes with "laws"). They discharge heat by panting.

18. A cat in a hurry can sprint at about thirty-one miles per ________.

DOWN

1. Calico cats are almost always this gender.

2. Among the seven ________, only icy Antarctica remains catless today.

4. The first seeing-eye dog was presented to a ________ person on April 25, 1938 (rhymes with "mind").

6. Cats can ______ 5 times their height (rhymes with "bump").

8. It takes 63 ________ for puppies to be born (rhymes with "ways").

9. The chow chow has a black ________. Other dogs have pink ones.

12. Cats have existed longer than ________.

14. There are 42 ________ in a dog's mouth.

15. Cats ________ on their toes.

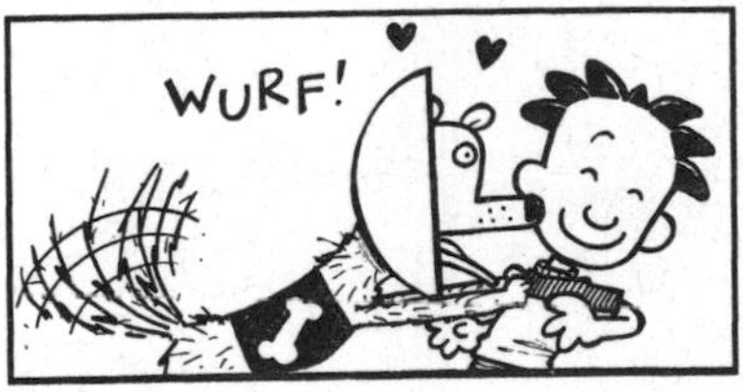
WURF!

FREAKY FACTS

Francis loves learning wild facts like these. Test your brain with these trivia questions, then uncover the answers using his secret code on page 58.

Q: What is the biggest planet in our solar system?

A: $\dfrac{}{4}\ \dfrac{}{10}\ \dfrac{}{2}\ \dfrac{}{20}\ \dfrac{}{6}\ \dfrac{}{8}\ \dfrac{}{14}$.

Q: What's the highest mountain on Earth?

A: $\overline{}\ \overline{}\ \overline{}\ \overline{}\ \overline{}$
   18 11 10 21 6

$\overline{}\ \overline{}\ \overline{}\ \overline{}\ \overline{}\ \overline{}\ \overline{}$.
 8 19 8 14 8 24 6

Q: What is the name of the closest
   star to Earth?

A: $\overline{}\ \overline{}\ \overline{}\ \ \overline{}\ \overline{}\ \overline{}$.
   6 1 8   24 10 21

JUICY GOSSIP

FACULTY
...and so then I
him that he'd be
not even THINK
acting as if he
even know wha
TALKING ab

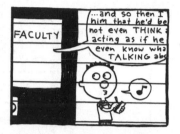

Nate writes a gossip column about his teachers, and it's a gas! Fill in the squares so that each teacher's initial appears only once in every row, column, and box.

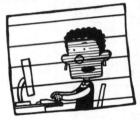

C = **MS. CLARKE**

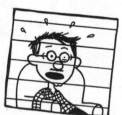

R = **MR. ROSA**

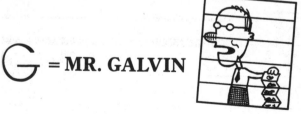

G = **MR. GALVIN**

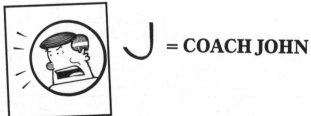

J = **COACH JOHN**

minor health problems.

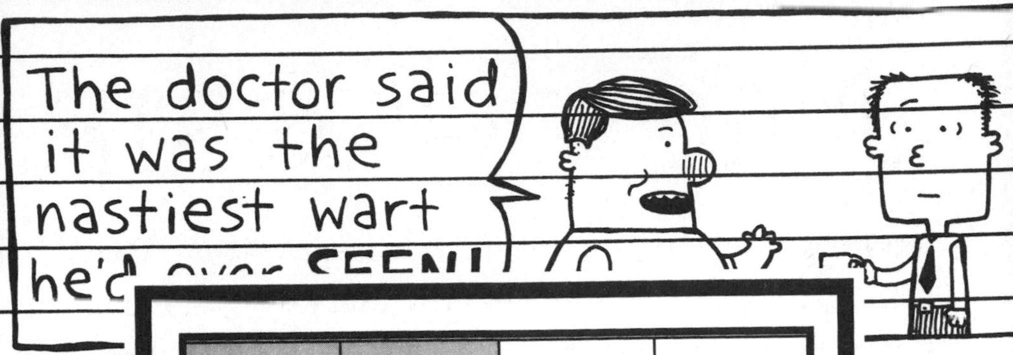
The doctor said
it was the
nastiest wart

C			J
J			
	C		
R		G	

• Ms ... stop

co

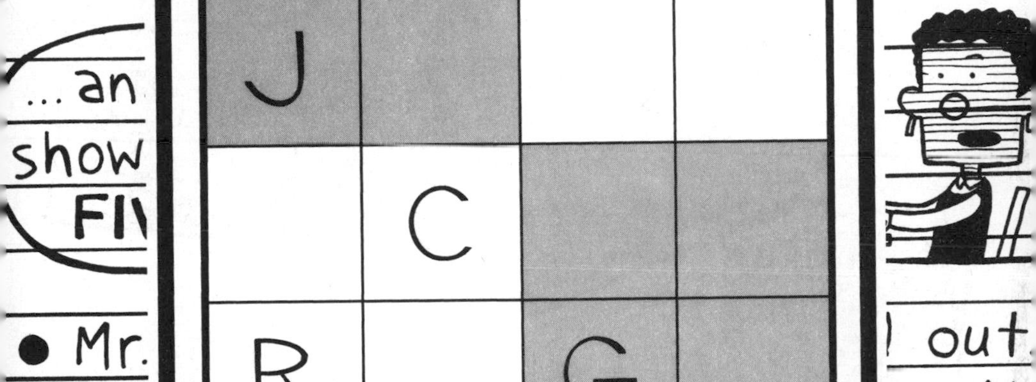
... an
show
FI

• Mr. ... out.

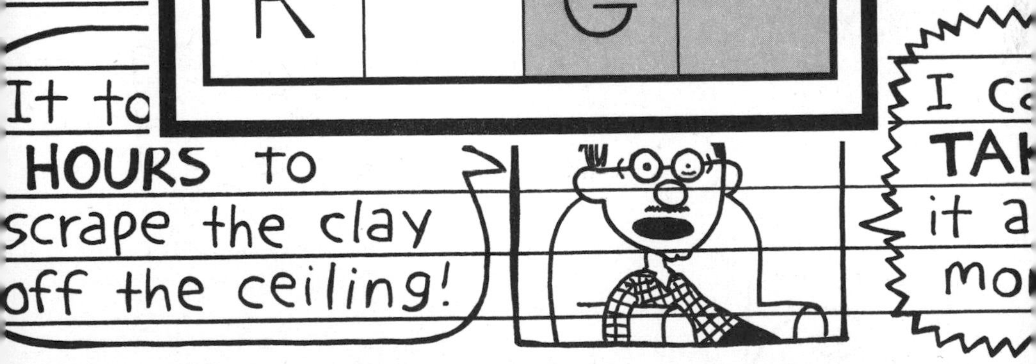
It to
HOURS to
scrape the clay
off the ceiling!
I ca
TA
it a
mo

• Mr. Galvin is very, very boring.

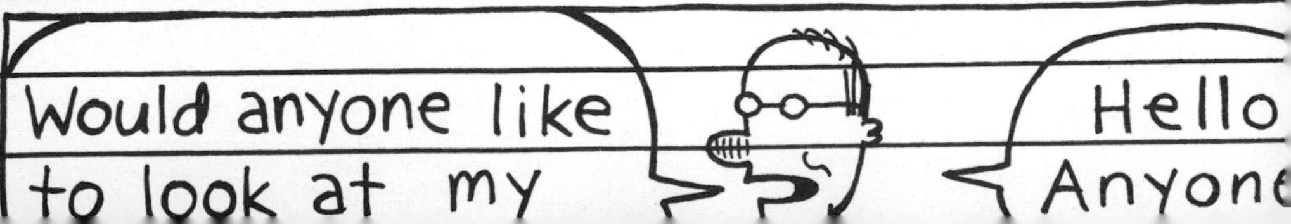
Would anyone like
to look at my
Hello
Anyone

NOTORIOUS NATE TRIVIA

1. Nate once called Chad by the wrong name. What was it?

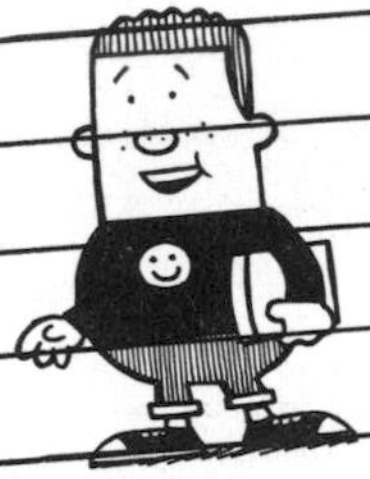

   a. Bob
   b. Randy
   c. Todd
   d. Gordie

2. Nate's Little League team was once sponsored by which business?
   a. Franny's Pizza
   b. Patsy's Pancake House
   c. Nate's Noodles
   d. Joe's Hot Dogs

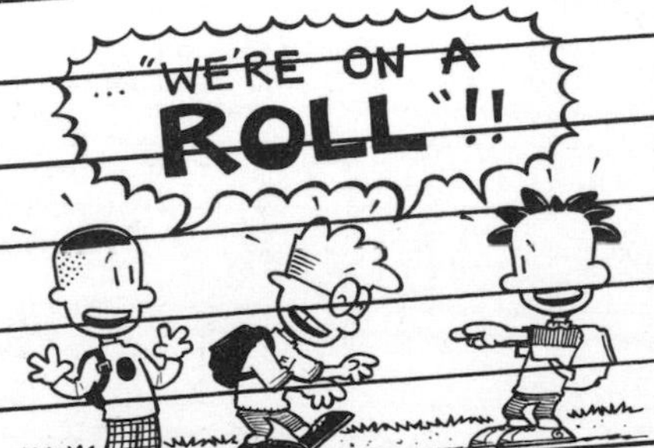
... "WE'RE ON A ROLL"!!

3. What was the name of the mascot for Nate's fleeceball team?

a. Puffy

b. Kuddles

c. Killer Bee

d. McWinky

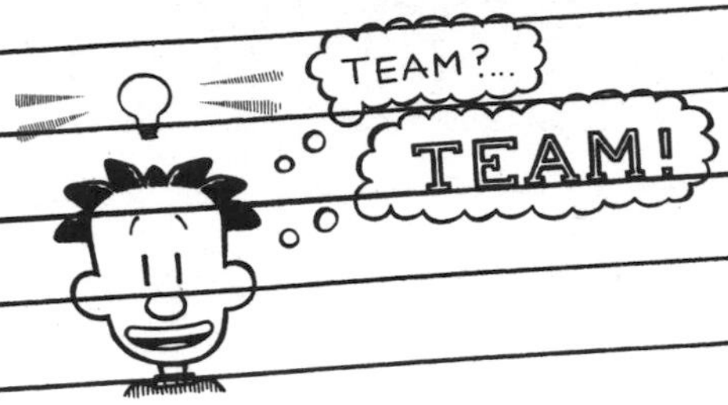
TEAM?...
TEAM!

4. Which of Nate's rivals gets a bloody nose?

a. Chester

b. Gina

c. Artur

d. Randy

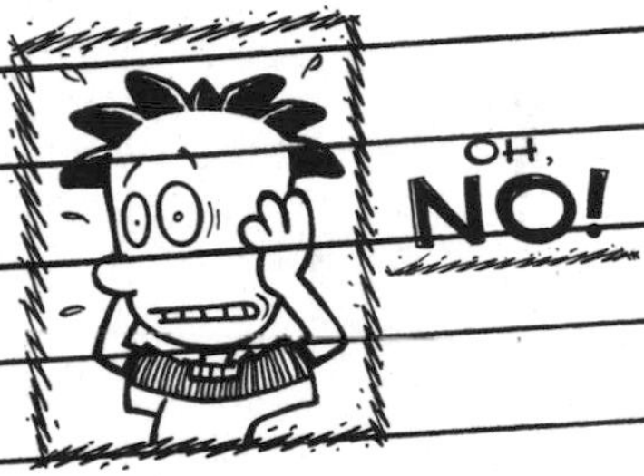
OH, NO!

5. What does Gina sometimes call Nate?

a. El Stupido

b. Spiky-Haired Kid

c. Pinhead

d. Ultra-Nate

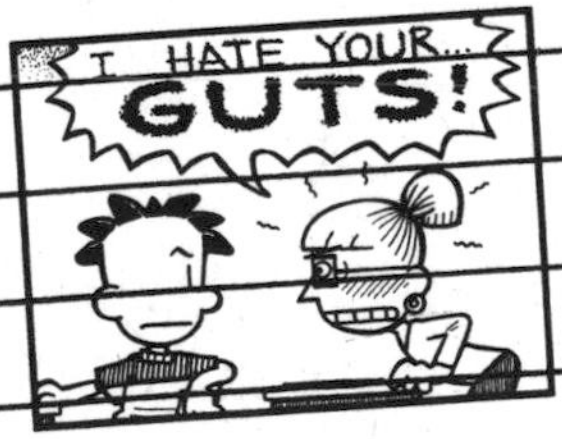
I HATE YOUR... GUTS!

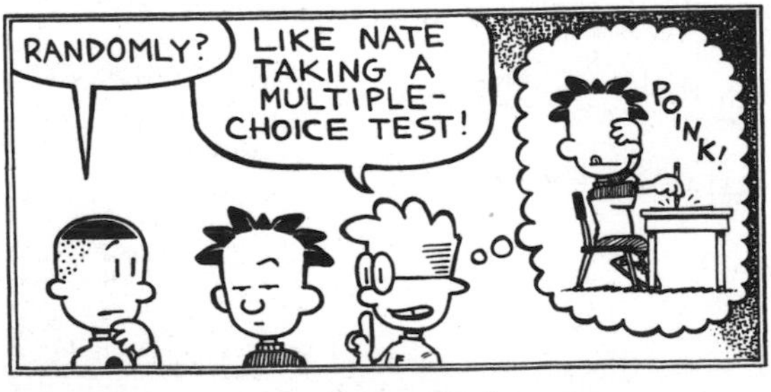
RANDOMLY?
LIKE NATE TAKING A MULTIPLE-CHOICE TEST!
POINK!

LOST IN THE WOODS

Help! Nate and his scout troop have gone down the wrong trail. Find all the camping words in the puzzle, and get Nate and his friends back to civilization!

MAP
FLASHLIGHT
TENT
TRAIL MIX
COMPASS
BACKPACK
SLEEPING BAG
HIKING BOOTS
CAMPFIRE
SUNSCREEN

INSECT REPELLENT
WATCH
OUTDOORS
BUGS
RAIN GEAR
BINOCULARS
WATER BOTTLE
MOUNTAIN
FIRST AID KIT
CANOE

N	R	M	R	H	E	B	F	T	D	A	U	W	E	T
D	F	G	T	P	A	U	O	N	E	H	W	G	X	A
O	T	R	A	I	L	M	I	X	G	N	A	S	A	T
S	T	O	O	B	G	N	I	K	I	H	T	R	S	I
I	S	G	U	B	G	I	W	M	T	H	E	E	U	K
T	R	C	N	T	E	N	O	E	G	O	R	C	N	D
A	A	N	A	O	D	U	I	I	H	R	B	O	S	I
N	L	B	N	M	N	O	L	P	A	U	O	M	C	A
O	U	A	A	T	P	H	O	I	E	A	T	P	R	T
H	C	P	A	C	S	F	N	R	N	E	T	A	E	S
C	O	I	N	A	K	G	I	B	S	P	L	S	E	R
T	N	E	L	L	E	P	E	R	T	C	E	S	N	I
A	I	F	L	A	A	K	A	A	E	O	F	A	C	F
W	B	K	R	K	T	S	O	C	U	E	M	G	B	U
S	A	N	N	F	P	A	R	S	K	N	C	I	R	U

GOSH, this is a steep mountain!
We're not even ON the mountain yet!

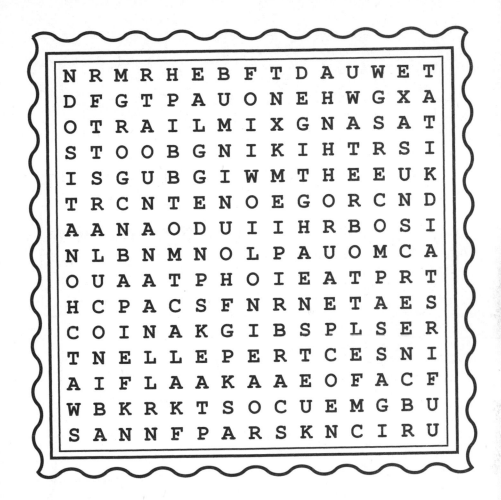

COMIX CAPER

Draw a comic strip featuring the following characters. Anything goes!

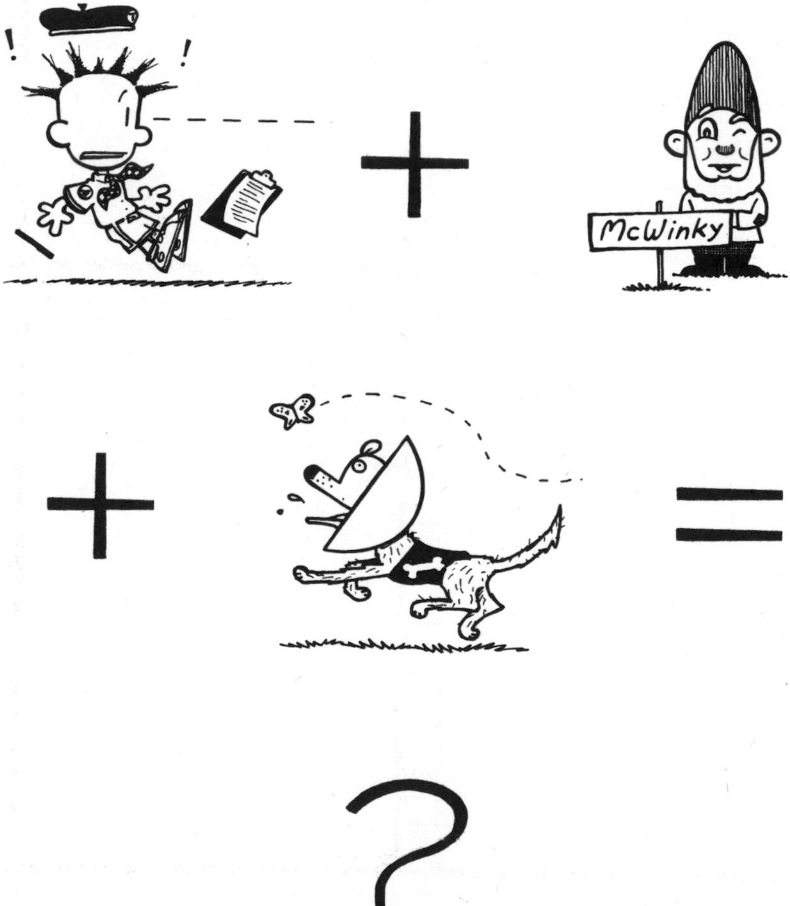
McWinky

YOUR TITLE HERE

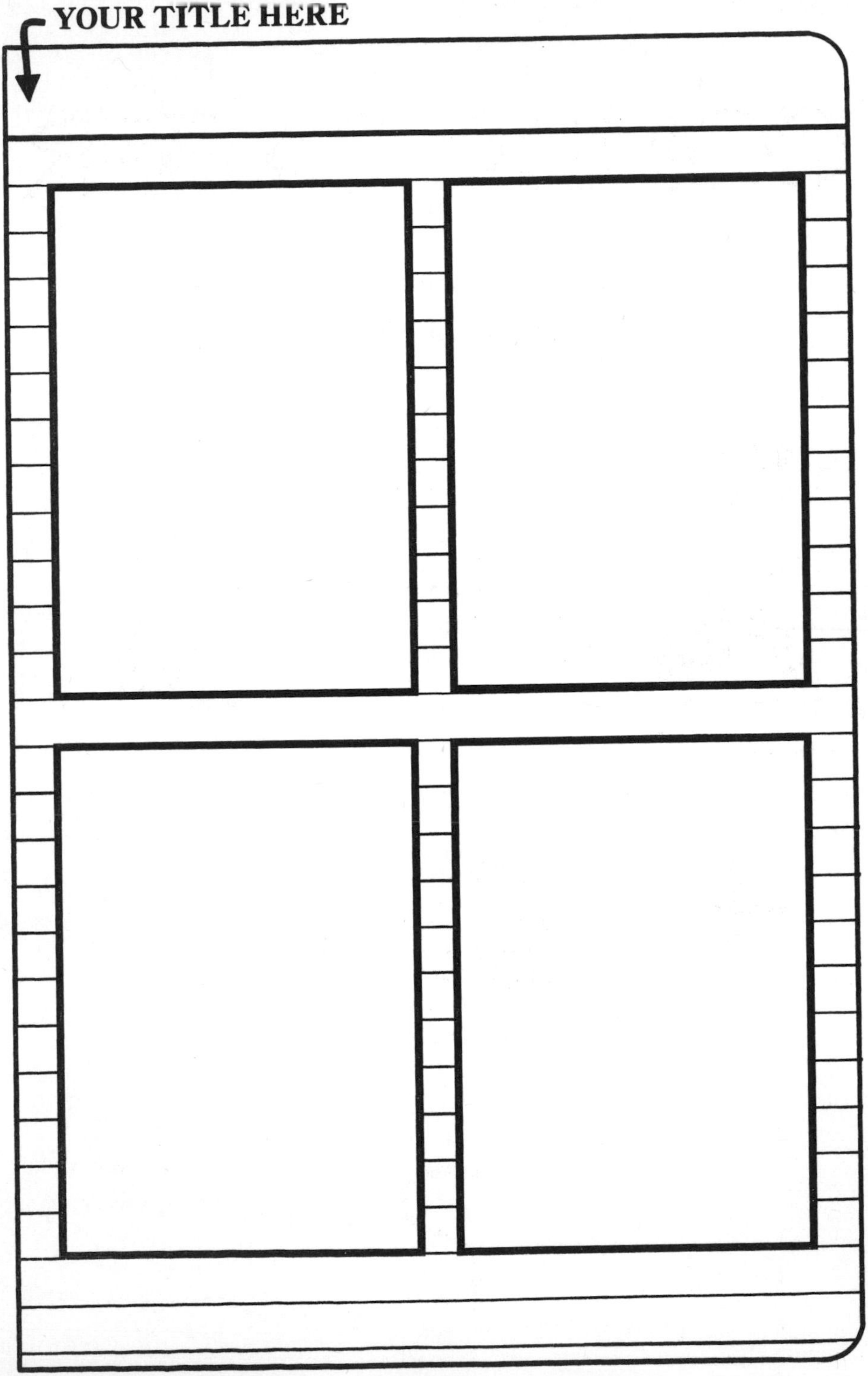

PRACTICAL JOKESTER

Teddy is a huge fan of corny jokes! Use his code on page 34 to find out the punch lines.

Q: What did the beach say when the tide came in?

A: $\overline{} \ \overline{} \ \overline{} \ \overline{} \ \ \overline{} \ \overline{} \ \overline{} \ \overline{}$
O L M T   G R N V

$\overline{} \ \overline{} \ \overline{} \ \overline{} \ \overline{}$.
M L H V Z

HEH HEH!

Q: What did one potato chip say to the other?

A: $\overline{} \ \overline{} \ \overline{} \ \overline{} \ \overline{} \ \overline{} \ \overline{}$
H S Z O O D V

$\overline{} \ \overline{} \ \overline{} \ \overline{} \ \overline{} \ \overline{}$
T L U L I Z

$\overline{} \ \overline{} \ \overline{}$?
W R K

HA HA

HEE

OPERATION CREATION

What went wrong with Doctor Cesspool's operation?

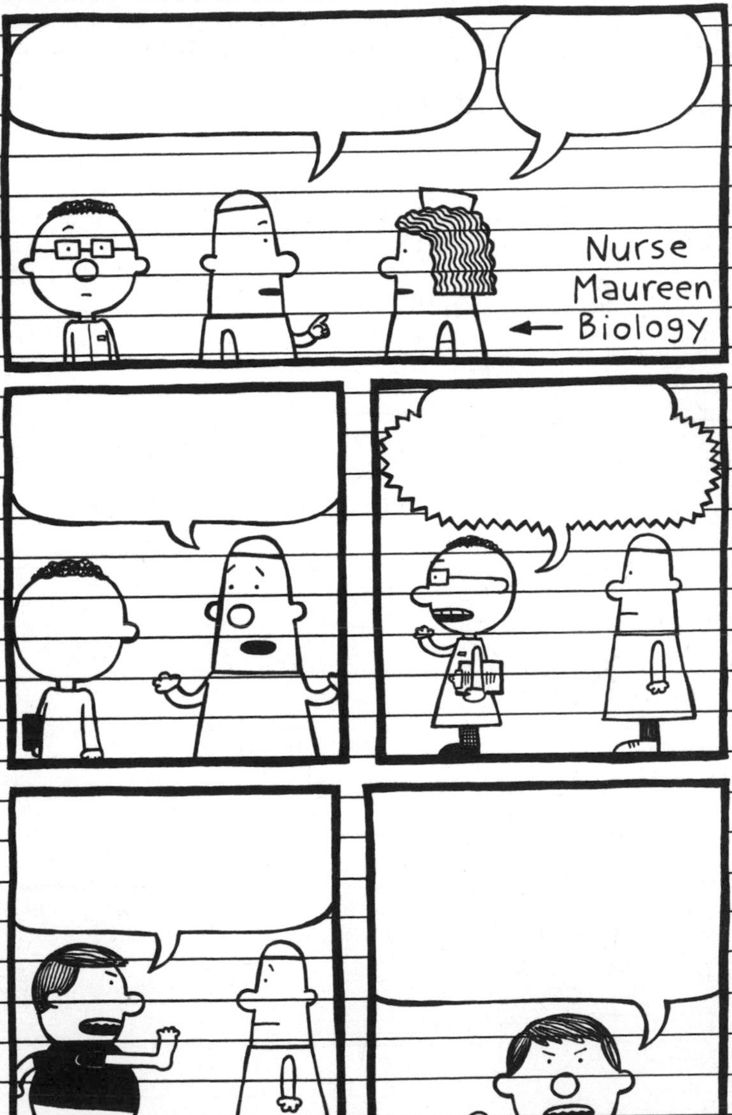
Nurse
Maureen
Biology

LUCKY DAY

**Do you lead a charmed life?
Write down your luckiest moments ever,
then rate them from 1 to 10, 10 being the best!**

LUCKY MOMENT	**RATING**
1.	____
2.	____
3.	____
4.	____
5.	____
6.	____
7. Your dad packs Cheez Doodles in your lunch.	____
8.	____
9.	____

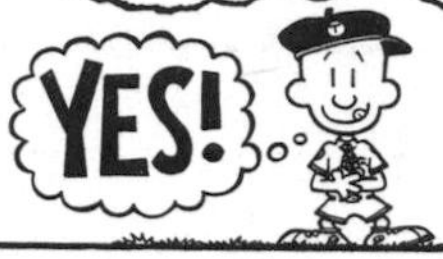
YES!

10. ______

11. ______

12. You find a 10-dollar bill on the way to school. ______

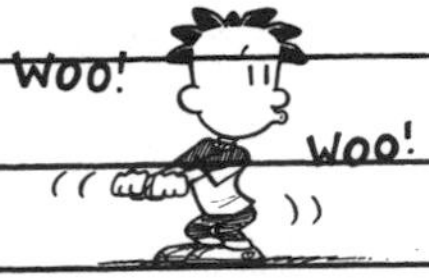
WOO!
WOO!

13. ______

14. ______

15. ______

16. ______

17. ______

18. School's closed for a snow day. ______

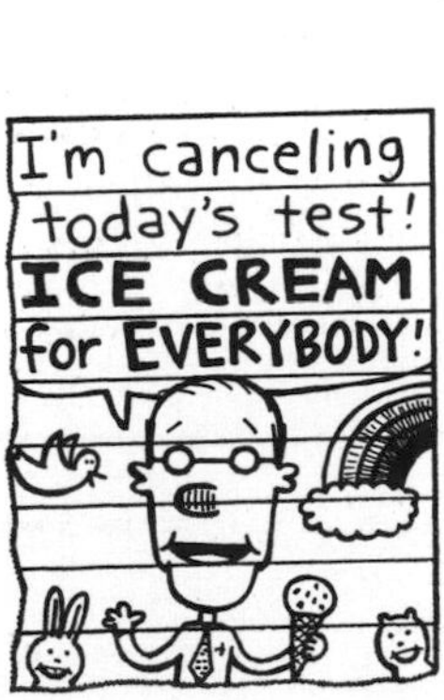
I'm canceling today's test! ICE CREAM for EVERYBODY!

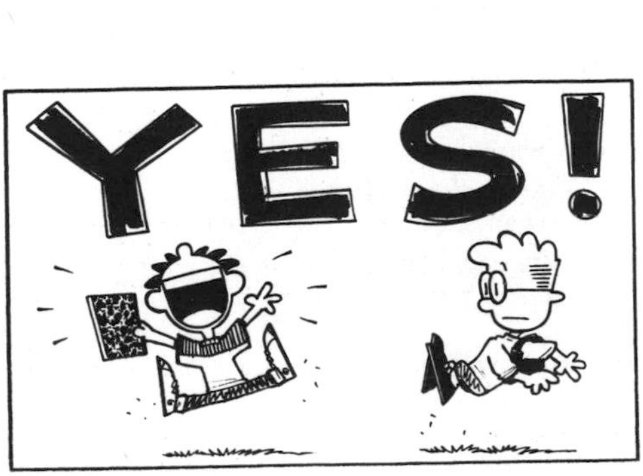
YES!

ANSWER KEY

HOW WELL DO U KNOW NATE? (pp. 1–3)
1. (d) Throwing a pie in his face
2. (c) Teddy pretended his science lab squid was a booger.
3. (b) Scorpio
4. (d) Ultra-Nate
5. (e) Psycho Dogs

CODE CRACKER (pp. 4–5)
Gina loves Francis. FALSE
Nate gets a black eye riding his skateboard. FALSE
Teddy's dad is troop leader. TRUE
Nate eats rice cakes. FALSE
Spitsy has a crush on Ketchup the cat. FALSE

SCOUT'S HONOR (pp. 12–13)

MUSIC
COOKING
SWIMMING
SCULPTURE
ROWING
ART
FISHING
WEATHER
NATURE
CAMPING
FIRST AID
WOODWORK
GARDENING
SKATING

MOST VALUABLE PLAYER (p. 14)

START
FINISH

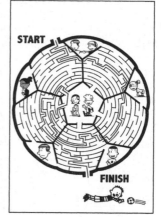

SEMAPHORE SUPERSTAR (p. 15)
Remember this page. You'll need it later!

UN-YUMMY TREATS (pp. 16–17)

K	O	S	P	J	W	C	I	L
J	I	C	K	S	L	O	W	P
L	P	W	C	I	O	J	K	S
I	J	P	W	C	S	K	L	O
C	L	K	I	O	P	S	J	W
S	W	O	L	K	J	P	C	I
W	K	J	O	P	I	L	S	C
O	C	L	S	W	K	I	P	J
P	S	I	J	L	C	W	O	K

IT'S SHOWTIME! (pp. 20–21)
Semaphore: What play is it?
Answer: Peter Pan

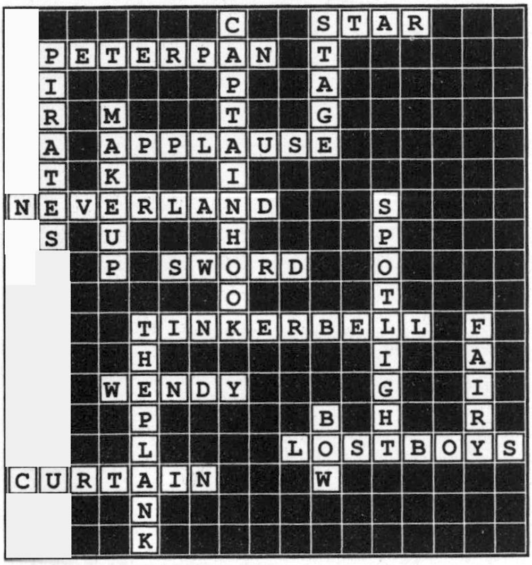

HIKE TO NOWHERE (p. 29)

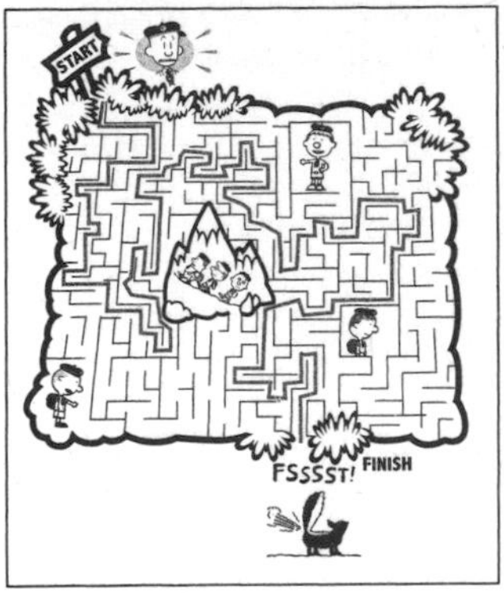
START
FSSSST!
FINISH

TIMBER SCOUTS
(pp. 30–31)

F	A	T	N
T	N	A	F
N	T	F	A
A	F	N	T

TIME TO RHYME (pp. 32–33)

3. Funny bunny
4. Calm mom
5. Mad dad
6. Crazy daisy
7. Funky monkey
8. Book nook
9. Wrong song
10. Fun run

TEDDY'S ULTIMATE SPORTS TRIVIA (pp. 34–35)
Shaquille O'Neal wears the largest shoes in the NBA. Size 22!
The Tour de France bicycle race lasts 21 days, and Lance Armstrong has won a record 7 times!

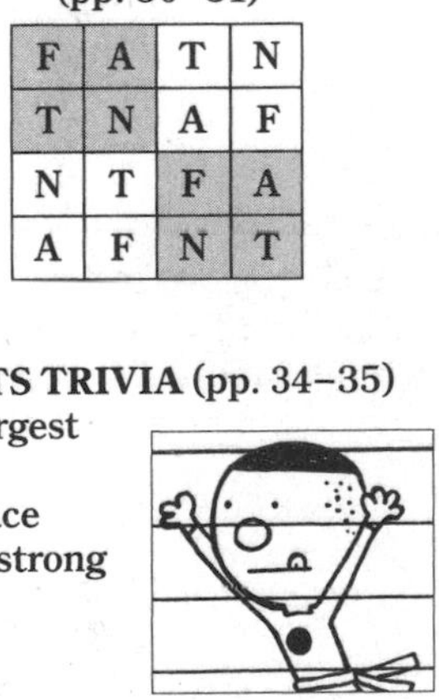

FRIENDS FOREVER (p. 38)
Semaphore: Best friends are the best!

DOG DAZE (pp. 40–41)

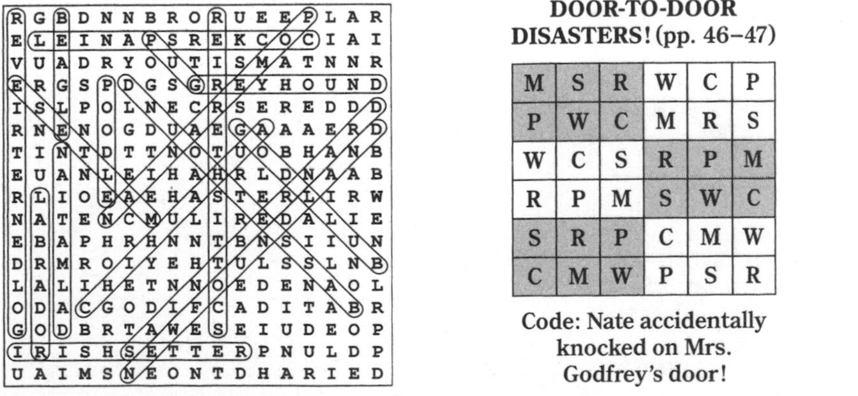

DOOR-TO-DOOR DISASTERS! (pp. 46–47)

M	S	R	W	C	P
P	W	C	M	R	S
W	C	S	R	P	M
R	P	M	S	W	C
S	R	P	C	M	W
C	M	W	P	S	R

Code: Nate accidentally knocked on Mrs. Godfrey's door!

LAUGH RIOT (pp. 50–51)
Q: What do you call a sleeping cow?
A: A bulldozer!
Q: Why did the booger cross the road?
A: Because he was being picked on!

FRANCIS'S CLASSIFIED CODE (pp. 58–59)
Scientists in Peru found a giant penguin that lived thirty-six million years ago.

BADGE BONANZA (pp. 60–61)

F	C	H	A
A	H	F	C
H	A	C	F
C	F	A	H

NAME THAT GNOME (p. 63)
1. Happy
2. Bashful
3. Grumpy
4. Doc
5. Sleepy
6. Dopey
7. Sneezy

ALIAS (pp. 66–67)

G	B	T	P	Q	I	D	A	V
Q	D	A	T	V	B	I	G	P
I	P	V	G	D	A	T	Q	B
B	V	D	I	G	T	A	P	Q
P	I	G	Q	A	V	B	D	T
T	A	Q	D	B	P	G	V	I
D	G	I	V	T	Q	P	B	A
V	T	B	A	P	G	Q	I	D
A	Q	P	B	I	D	V	T	G

SUPER SCOUT CHALLENGE (pp. 68–69)

G	H	C	G	I	O	I	B	R	O	C	G	H
N	A	A	S	I	I	A	L	C	H	M	D	P
I	N	B	B	R	D	I	A	T	P	R	W	K
K	D	I	G	G	O	M	A	I	E	O	P	C
I	S	N	E	N	P	O	H	H	L	F	L	L
H	H	S	S	F	I	S	D	L	O	I	C	P
A	A	U	I	M	D	P	A	T	M	N	C	O
R	K	R	L	N	N	M	E	B	U	U	O	O
R	E	V	E	A	H	W	I	E	O	O	P	R
K	C	I	T	S	G	N	I	K	L	A	W	T
R	R	V	R	S	G	T	N	Y	I	S	R	R
F	K	A	R	C	H	E	R	Y	A	O	O	G
S	M	L	G	T	L	A	A	E	F	B	N	N

YOU ARE THE INVENTOR (p. 71)
Code: This is genius!

FAR-OUT FACTOIDS (pp. 78–79)
Humans have over seven thousand different facial expressions.
In an average lifetime, you will breathe around six hundred million breaths.

ADVENTURES OF ULTRA-NATE (p. 83)
Code: Oh, the suspense!

MAD FOR BADGES (pp. 85–86)
Codes:
Make some noise!
A shooting star!
Mmm, yum!
Speed demon!

TOP 5 DOGGONE FACTS (p. 94)
2. Ellen
3. Squirrels
4. Go Fish

RHYME-A-THON (pp. 88–89)
1. New crew
2. King's ring
3. Shy guy
4. Great Nate
5. Pretty kitty
6. Clown's town
7. Gray day
8. Light kite
9. Slow crow
10. Big pig

DRAMATIC FLASHBACK (pp. 98–99)
Semaphores:
Ouch!
Uh-oh!

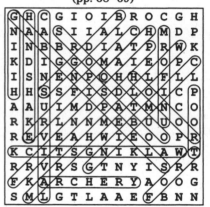

CREATE-A-COMIX (p. 91)
Semaphore: This should be funny!

SKATER SCRAMBLE (p. 93)
Semaphore:
If you find more than fifteen, Nate gets to go to the skate park!

THE FORTUNE-TELLER (pp. 100–101)
Semaphores:
You will live in the lap of luxury.
You will travel to the moon.
You have a secret admirer.

FACT-TASTIC TRIVIA (pp. 108–109)
A tiglon.
The dodo bird.
The black widow.

PSYCHO DOGS RULE (pp. 114–115)

N	C	T	M	F	G	W	S	P
M	W	F	P	S	N	C	T	G
G	P	S	T	C	W	F	N	M
S	M	C	N	P	T	G	W	F
P	N	G	C	W	F	S	M	T
T	F	W	S	G	M	P	C	N
C	G	M	W	N	P	T	F	S
F	S	N	G	T	C	M	P	W
W	T	P	F	M	S	N	G	C

THE HERO (p. 116)

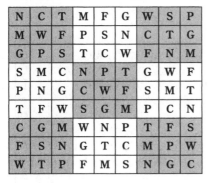

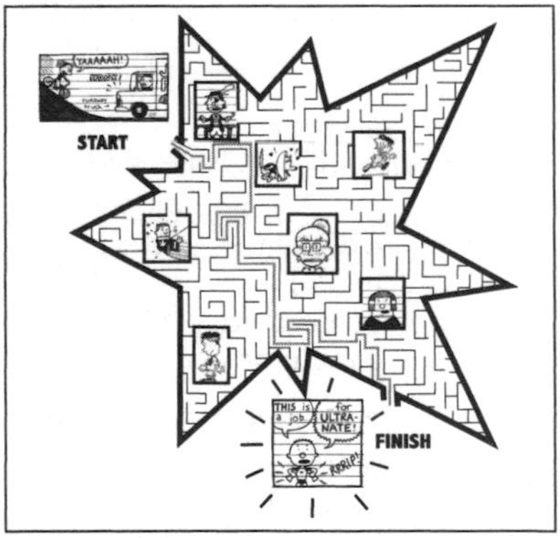

START
THIS is a job for ULTRA-NATE!
FINISH

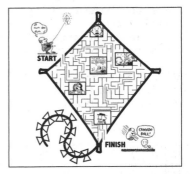

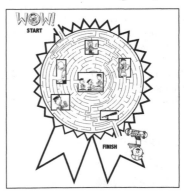

DESTINED FOR GREATNESS (pp. 126–127)

M	S	C	T
C	T	S	M
T	C	M	S
S	M	T	C

HIDDEN WORDS (p. 137)
Code: If you can make twenty-five words, you earn a whiz kid merit badge!

ZAPPED! (p. 106)

START
CANNON-BALL!
FINISH

JOKIN' AROUND (pp. 122–123)
Stinkerbell
I'm stuck on you.
The letter "T."

U R CAR2NING! (p. 125)
Semaphore: What's your favorite comic?

THE DOCTOR IS IN! (p. 128)
Code: Is he crazy?

THE GRAND PRIZE (p. 132)

WOW!
START
FINISH

BELIEVE IT OR NOT? (pp. 138–139)
Venus is the only planet that rotates clockwise.
A duck's quack does not echo.
Most dust particles in your house are made from dead skin.
The elephant is the only mammal that can't jump.

GREAT NATE FACTS
(pp. 140–141)
1. (b) Jenny
2. (c) Skateboard
3. (b) Pulling weeds for Mr. Galvin
4. (a) Maureen Biology
5. (c) Kevin

SCHOOL PICTURE DAY (p. 155)
Code: Say cheese!

LOTSA LIMERICKS
(p. 149)
Flu
My
Mama
Late
Nate
Doodles
Great

SPORTS SCENE (p. 151)
A diamond
Four
Seven

SAY IT LOUD!
(pp. 152–153)
Codes:
Is Nate in love?
Boring!
Why does Artur look scared?
Coach John explodes!

WHO'S A BRAINIAC? (pp. 158–159)
Some turtles can breathe through their butts.
Pearls melt in vinegar.
A butterfly has twelve thousand eyes.

LAUGH-A-THON (p. 160)
A watch dog!
Mice Crispies!
Drop him a line!

EXCLAMATION STATION (pp. 162–163)
Codes: What's wrong with Nate?
Check out Ellen's room!
One scary dude!
Boy, is he mad!

FUNNY BUSINESS (pp. 164–165)
For holding up the pants.
Because they are always stuffed.
The roles weren't good enough.

WHAT COULD GO WRONG?
(p. 161)

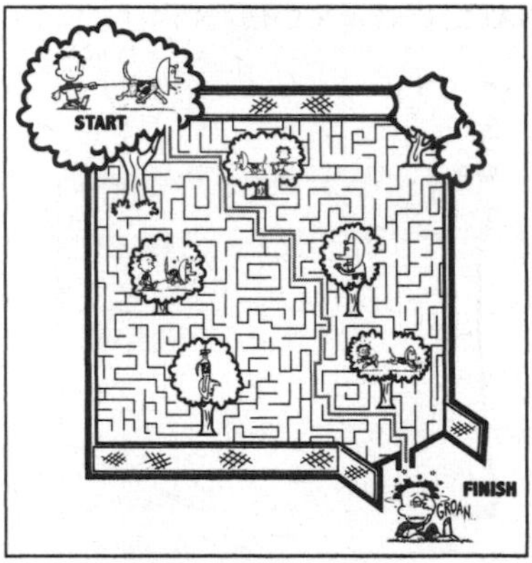
START
FINISH
GROAN

LOCKER DISASTER (pp. 170–171)

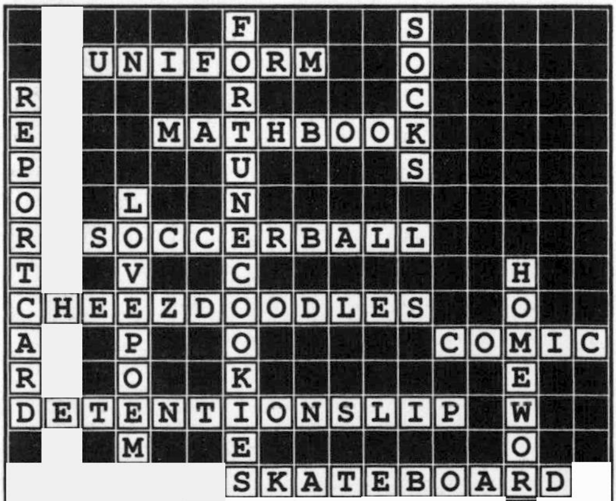
UNIFORM
MATHBOOK
SOCCERBALL
CHEEZDOODLES
COMIC
DETENTIONSLIP
SKATEBOARD
SOCKS
FORTUNECOOKIE
REPORTCARD
LOVEPOEM
HOMEWORK

WHAT WAS THE QUESTION AGAIN? (pp. 174–175)
Pacific Ocean
Iron and oxygen
The Sahara

HAPPINESS IS . . . WARM FUZZIES (pp. 176–177)

S	U	W	N	L	H	F	G
L	H	F	G	S	U	W	N
U	N	S	W	H	F	G	L
H	G	L	F	U	N	S	W
W	S	H	U	G	L	N	F
N	F	G	L	W	S	U	H
F	W	U	H	N	G	L	S
G	L	N	S	F	W	H	U

ALL MIXED UP! (pp. 182–183)

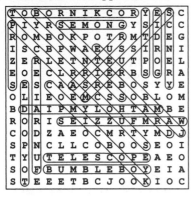

NATE'S COMIX CRACK-UP (p. 186)

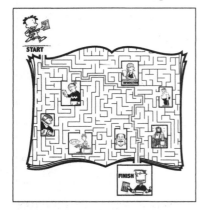

LOST IN THE WOODS (pp. 202–203)

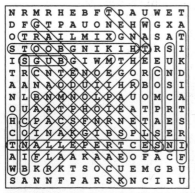

Semaphore: Dad's such a dork!

SUPER WRITER (pp. 188–189)

1. Nice mice
2. Bird herd
3. Sandy candy
4. Far star
5. New shoe
6. Pup cup
7. Red bed
8. Late mate

WHO'S A SPORTS GENIUS?
(pp. 190–191)
Swimming, cycling, and running
Soccer
Badminton
Hop, skip, and jump

CATS AND DOGS (pp. 194–195)

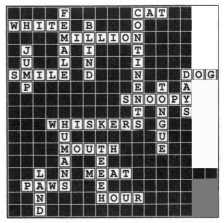

FREAKY FACTS
(pp. 196–197)
Jupiter
Mount Everest
The sun

NOTORIOUS
NATE TRIVIA
(pp. 200–201)
1. (c) Todd
2. (d) Joe's Hot Dogs
3. (b) Kuddles
4. (d) Randy
5. (c) Pinhead

JUICY GOSSIP
(pp. 198–199)

C	G	R	J
J	R	C	G
G	C	J	R
R	J	G	C

PRACTICAL JOKESTER (p. 206)
Long time no sea.
Shall we go for a dip?

READ ALL THE BiG NATE BOOKS TODAY!

NOVELS

READ ALL THE BIG NATE BOOKS TODAY!

ACTIVITY BOOKS

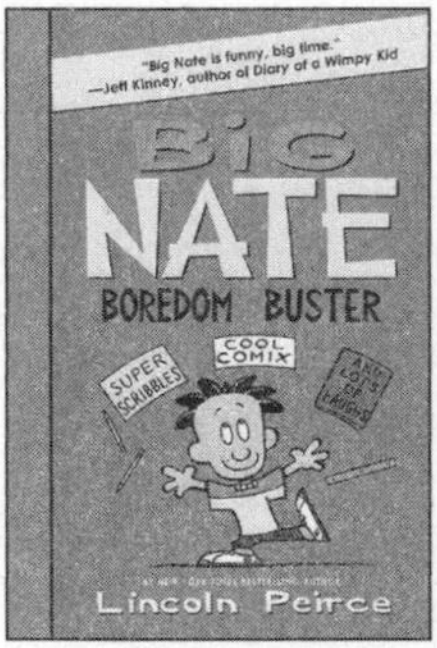
"Big Nate is funny, big time."
—Jeff Kinney, author of Diary of a Wimpy Kid
BIG NATE
BOREDOM BUSTER
SUPER SCRIBBLES
COOL COMIX
Lincoln Peirce

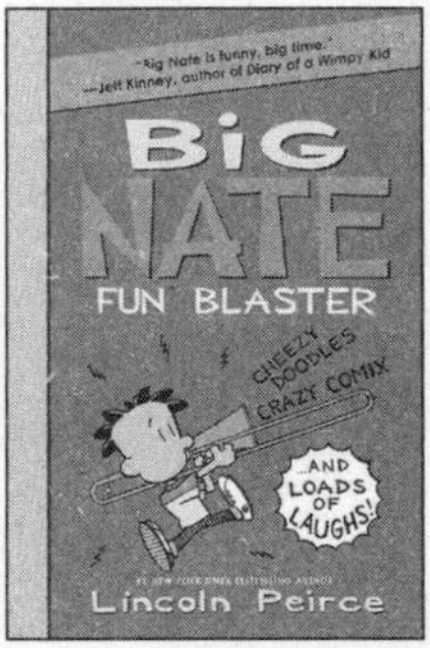
"Big Nate is funny, big time."
—Jeff Kinney, author of Diary of a Wimpy Kid
BIG NATE
FUN BLASTER
CHEEZY DOODLES
CRAZY COMIX
...AND LOADS OF LAUGHS!
Lincoln Peirce

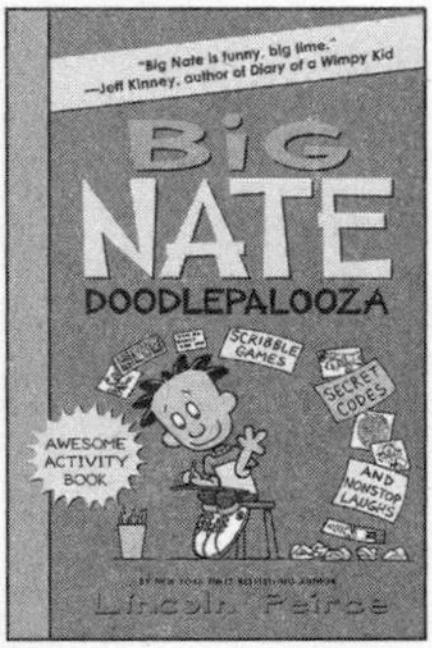
"Big Nate is funny, big time."
—Jeff Kinney, author of Diary of a Wimpy Kid
BIG NATE
DOODLEPALOOZA
SCRIBBLE GAMES
SECRET CODES
AWESOME ACTIVITY BOOK
AND NONSTOP LAUGHS
Lincoln Peirce

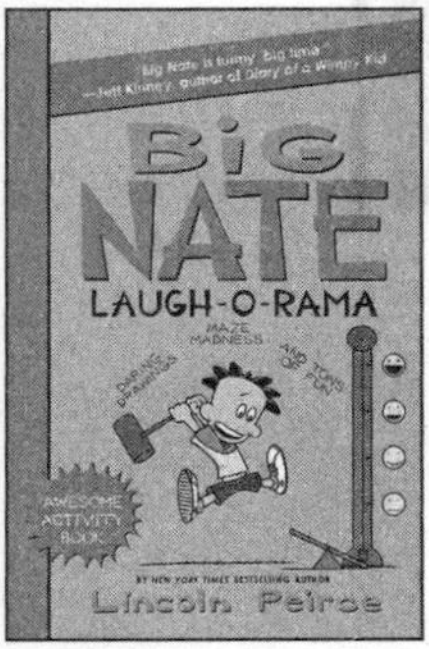
BIG NATE
LAUGH-O-RAMA
MAZE MADNESS
AWESOME ACTIVITY BOOK
BY NEW YORK TIMES BESTSELLING AUTHOR
Lincoln Peirce

COMIC COMPILATIONS

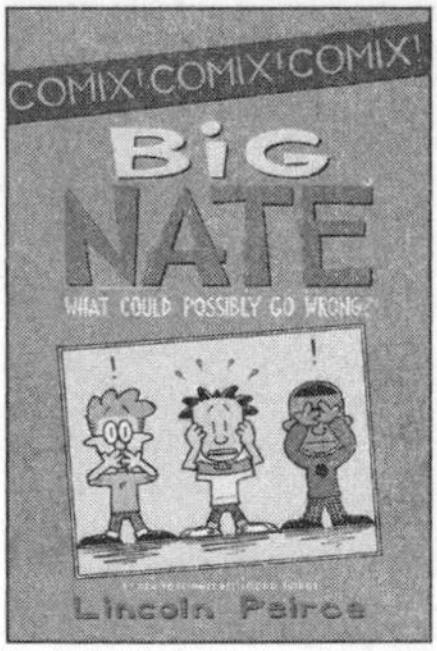
COMIX! COMIX! COMIX!
BIG NATE
WHAT COULD POSSIBLY GO WRONG?
Lincoln Peirce

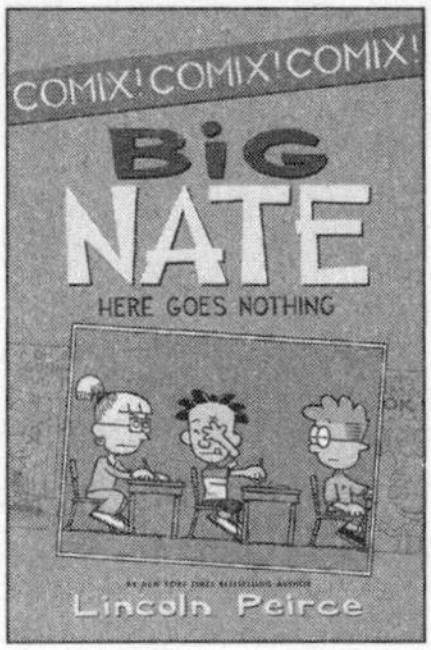
COMIX! COMIX! COMIX!
BIG NATE
HERE GOES NOTHING
BY NEW YORK TIMES BESTSELLING AUTHOR
Lincoln Peirce

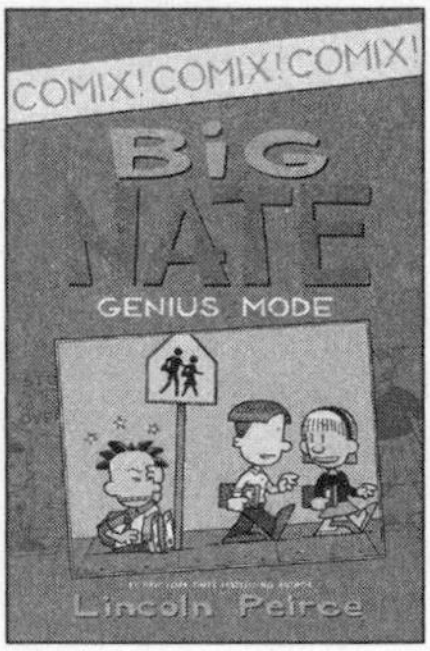
COMIX! COMIX! COMIX!
BIG NATE
GENIUS MODE
Lincoln Peirce

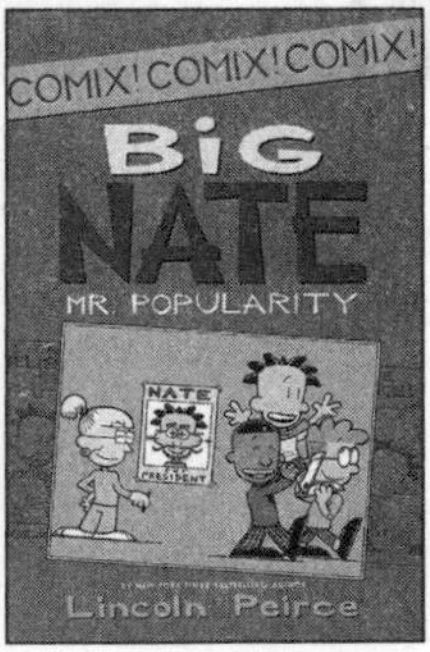
COMIX! COMIX! COMIX!
BIG NATE
MR. POPULARITY
NATE
PRESIDENT
Lincoln Peirce

HARPER
An Imprint of HarperCollins*Publishers*

WWW.BIGNATEBOOKS.COM